THE CULL

A novel by

Rachel Glickler

First Printing, 2019

ISBN 9781701201675
Registration TXu 2-182-248

Cover Design by Rachel Glickler
Printed in the United States of America

This is a work of fiction. Names, characters, evil corporations,
events, and incidents are the products of the author's
imagination. Any resemblance to actual persons, living or dead,
or actual events is purely coincidental. Okay, so the author might
have humoured a few friends and, after renaming them, had them
bumped off in a manner she thought might please them best, but
most of the characters stem solely from her imagination. Well,
sixty percent of them at least. If you think a character might have
been modeled after you, you might be right. Just remember that
you gave the author permission and most of you expressly
requested a fictional death by keystroke. If you don't like how
she disposed of you, better luck next time.

For my mother

We will remember her.

May her name be a blessing.

One

Dear James,

By the time you receive this letter, you will have already realized the consequences of what happened yesterday. I did not fully understand them myself until now and it is far, far too late to change anything. I have been around hundreds of people in the past several hours being jostled and innocently touched as so many do in passing. It is likely that, because of me, it is too late for them as well.

We shared communal spaces. We shared air. The small child in the seat next to me on the plane shared my drink while I was resting my eyes. I couldn't stop him and now it's too late. He will soon be nothing more than a memory and all because I closed my eyes for a moment.

We closed our eyes, too, James. We thought we knew what we were doing, but we didn't. We tried to save the world from those who meant to do it harm only to be the ones to damn it. Even so, please do not blame yourself. I don't. I know our motives were just.

I don't know when this letter will reach you or if it will at all. I will mail it as soon as I reach my parent's house. I am so tired and already showing signs of the first symptoms. I don't know how much longer I have. It is unlikely we will ever see each other again so please know that I feel the same about you as you do me. I always have. I should have told you earlier.

All my love,
Sharsti

THE MAN APPEARED quite suddenly from behind the play structure. He had not been there a moment before. Of this, Frankie was sure. She had only just come around from the other side a few moments before and there had been no one and nothing there except an expanse of well-maintained lawn. He was not exactly the sort of fellow one would overlook either. Most of the adults who frequented the playground this late in the afternoon were either stay-at-home-mothers in yoga pants eager to run off some of their children's energy before bedtime or men in basketball shorts or sweats getting in some quality time with their families after a long day wherever they worked.

Frankie and her husband were both of these in a way and neither all at once. Unlike the majority of their neighbors, their roles were reversed. While she was at that particular moment dressed in her favorite mermaid print yoga pants, it was Frankie and not her husband, Hugo, who spent most of the day stuck behind a desk in the name of the almighty dollar. Hugo, in sweatpants so ancient that the knees were beginning to wear thin, spent his days grocery shopping, planning meals, and hustling their two children to and from school and then on to their various activities. Still, while their roles were so different from what was considered the norm for their peers, they blended in very well with all the other adults on the playground.

Except for the man.

In a very expensive looking crumpled grey suit, he staggered in a drunken manner around the play structure, pausing briefly to swing his head from left to right as though surveying the area. His hair was almost completely white and stood on end randomly as if only select parts had been teased up. *Or electrified*, Frankie mused.

From the corner of her perception, Frankie was aware of the ring of children dancing around another child who lay prone within the moving circle, their singsong voices rising above the rest of the playground noises.

"Dead man, dead man, come alive!"

The man coughed, his chest jerking roughly. He wiped one arm across his forehead, the limb moving with about as much control and grace as that of a ragdoll. Frankie saw now the sheen of sweat on his face and the still wet stains on either sleeve. It was not just his age and attire that made him stand out; to Frankie, he looked ill and not simply drunk.

Frankie glanced over at Hugo. He was pushing their younger child on the swings and facing away from her so he had not yet seen the man. Her eyes searched the playground for her daughter, but she could not spot her. "Lydia?"

"Come alive by the count of five!"

The man was advancing slowly, moving as though his legs were becoming increasingly unfamiliar to him. He was starting to attract attention. A few heads had turned in his direction to watch his awkward progression around the structure. His left leg jerked with every other step and his right leg dragged as through numb. It left behind an uneven trail in the wood chips. Frankie glanced at her husband then called out again, her voice breaking slightly as she scanned the playground once more. "Lyds? Lyddie?"

"One, two, three, four..."

A small head crowned with jet black curls popped out from under the slide as a young girl came bouncing into sight at the same time the prone child leapt up to chase his friends. Lydia's attention was not fully on her mother just yet. She was grinning at the children in the circle. "I'm alive!" a boy's voice rang out and was immediately answered by shrieks and laughter.

"Five!"

Lydia swung around to face Frankie, a lopsided smile spreading over her rosy face. She opened her mouth to speak, her voice coming out as a wordless squeak as the man stumbled forward, his arms outstretched to break his fall. He had caught hold of the young girl's shoulder, dragging her down with him as he crumpled to his knees into the wood chips. Coughs wracked his body, spittle spraying over Lydia's face before she could pull away.

"Mommy!"

Eyes wide with shock, Lydia at last managed to pull away from the man's grip and dashed toward Frankie, wood chips flying up behind her. The frantic pitch of her voice had drawn the attention of all those around her who had, until that moment, assumed that the man was nothing more than a harmless drunk businessman on his way home after a particularly bad day.

Hugo spun around and ran toward the sound of his daughter's voice, closing the distance between them just before Lydia reached Frankie. He swept her up into his arms and, seeing the wetness on her cheeks and mouth, wiped at her face with the flat of his hand.

"What happened?"

Frankie did not respond. She didn't have to. Lydia was already awkwardly relating her brief frightening experience and making wild, exaggerated arm motions in a typically childish attempt to add flourish to the tale. Frankie's gaze was locked on the man who was now rising shakily to his feet. He had, clutched in one hand, what looked like a partially opened brown leather wallet. A few cards and slips of paper were poking from it at different angles, but he made no effort to tuck them back in as he shoved it inside his suit jacket from where it must have fallen when he collapsed. She watched with a sort of frozen fascination as the man continued his lurching walk across the playground.

Frankie, along with everyone within arms-length of the man, backed away instinctively as he passed by. His gaze briefly met hers, a quizzical expression flashing over his face as he shuffled past. His lips were moving, Frankie noted, but she could not make out what he was saying. No fewer than twenty pairs of eyes followed his progress as he stepped out of the wood chips and onto the sidewalk that ran along the front side of the park. He shuffled slowly up the path for several seconds then, as if gaining a sudden spurt of energy, lunged forward and continued staggering at a faster pace.

Most people had turned away as soon as the man stepped onto the sidewalk. He was going away. As far as they were concerned, his leaving meant that they no longer needed to be watchful of him. Out of their sight, but not out of Frankie's mind. She could not tear her eyes away from him. His figure became smaller and smaller and darkened into an indistinguishable blob at the far end of the street.

Something was different.

It took Frankie another few moments to realize what it was. It seemed suddenly quieter. The children in the playground were no longer shrieking, having been shocked into silence only minutes before. The adults were either still taking stock of their young or checking their phones. That was not what had struck Frankie.

Everything was quieter.

Frankie looked up. A swarm of flying bugs was swirling in a looping pattern like a rollercoaster. She stared, mesmerized for a moment by the intricate patterns they were forming. Against the backdrop of almost perfectly still leaves, they seemed even more out of place. It reminded her of something, but she could not place what. It was like the gentle tugging of a dream on a sleep-fogged brain the moment after waking.

You knew there was something important about the dream from which you had just woken, but the memory of it was frustratingly beyond reach. Frankie's mind was barely registering the faint humming the bugs were making when she abruptly came back to herself and remembered her daughter. She turned back toward her husband and reached out for the child.

"I'll take her," she said, nodding over at the small boy Hugo had left in the toddler swing several feet away. The boy was beginning to fuss as the swing slowed. "Colin wants you."

Hugo passed Lydia over to Frankie and jogged back toward their son. Frankie pulled her daughter closer, sinking her nose into the girl's dark curls and inhaling her scent. She smiled reassuringly at the child before lowering her to the ground. She was getting far too big to carry.

Frankie started to turn then noticed something white on the ground near where Lydia and the man had been. She was sure it had not been there before. The patrons of this park were pretty good about cleaning up after themselves. She walked over, Lydia skipping after her, and quickly scooped it up. It was a plain business card. It must have fallen from the man's wallet. The back was blank except for the initials *SF* embossed in gold and the front bore only a name and a phone number.

"Dr. R. Miller."

Frankie shrugged and slipped the card into the pocket of her lightweight sweatshirt. She would throw it away when they got home. She doubted Dr. Miller or the man who lost the card would miss it much.

She bent over and, brushing away a few wood chips from Lydia's coat, pressed a kiss against Lydia's slightly damp cheek. Smiling again, she took hold of her daughter's small hand. "Come on, Lyds. Let's see if those boys are ready to go home."

Two

Emmy-Ann: Hello, Oklahoma, and good morning! **[Audience claps]** Amos is out sick today so my good friend Tina will be filling in. Good morning, Tina.

Tina: Good morning, Emmy-Ann. Gee, I hope he doesn't have that flu that's going around! I hear it's pretty nasty.

Emmy-Ann: I know! It does seem to be going around pretty fast, doesn't it? Anyway, we have another great show lined up for you this morning. We have a special guest today who I just know y'all are going to flip over! But, before we reveal who it is, we will be learning how to make a super yummy soup just in time for autumn with world renowned chef extraordinaire Kym Mathias. Here she is now! Welcome, Kym! **[Audience claps and whoops]**

Kym: Thank you, thank you. It's a pleasure to be here. I can't wait to show you my newest version of traditional chicken noodle soup! It's sure to cure what ails you!

Tina: We should take some of that soup to poor Amos. I'll bet that would fix him right up!

Emmy-Ann: What a great idea. Tina! I'll take some right over after the show!

Hello, Oklahoma with Amos and Emmy-Ann, KBOK

RAIN TAPPED STEADILY, almost rhythmically, against the metal guttering. The sound echoed softly through the window panes and into the dimly lit living room where a man sat slumped alone on a battered brown recliner. The bulky old TV in front of him flickered. It cast flashes of light across the room. A woman with a toothy smile mutely explained all the wonderful things the food processor in front of her could do for him for only five easy payments of $19.99. Shadows danced over the bare walls around him attracting his gaze. It was late. He should have gone to bed ages ago.

A dull thud came from somewhere outside followed by the almost imperceptible tinkling of glass. A voice, muffled by walls and windows, barked something unintelligible. A door slammed then an engine roared and, tires screeching, a vehicle that sounded at least as large as a pickup truck sped up the street and away from the small house.

Before he knew quite what he was doing, Henry leapt from his seat and was down the dark hall to his unlit bedroom in a flash. He wrenched open the top drawer of the lone nightstand and plunged his hand in, his fingers closing tightly around the cool and familiar handle of his XD-40. Cocking it, Henry dashed back down the hall and out the front door into the chilly night. His bare feet slapped loudly against the wet pavement and he swore under his breath as he slid to a wobbly halt in a sizable puddle on the sidewalk in front of his house. The bottoms of his jeans were soaked trough. Far up the street, tail lights were disappearing around a corner.

Henry glanced over at his sun-faded tan 1973 CJ7. There was a large spider web break with a hole at its center on the driver's side of the windshield. Groaning, he ambled over and looked inside. A fairly large, round rock rested on the driver's seat. Why hadn't he just kept his damn gun on

15

him when he'd got home? He felt stupid for not having expected something and more so for not having been better prepared.

Across the street, a light appeared behind the kitchen blinds of a modest single-story home that was very like his own. Henry quickly shoved his gun into the waistband of his jeans and pulled his flannel shirt up over it. He patted his pockets for his cell phone and palmed it just as it began to vibrate.

"It's okay, Mrs. Rose," he said into it without waiting for her to speak, "It was just some kids messing around. Go back to bed".

He could just see her peeking through the slats at him. "Oh, Henry," her voice quavered, "Your truck!" Mrs. Rose was well into her eighties, but her eyesight often seemed sharper than his own despite the increasingly blue cloudy cataracts that were forming on either of her light grey eyes. He waved his hand at her and she disappeared again behind the kitchen blinds.

"Don't you worry," He replied, resisting the urge to correct her by informing her that it was a Jeep and not a truck he drove. His hand absently rested on the spot where his gun was hidden from sight. "It was just some stupid kids. I'll take care of it. You go back to bed, Mrs. Rose". Reluctantly, the woman hung up and, within seconds, her house was plunged into darkness again.

Henry heaved a sigh. He really did not have the time to replace his windshield, but he supposed he probably should. Driving without one was not exactly his idea of fun. Yanking open the stiff driver's side door, he made a mental note to call Freddie's Auto Salvage in the morning to see if, by any chance, they had any junkers from which he could rip a windshield. It would be a pain in the ass to do it himself, but worlds cheaper than having it done by some idiot kid at Perfect Fit Auto Glass who probably hadn't known the difference between a wrench and a ratchet before being hired and who probably still confused the two.

He grabbed an ice scraper from the passenger side floor and turned it brush side down. With careful strokes, he swept the glass shards that had sprayed across the seats and dash into a couple small piles then when to work on what had made it to the floor.

It had been his father's Jeep. Henry Lee Decker Senior, Hank to his friends, had bought it brand new the year he graduated from high school. He had been saving for his own car since he was ten years old. No lawn went unmowed, no newspaper undelivered. Hank had been determined to have his own vehicle so he could drive himself right out of what he called Podunkville, the town in which he was born and raised, and drive himself out he did that summer of 1973. Little did he know that he would be driving himself right back into "Podunkville" less than a year later in that very same Jeep with his heavily pregnant soon-to-be bride riding shotgun.

Hank had refused to give up his hard-earned Jeep in favor of a more practical family vehicle. He had sworn he would never be caught driving around town, a bunch of screaming kids bouncing round the back of a station wagon. Fortunately for Hank, but much to the disappointment of Henry's mother, Maggie, there were no more pregnancies after Henry's arrival in the summer of '74. It had not been an easy labor and, after both Maggie and her baby had shown signs of distress, Henry Lee Decker Junior was brought into the world via C-section. Neither Maggie nor Hank had ever been willing to discuss the details of Henry's dramatic entrance into the world. The most he knew was that something had gone very wrong and, while he was lucky to be alive, there had been some sort of damage to his mother's uterus that had made any future children a biological impossibility.

If either his mother or father had felt as though they had missed out having had only one child, they certainly never expressed it in any way to Henry. He had been the center of their attention from the moment of his birth and a great source of pride to both parents. Hank had been especially proud of his progeny who, by all accounts, was his spitting image. From the moment he could spend a decent amount of time away from his mother, Hank had taken his small son on camping and fishing trips as well as spending hours teaching him how to properly care for the Jeep. The two had been inseparable.

Henry had coveted his father's Jeep for as long as he could remember. Hank had driven it to and from work whenever the weather wasn't good enough for walking. Every family trip had been taken in it. Other than that, Hank had tried to drive it as little as possible so it would last.

When he was fifteen, after a whole lot of begging, Henry learned to drive in it. Everything he knew about fixing cars stemmed from the work he and his father did on that Jeep. Hank had been fond of telling his son each time they had to go to a junkyard or auto parts store for something how 'Jeep' actually stood for 'Just Empty Every Pocket'. Regardless, Hank had refused to sell the Jeep and buy something that required less time and money. Maggie had joked more than a few times how Hank had loved that damned thing more than he loved her. Still, as much as Hank had loved his Jeep, Henry never doubted how much his father had adored his mother.

Like his father, Henry was 18 when his dream vehicle finally became his own. Unlike his father, though,

Henry could not pride himself with having earned it. Instead, it came to him as inheritance. On his deathbed, in a morphine induced haze, Hank had mumbled something about Henry's being an only child having been his fault. When Henry pressed his father to explain, Hank had simply replied, "I shoulda just bought a damned station wagon".

Henry stared down at the little piles of glass he had made. No, he really didn't have time for this shit. He had a full week of work to look forward to complete with the promise of overtime as well as a couple side jobs that needed wrapping up. He wasn't entirely sure when he would be able to make it to the junkyard much less when he would be free during daylight to actually install the glass.

He straightened up, looking across the street. Mrs. Rose had a garage with very little in it. She didn't even have a car, having sold it after a doctor told her that she would not be able to see well enough to drive it without first having laser surgery on her eyes to remove the cataracts that had formed on each. She confided in Henry that it was not cowardice that prevented her from getting the surgery so much as her lack of desire to see much more of the world than she absolutely had to. "Henry, love," she whispered, "the things I have seen in my life would shake even you to your very core". He wondered if she would mind him borrowing her empty garage one evening.

"Oooh…"

Henry jerked his head to look back up the street, his hand resting on the spot under his clothes where his gun was tucked. It suddenly struck him how still it was. Despite being smack in the middle of a more residential area of town, everything was almost disturbingly quiet tonight. Not even that damned stray cat that liked to ransack trash containers was around.

"Ooooooh…"

The voice was growing louder, echoing strangely against the houses and causing Henry to spin halfway around before correcting and facing so that he was staring up the street again. Chills shot through him. For some reason, the voice was unnerving him more than it should have. It was probably just some drunk stumbling home. The timbre of it did not sound masculine. Better safe than sorry, he backed slowly around to the rear of his Jeep and crouched between it and the wall of the house. He was already on edge. Whoever or whatever was making that noise was not helping ease him in the slightest.

Henry peered around the bumper of the Jeep, resting one hand on it for balance and the other on the waistband of his jeans where his gun waited. A twinge shot through his right knee making him wince. He was too old for this shit. Hell, he was too old to be hiding behind anything from what was very likely, now that he was thinking about it, just those idiot kids he had managed to piss off that morning. He had known it would only be a matter of time before they found him. Maybe if he had been driving a minivan, they would have had a harder time. Vehicles like that littered most residential areas in town. Old CJ7s? Not so much. Sure, it was a plain flat black, but that hand painted red alien landscape on the front bumper, while only about four inches long, made the vehicle even more distinctive.

It obviously had been earlier that day when a carload of teen boys had been swerving in and out of traffic behind him. Henry, not wanting to read about how a bunch of idiot kids had crashed and killed themselves or, even worse, an innocent bystander, slowed down enough so that they were unable to squeeze between him and the red Honda next to him. He had maintained his position until spotting a police car whereupon he moved over and let karma intervene. With their middle fingers thrust in Henry's direction, the teens, frustrated at having been blocked, sped up so suddenly that the action attracted the attention of the officer in the police car who pulled out behind them and signaled them to stop. There was no way a ticket for reckless driving had not been in their future.

Wincing again, Henry shifted his weight over to his left leg to relieve the pressure on his right knee. It was still sore from spending so much time kneeling without protection at work. He'd let a new guy borrow his kneepads a month before and had not seen them since. Come to think of it, he had not seen the new guy again either. He'd just been trying to be nice and now he needed to buy new kneepads. He should have known better. He was old enough to know better. He shook his head slowly knowing that he would probably do the same thing all over again for the next new guy. It was who he was. He was not stupid or gullible. He just liked to help others.

He was definitely way too old for this shit. If it was those idiot kids, what did he have to be scared about? The worst thing they were apt to be armed with was another damned rock. He leaned harder against the bumper and started to rise, but froze halfway up.

A slender woman was leaning against the nearest lamp post. She was wearing jeans and a loose dark blue blouse that, without a jacket, could not possibly be warm enough in the chill that the rain had left. However, she was not shivering. In fact, she seemed completely oblivious to the chilly, wet weather. She groaned softly and turned her head jerkily to the side, her long black hair shifting away from her face. There was a distinct sheen of sweat on her ashen cheeks and forehead and strands of hair that almost seemed to shimmer white in the street light were plastered

21

to her skin like some sort of strange modern art picture frame. She had a sort of exotic look about her that did not quite match the pallid tone of her skin. He thought she might be Asian. There were scratches all over her face that looked pretty fresh.

Henry pulled himself all the way up and took a couple steps around the Jeep toward her. "Miss?"

The women jolted as though the sound of his voice had sent shockwaves through her. She swiveled her whole body in his direction and stood swaying silently. Although he was only a matter of twenty or so feet in front of her, she gave no other sign that she was aware of him. Her mouth was moving soundlessly, but Henry had never been good at reading lips. His eyes flickered to a long scratch that ran down the side of her left cheek. It was deep and, by the puffiness surrounding it, untreated. The expression on her face reminded him of a wild animal and her eyes, unfocused, were an icy blue, but it was her mouth that truly bother him. It was like something out of a B-Horror flick. Drool seeped from the edges and he saw now that she was not trying to speak at all. Instead, her jaw was moving as if she was chewing on something.

"You okay there, Miss? You need hel-" The woman had pitched forward and was staggering slowly toward him as if she could not see him but, rather, was drawn to his voice.

Before she could reach him, he leapt away from his Jeep and watched with confusion as the woman crashed into the side of the vehicle and began to paw blindly at it. "Uhhhng...Jaaay..."

Henry backed slowly away from the woman and edged toward his front door, his feet slipping slightly in a puddle. He had never been prone to flights of fancy nor had his imagination ever been something to write Stephen King about, but this, in his opinion, was some spooky-ass zombie shit. He wondered if it was that drug he kept hearing about that was making kids in Florida act like zombies. He wracked his mind trying to remember anything about it other than the fact that it was making druggies eat people's faces off.

Just as his hand touched his front door handle, a spotlight lit up his street and swung into his driveway. The woman, unfazed, kept banging her body against the Jeep, her hands spasmodically searching it. She was now repeating the same sound with increasing urgency despite the obvious effort it was to form the words. "Jaaaay....heeeelll....p....jaaay".

An unmarked black vehicle pulled up quickly to the curb, the soft purr of the engine only now reaching Henry's ears, and a couple of men in dark suits jumped out of either side. The driver headed straight for Henry, one hand up in a friendly greeting, while the other went in the direction of the woman. The second man had a mask like the one's Henry had seen doctors on TV shows use covering his mouth and nose and was hastily pulling on what looked like latex gloves. Henry tried to keep his eyes on both, but the first man positioned himself between Henry and his Jeep.

"Evening, sir," the man said, a wide smile spreading lazily across his face, "Sorry to disturb you. There was a lapse in security up at the hospital and this little lady managed to squeak through the cracks and went for a walk. We've been looking for her all night."

Henry frowned and leaned to the side to peer over the man's shoulder, but the man leaned with him. "What's wrong with her?" he asked.

"Don't you worry about her, sir. She'll be fine." He

glanced back quickly. Henry caught a glimpse of the man's partner. He appeared to be struggling somewhat with the woman. The man turned again to Henry, shifting with each movement of Henry's eyes to obscure his vision. "She'll be fine, sir. Just going to get her back to her nice, comfy room up at the hospital."

"Heh," Behind the man, Henry could hear the woman groaning and grunting louder and with more purpose. There was an urgency developing in her voice, but he could not see past the man in front of him well enough to get a better picture of what was happening. "Heh!"

There was a soft clinking noise like metal joining together. He didn't have to look to know what that sound was. One more time, the man glanced over his shoulder and, seeing his partner guiding the woman over to their car, started to back away from Henry. "You have a good night, sir."

That nixed all thoughts of zombies for Henry. No one in any movie he had even seen bundled a handcuffed zombie into the back of a car to return it to a hospital. They just shot them in the head and called it a day. But, then, he wondered, was that how sick women are typically handled? Something was off. Aside from being very obviously ill, she did not seem to pose much of a threat to anyone. Then there was the two men. Neither looked remotely like paramedics or even doctors to Henry. They were more like businessmen or, he mused, like a couple of guys from that movie about the secret agency that deals with aliens disguised as humans. He furrowed his brow in thought. Whether she was a zombie, an alien, or just a sick woman, something was definitely not right about all this.

"Jaaaay! Heeeelp!"

Zombies also did not cry for help.

He watched as the second man closed the passenger side door on the woman and hurried around to the driver's side. The first man, reaching the passenger door, paused with his hand on the handle. He turned back slightly and stared at Henry for a moment.

"You, uh, you didn't touch her, did you?" he asked in what he must have thought was an offhanded manner. "She didn't spit on you or anything, did she?"

Henry shook his head. "No, why?"

"You're sure?"

"Yeah," Henry frowned at the man. "I'm sure. But why? Is she contagious or something?"

The man nodded curtly once, satisfied with Henry's answer. Without another word, he opened his door and slipped into the car. As soon as the door shut, the car pulled back onto the road and headed down the street. Henry watched it go all the way down, making no sign of turning to head uptown. Lips pursed into a frown, he shook his head.

The hospital was in the other direction.

Three

Boomer: Gooood morning, good morning, good morning! What a beautiful day it is here in southern Colorado! It's a little cloudy out there with a high of 75° and a low of 41°. That's slightly chillier than expected for this time of year and we're looking at an 80% chance of rain, but that's nothing we can't handle, is it? Maybe it means we'll have a good snowfall this year so we can all hit the slopes a little earlier. Just take care not to get sick. There's a nasty flu going around. My kids are home with it right now driving my wife crazy, but, boy, does she ever pamper them! They never want to go back to school because of how she spoils them when they're sick. Hey, I think I feel a sniffle coming on. Maybe I can get in on some of that spoiling. **[Boomer sniffs loudly]** Shh! Don't tell the wife! Here's one of my favorite oldies 'Somebody Get Me a Doctor' by Van Halen!

The Boomer Gallagher Morning Show, 93. 9 KZCO Rocky Mountain Oldies

"MOMMY?"

A shaggy brown dog was sitting across the street, unmoving and staring at Frankie. She had been pulling weeds from the path that led between the joint front porch of their duplex to the sidewalk when Lydia called to her from where she had been sitting on the lawn stringing daisies together to make necklaces. The girl had stopped and was looking, not at her mother as she spoke, but at the dog.

"Mommy?"

Frankie tucked a stray black curl behind her ear and stood up, dusting off her knees before straightening completely. The dog did not seem to be wearing a collar and she did not recognize it as being from their neighborhood. Still, it looked friendly enough. Frankie wondered if she could convince it to go with her into their backyard so it would be safe and secured while she called Animal Control.

She was good with animals. She always had been. When she was little, she had wanted to be a vet and had spent all her free time right up into her mid-teens up the street at the Parker's small farm helping Mr. Parker with his animals. The Parkers farm produced barely enough to support the farm and themselves, but they never seemed to want for anything.

At first, Frankie had thought it was because Mrs. Parker also worked at the library, but Frankie discovered much later that this was due to a lot of support from her own parents. Mrs. Parker had been her mother's closest friend since childhood and Mr. Parker had become fast friends with her father soon after he had moved to town in his late teens. As a result of the friendship, Frankie had pretty much grown up alongside Janie, the youngest of the

Parker's children. The two were inseparable and found in common a natural talent for caring for and communicating with animals.

Frankie walked toward it calmly offering her hand and making soft clicking noises with her tongue. "Here, boy. Here, doggy. It's okay. Come here".

"Moooommmy?"

The dog rose suddenly, the hair on the back of it head and neck prickling up. A low growl rumbled from it as it took two warning steps forward. Frankie froze. Natural talent meant little when it came to feral animals. What was that her mother had said about dealing with mean dogs? Was she supposed to back away? Make herself bigger and more threatening? She suddenly couldn't remember. Palm out toward her daughter, her eyes darted about to see if any gardening tools had been left out that she could use for protection if necessary. "Stay still, Lyds. Don't move".

But Lydia was already moving and the dog's attention was shifted from Frankie to her. Its head spun to follow Lydia's movements. Frankie could now see the white foam bubbling and dripping from its mouth to the sidewalk. Without warning, it leapt forward so rapidly that Frankie did not have enough time to react.

She flung herself sideways in a hopeless attempt to place herself between the dog and her child, but it was too late. The dog was past her, snarling and barking as its dark form covered her child and blocked her completely from Frankie's sight.

Frankie's shrieks melted into Lydia's. Too late. It was too late.

"MOOOMMY!"

Frankie jolted awake, blinking at the darkness and panting from fright. Sweat sliding down her face, mingling with the tears that were streaming down her cheeks. Relief flooded through her. It had only been a dream.

She wiped at the sweat that was dripping from her face. It was hot. Why was it so hot? By September, the nights were usually noticeably cooler. She shoved the comforter off herself and blinked into the darkness. No. It wasn't hot. She could feel the iciness of the air in her lungs as her breathing began to slow. She must have forgotten to turn up the heat for the night. Next to her, the shape of her husband rose and fell with the gentle rhythmic abandon of deep, undisturbed slumber.

"Moooommmmy!"

He would sleep through an earthquake, Frankie thought as she swung her legs over the side of her bed. Her bare feet touching the cold wooden floor sent waves of shock through her overheated body. Her entire body ached as she shivered violently.

She swore under her breath. This was no time to get the flu. There was a big meeting at work in the morning that she simply could not afford to miss and she had promised Colin that she wouldn't miss his first soccer match. She knew it would just be a bunch of boys and girls between two and four years old darting wildly and without real direction around a pitch, but it was important to him that she be there.

Sighing, she picked up an elastic hairband from her nightstand and pulled back her unruly damp hair. Then, leaning heavily on the nightstand, she pushed herself up. She stumbled down the hall to the children's room and clicked on the small bedside lamp that sat next to her daughter's bed. Dim yellowish light brightened the room a bit, stinging Frankie's eyes. She rubbed at them as she sat on the end of Lydia's bed. "What's wrong honey?"

She was answered with muffles rattling breaths.

Lydia's head was mostly covered by her Spiderman duvet. The girl had been obsessed with the wall-crawling hero since her second birthday when someone, not knowing what to get her, had gifted the girl with a six-inch tall Spiderman action figure. It was love at first web. That very same doll was propped up in a defensive pose against the wall on the nightstand. He looked ready for anything. Lydia liked to keep him there to protect her against what she called "night bumps".

Still bleary-eyed, Frankie pulled the covers back from her child's head, her cap of dark curls spilling across the pillow. Frankie blinked again to banish the sleepiness from her eyes. There was something white all over those luscious black locks. "Mommy?"

Frankie wiped the hair from her daughter's face, her hand coming away wet. Lydia, like her mother, was covered in sweat. "Great. Now there's two of us".

Lydia struggled to sit up. She twisted toward the sound of her mother's voice, her eyes fluttering open and closed. Frankie's own vision was finally clearing a little. She brushed again at Lydia's hair wondering what in the world the child had got in it. It seemed to move with her hair almost like it was part of it. She pressed her fingertips gently to the child's scalp and, wiggling them a bit, ran her fingers through the hair to dislodge the white objects. Again, the white things moved as one with her daughter's dark locks. Then it struck her; It *was* Lydia's hair.

Streaks of white permeated her thick, ebony curls. Frankie shook her head, confused. She cupped Lydia's hot cheeks in her hands and tilted her face up. The child's eyes were now open, but there was no trace of their familiar chocolate brown hue. Cloudy blue masses covered the entirety of the irises and pupils. A groan escaped her parted lips and she reached up, clawing weakly at Frankie "Moommm-uh…. Mommmm…"

Involuntarily, Frankie's body jerked away from her daughter. She staggered backwards, banging her shoulder so hard against the half open door that it slammed against the wall. Her eyes passed over Colin's bed. He was curled under his own blankets, unmoving despite the racket she was creating. He was just like his father. Elephants could have marched through the room and he would have slept on.

Frankie pushed against the door and pitched back, crashing into the hallway. "Hugo!" she yelled, feeling dizzy. It felt like one of those dreams where you could scream as loudly as you wanted and never be loud enough. Hugo wouldn't hear her; he slept like the dead. She shrilled his name again, banging her fist against the wall as hard as she could. Was this really a dream? Would she wake shrieking so loudly that the neighbors would wake as well?

To her surprise, it was enough. Hugo came stumbling through their open bedroom door and tripped into the hallway. He braced himself against the wall and flipped the light switch. Light flooded into the hallway, its brightness stinging her eyes. She blinked furiously against it until her husband became more than a painful blur. Hugo was gaping at her, shock widening his sleep crusted eyes. His mouth flapped comically for a moment before he found words. "Jesus…Fuck! Fuck, Frankie! Are you okay?"

He ran to her, gripping her by the shoulders as she slumped against the wall for support. His eyes were darting from her face to her hair repeatedly. "What's wrong with you? What did you do?"

He looked wrong. Hugo looked older. When had his hair gone salt and pepper? She shook her head and squeezed her eyes shut to block out the blinding hall light. "What did I…? Not me…flu," she said dismissively, pointing back up the hall to the children's room, "There's something wrong with Lydia."

Hugo released his wife and followed her finger, but his eyes remained on her until he disappeared through the door. There was silence for a few seconds then Hugo swore loudly. "Call 911! Jesus! Frankie, call 911!"

Frankie was already stumbling back to their room. Her phone was plugged in to charge on the nightstand next to her side of the bed. She grabbed it, but her fingers felt numb and it slipped through them and clattered to the floor. She dropped to her knees and fumbled for it again, this time managing to maintain a grip on it. She unlocked the screen and stared at it for what seemed like ages before releasing a sharply barked involuntary laugh. She had briefly forgotten the number for 911.

Frankie jabbed her finger at the screen of her phone and lifted it to her ear. She didn't even hear it ring before a pleasant male voice sounded in her ear. "911. What is your emergency?"

"My daughter," Frankie slurred. She was so tired now. A surge of guilt swept over her as she thought how nice it would be if she could just lay her head down against the cool floor and go back to sleep.

"Ma'am?" The voice. How many times had he said that? Frankie wasn't sure. She could hear Hugo saying something from down the hall. She wondered if he was talking to her. "Ma'am?"

She squeezed her eyes shut again and tried to focus on the voice at the other end of the phone. "My daughter…"

"Has your daughter been hurt?"

"She's sick…She's…," Frankie's lips felt dry and her tongue heavy. The word she was trying to come up with escaped her. "She's different…I…we need help".

"Is she breathing?" The line crackled loudly in her ear.

"Yes."

"What is your-" The line crackled again and a deeper, gruffer voice continued. "Is your front door unlocked, Ms. Reed?"

"I…I don't know…I don't think…" *Reed*? She could not recall having given her name yet and, in any case, Reed was her maiden name. Surely, she would have said Krause. She did not have time to think any more about it. The man was speaking again, asking her questions she found difficult to get her mind to focus on much less answer.

"We're on our way," the man assured her. Frankie tried to respond, but she kept drifting away then back again, honing in on the man's voice each time the pitch of it changed. Her head was swimming now and the man's words were beginning to sound garbled. It occurred to her that she had never given her address either, but, then, did anyone have to anymore? *Technology these days*, Frankie thought. *Big Brother always knows where you are.* That was her last thought before the phone slipped from her fingers and everything went black.

FRANKIE'S FATHER HAD been what some people called a Prepper. He called it common sense. For as long as Frankie could remember, her father had always made sure they had extra of just about everything. "It never hurts to be ready," he often quipped while the two of them pushed a shopping cart up and down aisles at the grocery or hardware store. But ready for what, exactly, he never said.

Frankie really enjoyed shopping with her father. Her mother had little patience for getting anything more than what was needed when it came to shopping and would opt to stay home to watch one of her daytime soaps whenever her husband announced it was time to go to the store to stock up. Frankie, however, never passed on a trip anywhere with her father. He traveled for work and there were times he was gone for weeks in a row. They spoke often on the phone, but it never felt to her like it was enough. Because of this, she leapt at every chance to spend even a few minutes with him.

As odd as it always had been to outsiders, Frankie's father's behavior became noticeably strange to Frankie after he arrived home from one of his business trips in 1989. Frankie had been about to finish up kindergarten and had been looking forward to the summer with mounting excitement.

Her father had been gone for well over a month and had promised to take her and her best friend Janie Parker on a camping trip just as soon as he got home. When the day arrived and his car finally pulled into their driveway, Frankie could barely contain herself. She had raced to see him and had flung herself into his arms just as soon as he stepped out of his car.

There were two things about that day that Frankie would never forget. The first was how fiercely her father had hugged her. It was a desperate sort of hug like he was drowning and she was a life vest. Frankie had made a squeaking noise and wriggled until he finally released her. The second thing was his appearance.

Franklin Ray Reed was a very handsome man. He had high cheekbones and a broad, prominent nose that he had always felt too big. Frankie had always thought it made him look distinguished. Secretly, though, she was glad her own nose was more similar to her mother's. She doubted a nose like his would have looked quite as nice on a girl.

His jet-black tight curls were kept neatly cropped and always glistened slightly from the sweet-smelling pomade he used in them. Frankie's hair was a lot like his except in color. She also favored her mother this way, but was less pleased about it than she was about sharing a nose shape. Her mother's side of the family was littered with redheads. While she did think the color was pretty, she had always thought it looked strange on her. She thought it did not match her skin tone the way it did for her mother. Adults had always told Frankie that her hair made her look a bit exotic. This was something she probably would not have minded as an adult, but, as a child, it was difficult to look so different. It was, more often than not a reason for other children to pick on her. Her mother was always against the idea of Frankie dying her hair, but the taunting was the main reason she finally did the night before she moved out to go to college. She had been determined not to stand out so much.

Frankie's father was always impeccably dressed. He tended to choose expensive suits with brightly patterned ties that went well with the silver framed glasses that he wore halfway down his nose so that he could peer over them to talk to people and look down through them to read. Everyone said Frankie was the perfect combination of her parents, but, as beautiful as she thought her mother, Frankie secretly thought with pleasure that she favored her father more. As she got older, it became obvious that this was not true.

That day, though, her father appeared very little like his usual self. She had stared at him once she had stepped back from his embrace, a skeptical look on her face. She was not even certain that the man in front of her was, indeed, her father. He was very like her father, but parts of him were different. His skin, for one, usually a rich and deep brown, was distinctly paler. It was still darker than her own skin, but it was a sort of sickly ashy color that reminded Frankie of how the chalkboard at school looked after a long day of constant writing and erasing. He was sort of dusty, she thought. His hair, once the deepest shade of black, was now flecked with white like he had just stepped in from being out in the snow and it had yet to melt. She wanted to brush it away, but he was so tall that she would never reach his head without clambering up him and, right now, he did not look like he could support her weight. In fact, she realized, the real difference in him was that he looked sick. She frowned. Franklin Reed never got sick.

Strangest of all were his eyes. They were normally a beautiful pure brown. Frankie had risen onto the tips of her toes and leaned over the back of their station wagon to get a closer look as her father unloaded his suitcases from the trunk. She could not quite see them, but his eyes were definitely not pure brown anymore. She would discover later, when he tucked her into her bed, that she had been right in thinking she had seen some blue in them. Those wise eyes, she saw as he wearily read her a bedtime story, had the most peculiar swirls of blue throughout his irises.

When her father rose from her bed and slipped the book back into its place on the bookshelf, Frankie had asked him why he looked so different. He had paused for several seconds before answering, "People change, Frankie, as they get older. I got older".

It felt like a lie. This really bothered her because her father had always impressed on her the importance of truthfulness. Besides, how could he possibly have aged so much in such a short amount of time? "You sick, Daddy?"

Again, he paused. "Maybe a little, princess. I'm tired. Work was…hard".

Frankie, as a child, had asked her father several times what he did for a living. She knew that he was a doctor, but not the sort that saw patients. He never really gave her an answer that satisfied her curiosity. In fact, he never spoke about what he did for work except to tell her that it was just "boring government stuff" that she wouldn't be interested in. She did not believe that in the slightest. Frankie was interested in all things involving her father.

That summer was meant to have been so much fun. Frankie's imagination had been wild with thoughts of fishing and hiking as well as learning how to tie knots and carve miniature figurines like her father did when he was in Boy Scouts. He had promised all this and more. Her little heart would skip beats as she thought of all the wonderful things she and her father would do. Janie had been excited, too. It was all they had spoken about for the whole month before school let out for the summer. However, her father had spent the summer before Frankie's sixth birthday building a bunker beneath their backyard instead. He then began purchasing various nonperishable supplies with an urgency she had never seen in him before. He was so wrapped up in his project that he almost forgot about Frankie's birthday when it rolled around late August.

There was no camping trip that year or the next either. There were no camping trips with her father ever again.

Years passed and, eventually, Frankie's father appeared to become less obsessed with the bunker and keeping it stocked. He never really stopped adding to it or replacing things as time went by, but he spoke less about it and made far fewer references to being ready. The last thing Frankie recalled him actually doing to it was when he planted bushes near the entrance hatch. Once the hatch was hidden from sight, Frankie found it easier to forget altogether that the bunker ever existed.

Her father became quiet and withdrawn, often spending evenings at home out on the front porch staring out into the darkness. Frankie had tried, at first, to talk to him. Their conversations were clipped and more forced than they should have been so, eventually, she gave up altogether and left him to it.

Despite the lack of communication, Frankie would still join her father on the front porch. She would take a book or her homework and lean her back against the wall under the kitchen window so that the soft light would spill out from over the sink where her mother stood washing the supper dishes. She tried not to mind that they never spoke. She tried to convince herself that it was enough just being near him, but the silence was painful to her. Often, it made him seem secretive. It was as if he knew something, but could not or would not share it with anyone around him.

Frankie often felt locked out of her father's life. When she was sixteen, her mother had tried to console her, assuring her that whatever was going on with her father had nothing to do with her. She speculated that her husband was simply preoccupied with thoughts of work and that this would soon change. He had been talking about retiring and, she was sure, would start spending more time with them. She was so sure of it. Maybe they would even go camping.

Her mother said this just about every year after that first missed camping trip. It never happened, at least not with her father. Frankie went a handful of times with friends and, at the insistence of her mother, attended a religious summer camp for five years in a row. It wasn't the same, though. It never was. No experience ever lived up to Frankie's memories and the promises of fun and adventure her father had made so many years before. She often wondered if anything ever would.

MA'AM?"

Frankie groaned. Her head was throbbing and she could not make her eyes focus. There was a sort of blobby shadow in front of her, illuminated by light behind it. This much she could tell; she was sure it was the blob that was speaking to her. She opened her mouth to answer, but only another groan escaped her lips.

"Ma'am?" The blob spoke again, gently, but more insistent this time. It prodded at her forehead with something long and smooth. "How many people are in the house with you? Is there anyone else?"

Another voice spoke, deeper and with more authority than the first. It was familiar to Frankie, but she could not place where she had heard it before. "There was a boy, too, Mendez. You and Johnson, clear this room. Where's the husband? Did someone escort him out yet?" Frankie heard heavy thumping retreating from the room.

Four

Tina: Hello, Oklahoma, and good morning.
[Audience claps] Emmy-Ann is out sick today.
Before we begin our show, it is with great
sadness that I have to tell you that our very own
Amos McGuire has unexpectedly passed away.
Amos had been with KBOK since 2001 and on
Hello, Oklahoma since 2012. He was an integral
part of the KBOK family and will be missed.

**Hello, Oklahoma with Boomer and Emmy-Ann,
KBOK**

HENRY WOKE FEELING stiff. He had fallen asleep for
the third night in a row in front of the TV. The morning
news was on, but, as usual, the sound was off. He rarely
bothered actively watching anything these days. There was
nothing much worth watching. Even the news was filled
with mindless drivel when it wasn't showing horrific
images of yet another mass shooting or some catastrophic
natural disaster. There was too much sadness, too much
pain in the world. He'd had his fill of that and then some.

He stretched and sat up, reaching forward for his cellphone to check the time. Turning the screen on, he squinted at the white numbers in the top right corner. *They make the font on these things so damned small,* he thought as the time slowly came into focus. 6:23 a.m. It was a Wednesday and, for once, he did not have to work. His boss had called the night before to say that he and a few others on the crew were suddenly not feeling well. He had thought it best to cancel the job for at least a day in case it was something contagious.

Henry still managed to wake up right before his alarm was set to go off. He silenced it, knowing he had forgotten to turn it off the night before, and dropped the phone back onto the rickety coffee table then ran his hands through his hair. He supposed he might as well get a start on his windshield. He had been driving it around with a hole in it for a few days now. It would be stupid to waste a surprise day off when he had no idea when the next would roll around. Work had been busy lately and looked like it would stay that way. It would be even busier if half the crew was knocked out by flu. Part of him wished work hadn't been canceled. They would be a day behind at best now and he knew he could have kept things going until whatever was going around passed. He was not worried about himself. He rarely got more than a cold.

Henry ambled down the hall and into the bathroom where he turned on the shower and pulled off his shirt. The one really nice thing about his house was his hot water heater. That thing could make the water go from icy to scalding in sixty seconds flat. Sure enough, steam quickly began to rise and spill over the top of the shower curtain. He reached through and adjusted the cold water tap then, stripping off the rest of his clothes, he stepped into the shower. Head back and eyes closed, he let the water flow over his forehead and down his face.

41

There was a faint buzzing from the other room, but he ignored it. Whoever was calling could wait. It was probably just his boss changing his mind and calling people in. Usually, he enjoyed taking extra hours. The more hours he spent working, the fewer he was free to let his mind wander. Today, however, he had things to do that would be just as distracting.

The phone buzzed again.

Henry squirted some shampoo into his hand then worked it through his hair. Its minty smell quickly permeated the whole room and sent his thoughts back to his father as it always did. His father had loved the smell of mint. He said it made everything seem fresh even if it really wasn't. He had always followed this by offering his son a stick of gum.

His father had died twenty-five years ago and Henry would still chuckle whenever he thought about some of the things the man would say. Hank had called them Dad Jokes. His mother told him once that she regretted laughing at any of the ridiculous things her husband said or did. "Laugh once and they never stop," she had whispered to Henry as she lovingly watched her husband saunter away, still laughing at a joke he had just made for the hundredth time.

Henry smiled at the memory. Then, as it always did, the smile faded as he thought about his mother.

Maggie had doted on her only child. It didn't matter how many times she was told by other mothers that her attentions would ruin her son. Maggie believed it was important for Henry to know every day that he was loved. She made it obvious that she lived to care for him and would do just about anything to make him happy. She was constantly hugging and kissing him which never really bothered him even when his friends laughed and made fun of him for it. He felt loved. His mother made him feel special. Her love made him feel powerful and courageous and often helped propel him down steep hills and up tall trees. Her love made him feel like there was nothing he could not do.

Then, when Henry was ten, Margaret Mae Decker was struck by a car as she stepped out onto the crosswalk from the grocery store to make her way home. She didn't even make it to the hospital. The driver, a young man visiting from out of town, was said to have been well over the legal limit. One witness had commented that she could smell the alcohol on him stronger than if she'd had her head over a bucket of whiskey.

Growing up without her had not been easy. Henry had been surprised at how angry he felt at her. He knew that the blame fell directly on the drunk driver and nowhere near his mother. She had been exactly where she should have been. She had broken no laws, bent no rules. She had been taking home groceries just like she had done at least twice a week for several years before. Henry knew it was irrational, but he had been angry with her nevertheless. She had left him. He hadn't even got to say goodbye.

Hank had not known what to do with his suddenly angry son. Henry had always been happy and good natured. He had been an easy child which Hank had been grateful for. He didn't exactly have much patience for children despite being pretty easy going to begin with and had left Henry's rearing mostly to his wife. With her taken so suddenly from them, Hank found himself drowning in his own grief and with absolutely no idea how to handle his son. Because of this, he withdrew from his only child and rarely came into contact with him except to put food in front of him or when they passed in the hallway. The last real moments of closeness Henry could remember them sharing had all taken place while he was either learning to drive or fix his father's Jeep. Even then, the closeness felt forced.

Henry had grown resentful of his father's emotional absence. He had needed his father to step into the space his mother had vacated and, when he did not, Henry assumed it was because he had not wanted to. It didn't occur to him until much later that his father had been just as angry about Maggie's death as he was and, like him, had had no idea how to cope with it.

By the time Hank's grief became less consuming and Henry's anger had dissipated, too much space had formed between them. There was still love, but with markedly less affection and closeness than there might have been. The realization that they had missed out on each other left Henry feeling even more empty and lost.

Henry's phone was buzzing again. Whoever was calling was determined to reach him. He shut off the water and, grabbing a dingy looking towel that long ago had been a soft shade of cream, rubbed himself dry. In the time it took for him to get to his bedroom and haul on a clean t-shirt, a blue flannel button up, and a pair of jeans, the phone had gone off three more times. Each time, it buzzed for several seconds before going to voicemail. Judging by the amount of time between buzzing, it didn't even seem like whoever was calling was bothering to leave a message anymore.

Henry went back up the hallway to the living room and scooped it up. Turning the screen on, he saw sixteen missed calls. Only one was work related. He recognized the number as belonging to one of the newer crew members. He had meant to add it to his contacts after getting six calls in one day for help concerning the same problem, but had forgotten and now he couldn't even remember the kid's name. The young ones never lasted very long anyway. They were headstrong and impatient and that sort of combination was dangerous.

The rest were all from Mrs. Rose across the street. Guilt shot through him. Mrs. Rose never called unless she really needed him. She was always too afraid of bothering him even though he had told her on numerous occasions that he was available to her whenever she needed. She reminded him of his maternal grandmother and, in a way, of his mother herself. More often than not, Henry would have to either call her or stop by her house to check on her. He did this at least twice a week.

Guilt swiftly turned into worry as he hit the redial button and lifted the phone to his ear. What would have caused her to call him fifteen times? Was she hurt? He scowled at himself. He would be really pissed at himself if it turned out she had fallen and was lying on the ground waiting for him to rescue her. It briefly occurred to him that she probably would have called emergency services and not him had that been the case. The phone didn't even ring once before the woman picked it up.

"Henry!" Mrs. Rose's voice shot into his ear so unexpectedly loud that Henry jerked the phone back from his head with a wince before returning it his ear. She was still talking, obviously not having waited for him to respond "-and I don't know what to do! They're everywhere, Henry! There's one at my front door and he won't go away! Henry! What's happening, Henry?"

"What?" Henry furrowed his brow, trying to make sense of what she was saying. "Who's at your door?"

The old woman still had not stopped talking. "What's going on?" She had barely paused for breath.

Henry moved to his window, the phone still against his ear, and used his thumb and forefinger to spread two slats on his miniblinds apart. Bending slightly, he peered through them and nearly dropped his phone.

The scene outside was like something out of a horror movie. Dozens of people were in the streets in various states of disarray. Many were in pajamas or sweatpants and t-shirts like they had been asleep in their beds only moments before while others were in uniforms or other sorts of work attire. All were disheveled as if a tornado had swept them up from wherever they had been and given them a good trip around Kansas before unceremoniously dumping them on this Oklahoma street. Henry noticed that each and every one had white hair. Almost all of them had mostly white hair with a few streaks of differing colors throughout, but a few looked as though they had been randomly sprayed with some sort of white hair dye. No matter what race they appeared to be, all had a sort of ashy discoloration on every visible inch of skin.

Across the street, there was a man with hair that reminded Henry of Albert Einstein who was pawing in a somewhat lazy manner at Mrs. Rose's front door. There was no urgency in his actions, but Henry could understand how it would unnerve the frail old woman. A few were sort of milling around his front yard. Several were wandering aimlessly in the street, sloshing through the puddles that remained from the rain the night before as if they had no awareness of them. The way they were shuffling about with little control over their limbs and no apparent direction put Henry in mind of an old black and white zombie movie.

At this thought, Henry's stomach suddenly felt very heavy as a realization swept over him; they all looked like the woman from two nights ago. Many looked even less coherent.

"Henry?"

She had been, according to the man in the suit, just sick. Did this mean all these people were all sick and, if so, with what? What sort of contagion would spread so rapidly and have such a strange effect on so many people so quickly? He remembered that one of the men who had dealt with the woman had put on a mask and gloves before getting anywhere near her while the other had not bothered. *It mustn't be airborne, then*, he concluded.

"What should I do, Henry? I can't get through to 911. I keep getting a recording telling me that all the circuits are busy. What should I do? Henry, there's a man trying to get in!"

Henry released the blinds and took a step back. He had absolutely no idea what she should do. It did not look like the man outside Mrs. Rose's door was making any real effort to get in. It looked more like he just couldn't figure out why there was a door in his path. Regardless, the man was frightening her and Henry knew he couldn't not help her. "Hold on, Mrs. Rose, hold on. It's okay. Everything is going to be okay." He repeated the platitudes a few times, but wasn't sure the woman was actually listening to him. She continued fussing on the other end of the line.

"Stay put," he said louder and then, louder still, "I'll come over. You hear me, Mrs. Rose? Stay put. I'm coming".

She was still talking when he pressed the button to end the call. His eyes shifted to the muted television. The news was still playing and a pretty newscaster was silently talking directly to the camera as words scrolled across the bottom of the screen. He barely caught the words 'state of emergency' before he swept up the remote and jabbed at the volume button, unmuting her so that her voice flooded into the room with a shock of increasing intensity. He hastily corrected it and, as the volume lowered to a more reasonable level, his attention zeroed in on her words.

"...in your homes. Again, the Centers for Disease Control is advising that you stay in your homes or remain inside your places of business until further notice. If you are near anyone exhibiting any of the symptoms previously detailed, please refrain from making physical contact with them. Keep your distance and avoid coming into contact with bodily fluids as it is believed this is how the contagion is spread. It is advised that-I'm sorry. I'm just being informed that the President of the United States is about to address the nation. It is likely that he will make a formal declaration of a nationwide state of emergency. Darcy Bannister, our White house correspondent, is live..."

Henry was not listening anymore. The remote had fallen, forgotten from his hand and, bouncing off the arm of his recliner, fell to the floor and disappeared from sight. He jammed his cell phone into his pocket and retrieved his gun from its normal resting place in his nightstand then ran to the front door. He paused with his hand outstretched to open the door as he remembered again the man with the mask and gloves. Even the newscaster had said to stay away from them and avoid contact.

"...conditions around the White House have resulted in the removal of the President by..."

He cautiously moved the blinds aside once more and stared out. Were there more of them than before? It certainly seemed like it. He was not sure how he would get through them all without making at least a little contact. Glancing around, he pulled a heavy work jacket off a hook and hauled it on. He fished around the pockets and found a dirty bandana which he tied around his mouth and nose and topped with a pair of sunglasses. Finally, he put on a baseball cap and his work gloves.

A ripple of laughter escaped his lips. He was sure he looked ridiculous. He must look like he was about to rob a bank.

"...*advising that you stay in your homes and avoid all contact with anyone who appears sick or who has come into contact with someone who is sick. Back to you, Jessica.*"

Without further thought, he opened up his front door and slipped out into the crisp early morning air. His ears were immediately assaulted by what the walls of his house had somehow managed to mask. The people were moaning softly. None seemed to be making any effort to speak. One or two were standing completely still as if frozen to the spot.

There were undeniably more of them than there had been when he was on the phone. The street and sidewalk were thick with them. They were bumping into each other and, each time, clinging to or practically clawing at whoever or whatever they touched. Henry watched as one, a young girl in blue pajamas with some Disney princess on them fell to her knees and disappeared behind the shambling legs around her. The man next to her tumbled down suddenly and was followed almost immediately by another man. It was like watching dominoes fall.

Henry gently closed his door behind himself, listening for it to click before he started down the path toward the sidewalk. He paused several feet away from the closest of them. Her eyes were mostly closed and, aside from wobbling like she had a decent sized bottle of booze tucked into the oversized purse she carried slung over her shoulder, she did not move. His eyes passed over her, taking in her disheveled appearance. She was somewhere in her mid to late forties and, judging by her gray uniform complete with a well starched white apron and her sensible white sneakers, he guessed she had been on her way home from work when the sickness became too much for her.

Or on the way there.

Her clothes were damp. As far as he knew, the rain had slowed to a drizzle sometime around nine p.m. and had stopped completely by ten when he had gone to bed. If so, then she had likely been out all night. He stared at her for several seconds, before edging warily around her and stepping off the curb into the street.

He snorted quietly as he realized he would have to wend his way through the mass of people like he was the frog in a vintage video game avoiding cars. The main difference was that most of the cars he could see were still parked in driveways and none of the people in the streets were moving fast enough to pose much of a challenge to avoid.

There was room to walk between most of them, but he really did not care to get too close. He would have to go up the street a bit before he could cross over and come back to reach Mrs. Rose's house. He had never cared for crowds, generally avoiding all sorts of public gatherings like county fairs and carnivals even as a child. No attraction ever seemed worth dealing with hundreds of other people all clambering to get into line for a ride or cotton candy or whatever else was so important to their experience. He always opted to stay home where it was nice and quiet. As much as he disliked celebratory crowds, he would have rather been dropped smack in the middle of a state fair than walk through this. At least with a state fair, no gun or patched together workman's hazmat-chic look were required. Well, not usually.

As an afterthought, he tucked the gun safely away and moved cautiously diagonally across his lawn. No one so much as glanced in his direction, but, just in case, he was sure that each footfall was as deliberate and quiet as he could possibly make it. Reaching the sidewalk after what seemed like ages, he sidestepped a woman as she staggered forward and ducked just in time to avoid someone's arm as it flailed at his face.

His breath caught in his throat and he stared back over his shoulder at the still floundering arm. No, it had not been intentional. The owner of the arm was no more aware of him than were any of the others. He expelled the breath and rolled his shoulders back. He was even more jumpy than he had thought.

With renewed determination, Henry moved on, his eyes scanning the peculiar crowd for the best place to cross the street. Spotting an opening, he dashed toward it and spun to avoid a man who was not moving at all. He was, instead, standing perfectly still with his sweat-soaked face tilted up at the sky, his cloudy blue eyes staring blindly. Henry had forgotten about the eyes. For some reason the eyes made everything that much worse.

Then, without warning, the man collapsed like a ragdoll to the ground in a pile where he remained completely motionless. He did not even seem to be breathing. All around, the pale people rambled as if nothing at all had happened. No one except Henry took notice. It was as though everyone else had been struck totally blind.

The man had not made much noise at all when he had fallen. Henry thought back to how the woman from a few nights ago had turned and come at him when he had spoken to her. He decided that it was probably a very good idea if he made as little noise as possible. He wondered how much noise he would have to make in order to attract

51

their attention. Maybe about as much as a raised voice, he mused. Perhaps they were drawn specifically to human voices. Perhaps the woman had not been as sick as these people were. Either way, he was not about to test it out while they were clogging the street like a flash mob gone very wrong.

Instead, he continued winding his way across the street, sidestepping and dodging wherever necessary. Through the mass, he spotted a familiar shock of bright green spiked hair. He leaned around an older man to get a better look. Could someone else be trying to make their way through this horror show? The barer of the punk rock hairdo wobbled as he turned a little. Henry could not yet see his full face, but he did not need to. He recognized him even from the side. This was the kid who delivered him pizzas. *Used to,* Henry corrected himself. From his colorless, sweaty face, Henry doubted the kid would be delivering pizzas any time soon if ever again.

Reaching the curb, he stepped up onto the sidewalk and came practically nose to nose with a rather athletically built old woman. He immediately leaned the top half of his body back, shivering involuntarily as he stared into her icy blue eyes, and swung his arms out to catch himself. Her eyes seemed to lock on to his and follow him as he tumbled backwards, crashing into someone or, more likely, several someones, as he fell.

He landed atop a pile of sweaty bodies, the heat rising off them with such startling severity that Henry, had he not felt the need to get up and away as quickly as possible, had the urge to strip off his heavy coat. Arms and legs swung wildly beneath him, shifting the heap of squirming bodies so that, despite his efforts, he started to sink further into the tangle of limbs.

The once soft groaning had increased to pained and almost frightened sounding moans. Henry pulled his arms and legs into his chest and flung himself to the side, rolling and, in the process, having a very bowling ball-like effect on several people nearby. Once he was no longer on his back, he breathlessly scrambled to his feet and wobbled gracelessly back toward the sidewalk on Mrs. Rose's side of the street. He sped up, throwing caution to the wind and sprinted across the lawn next door to her house. His bum knee twinging, he hurled himself over a low hedge and into her yard. Aside from the man who was still bumping, albeit with less insistence than before, into the front door, there was no one else nearby.

Henry paused several feet away and bent over, resting his hands on his legs just above his knees. He sucked in a few deep breaths and, for the first time he could recall, wished that he had joined a gym ages ago. He was too old for this shit as well.

Straightening, he surveyed the house and yard, wondering how he might create a distraction to get the man away from the door. The people he had knocked over in the street were still squirming in the pile. None appeared to be making any real effort to correct themselves. He doubted they were able. His breathing regulated once more. He began to calm. While the whole situation was beyond creepy, it could be a whole lot worse.

Those affected by whatever this was could be violent. *Hell*, he thought with a snort, *it could have been a zombie apocalypse instead.* At least no one was trying to eat him. Still, he decided to err on the side of caution now that he was thinking a little more clearly. No need testing any theories right away. First, he had to get to Mrs. Rose who was probably beside herself at this point.

He knew for a fact that some level of noise caught their attention. He scanned the yard and spotted a baseball-sized stone bordering a flowerbed close to the sidewalk. He started to backtrack to collect it, then froze.

The old woman who had startled him before was turned completely around so that she was facing him, but it was that she seemed to actually be looking right at him that gave him pause. She was the first that he had noticed to make any sort of eye contact. In fact, aside from the ones he had barreled into, she was the first who appeared aware of him at all. Giving himself a mental shake, he took another few steps toward the stone.

The woman took a step toward him.

While he would never admit it to anyone, Henry damn near pissed himself. His mind was racing. The woman had only taken one step. It was a coincidence; he was sure of it. Still, there he stood, a grown man, unwilling just yet to take another step for fear that she might as well. He was glad that the only people around had no more consciousness than earthworms. It would be easier to contain his embarrassment.

The last time Henry had been this unnerved had been in high school, but, unlike now, there had been plenty of people around who were far more aware of his actions than he would have liked. None being aware would have been nice.

That time had involved a girl as well. However, she had been a lot younger than the pale woman who stood a few short lengths from him now and she had been making eye contact for sure. He remembered how her eyebrow had risen quizzically at him while he stammered out an awkward invitation to a school dance. He had not meant to ask her in front of all her friends. It had just sort of happened.

He would have given anything back then to have just disappeared. Now, he would have given anything to have time-traveled away from the icy gaze of this pale woman back to that other uncomfortable experience. At least he'd had a vague idea of how that pretty young girl might respond. He had no idea what to expect in this situation. He was unsure what to do next.

"Henry!"

Just like that, the decision was taken from him. In unison, Henry and the pale old woman jerked their faces around at the sound of Mrs. Rose's voice, but it was the woman who moved first. With surprising strength and speed, she flew in Mrs. Rose's direction. Her mouth stretched wide, lips curling up over yellowed teeth, and shrieked at such a high pitch that Henry's ears felt as if they were being stabbed with some sharp instrument.

He spun around on his heel and, stone forgotten, raced toward Mrs. Rose's house. He could hear footsteps thudding and squelching in the wet grass not far behind him.

"Henry!" Mrs. Rose was leaning out her kitchen doorway at the side of the house, one hand on the metal screen door and the other clutching the doorframe for support which she released as he got closer. Henry dashed at her and, covering the space between them faster than he would have thought he was able, flung himself past her and through the door. He grabbed his neighbor's wrist and hauled her in after him, the side door clanging loudly after them then swung the heavier wooden door shut.

Just as it closed, something slammed heavily against the metal screen causing both doors to rattle. He pressed his body against the door and slid the deadbolt into place. There was another piercing shriek followed by what Henry now understood to be the body of the pale woman hitting the outside door again.

He grabbed a nearby chair and, turning it around, jammed the top of the back under the door handle. It was not a great fix, but it was better than nothing. He doubted anyone could break through both doors anyway, especially not a sick old woman regardless as to how fit she might have been before.

Henry turned and scanned the kitchen taking stock of anything that could be used as a weapon. While he did have his gun, it never hurt to be as prepared as possible. Mrs. Rose, he noted, had an extensive set of kitchen knives displayed in two wooden racks on either side of a large wooden cutting board. Hanging from beneath the cupboard above the cutting board was a set of meat cleavers. Henry had mental flashes of a particularly humorous old horror movie and snorted with laughter despite himself.

"Henry," a frail sounding voice whispered. Henry ripped his gaze from the knives and saw Mrs. Rose bracing herself against the kitchen sink. She was staring out the window, a look of horror spreading over her wrinkled face.

"Henry?" Her voice was barely a whisper. "They're coming. They're all coming."

Five

Ivan: Good morning, Colorado. My name is Ivan and I'm filling in for Boomer McGuire who has had a family emergency. **[Ivan coughs]** Excuse me, Boomer had lined up a great show for you today and I plan on following through with his plans to give away tickets to **[Ivan coughs]**, excuse me, give away tickets to see **[Ivan coughs]**. Wow, sorry about that. I just need a drink of water...and maybe some better air conditioning. Boy, it's **[Ivan coughs]** hot. Here, let's hear from our **[Ivan coughs]** sponsors and **[Ivan coughs]** and I'll be right **[Ivan coughs]** back.

The Boomer Gallagher Morning Show, 93. 9 KZCO Rocky Mountain Oldies

IN HER MID to late teens, Frankie had secretly been a bit wild. She had always maintained above average grades and participated in all sorts of extracurricular activities including softball, 4-H, her church youth group, and the school newspaper as a photographer. Her days were fairly full and she rarely had a lazy one. She was certainly not the sort of girl who spent her free time roaming the mall in a pack of other girls discussing boys or outfits. It was not that she would have necessarily minded doing that sort of thing. She just did not have the time or the girlfriends with whom to do it. She had Janie Parker, of course, but her best friend was just as busy as she and, in the little spare time they did have, they could usually be found at the Parker's farm helping care for the animals.

Nights were different. Both she and Janie would sneak out their respective windows and meet on the corner across from the convenience store by their high school. It was the midpoint between their homes and the perfect spot for Corbin Watt to pick them up in his beat up blue 1990 Chevy Blazer. He was a senior when he first started hanging out with the girls. He had met them through his little brother Matt, who like them, was only a sophomore. When Corbin graduated and went off to college, Matt took over use of their father's Blazer as well as the job of picking up Frankie and Janie.

Hanging out with Corbin opened a lot of social doors for the girls. While they were never considered popular in the traditional sense, they were certainly well known and liked. They quickly developed a reputation for being the sign of a good party. If Frankie and Janie were there, it was bound to be a fun time.

The first year of partying with Corbin was spent learning how to drink without putting themselves in more danger than they could handle. The girls promised Corbin that, after he went to college, they could always be sure that one of them was sober if Matt was not with them. The second agreement was that one of the three had to be sober every time they went out. That way, even though Matt was the only one with a license, there would always be a designated driver.

Frankie had her fair share of hangovers during her high school years. By the time she reached college, the novelty of drinking or partying in general had just about worn off. From college on, she could count her hangovers on one hand. Still, she never forgot what they were like and, from the throbbing in her head and the nausea threatening to rise up in her throat, Frankie could have sworn that what she was currently experiencing was nothing short of the single worst hangover she had ever experienced.

She just couldn't remember drinking.

Frankie tried to reach up to cradle her aching head in her hands, but found she could not move her arms. Panic began to well in her chest and throat. Was she paralyzed? Had she been in an accident? Scenario after scenario ran through her mind as she blinked furiously to clear her vision. Everything was blurry.

She stopped abruptly. Blurry vision. This reminded her of something. She swam through the depths of her fuzzy mind, trying to think of the last thing she remembered. Then, suddenly, it all came rushing back. The flu. She had woken in the night with a really bad flu. Lydia. Lydia had been sick as well. Frankie recalled going to her then frantically waking her husband. She had called emergency services and…

Was that where she was now? Was this a hospital?

Her sight was returning excruciatingly slowly. To make matters even more frustrating, just about everything around her seemed to be almost entirely white. The walls, the counters, the bedside table, the sheets covering her, and even the straps restraining her wrists were all the same glaring shade of white.

Straps? Frankie opened her mouth to speak, but immediately began gagging. There was something in her throat. Again, panic threatened to consume her and she pulled with all her strength against her restraints. A loud rhythmic beeping ensued, matching the racing beat of her heart. Flinging her head to the side, she saw the source of the beeping; a machine that appeared to be tracking her vitals.

A door swung open and the form of a slender red-headed woman hurried in, followed closely by what was either a couple of men or two very thickly built women dressed all in white. One was almost abnormally tall and ducked slightly as he entered the room. All three were wearing hospital grade gloves and had on masks that covered their mouths and noses. As she approached Frankie, the woman pulled up a pair of goggles that had been dangling from a plastic rope around her neck and swiftly adjusted them over her eyes. The men went to either side of Frankie and pressed down firmly on her so that she could not move no matter how hard she struggled. The woman then began checking the readout the machine was spitting forth before taking a little metallic cylindrical object from her pocket and, leaning around one man, pointed it directly at Frankie's eyes.

An unexpected burst of light burned Frankie's sensitive eyes causing her to squeeze them shut and turn her face away. "What the…" she heard a male voice say.

"Did she just react?" Another male voice asked.

There was no immediate response. Then, without warning, someone grasped Frankie by the chin and jerked her face back so that it was facing up again. "Hold her here.

Like this," the woman said and, as her hand was replaced by someone else's gloved hand, she pried open one of Frankie's eyes and shone the light in it again. Frankie winced, feeling tears spring up and threatening to spill. She heard a soft moan, but could not be sure if she herself had uttered it or if it had been from someone else entirely.

"Looks like his research was accurate," the woman muttered. She clicked the light off and leaned forward so that her face was closer to Frankie's. In no more than a whisper, the woman asked, "Hello…is there anybody in there? Just nod if you can hear me".

Is there anyone at home? Was this bitch seriously quoting Pink Floyd at her? Frankie gagged again, but did her best to move her head up and down while still being held still.

The woman quickly removed the thing in Frankie's throat and, trying not to throw up, Frankie gasped. Her chin was released and she swallowed hard several times before attempting to speak. Her mouth was so dry and her throat felt raw. "Wa…"

One of the men jumped back at the sound of Frankie's voice. Both the other man and the woman turned at his sudden movement, but returned their attention almost immediately to Frankie as she took advantage of not having extra weight on that side of her to try ineffectively again to pull away from the straps. "Waaa," she said hoarsely.

"Water," the man still holding her down said. His voice was deep and resonating. "She wants water".

"So, go and get her some," the woman sounded distracted and, when the man did not move, she heaved a sigh and addressed him directly. "Look, she's not going anywhere. She can't hurt me. Not anymore. Just go get some water, okay?"

61

Hurt her? Frankie could not imagine why anyone would think she would want to hurt someone. She just wanted to sit up and, like the man who was now leaving the room had surmised, a drink of water. There was another soft moan and, this time, Frankie was sure it had not come from her. Before she could ask, a petite girl dressed in soft blue scrubs walked in and, upon instruction from the redheaded woman, removed a line that had run from an IV to her arm. Then, much to Frankie's embarrassment and discomfort, the girl lifted up the bedsheet and, while the remaining man assisted, removed a catheter from her. Frankie winced and tried to focus her attention elsewhere. She tried again to speak, her voice stronger this time. "Where...?"

"You are in..." The woman paused. Frankie, whose vision was almost back to normal, could see that the woman was searching for what she should say. *So not a hospital, then.* If it were a hospital, the woman would have had no issue telling her. Could it be a prison? She could not imagine why it would be since she had done nothing wrong as far as she knew. Was it a government facility? If so, why not just say? The woman's lips were pursed in thought. She was silent until the girl left the room, taking the IV stand, catheter, and lines with her. Then, seemingly having come to a decision on what to say, she spoke again. "You've been very ill. We have been taking care of you."

Short, sweet, and everything Frankie either already knew or had figured out herself. It did not answer her question at all. In fact, it opened up a few more, but the man had returned with her water and offered it to her through a straw. She wondered why his uniform looked like it was at least a full size too small. It clung to him leaving very little to the imagination. Maybe they did not make them in his size. He was rather tall and broad in the shoulder. She pushed all her questions back. Her thirst took

62

precedence. Frankie sucked desperately, gulping the water and spluttering as she choked on it. The man was watching her with what appeared to be interest. When he took the cup away, Frankie looked over at the woman. "How long?"

The woman did not answer right away. She was consulting a chart and making marks all over it. She slipped the pen she had been using into the space at the top of the clipboard and answered offhandedly, "Well, they brought you in on Tuesday morning and it's Friday so…"

Four days. Frankie had been here for four whole days. She tried to sit up, but found she could not. "Here," the big man placed one hand over the strap on her left wrist as he leaned to press a button on the side railing near her head. As the top half of the bed began to fold upwards with a loud whirring noise, he pulled his hand away from her wrist. The strap jerked slightly as though something had been caught in it. He released the button when Frankie was in a more upright position. "Better?"

Frankie nodded, looking around the room. Everything was clear now and she could see that there was not much more to the room than what she had been able to see when she had first woken. There was a single curtain on her left dividing the room. There was no artwork or medical posters as she might have expected. There weren't any signs advising her of patient rights either. There wasn't a TV or so much as a magazine rack. The lone bedside table held a silver tray with various instruments and, other than the machine which had gone from urgent beeping to a slower, more rhythmic beeping as Frankie herself calmed, there was absolutely nothing at which to look. There wasn't even a window. The only way in or out of the room, unless the other side of the room that she could not see was more interesting than her own, was through the single door in front of her bed.

Both men, no longer holding her still, were hovering nearby. They were watchful of her, the larger with interest and the smaller as though he expected her to suddenly grow fangs and claws and to tear herself free with superhuman strength. The one who had leapt away from her before now looked as if he half expected her to try to kill them. She turned to him and studied him for a moment. He was not especially intimidating, but he certainly did not seem the sort to be frightened of a slimly built woman who barely scraped 5'5 when she wasn't strapped down to a hospital bed. Still, he was obviously wary of her.

Frankie frowned at him. "I don't bite".

The man cringed visibly at her words. Or maybe she did bite. She had been asleep for four days. It was quite possible that she had done a plethora of things while she was unconscious that she would not normally do while in full control of herself.

The red-headed woman had been checking the printout that was still coming out of the machine. She spoke absently, her eyes scanning the paper, "No," she mumbled, "No, she doesn't. Most of them don't".

"Most of who?" Frankie turned to the woman who met her gaze, a look of surprise on her face.

"How peculiar," she said almost dully, peering again at Frankie's face, "I would have thought you'd know."

A chill ran through Frankie. "Know what?" The chill became a violent shudder as the memory of what had happened four days ago came flooding back full force. "My family! Where's my family? Are they here?"

The woman opened her mouth then snapped it shut and rose with new conviction. She turned and headed toward the door, her hand beckoning to the men to follow. "Come on. We have rounds".

The men followed her without speaking. Frankie tugged at the straps. "Where is my family? Answer me!" Frankie screamed after them. Her panic was gaining momentum. The man who had brought her water glanced back at her, his brow furrowing slightly, but said nothing as door swung shut behind them. Frankie was left alone.

"Come back! Tell me where my family is! Where are my children?"

A moan, low and prolonged this time, came from behind the curtain that separated the room, drawing her attention away from the door. She was not as alone as she had initially thought. "Hello?" Her throat burned.

The moaning continued for moment then, as if the person behind the curtain was walking away, the sound became softer and softer until it had faded out completely. She tried again. "Hello?"

No response came from behind the curtain. Frankie stared down at the straps. Red marks were forming on her wrists where the straps had begun to cut at them when she pulled. With curiosity, she looked down her blanketed body to her feet. She couldn't shift them much either. Now that she was regaining full mental control, she was realizing how little physical control of herself she had. Anxiety was throttling her. She was completely trapped in a place she did not know and no one seemed willing to tell her anything useful.

"Hey!" She swallowed hard. She might not be able to move, but she had her voice back. "Hey! Anybody! What the hell is going on? Someone answer me! Hey!"

She stopped and listened as footsteps sounded outside her door in the hall. They paused just outside and the door handle turned slowly. Then it clicked back into place and the footsteps resumed. She could hear muffled voices in the hall getting quieter until both they and the footsteps were gone altogether. Whoever had been about to come in had been interrupted or called away. Frankie tried to relax, but the anxiety was causing every nerve in her body to prickle uncomfortably.

What the hell is going on?

Frankie twisted her wrists while she thought, tucking her thumb inward and folding her fingers in toward her palms. The strap on her left wrist felt looser than the one on her right. They were both cutting into her wrists making her wince, but, after a few minutes, they gradually began to slide up.

She had taken yoga a few years ago after she had experienced postpartum depression following Colin's birth. She had not realized that was what she was suffering from until another mother pointed it out. She had always thought postpartum depression was feeling sad and resenting or even hating your baby. She had felt none of that and had been dismissing the bouts of anxiety and the panic attacks as flukes or coincidental. After all, who wouldn't have been nervous driving around in rush hour traffic with a toddler and a newborn? When the other mother gently suggested Frankie see her doctor about postpartum depression, she had laughed, but the other mother had insisted and Frankie decided to humor her.

Sure enough, she received a diagnosis of postpartum depression. Her doctor had recommended that she try yoga as well as therapy and, to Frankie's surprise, the combination had worked very well. The medication didn't hurt either, but that was not an option at the moment.

Instead, Frankie settled for regulating her breathing and trying her best to clear her mind. She managed the latter with little difficulty. The former, however, was all but impossible. Her mind kept racing with questions and memories.

A strap slipped off.

Frankie gaped at it, shocked that her efforts had actually worked. Her left wrist was raw and bleeding a bit in spots, but it was free from the restraint. Then, unsure how much time she had before someone came back, Frankie reached over and unbuckled the strap on her right wrist. Both arms free, she scooted hastily down the bed, shoving the thin white sheet off her legs as she went. Legs uncovered, she fumbled with the buckles on either ankle before swinging her legs off the bed and tumbling to the floor in a heap. Her legs had given out from lack of use.

The wires that had run from the machine next to her bed to spots on her chest were unceremoniously ripped free causing the machine to issue an obnoxious buzzing as the electronic screen flatlined. She held her breath for several seconds. If the din she had made had somehow not been heard by anyone, the racket coming from the machine would surely draw attention. She scrambled across the floor and yanked the power cord from the wall, silencing her machine. The only things she could hear now were the beeping of machinery on the other side of the curtain and the pounding of her own heart which she could have sworn had jumped up into her throat. She exhaled forcibly and reached up to take hold of the edge of the bed.

Just as she managed to pull herself to her feet, the floor so cold on her bare feet that it burned, she heard footsteps returning. Frantic, she scanned the room. She would never be fast enough to get back up into the bed and would not have time to adjust the straps well enough to convince anyone they were still on her. It was a weapon she needed.

The table was too cumbersome. The tray, however, held an assortment of medical instruments, a few of which Frankie recognized. Her heart leapt as she spotted a needle with a clear liquid still inside. She grabbed it and bit off the cap to expose the needle. She had absolutely no idea what was in it. With luck, whoever was now turning the door handle to her room would not know either.

The door opened and a man appeared. Halfway in, he looked up and, meeting Frankie's wild-eyed gaze, froze. He raised one hand, palm side toward Frankie and mouthed for her to remain silent. He slipped all the way through the door and closed it behind him carefully so that the click it made was barely audible. Frankie raised the needle and pointed it at him. It was the man from earlier, she realized, the one who had brought her water. He was now wearing a dark jacket over his scrubs.

"Shh," He placed a finger up to his mouth and took a tentative step toward her. "You make too much noise and Dr. Asmussen will hear. Then you'll never get out of here."

He took another step closer. Frankie brandished the needle at him, but he did not stop. She scrambled backwards, almost dropping the needle. The man continued his advance while yanking his arm out of his jacket sleeve. He did not seem to care in the slightest about the needle. She might as well have been threatening him with a wet noodle. Frankie jabbed it in his direction causing him to sidestep as he reached her. He took hold of her forearm and squeezed until her hand opened and the needle fell to the floor. "It's ok. Really. I'm trying to help you."

"Let go of me!"

The man shushed her again, shrugging his jacket off completely while maintaining a firm grip on Frankie. "Here. Put this on. We have about fifteen minutes before Dr. Asmussen gets back. We have to get all the way across the building to the service entrance in that amount of time and we aren't going to make it if you make things difficult."

Frankie did not know if she could trust this man, but her options were limited. She could either go with him into the unknown or stay here in the unknown. A moan came from behind the curtain once more. Her eyes shot toward the sound. The man either had not heard or was simply ignoring it. He had given up trying to convince her to put the jacket and was roughly stuffing her into it. She was suddenly exhausted, her will to fight him evaporating. It would be easier to go with him and, besides, she might see an opening to get away that she very clearly did not have while stuck inside this room.

The man bustled Frankie to the door, supporting and guiding her with one hand on her elbow. She looked back over her shoulder as he opened the door and saw another bed on the other side of the curtain. An ancient looking woman was strapped down and hooked up to a machine just as Frankie had been.

"What about her?" The man frowned and tugged her through the doorway, the old woman in the bed disappearing from sight as the door clicked shut behind them. "We can't just leave her!"

"We don't have a choice," the man whispered, pressing his hand into the small of her back to get her moving.

"There's always a choice! We have to-"

"We have to get out of here now. That kid doesn't have another hour left in her, I guarantee it. If we don't get going, we'll have even less. Now move." He grabbed her arm and pulled her along with him.

Together, they ran down the hall, Frankie still stumbling on shaky legs, and through a set of double doors. Frankie's bare feet slapped against the chilly tile floor as they raced down one corridor after another. She lost track of how many doors they had gone through and, before long, had lost all sense of direction as well. Every hall looked just like the last and was devoid of all signage saving small plaques next to each door with room numbers printed too small for Frankie to make out as they hurried by. For all she knew, they were going in circles. The man, however, seemed to know exactly where he was going which was good, Frankie supposed, as an alarm began to blare through loudspeakers attached to the ceiling.

"Shit," The man sped up, scooping Frankie up and flinging her over his shoulder. She squawked as she flopped against him, and felt the heat of embarrassment rising to her cheeks that contrasted the cool air that was now shooting up into the thin hospital gown. She was grateful for the man's jacket. It was the only thing preventing her from being completely exposed. The man let out a low frustrated grunt. "Shit, shit, shit!"

They had just turned the corner and were racing down a darkened hallway. Frankie, unable now to see what lay ahead of them, watched the light from the hall behind them recede as she was bounced into the darkness. There was a loud creak and light spilled into the hallway. A feminine voice called out for the man to hurry as they burst through an exit into what looked like a loading bay.

Crisp air bit at her exposed cheeks. Frankie braced herself against the man's back as he ran down a set of stairs so that her head was no longer bobbing furiously with every step he took. At the bottom of the stairs, the man pulled her from his shoulder and shoved her through the side door of a plain white van. She tumbled in, landing with all the grace and refinement of a sack of potatoes, and had just enough time to see that there were two other people crouching against the side before the van's door was slid shut and she was plunged into darkness.

Frankie heard two more doors slam shut. Then, without warning, the van lurched forward flinging her toward the rear of the vehicle. Someone in the dark reached out with gloved hands and caught hold of her shoulder hard, stabilizing her before she had flown very far. They pulled her toward themselves and held her as the van veered suddenly. She clung to the person, shoving her face down into them and planting her feet as firmly against the floor of the van as possible.

Her heart was pounding in her chest. She had never been particularly fond of rollercoasters and that was exactly what this felt like except without the security of the thickly padded bars that held you firmly against the seat. She focused on the beat of her heart and the rumble of the van's engine. This was no easy feat as the van bumped along over an uneven road, but it was better than freaking out about who these people were, where they were taking her, and, most of all, what the hell was going on.

Whoever was up front in the cab of the van was talking now. Frankie could not make out any words, but the tone was urgent and questioning. Another voice interrupted the first. She recognized it, by its deepness, as being that of the man who had taken her from her room. By the sound of things, Frankie wagered that the man was the one in charge even though the job of dragging people from hospital rooms seemed, at least to her, more like grunt work. He was quite tall, although most people were compared to Frankie, and built like a brick. She was swimming in his jacket, but glad for it nonetheless. Her hospital gown offered little protection on its own.

The urgent voice sounded again followed by the man's again. He was more insistent this time as if demanding something. A moment later, the van lurched forward as that driver increased their speed. The person holding her gripped her more tightly and shifted so that they were braced against the walls of the van. Then, without warning, the van hit something that crashed over the top of the van with resounding metaling clangs. Up front, someone hooted with unrestrained glee while the clanging sound continued behind the van as they continued without slowing.

The van swerved once more then evened out. The surface they were on was smoother than the last and their path far straighter. She figured that they must now be on a highway. She could hear swishing noises as they passed what she assumed were other vehicles. As far as she could tell, they were going very fast.

The voices up front had stopped and no one in the back with her had spoken so she thought it best, for now, to remain silent herself. She listened to the sounds of the van and other vehicles and stared into the darkness for several minutes. She was beyond exhausted. Still clinging to some unknown person, she closed her eyes. It was no time at all before she drifted back into the comforting blackness of sleep.

Six

Joanna: Good evening and welcome to another addition of The Newsroom. I'm Joanna Watson. Reports of what is beginning to look like an epidemic, the exact cause of which is as of yet unknown, are sweeping the nation. The majority of reports of illness are in London leading experts to believe that this unnamed virus might have been brought into the country through Heathrow. Some sources are claiming that the virus originated in the western part of the United States while others theorize that the Centres for Disease Control located in Atlanta, Georgia is to blame. The exact number of cases of what appears to be the deadliest flu since the Spanish influenza pandemic of 1918 is not known at the moment. However, since the first report two days ago, the number has risen to somewhere in the thousands. Sources suggest that, at this rate, the number of cases will double within the next twenty-four to forty-eight hours if it is not immediately contained. The PHE, Public Health England Centre of Infectious Disease Surveillance and Control, is advising that extra precautions be taken to avoid contracting the virus. Wash your hands regularly and avoid contact with those who appear to be ill. Wearing gloves and face masks is also suggested. If you believe you or someone you know has contracted this virus, please call....

The Newsroom, RBC (Royal Broadcasting Company)

FEAR CAN BE bought for the price of a movie ticket. It can be found lining shelves in bookstores or anywhere DVDs can be rented, covers pointing outward to inspire excitement at the prospect of being drawn into brief moments of terror. For many, the fear brought on by movies or books lasts for some time after. The very memory of a character or situation will have them shivering with dread and cause them to search every shadow for monsters even years later. Henry, however, was not one of those people.

He had never been very interested in horror films or novels, but not because they scared him. On the contrary, for him, they rarely caused so much as a jump. All too often, he found the horror genre to be formulaic and, as a result, woefully predictable. Without the element of surprise, horror was simply not entertaining to him as it seemed to be for the majority of people he knew.

It was not as though he hadn't given horror several chances. He was just never the sort to cling to the armrests in movie theaters nor was he the type to peek around corners after watching movies that promised to leave the viewer with nightmares. He certainly never had nightmares inspired by a work of fiction. He supposed that was the reason he was virtually immune to horror; he was never able to forget that none of it was real. He could never lose himself enough in a novel or movie to the point that he forgot it was only the creation of another person's mind. No matter how he tried to relax and just get into it, he always maintained a stranglehold on reality.

At the moment, there was only one thing that had the power to truly frighten Henry and, at the moment, it was swarming all around him. He had joined Mrs. Rose at the kitchen window and was staring out across her lawn as what must have been no fewer than fifty people, all ashen skinned and snowy haired, slowly advanced on the house. They jerked awkwardly with each step as if being pulled along like puppets on strings. Their mouths were gaping and their icy blue eyes were vacant. It was as though they were completely unaware of their actions.

These were real people. This was actually happening. This was reality and Henry was terrified.

Henry swallowed hard, scanning the crowd. He was beginning to recognize faces. He spotted Mr. and Mrs. Zimmerman from the house on the far corner. Both still dressed in pajamas and no longer dark haired, they were staggering forward, bumping unconsciously into each other. Behind them, Henry could see their teenaged son, also dressed for bed, and a man in running shorts who Henry often saw jogging through the neighborhood early each morning. Coming up the walk was a woman whom Henry only knew as the snooty-looking owner of an ostentatiously groomed poodle that liked to relieve itself on his lawn whenever the two passed by on a walk. The woman never cleaned up after the dog.

Face after face was suddenly familiar to him. He had not recognized any of them when he had made his way through them before. They had been so close and, yet, somehow not real to him. Henry's eyes leapt from face to face. They were real now.

They were real people.

They were real and, as Mrs. Rose had said, they were all coming. With a shock of dread, it occurred to Henry that the screeching woman was no longer throwing herself at the side door nor was she screeching anymore. He did not care to wait to find out why she had stopped.

Grabbing Mrs. Rose by the hand, Henry ran from the kitchen into the hallway. Much like his own home, there was no attic or basement in this house. Unsure where to go, he hurried the old woman down the hall and into a back bedroom. There was an open door to a bathroom at the far end of the room. He had never been this far into her house. He hoped that the bathroom was similar to the one in his own home.

Sure enough, the small room was equipped with a tiny window and a skylight. Henry locked the door behind them and went to the window. He pressed both hands against the cold glass and eased it open slightly as quietly as possible. Peering out, he saw that a few of the pale people had entered the backyard. They were no longer advancing, but had returned to the randomly wandering and moaning state they had been in when he had first spotted them through his living room blinds. They seemed so innocuous now, like life-sized toys left out on the lawn. Still, he did not want to risk a repeat of what had happened out front.

They could not stay locked in a bathroom, either. He had to get them to somewhere safe until he could figure out their next move. He slid the window shut again and looked up at the skylight. He wondered how, if need be, he was going to get an eighty-year old woman up through it without hurting her.

He didn't even know for sure how dangerous the people outside were. They were, after all, just very sick people. In their weakened states, how much damage could they really do? Still, they were, for lack of a better description, acting very like zombies. Or, at least, they were acting mostly like how he understood zombies to behave. But if they were zombies, wouldn't that mean they would attack anyone not like them? He could not recall seeing blood on any of them. Henry tried to think back to the morning news. What was it the newscaster had said?

76

Henry looked over at Mrs. Rose. She had seated herself on the lid of the toilet and was staring wide-eyed at him, her fingers pressed to her lips. She had lived in this house for as long as Henry could remember and she'd had white hair for at least half that time. He found himself staring at her eyes. If not for the fact that he could clearly see the soft grey of her irises surrounding her the slight clouding the cataracts was causing over her pupils, he might have mistaken her for one of people who were now on both sides of her house.

The people outside were contagious. This much, he knew. However, he had known that before the news had told him, hadn't he? They were contagious, but he was almost positive that they were alive. If they weren't, surely the news would have said something. And what if they weren't alive? He shook his head, but the irrational thoughts were still racing through his mind. Horror movies were not frightening to him. The fact that his life was rapidly resembling one absolutely terrified him.

Henry yanked the bandana down from his mouth and turned on the faucet in the sink. He removed his gloves and cupped his hands under the cold water, catching it in a pool between his palms. He bent and greedily slurped at it, his eyes flickering up to his reflection in the mirror. Unlike the people outside, his dark hair was speckled with silver that had come naturally with time. Someone had once told him that it made him look distinguished, but he had been pretty sure that was just a polite way of saying 'old'.

Shutting the faucet off, he turned back around and leaned against the sink. Mrs. Rose had dropped her hands into her lap and was gawping at him. He offered her what he hoped was a reassuring smile and turned his attention back to the skylight. Whatever was going on outside, whether or not the pale people were a real threat, they could not risk staying here in this tiny bathroom.

WHEN HENRY WAS eight, a few of his friends had dared him to climb through a rusted and forgotten pipe that ran under the bridge that led out of town. He had not wanted to go into it, but one of the other boys had started clucking like a chicken. That had set the others off and, if Henry was anything, he was brave. It would not do to let the guys think he was scared of something as silly as the dark. Henry had stared as far into the darkness of the pipe as he could for only a couple of seconds before puffing out his chest and announcing to the excitement of his friends that he was going in.

He had only managed to go a couple of feet in before he realized that taking his friends up on this dare was probably the least sensible thing he had ever done in his short life. The pipe reeked of mold and decay. Being so close to the small stream below the bridge, the pipe was likely flooded every time they had a good rain. There was a good deal of vegetation, most of which was covered in a thick, slimy substance. Henry's hands and knees slipped with each movement further into the pipe, but he pressed on, blinking against the darkness. Behind him, the other boys were cheering. No one was clucking anymore.

Eventually, the sound of his friends' laughter and encouragement lowered to nothing more than a faint buzzing. Henry's head bumped into something hard, but somewhat squishy. The smell inside the pipe was so strong now that it stung at Henry's nose and brought tears to his eyes. He reached forward, the odor turning his stomach and making him gag. His hand met the hard and squishy thing and, as he pulled it back, came away sticky.

He had paused to think, his fingers rubbing against themselves and the goo on them. He should have reached the other side of the pipe by now. The bridge, while having room enough for vehicles to cross it going in either direction at the same time, was not really all that wide. Whatever was in front of him was blocking where the pipe opened on the other side. He considered simply backing up and going around to see what it was, but was sure the clucking would start again if his friends saw him come back out the way he came. Besides, he figured they were already on this side by now. They were probably just on the other side of the thing blocking the pipe, waiting for him to emerge.

Feeling like he was going to throw up his breakfast, Henry balanced on his knees and, with all his strength, pushed the object forward. It tumbled away from him with a sickening squelch. It fell from the pipe and rolled down the embankment, coming to a stop right at the edge of the water. Henry squinted and shielded his eyes from the sunlight that now flooded into the pipe. In front of him, he could see several familiar pairs of shoes, all standing facing Henry and the entrance to the pipe. As he looked up, though, he saw that all of the boys' bodies were twisted so that they were pointed down toward the water.

Henry followed their gaze.

Lying next to the water was what looked like a pile of old clothes. Henry pulled himself from the pipe and took several steps down toward the pile, his friends following cautiously behind him. When he reached it, his stomach turned once more and the urge to vomit became all but overwhelming. Without going around for a better look, Henry could tell what this was.

Henry had dislodged a body from the pipe and, from the look and smell of it, it had not been alive for a very long time. This was nothing like the movies. This was all too real. From behind him, someone screamed, high pitched and desperate. Henry, for the first time ever, felt inclined to join in.

"HENRY?"

If those childhood friends could see him now, in his forties and hiding in a bathroom, there would be a whole lot of clucking going on. Mrs. Rose had never looked more frail to Henry than she did at that moment. She wore her fear like a mask and was looking at Henry as if he was the only person who could remove it from her.

"What are we going to do, Henry?"

Henry pressed his lips together, biting the inside of his cheek as he thought. He had absolutely no idea what they were going to do. Even going through the skylight posed issues. For one, assuming he got them both up and through it unscathed, where could they possibly go from there? It was not like she could shimmy down a drainpipe or leap from one roof to another. He stifled a laugh at the thought.

"Might wait it out," he finally responded, "I mean, the news said it's a sickness. Someone at the CDC's gotta be on this."

"In here? Wait it out in here?"

Henry looked around the small bathroom. There was plenty of water and, if he lined it with towels, the tub might make a decent bed for the old woman. He would have to prop himself up to sleep as there was not space enough for a man his size to lie down. As for food, he supposed he could make a quick trip back to the kitchen assuming the pale people outside stayed as docile as they now seemed to be.

"Yeah," He, nodded, trying to sound confident. "It's probably the safest place we could be."

Mrs. Rose looked skeptical. "Who were they, Henry? What were they doing?"

Henry was not entirely sure how to answer her. Anything he said beyond pointing out that he had seen a few of their neighbors in the crowd would be almost pure guesswork. He had no clue what they were doing or why they suddenly appeared driven when the pale woman had begun her shrieking. He pulled out his phone and unlocked the screen. "I'll see if I can get the news on this thing. Never was very good with them. Guess you have to be smarter than the smart phone."

Mrs. Rose did not respond to his attempt at humor. Instead, the old woman slumped against the back of the toilet. She looked so drained that Henry felt a surge of pity for her. If what was going on outside was this hard on him, he could only imagine how she was handling it.

He refocused his attention on the screen of his phone, finding an internet search application and tapping on it. He searched for news sites and was relieved when several came up on the first attempt. He scrolled the screen down, his eyes scanning the page until he found a media source he recognized and tapping on its link. The home page loaded quickly, the headline leaping out at Henry in bold, black letters. He tapped on it which send him to another page with a video at the top and an article below. He skipped over the video and scanned the article.

SUPERVIRUS SWEEPS NATION

The Centers for Disease Control and Prevention (CDC) confirmed earlier this morning that a supervirus is rapidly spreading throughout the United States. Margaret Spencer of the CDC's Emergency Operations Center announced the CDC's Emergency Operation Center has been activated at Level 1 to respond to the supervirus. This is the fifth time in American History that a level 1 response has been necessary and, according to Spencer, it is the most serious. Level 1 responses require a 24/7 agency-wide effort.

Since Monday, the number of reports of illness across the country has ballooned from 68 to over 5,000. The current known death toll stands at 4,585, but, due to the ease of infection and the swiftness of its progression, is estimated to double if not triple over the next few days if the supervirus is not contained. As of yet, there have been no reports of infection in any country other than the United States, but it is believed people from infected areas have traveled overseas since the first infections were reported. Spencer noted that the contagion spreading to other countries would be nothing short of catastrophic.

Reports of symptoms vary; however, several sources have stated that the most common indication of infection is the appearance of flu. This includes, but is not limited to fevers, chills, lethargy, a loss of pigmentation (unspecified), and migraine-like pains.

According to Spencer, there is no known treatment for this as of yet unnamed supervirus, but efforts to contain the spread of infection as well as the eradication of the virus is well underway. The CDC is advising that people remain indoors and avoid all contact with anyone exhibiting symptoms as it is believed the virus is spread through bodily fluids. Spencer stressed that the supervirus is so contagious that even the smallest amount of bodily fluid would almost guarantee infection. If you have come into contact with someone who is infected or believe you or someone you know might be infected you are urged to contact the EOC immediately.

The President is set to address the nation at 9 am CST from an undisclosed location.

Henry stared at the screen, shaking his head. The article really had not told him anything he did not already know or had not figured out for himself. He searched for a time stamp and found the article to been released several hours before. A lot could have changed since then. A lot probably had. He backed out of the site and typed "supervirus" into the Google search bar. Numerous articles with similar time stamps came up immediately. He clicked on a few and, after a quick perusal, found their content to be no more helpful that that of the first article. Swearing under his breath, he jammed the phone back into his pocket. "Shit."

Henry's eyes shot up at Mrs. Rose. "What?"

"It's okay to swear, Henry. I won't be offended." She looked up at the frosted glass of the window as though she could see out it. "Considering what we've seen and heard today, a curse word or two might just lend a little normalcy."

When he didn't respond, Mrs. Rose turned and looked him in the eye. "Hell."

"Crap," he answered without thinking.

"Shit."

"Damn."

A smile tugged at the corners of Mrs. Rose's lips and her face took on a mischievous look so out of character for her. She leaned forward and, speaking clearly, she drew out the single syllable of one final word, "Fuuuuuck".

Henry burst into laughter, feeling a sort of mild relief spread through him. If old Mrs. Rose could find levity at a time like this, then he could find courage. They both fell silent for a moment, smiles remaining on their faces. Then, Henry quietly slid the window open a crack and peered through. Outside, sluggishly roaming through the immaculately kept flower beds, their feet tramping down plants as they went, were six people. They looked like careless tourists in a botanical garden. Mrs. Zimmerman was among the ghoulish tourists, but neither her husband nor her son were in sight. They all seemed so harmless to Henry just then. It wasn't as though they were attacking the house or showing any signs, for that matter, of aggression. Henry closed and locked the window once more.

"Right." Mrs. Rose was still watching him, but the jovial smile had disappeared, replaced by a grim expression. Henry cleared his throat and continued, "I'm going back to the kitchen. I'll get some food and a couple other things and then I'll be right back. You stay here, okay?"

Mrs. Rose nodded. "If you could move my dresser in front of the bedroom door, we might be able to make ourselves a bit more comfortable. It's rather heavy, you know."

It was not a bad idea. Henry thought he remembered seeing a TV in her bedroom. If he could secure the window above her vanity, then the room might serve them well at least until he could figure out what to do next. They would be able to watch the CDC's containment progress in relative comfort. "I'll do that when I come back. You keep this door shut and only open it when you hear me, got it?"

Mrs. Rose nodded again and folded her hands into her lap. Henry turned from her and took a deep breath. Then, knowing that his courage would not grow any more the longer he stood there, he unlocked the bathroom door and, opening it, came face to face for the second time that morning with the pale old woman.

Seven

Alisha Marquez
U guys, I don't know whats going on. It took
forever to connect to LifeFeed. I don't know if
its my internet connection or if its cause
everyones on evry social media sight blowing up
about this crazy flu everyones getting. My mom
got sick yesterday and wanted to send me to
my dads house, but he said he couldn't watch
me and his other kids because their sick, to. I
guess I'll just chill hear. Anybody want to hang
out? I'm bored!
(25 minutes ago)

Alisha Marquez, LifeFeed (Social Media Site)

TIME IS A STRANGE thing. People are taught from a
very early age that it is unquestionably real and then,
unconsciously by the actions of those around them, that it is
something that essentially controls them. You must be in
certain places at certain times, do particular tasks at

particular times, and you must always be mindful that you do not run out of this thing someone decided to call 'time'. No matter how hard a person tries to manage it, time always seems to have the upper hand. Each generation is all but controlled by something that was created in the minds of people long before them. Its parameters are entirely man-made causing the makers to become like rats racing against something so abstract while never truly considering it analytically, unable to simply accept that it is.

Time is also strange in that no two people truly experience it in the same way. Whether they sit watching the seconds tick by on a clock or attempt to pass it blindly, the experience will differ immensely from one person to the next. Add a little darkness and even the bravest of men can feel as though they are being swallowed by it.

This is what it felt like for Frankie when she woke with a gasp into blackness. In response, the man she was resting against squeezed her arm gently as if to reassure her. It took her a moment to remember where she was and another to collect and calm herself. The van was still rumbling along, but she could now hear music coming from the cab. She had absolutely no idea how long she had been asleep.

Her ears were still echoing with the memory of her husband's screams in her dream. They had seemed just as real as they had been the night she had discovered Lydia ill in her bed.

She forced herself to settle and lay motionlessly against the person against whom she had fallen asleep. His chest rose and fell rhythmically and Frankie could feel the slow steadiness of his heartbeat. She counted the beats in increments of sixty and tried to breath along with the man. After cycling through for the fifth time, Frankie decided it was probably better not knowing how much time was passing and stopped counting. She wondered how much longer she could remain this calm without knowing what was going on.

Not that she was all that calm, considering.

Sometime later, hours or minutes for all she knew, the van began to slow. It turned a few times before jolting so hard that Frankie's body jumped up and away from the man. He grabbed her and steadied her as the road became rough and uneven. The van bumped along for quite a while and then slowed until it stopped. There was a pause then the engine cut and the doors to the cab opened, killing the music that had been playing. Footsteps crunched softly from the front of the van and halted next to it. The side door slid open revealing more darkness brightened ever so slightly by gentle beams of moonlight through the leaves of tall, thick trees and a yellowish light that shone through a window of a nearby cabin.

A woman wearing a plain black beanie that looked handmade was peering in at them. The hat was barely concealing her blonde hair and several strands were escaping in wisps around the edges of her oval face. It took a moment, but Frankie recognized her as being the woman who had met them in the loading bay where the van had been waiting. "Mack."

"Mick," the man clutching her, responded. He rose, pulling Frankie with him and handed her out the open van door to the woman who helped her to the ground. Frankie's footing was far less than sure. She felt wobbly, but better than she had before she had fallen asleep. *This sure has been one killer flu,* she thought grimly, allowing herself to be led toward the cabin.

She wondered when she had become so trusting. She preached Stranger Danger to her children, instructing them to be polite, but wary and here she was practicing almost the opposite. Her breath caught in her throat. Where were her children? Where was Hugo? She still had no answers to her questions and no one seemed inclined to even speak to her much less ease her concerns with a few simple words. Why would no one tell her where her family was? The longer she went without answers, the more questions she had and the more panicky she felt.

Judging by the fact that it was now nighttime, she had just travelled several hours with people she did not know into the middle of the woods. What woods they were in, exactly, she had no clue. Still, she supposed that if they had meant her any harm, she would have known hours ago. Also, it was not as if she had had much choice in the matter. From what she could see, it did not look like there was anywhere for her to go if she were to run and she was definitely not dressed for an outdoor excursion of any sort. She shivered beneath the tall man's jacket.

Still barefoot and accompanied by four others, she gingerly made her way gingerly across an unpaved driveway and up wooden steps. The front door swung open and an older rotund woman with a mass of perfectly coifed blonde hair greeted them with a wide grin. She looked first at the younger blonde woman and then the man supporting Frankie. "Mick. Mack."

"Ma," they intoned together.

Frankie, from between the two, raised an eyebrow. "What is this? HeeHaw?" she asked, becoming the opposite of how she expected her children to behave by sending whatever remained of her politeness away to wherever her sense of caution had gone.

A sharp bark of laugh escaped the large woman's lips. The suddenness of it made Frankie shrink away involuntarily. "Now *that's* funny! Oh, Lort! Look at you, girl! And look at me, forgettin' my manners. Lort, oh, Lort!" Her thick southern accent, combined with her pronunciation of "lord" all but confirmed for Frankie that she had, indeed, been zapped into an episode of the old comedy show. The woman stepped aside, waving them in. "Come on in, y'all. I have some supper on."

THE CABIN WAS warm and inviting. The kitchen and dining room were separated by a high wooden island with tall rustic barstools tucked neatly underneath, the seats of which were dressed in kitschy farmscape-printed quilted covers. There was a rather impressive display of ceramic chickens carefully arranged along a shelf that ran along the top of the wall around the dining area. Matching chicken dishtowels and potholders were strategically placed around the sink and stove. Even the curtains that lined the windows of the kitchen and dining room were of happy chickens pecking at seed or in mid-flap atop white picket fences. Topping off the look were a few paintings that hung over the dining room table that were, unsurprisingly, of farm scenes complete with chickens doing what chickens do. Both rooms were decorated exactly how Frankie expected they would be if the owner had shopped exclusively in the gift shop of a Cracker Barrel.

Frankie was curled up on an overstuffed couch in the living area. From her vantage point, she had the perfect view of every part of the cabin short of whatever rooms were down the long hall next to her. Having been instructed to make herself comfortable she had promptly chosen this particular seat for just that reason. It didn't hurt that it also had a heavy crocheted blanket and an invitingly plump pillow resting on it. Frankie had sunk into the couch, tucking her feet up underneath herself, and pulled the blanket around her shoulders. Another benefit of her chosen spot aside from being able to keep a watchful eye on the others who had scattered themselves around the cabin, was the basket of yarn with long knitting needles protruding from it that sat on the floor within reach. No one had come across in a threatening manner yet, but it never hurt to be cautions and prepared.

She was doing her best to appear calm. The last thing she wanted right now was to appear like a crazed woman in front of a bunch of people whose intentions she still did not know. Inside, however, crazed was exactly how she felt. She had no idea where her family was and, the longer she went without knowing, the more she began to fear the worst. Her memories of the events right before she woke attached to machines was fuzzy. She remembered going to the playground and something about a strange man, but nothing much after. Frankie felt her stomach knot. She licked her lips and took a slow breath as she surveyed the room. She needed to think about something else.

Mack, the young man who she had pretty much used as a bed the entire way to the cabin, had kicked off his boots at the front door and settled himself atop a barstool facing away from her. The large woman had positioned herself in the kitchen and was fussing about the stove and oven. From the way she moved about it, Frankie wagered the woman probably spent more time there than anywhere else in the cabin.

Both the man who had carried her out to the van and whoever had been in the back of the van with her had vanished down the hall. The blonde woman had removed her beanie and was fixing her long, straight hair into a high ponytail. She made eye contact with Frankie then, scowling, swept up magazine from the coffee table and flopped onto the couch opposite where she proceeded to pretend Frankie did not exist.

Frankie's eyes wandered around the room once more, pausing again on the ceramic chickens. She wondered what sort of person could possibly like chickens this much.

"You like my chickens?"

The twanging question answered Frankie's musing. The large woman was standing at the edge of the kitchen, wiping her wet hands on a chicken print apron Frankie had somehow failed to notice before. Frankie fought for something to say then settled on, "They're...um...very nice."

Her response garnered another sharp laugh from the round woman. She shook one finger at Frankie as though scolding a small child and drawled, "Don't you lie to me, girl. Mama Jean can smell a liar a mile away. Besides, you seem the sort who prefers her chicken breaded crispy next to a heaping pile of hot mashed taters and a side of corn. Well, it's your lucky day, girl."

She scooped up a plate from the island and shoved it into Mack's hands. She waved her hands in a sort of "go on" gesture to the young man who, in response, hopped off his barstool and delivered the plate of food to Frankie. He smiled down at her as he offered her the plate. She took it with a measure of caution and watched as he returned to his spot at the island. Once he was settled, she looked at her plate. It was just as promised; two crispy drumsticks, corn still on the cob just the way she liked it, and a steaming pile of mashed potatoes.

Frankie stared down at her plate. She wasn't sure how she would manage to eat at all. She felt a bit like throwing up. People watching and chicken admiring had done little to distract her from thoughts of her family.

It did look good, though. She swirled her fork through the potatoes then took the smallest of bites. It was delicious. Her stomach rumbled and she dug right in, realizing that this was the first solid food she'd had in about five days now. Mama Jean was making tutting noises from the kitchen as she watched Frankie wolf the food down. She heard the older woman mumble something about "those people" at "the facility" before setting about plating more food for the others.

Mack ran one hand absently through his short blond hair and pulled a freshly loaded plate toward himself. "Thanks, Ma," he said around a mouthful of potatoes, earning himself a swat. Now that she was getting a better look at them, she was sure that Mick and Mack were twins or, if not, brother and sister who were very close in age. In fact, Mama Jean looked an awful lot like both Mick and Mack, Frankie was just now noticing. She wondered if they were actually related.

"Michaela, get your tush over here and have some supper." The younger woman, still ignoring Frankie, heaved a sigh and, throwing the magazine aside, joined Mack. She, too, pulled the plate Mama Jean set down in front of her toward herself and began poking randomly at bits of food with her fork. Judging by the look Mama Jean was giving Mick, Frankie was sure now that the three were, indeed, related.

"Jimmy!" Mama Jean called down the dark hallway. "Jimmy! Earl! Come and get some supper before it gets cold!"

A door down the hall opened and the sound of muffled voices became audible. Frankie crammed another forkful of potatoes into her mouth and watched as the two men reappeared and claimed barstools at the island. She wondered which was Jimmy and which was Earl.

The man she had not really seen yet was seated next to Mick. He had scraggly black hair and what he must have thought passed for a goatee. He was tall and almost painfully slender with a stoop in his back. Dressed in blue jeans and an unadorned green t-shirt, he reminded Frankie of Shaggy from "Scooby-Doo". He certainly ate like the cartoon character. Frankie half expected a large cartoon talking dog to come in and beg for snacks. She held back a laugh at the thought, trying not to choke on potatoes.

Next to Shaggy sat the man who had carried Frankie out to the van. He was no longer wearing all white as he had done when they first met, but had changed into jeans and a dark grey button-up shirt. He was the tallest of them all by about a foot and had a head full of thick reddish-brown hair. She recalled him being big, but he seemed broader in the shoulders and more barrel chested than when he had been clothed in scrubs. Frankie could have sworn it was black and not white that was slimming. She mentally shrugged it off. To be fair, her first assessment of him had been under duress.

Having finished her dinner, Frankie rested her plate, empty all but for two picked clean drumsticks, in her lap and leaned back against the pillow. She felt better for having eaten despite having some mild nausea from not having done so in quite some time. The men were either well into their own meals or holding out their plates for seconds. Mama Jean was happily refilling plates and chattering on about something inconsequential she had read in a magazine. Mick had taken a few bites, but was still mostly prodding her food and pushing it around her plate.

The atmosphere was very comfortable to Frankie, like a family reunion.

At this thought, a jolt of pain stabbed at Frankie's chest. Guilt swept over her again for having once again forgotten her own family no matter how briefly. She cleared her throat, attracting everyone's attention. Even Mick glanced over her shoulder at Frankie with mild interest.

"Does anyone know," she began hesitantly, her voice threatening to crack from disuse, "where my family is?"

No one spoke. Mack and the tall man both put their forks down and looked away. Shaggy's eyes darted to Mama Jean, who had just then decided to busy herself with washing dishes, then back to his plate. Only Mick's gaze remained steady, but Frankie could not read her expression. The whole room had become hushed. Frankie listened to the clinking of dishes in the sink then tried again more firmly.

"Where is my family?"

"Well, honey," Mama Jean's voice had taken on an unnatural cheerfulness, "That's a good question, but it's late and- "

"I need to know," Frankie interrupted.

Mama Jean set down the dish she had been cleaning and dried her hands on her apron. "I really think," she began again, but Frankie had risen suddenly to her feet, the plate in her lap falling to the floor and clattering noisily.

Shaggy slithered off his barstool and loped from the room muttering, "'scuse me". Frankie watched him go, her puzzlement growing. The tall man rubbed his hands firmly down the front of his jeans and, swiveling on his stool, rose and lumbered toward her. He pulled up a chair and placed it next to Frankie. Then, perching awkwardly on it, he looked directly at her, his dark brown eyes searching hers.

"What?" Frankie's face suddenly felt warm.

Mama Jean stepped around the island quickly and hastily repeated herself, "Now, Jimmy, it's frightful late and I really do think the girl should be gettin' to bed. There's time enough for talk tomorrow."

He leaned around to look at the older woman and shook his head slowly. "No, Jean," he rumbled, "Now. She needs to know. You would want to know, wouldn't you?"

Mama Jean, looking less than pleased, but resigned to his decision, lowered herself onto the couch opposite and watched them, her face full of concern. She looked ready to leap up at any moment. The man turned back to Frankie and regarded her for another moment. Frankie felt a large lump growing in the pit of her stomach.

"I'm guessing they didn't win tickets to Disneyland."

Behind the man, Mick snorted and was rewarded with a sharp look from Mama Jean. The man, however, remained expressionless, the attempt at levity having fallen short with him. Humor, regardless as to how morbid, was her coping mechanism. It did not appear to be his.

"Francine," he began.

"Frankie," she interrupted again, "No one calls me Francine. Not even my parents."

He nodded slowly and started again, "Frankie, this isn't easy to say…"

Frankie knew that nothing good ever began with 'this isn't easy to say'. The last time anyone had said that to her, it had concerned the death of her mother. Her father had uttered those very words over the phone three years ago and paused just as this man was now before delivering the blow. Even then, she had known what was about to be said.

She tore her eyes away from his, suddenly fully understanding where this was going. Her memories of the last time she had seen her family were blurry, but, deep down, she knew. Her daughter's ashen face, clammy with sweat, and her strangely clouded eyes flashed in her mind. The broken howl her husband had made followed by a voice mentioning her son echoed in her memory. She knew what was about to be said. How could she not?

"Frankie…" The man had risen and was towering over her. He placed one hand on her arm supportively, but Frankie knew he meant to catch her when she collapsed.

She planted her feet and tilted her head up to him. She knew already what he was trying to say, but she would not crumple. She would not let this defeat her. Steeling herself, she took a deep breath and asked anyway, "They're dead, aren't they? All of them…They're all dead."

YOU CAN PROMISE your mind the world, Frankie thought, *but your heart has its own agenda*. Frankie's promise to her own mind that she would not fall apart was only half achieved. She and the tall man had stood there for several seconds with his hand on her arm, waiting for her to collapse or faint when she found out the truth. Instead, she had stood firm, her eyes not leaving his as he confirmed

97

what, in her heart, she had already known; her family was dead. Her husband and children had died.

As far as the rest of the people in the room could tell, Frankie was taking everything far better than would have been expected of anyone. Inside, however, Frankie felt as though she was drowning. Her heart was aching.

The tall man had been visibly surprised when she had remained standing. He was looking at her like he was wondering if she truly understood what he had told her. Removing his hand from her, he stepped back and, breaking eye contact, spoke lowly, "Why don't we go talk in the back?"

Frankie nodded. The man turned stiffly and led the way down the hallway. Frankie followed mutely, aware of the hushed voices rising in their wake. She focused on the man's back as she willed her legs to not turn to jelly.

He pushed open a door at the end of the hall and, stepping back, motioned that she should go in first. Frankie squeezed between him and the wall to get through the doorway and made immediately for the bed. A bedside lamp and the moonlight from beyond the drawn curtains dimly illuminated the small room. Sitting on the edge of a queen-sized bed, she released a breath she had not realized she had been holding. The bed lowered noticeably under the man's weight as he sat next to her. Frankie's fingertips stroked absently back and forth over the quilted bedspread. It did not, she noted, have any panels with chickens on them.

At first, they sat in silence. Then Frankie folded her hands into her lap and, with a good measure of effort, addressed the man. She thought her voice sounded strangely muted and strained. "Jimmy," she started, unable to continue.

"It's James," he replied softly. "No one calls me Jimmy except for everyone I've asked not to."

Despite herself, despite the whole horrible situation, Frankie found a smile pulling at the edges of her lips. James reached out and placed his large hand on her leg. She stared at it, unsure how to process the familiarity. He was only trying to be kind.

"It was quick," he said, "Your children. They went quickly."

It was grim solace and likely the best she could expect. She swallowed hard. She had to remain calm. "How do you know?"

"Your husband was brought in to the facility with you. He died two days before you woke. Your son was gone before any of you were transported and your daughter died on the way. It was all in your file. I had access to it among many others."

"But what happened? Was it the flu? I mean, I know it can be bad, but…"

James drew a deep breath, his chest expanding slowly. He released it gradually and purposefully, collecting his thoughts, before answering her.

"It's a virus. A bad one. It's been all over the news, not that you've been awake for that. They're calling it a supervirus because, so far, there's no known treatment and no one seems immune. Only a small percentage of those infected have proven any measure of resistance to it. It's the most lethal virus the world has ever experienced and, if you want honesty, it's going to take a long time for the world to recover."

He seemed to be picking up steam with his explanation and was beginning to remind Frankie of one of her old college professors. "You see, there are pretty much two main group of people to consider when it comes to this virus; The first group is the largest. The majority of people who become infected will die regardless of treatment. It happens pretty fast. It is a lot like a flu for many. It begins with fever and disorientation. The infected experience lethargy and, if they are not in the best of health to begin with, sometimes coma. If they are old, young, or immunocompromised, they go even quicker. The second group is very small. They become infected and experience many if not all of the symptoms before making a recovery. I believe there is a third group that is even smaller, but I don't have any concrete evidence yet. I believe there are people who might be completely immune. Whether or not those who are immune are carriers…well, I need real evidence of them first."

He patted her knee gently. "You, Frankie, appear to be in the second group and I have a theory as to why."

Another long moment of silence passed wherein Frankie expected him to explain this theory of his, but he did not. She thought about the symptoms she had experience in herself and witnessed in her daughter. They both had fevers with chills and sweating as well as extreme lethargy. It was these symptoms that had led her to the conclusion that they had nothing worse than a serious flu. The other symptoms, she assumed, must have been unique to this particular supervirus however odd they seemed. James had neglected to mention these.

"So," Her head was swimming with the information he had given her. Question after question was springing into her mind, but she was not yet able to order them. It was all so confusing. "It is a flu."

James rose and went to the window. He stared out into the night, his eyes not appearing to focus on anything in particular. Frankie watched him as he crossed his arms over his chest, a giant of a man drawing inward and becoming somehow smaller and more childlike. She wondered what he did for a living. His size alone would have made him an asset on a football team.

She studied him with growing interest. He certainly did not talk like a football player. Well, not any she had known. Considering where she had met him, she thought he might be some sort of medical professional. He also spoke like a professor, she reminded herself. Whatever he was, he obviously knew a lot more about what was going on that he was letting on. Even with all her own sorrow, she felt a pang of sadness and sympathy for this man. Something more was weighing on him.

When he finally spoke again, his words were thick and strained. "Yes and no. Calling it 'flu' is a gigantic understatement. Thousands- No, hundreds of thousands of people are already dead, Frankie. It is spreading faster than any virus the world has known. It's spreading far faster than anyone guessed it would. Millions more are already infected and dying. And it won't stop there. It won't stop. This is nothing short of a biological weapon and the whole world is under attack."

Eight

Okay, people. The Nick Nolte after a dip in a swimming pool of cocaine impressions can stop now. Even I don't find them funny anymore.
#backofftheflakka
#zombieapocalypse
#livingghosts

June Posey, Comedienne, Shout It (Social Media Site)

A SHRILL SCREECH filled the small bathroom, the unexpectedness of it causing Henry to stumble backwards with shock. The pale woman, mouth stretched impossibly wide, stepped forward, matching his motion. Henry caught himself on the sink and, without thinking, leaned down slightly and rammed himself into the old woman.

The two went flying together across the bedroom and the woman slammed into the wall on the opposite side of the room with Henry smashing into her like a linebacker. She reached up, wrapping her long damp fingers around his neck and, digging her manicured nails into his flesh, squeezed. The force of the impact seemed to have little effect on her. The piercing wail, uninterrupted, echoed throughout the bedroom and down the hall. A quick glance confirmed for Henry what he had feared; the noise she was making was attracting the other pale people.

Ripping her hands from his neck, he leapt back, his eyes fixed on her as she started forward again. She seemed to have gained strength and was coming at him faster than before. He dashed back through the doorway and slammed the bathroom door shut just as she reached through. The edge of the door bounced off the old woman's strangely pale arm as she tried to push her way in.

One shoulder against the door, Henry drew back his left arm then swung it as hard as he could, his fist smashing into her face. There was a resounding crack and blood splattered from the woman's nose. She wobbled backwards, her arms flailing at her sides. Just as his fist connected with her sweat-sheened face, Henry realized something he had not when faced by the woman before; in spite of the shock of pure white hair and her cataract-like blue eyes, she could not have been more than twenty years old.

The pale woman stumbled back and Henry, taking advantage, slammed the bathroom door shut again. He locked it and pressed his back against it. The screeching grew louder as the pale woman threw herself against the closed door. Henry's body bumped away from the door a bit, but he jammed one foot against the base of the cabinet under the sink and held himself firmly once more against the door. His eyes searched the small room for Mrs. Rose. She was no longer perched on the toilet lid.

"Mrs. Rose?" He kept his voice low. Maybe the pale woman would somehow forget about them if she could not hear them. He would have laughed at this thought if he

103

could. Anything was possible, he supposed. Nothing was making sense anyway. He might as well have woken on another planet. Who knew what rules applied anymore?

Mrs. Rose's head poked out from behind the door of the shower. Her hair, normally carefully pinned up in a bun, was sticking up randomly and terror was spread over her ancient face. She was whispering something over and over. Henry looked up at the skylight. The bathroom door would not hold much longer and, judging by the shadowy forms that were now pressing themselves up against the window, this was their only way out.

"What do we do? What do we do?" Mrs. Rose's voice was louder and become more panicky with each thud against the bathroom door and scratch at the window.

Henry waited for the next thud then climbed up onto the countertop by the sink and punched up at the skylight. He'd expected more resistance, but the house was old and the cover went flying up into the space above like he had hit a sheet of thick paper.

Thud

"Mrs. Rose!" He whispered loudly as he reached down to her, but the old woman was frozen with fear.

Thud

"Mrs. Rose!" Henry raised his voice. Her eyes were fixed beyond him at the door. He had to get her moving. He could see a crack spreading across the wood from where locking mechanism was held.

Thud

Thud, thud

There were two of them now, heaving themselves at the door. Any noise he and his neighbor made in the bathroom was of no consequence. He knew that now. The things outside the door were not going to stop. With a deep breath, he yelled her name again and was rewarded for his efforts. Mrs. Rose looked up, and seeing his outstretched hand, clambered out of the shower. She caught hold of him and, as he yanked her up, there was one finally thud and the bathroom door came flying open, the wood at the lock splintering.

Henry grasped Mrs. Rose by the waist and boosted her up toward the skylight. She cried out as she was shoved up through the hole and into the space above. The pale woman was kneeling on the bathroom floor, her face pointing down and dripping bright red blood onto the tile floor. A man with white streaked hair was on top of her back, having tumbled into the small bathroom after the pale woman. Henry bent his knees and jumped up, grabbing hold of the ceiling around the hole and hauling himself up through it.

Henry was surprised to find himself and Mrs. Rose in a crawl space that seemed to cover the most, if not all, of the top of the house. Because of the skylight, he had not been expecting a crawl space and yet, here they were. It was mostly dark. Light from outside shone down through a second sheet of plastic above the hole where the skylight had been. Against the far wall, there was a small window that Henry assumed was on the side of the roof. It wasn't much, but it illuminated the space just enough for Henry to be thankful for the lazy, and somewhat confusing, builders. They had created this space, but had not seen fit to clear it completely.

There were a few sheets of inch-thick wood lying forgotten under years of dust. Henry scrambled for them and, grabbing the lot, pulled them over the hole in the bathroom ceiling. As the wood slid over the opening, Henry saw the woman rising to her feet. The man who had fallen on her tumbled to the tile floor like a pile of used rags and did not move again. The pale woman disappeared from sight as the wood slid into place.

Henry froze, one knee planted firmly against the wooden sheet, his breath catching in his throat. Mrs. Rose was lying on the crawl space floor, light from the window illuminating the lower half of her face. He could not see her eyes, but her mouth was beginning to open as if to speak. He hastily placed one finger to his lips to silence her and listened carefully. He could not hear anything from below. Was it possible that the pale woman had not actually seen where they had gone? Had they really been so lucky?

Several minutes passed. Henry felt his leg beginning to cramp from being held in an awkward crouch for so long. Still, he did not want to move. It felt too risky. He had not heard anything to indicate that the pale woman had left the bathroom. There was not much else they could do except wait and hope for the best.

MRS. ROSE WAS not doing well.

The soft moonlight that shone through the window was not bright enough to help him see more of her in the darkness than the soft outline of her prone body. Still, Henry could tell that she had fallen ill. Whether it was from the chill of the crawl space and the lack of food and water or from the supervirus, he did not know. Her breathing had been labored for quite some time now and she had not responded to his whispers for even longer. Apart from the sound of her breathing and a few stray moaning noises from out on the front lawn, it was quiet.

Henry's neck had finally stopped stinging from where the pale woman's fingernails had pierced his skin. He shivered and felt his forehead and cheeks with his wrist, but both were cool. He did not have a fever. Nothing online had said how long it would take once infected to fall ill.

He had carefully shifted himself to a seated position hours ago and had propped himself up against the wall with his head tilted oddly to one side due to the lowness of the roof above them. He could just see out the angled window to the street below. There were far fewer pale people now than there had been that morning. Only a few were still roaming slowly. Others were standing relatively still, their occasional gentle swaying the only real sign of life. Some must have wandered away, but most, it seemed, had simply dropped to the ground. Those ones were no longer moving at all.

More unnerving than the motionless human-shaped lumps outside or the uncertainty of Mrs. Rose's or his own health was the fact that he had not seen the pale woman since sliding the wood over the hole where the skylight had been. He could not be sure she had ever left the bathroom. Because of this, he had decided that silence would be the best course.

He had had nothing to do all day except watch the pale people drop or disappear and occasionally check his phone for updates. As the hours passed, far more of the former happened than the latter. It was past eight and there had been no new updates for at least two hours. The last update had been just as uninformative as the ones before it, advising for the umpteenth time that people stay indoors and avoid contact with anyone who appeared to be infected.

It did not stop him from checking. He was sure that someone who actually knew what was going on would eventually take control of the situation. Every time he checked, he had to turn his phone on then power it off when he was done to conserve the battery. He wasn't sure when he would next be able to charge it.

One thing was for sure; he could not sit here forever. He gently stretched his limbs and rolled his head to get the cricks out of his neck. It struck him then that he could not hear Mrs. Rose breathing anymore. Frowning, he twisted as quietly as possible so that he was on his hands and knees. Channeling his inner sloth, Henry began to move slowly and cautiously across the crawl space to where Mrs. Rose lay.

She did not seem to be moving. Leaning in, he checked to see if she was breathing. He placed two fingers on her clammy wrist and felt for a pulse. Not finding one, he put his hand on her abdomen. He breathed a sigh of relief. It was moving, but barely.

Henry took his cell phone from his pocket and turned it on. The phone buzzed to life and the dim light brightened the small space just enough so that he could see his neighbor. He turned the phone so that the light shone directly at her and looked her over. Her hair was just as white as it always was and he was sure that, were she awake, her eyes would be as they always were; just as cloudy with cataracts as ever, no more, no less. Everything about her was the same except her skin. It had taken on an ashen hue and was gleaming with sweat.

Moving his phone down the length of her, he saw a long scratch starting at just below the hemline of her dress. It ran down the back of her calf to the middle of her ankle and had streaks of dried blood staining either side of her split pantyhose.

Henry let himself fall back from her into a hunched seated position. He turned the phone back off and roughly pocketed it. Rubbing one hand down his face, he allowed himself one strangled sob before forcing his emotions back within himself as far as they would go. He had known this woman for the better part of his life.

It occurred to him for the first time that she had been his constant whenever everything else around him was falling apart. Mrs. Rose had often stepped in and filled an emptiness he had not truly understood was there until now. Every time she had popped by with dinner for him and his father, every time she had called him for help had been during a moment when he had really needed the one person he could not have. Mrs. Rose, while never his mother, had become like family to him, watching as he grew from a sad young boy into a man.

She had watched him live and now he was going to watch her die.

LOSING MRS. ROSE was a lot like losing his mother. Both had died so quickly that he had not been given the chance to say goodbye. Or, rather, he had not had a chance to hear them say goodbye to him. Both had also died unnecessarily. Granted, his mother had still been very young while Mrs. Rose had lived a long and full life. He was sure, though, that she would have made it well into her nineties running on pure willpower. She, much like his mother, had been stubborn as a mule. He was sure death would have had to chase her down. In a way, he supposed grimly, it had.

Henry had sat in the dark and, in the moments before Mrs. Rose took her final breath, he had held her

109

hand and whispered to her, recounting his favorite memories and promising to take care of things as best as he could for her after she was gone. This goodbye, falling on her deaf ears, would have to do.

It was very late when Mrs. Rose's body finally gave up and, even after she was gone, Henry kept hold of her hand. He was not worried, as the news had warned him to be, of touching her. The pale woman had touched him. Her sweat was already on his skin. It didn't seem to matter now if Mrs. Rose's sweat got on him. His neck still bore wounds from the fingernail punctures the pale woman had left. He was already infected.

It could only be a matter of time before he followed Mrs. Rose into oblivion.

Nine

Susan Ballentine
Has anyone heard from my son **Matt Ballentine**
or his wife **Sarah Ballentine**? They took the
baby to the ER last night and now they aren't
answering their phones. I can't get through to
the hospital either.
(5 hours ago)

Susan Ballentine
Hello? It's been four hours. Why is no one
answering me? **Jenny Kaufman**? **Kaycee Lee**?
Mike Ballentine?
(1 hour ago)

Susan Ballentine
Hello?
(1 minute ago)

Susan Ballentine, LifeFeed (Social Media Site)

"YOU MAKE IT sound like aliens are taking over."

James shrugged, still gazing out the window. "The
effect is just as catastrophic. Let's equate this supervirus to

an invisible alien armed force that is discriminatory against the majority of humanity. We cannot see them and we have no weapons that match theirs. They have one goal and we literally have no known defense against them. It's sort of a means of racial cleansing, the race targeted being humanity. If my theory is correct, very few people will survive this."

"How do you know all this?"

"That's a long story. The short version is that I was once an assistant professor at Stanford University. I taught courses concerning epidemiology and clinical research. Well, I did before I started stirring the pot." His words tailed off and left the room in silence.

Frankie drew her legs up onto the bed. She was physically exhausted, but her mind was wide awake. Images of her family kept tugging at her, threatening to overwhelm her. Not wanting that to happen until she could face her grief more privately, she decided to focus on James and what he could possibly tell her. At the moment, this was as good a distraction as any. "You've mentioned this theory of yours twice now. You gonna elaborate?"

James turned and leaned against the wall, staring straight ahead at a painting of a vase filled with sunflowers. After collecting his thoughts, he nodded slowly and looked over at Frankie. He took a deep breath and began hesitantly, "Well, like I said, this virus - this supervirus - has the capability of affecting most of the world. For example, in the United States, there are more than 300 million people. Of those, assuming all are infected, I predict that no more than 6% have a chance of survival. And that's only a chance. Gauging the effect on the world as a whole is a little more difficult as not all countries have or are able to conduct clear censuses. However, assume the world's population stands at about seven and a half billion. Of that, I estimate that only about 3% have the possibility of being resistant once infected. Not all of them will actually survive, though, but I believe they have the capability. Again, these numbers are only a rough guess."

Frankie's brow furrowed thoughtfully, "And what are you using as a measure? I mean, what makes them resistant?"

He raised one finger at this, his eyebrows shooting up slightly. The sheer ridiculousness of the 'ah ha' motion made her want to giggle again. She could see how this giant of a man could be a professor. She could just about picture him pacing in front of a class of aspiring doctors and researchers wearing a sweater vest and bowtie.

"Blood," he replied, jabbing his finger in the air at her.

"Blood."

"Yes," he continued, stepping away from the wall and becoming animated, "I believe that resistance to the supervirus lies in a person's blood type. I've been following this for a few years now and-"

"Wait," Frankie held up a hand, "You've been following this for a few years?"

He looked uncomfortable. "Um…yes."

"Years?" Frankie's voice had taken on a manic quality. "You've known about this for years and we're only just hearing about it now?"

James dropped his hand and shoved it into the pocket of his jeans as if the hand itself hand been the source of offence. "Frankie, you have to understand, I'm one man. As soon as I found out about this, I started doing independent research. I did everything I could to learn about it, to follow what was going on with it which was difficult in and of itself. I even gathered a group of trusted friends and colleagues to help me formulate a treatment separately from the group at the Swass Research and Development Facility. But as soon as I started speaking publicly about it…" His voice trailed off again.

"I should have stayed silent," he murmured. "I should have kept the whole thing quieter. I just needed a little more time."

Frankie stood up and took a step toward him, she could feel herself start to shake. "You've known about this for years," she said lowly.

He pursed his lips and forged on, "Frankie, they came after me-"

"You could have gone to the media with this."

James shook his head. "And look like a mad man. Who would have believed me?"

Heat was rising to Frankie's cheeks. She fought to keep her voice calm. "You should have tried."

"They came after my career, Frankie, my family…everything. They ruined me to silence me. They-"

"My family is dead!"

The force of her voice startled even Frankie herself. Anger had welled up inside and was threatening to explode from her. She marched toward James, fury spreading across her face. Her husband, her best friend was gone. Her sweet little girl was gone. Colin, barely two years old and coming into his own personality was just gone. They were all gone and Frankie had not been afforded the opportunity to say goodbye. There was nothing she could have done to prevent it.

But James could have.

"My family is dead," she raged at him, "and you *knew* it was going to happen! You knew and you didn't stop it! You knew!"

"Frankie…"

An unfamiliar noise, a guttural roar escaped her lips. She surged forward and railed her fists at him, beating them against his chest. James, stoic in his acceptance of the attack, remained still. He took each fist fall, making no attempt to stop her or defend himself, and watched as Frankie unleashed all her grief and anger upon him.

Then, as suddenly as it had begun, it was over. Anger abated, Frankie's fists dropped and her body followed as she collapsed into his arms. James held her against himself and lowered both their bodies to the crocheted rug at their feet. For a while, they sat like this, he in silence and she sobbing uncontrollably. He held her and listened as her sobs become muted, her body jerking and tears soaked his shirt. Soon after, as if completely drained, Frankie fell asleep right there on the floor in James's arms. The silence must have attracted attention because a soft knock sounded at the door.

James looked up from Frankie's nest of snow-streaked black curls to the door as it edged open and Mack's blond head appeared. He gave James an inquisitive look, pointing his chin at Frankie whose face was buried against James and shielded by her hair. James nodded once in return. Mack's face disappeared as the door shut again. Presumably, he was the envoy, sent to make sure no one had died.

James sighed. That was the problem, though. Someone had died. A lot of people had and millions more

115

would in a frighteningly short amount of time if he did not do something about it.

FRANKIE AWOKE HOURS later to sunshine and the sound of birds chirping happily outside her window. She, herself, had not awoken anywhere close to as happy as they sounded. She had jolted awake, the image of her daughter's ashen face burned into her mind. Pulling herself up, she leaned on one arm and rubbed the sleep from her eyes. It took her a moment to remember where she was and another several to break from the memory of her nightmare enough to recover the conversation she and James had had the night before.

Across the room, in an old wicker chair looking less than comfortable, sat James. He was slumped in the chair with his eyes still closed and his arms crossed over his broad chest. She was not sure if he was actually asleep and wondered if he had been sitting there all night. Had he served as guardian over her while she slept? She watched him breathing before speaking.

"Last night," Frankie said without waiting for him to open his eyes, "you said some people are resistant to the virus. I get that. I mean, here I am, right? You also said you think some people might be completely immune."

She paused, watching his rhythmic breaths before continuing. "You don't know? You seem so sure about everything else."

His chest kept rising and falling rhythmically for almost a full minute. She had just decided that he was still asleep when, eyes still closed, he responded, "I have no clear evidence of complete immunity. Not from my own research, anyway. Yet."

Frankie pulled the covers up and hugged them to herself. She had spent an awful lot of time sleeping lately. She was ready to do something, but did not know what. What was there to do? It had been over a week since she had gone to work and it was likely that, at this point, her job was not there for her anymore. Even if the world was not falling apart as James had essentially said, what was the point of going back to her old life? She would still have somewhere to live. The house would surely still be there, but there was no one except her to return to it. She had no family to support now. She only had herself to think about. She choked back the lump that was forming in her throat.

"I mean," James said suddenly, sitting up and opening his eyes, "it's altogether possible that there are people out there with an immunity to the supervirus, but, based on my research, I can't see how. All the completed research we did suggests that only people with an O-negative blood type have any sort of natural defense against the infection and, even then, it isn't a guarantee."

Frankie studied him. "O-negative," she murmured, "like me."

"And me," he added.

Frankie pointed at the door. "What about them?"

James winced, leaning forward and resting his elbows on his knees. It was clear that this was not something he cared to think about. He clenched his hands together into a tight fist, his knuckles turning white with strain. He sucked in a breath between his teeth and shook his head. "At first, I thought it was all negative blood types that were resistant to the supervirus, but that was swiftly disproven when all A and B samples reacted adversely to

117

the virus. Then I thought it might have to do with the antigen or, rather, the lack thereof. You see, blood types only have two kinds of antigen: A and B type. O means zero. It is a blood cell that lacks either the A or B antigen coating.

"We conducted a series of tests wherein each blood type was exposed to the supervirus. All positive blood types reacted almost immediately and within a matter of one or two days, all the white blood cells were mutated and systematically destroyed. Samples that were without A or B antigens, that is to say the O samples. responded just as swiftly to the attack, but did not submit when the other samples did. This is what led us to briefly speculate that it was the antigen that determined whether or not it was resistant to the supervirus."

He unclenched his hands and stared at them, palms pointed up. "This was disproven within six hours. Every O-positive sample yielded to the supervirus. Essentially, in every trial, every positive blood type was mutated and then overrun. It turned out to be a fairly accurate indicator of what to expect should the supervirus ever be released."

He tilted his head and coughed into the crook of his arm, clearing his throat before continuing, "The trials run on negative blood types gave us false hope. When infected, most of the negative blood types appeared to react the exact same way the positive types had, responding to the attack right away, but it became apparent after the third day that the white blood cells, while mutated, were not being killed off. In fact, the white blood cells were not even attempting to eradicate the supervirus anymore. They became …docile, in a sense, and seemed to be almost coexisting with it. The supervirus was developing a sort of bond with all the negative blood types. This led us to believe that resistance was likely determined by the RH factor." James paused, rubbing the side of his head thoughtfully.

Frankie clasped her hands together "A bond? So, it's still in me? The supervirus?"

"Yes, but-"

"But you said the tests gave you false hope." She interrupted, confused. How was it false hope when she, the carrier of O-negative blood type, was sitting here alive a week after the initial infection?

He sighed deeply, but took his time responding. Frankie could now hear sounds coming from other rooms up the hall and, beyond, in the kitchen. Her stomach growled noisily, but James did not appear to have noticed. He looked completely lost in thought. Then, as though he had never stopped speaking, James leapt right back into his mini lecture.

"Yes," he said patiently. "All negative blood types lasted past the two days it took for the supervirus to destroy the positive samples. On the fourth day after infection, however, all samples that were infected negative blood types showed new changes. The change made us think there was more hope than there actually was." He rose and began to pace the room.

"We saw the O-negative samples first. They had started to show signs that they were fighting the infection. We were excited – so excited. We thought that the negative blood types were proving to be resistant. We had thought we were closing in on a treatment. Then we checked the other samples. All the A-negative and B negative samples had white blood cells that were beginning to behave erratically. We weren't sure what this meant. The supervirus did not appear to be actively attacking the white blood cells anymore, but what they were doing...We weren't sure. As for the AB-negative samples..."

He was silent again, still pacing. Frankie, growing impatient, asked, "What about the AB-negative samples?"

"I had thought I'd found something different about the AB-negative samples, but the trials run on them were inconclusive as far as I'm concerned. I believe they were tampered with, but I don't have proof. We had this lab assistant, a guy by the name of Cabot. My buddy Robert had brought him in. Promised he was trustworthy." James scowled.

"Not so much?"

"Not so far as I'm concerned." James was becoming angrier, "He had been assisting with the process of infecting the samples with the supervirus. I was sure I had seen him messing with one of the samples, but he swore he'd followed procedure and Robert stepped in before I could check. Anyway, on the fourth day, the AB-negative samples were all responding like the A-negative and B negative samples. They all submitted completely. No one else questioned it. It made too much sense to them. I just...I'm just not so sure."

Frankie could smell something amazing being cooked up the hall. Her stomach growled loudly again and, this time, James noticed. He grabbed a fluffy looking robe that had been hanging on a hook on the door and handed it to Frankie who swung her legs from the bed and slipped it on. She followed him to the door then stopped short, her hand pressed firmly against the wood to prevent him from opening it.

"And it's still in me?"

James sighed, but continued patiently. "All viruses leave a trace, Frankie. They all do. This is no different. But, if you are concerned that you will infect me or the others, you can relax. I know someone else who was infected and recovered and he never infected anyone else."

"Will I meet him?" Frankie was suddenly eager. The idea of meeting someone else like her who had gone through the infection and come out relatively no worse for wear was a relief.

James met her eyes and fixed on them. He looked more solemn than she had seen him yet. "You already know him, Frankie," he replied softly, "He's your father.

Ten

'Infected Turned Away: Mount Sinai Among First to Close Doors, Over Capacity'

Mount Sinai Hospital, one of the nation's largest and oldest teaching hospitals closed its doors last night, turning away hundreds of people seeking assistance. Many were redirected to surrounding hospitals only to find them just as overcrowded. Over two-thirds of hospitals in New York state have reported having to refuse aid due to being well over capacity. Patients are reported to be sharing rooms with upwards of a dozen others while more still have been lined up in hallways to await a treatment that might not yet exist.

Nina Paul, National News

HENRY STAYED BY Mrs. Rose all night, holding her clammy, wrinkled hand until it became cold and began to stiffen with the onset of rigor mortis. It was the least he could do as it was becoming increasingly obvious that the woman would have neither wake nor funeral. It was up to him to show respect for a life well lived. Then, exhausted and hungry, he lay on his side next to her, his back to her lifeless body, and tried to sleep. The sound of his stomach growling seemed to echo across the dark crawl space, making it that much harder to drift off, but sleep eventually claimed him.

With sleep came dreams. Henry could not remember the last time he had had a dream much less a nightmare. The ones that came now felt endless. First, he dreamt of his mother and then Mrs. Rose. They ran in cycles, looping over and over again. Each time, one of the women would be in mortal danger and it would be up to Henry to save them. However, every time he tried, he would get to them seconds too late. No matter what he did, no matter how hard he tried, they always died.

He woke drenched in sweat and, for one terror-filled moment, thought he was finally showing symptoms of infection. He scrambled for his phone and, nearly dropping it twice while trying to turn it on, waited anxiously for it to come to life. The phone lit up, vibrating in his hands. He tapped the camera function and adjusted it so that it was aimed at his face.

"Let me take a selfie," he muttered to himself as he moved the phone around so that he could see all angles of himself on the screen. His face was flushed and his hair still the same boring salt and pepper that it always had been. Most importantly, his dark blue eyes where still dark. He was showing no sign of infection whatsoever.

Baffled, he clicked off the camera and pulled up Google. Articles popped up right away under the search bar. Breathing a sigh of relief that the internet was still up and running despite the chaos the world was sinking into, he scanned the titles and read them aloud under his breath.

123

"'Supervirus Death Toll Rises to Over 50,000'…'Dead or Alive: Thousands of Infected Roam Streets'… 'Infected Turned Away: Mount Sinai Among First to Close Doors, Over Capacity'…'White House Silent in Wake of Supervirus'…".

Henry snorted at the last headline. "Of course, they are," he spat, "Every politician for himself." He skimmed a few articles then powered his phone down. Returning it to his pocket, he stretched and began crawling back in the direction of the wooden sheet that covered the hole where the sky light had been. He refused to look back at the body of his neighbor. He couldn't. He was afraid he'd lose it if he looked at her again. A twinge of guilt ran through him and, to pacify himself, he promised to return and remove her from the crawl space just as soon as this was all over.

Reaching the wooden sheet, he cautiously prodded it and peered through the small crack as it widened. The pale man was still in a heap on the bathroom floor, but Henry could not see anyone else in the room. He pushed the cover further off and listened. The house was silent. Carefully, he poked his head through the hole and, upside down, peered into the bedroom. It looked empty as did the hallway beyond it.

His stomach rumbled. There was nothing else for it. He could not stay up in the crawl space forever. Besides, he really needed to pee and doubted his aim was good enough from so high up. Not that it really mattered at this point.

Henry righted himself then slowly lowered his body through the hole and onto the counter next to the sink. Remembering the shower, he twisted until he could see into it from where he was and, finding it empty as well, jumped lightly to the tiled floor. He skirted the man on the floor and, one eye on the unmoving mass, relieved himself with a heavy sigh into the toilet. He returned to the sink and turned on the faucet, running it until the water became hot. With his sleeves pushed up as far as he could get them in his bulky attire, he scrubbed at his hands and wrists before moving to his face. The hot water felt amazing on his skin.

He looked up at himself in the mirror. Water was dripping from his chin into the sink. His hair was unkempt, but appeared to have no more gray than usual. His face was another story. There was already enough stubble on his face to forego calling it a five o'clock shadow and go straight to accepting that it was well on its way to being a beard. His eyes looked tied, though, and there seemed to be more creases around them than there had been the last time he had looked closely at himself. He sighed a second time and dried himself on one of Mrs. Rose's decorative flower-print hand towels before heading to the door.

Pausing in the doorway, he glanced back at the man on the floor. With one foot outstretched, he prodded him with his boot. The body wobbled then fell on its side where it lay frozen bent in the position in which he had found it. The man was definitely dead, no question about that. Henry searched his face, trying to figure out if he knew him, but nothing about the man was familiar. It was a small town, but Henry had always made a point of keeping to himself. The only reason he knew any of his neighbors at all was due to constant proximity or having had them insert themselves in one way or another into his life. The effort was rarely, if ever, his own.

Henry turned from the body and made his way through the bedroom and back up the hall, his eyes darting from shadow to shadow as if they would somehow come alive and turn into screeching pale people. None did, of course, but he stayed watchful as he entered the foyer that broke off into the living room to the left and the kitchen straight ahead. He pressed himself up against the wall and peeked into the living room. There were a couple of bodies, each in its own pile on either side of the room. The kitchen did not contain any bodies at all. The house was empty except for himself and three dead bodies.

Four, he corrected himself, remembering Mrs. Rose.

The kitchen door was wide open. That explained how the pale people had got into the house. The door must have given out from the strain just as the bathroom door had. He marveled that he had not heard it. He did not think the house was so large that the sound of a door being forced open would not carry to the other side. He tried to think back. Had he and Mrs. Rose been making enough noise to mask the entry of the pale people?

Out the kitchen window, Henry was met with a horrific scene. There were dozens of bodies scattered about the front lawn, sidewalks, and in the street. Aside from a large black crow sitting on a low branch of the tree next door, there were absolutely no signs of life. He rubbed his eyes and peered through the window again. He was not sure which was worse; watching the pale people roam mindlessly or seeing them all dead.

A whimpering golden retriever appeared from behind a pile of bodies. It was making its way almost frantically up the street, its head swinging back and forth as it bent to sniff at each body as it passed. Although he could not hear it through the glass, he was sure the dog was whining as it searched. This, he decided, was worse.

Henry yanked himself from the window and searched the cabinets for a glass. Finding one, he filled it from the sink and drank it in four large gulps. He refilled the glass and, placing it on the counter, went to inspect the contents of the refrigerator. Mrs. Rose had always been an excellent cook. Henry had looked forward to the dinners she would occasionally deliver to him and his father after his mother's death. They certainly beat the PB&Js and TV dinners that his father tended to serve up. His father was many things; a chef was not one of them.

He was not disappointed. Neatly packaged in a rectangular Tupperware with a red lid was a lamb chop with a side of fried potatoes. He popped the lid and, discarding it, scooped up a handful of the potatoes with his fingers and crammed them into his mouth right there in front of the refrigerator with the door wide open. They were gone in seconds. He tore at the chop with his teeth, his eyes already searching the shelves of the refrigerator for more. He couldn't remember the last time he had been this hungry.

Leftover creamy potato soup was consumed cold and, like the lamb chop, straight from the tub. He tossed the containers into the sink and crossed over to the pantry, leaving the refrigerator door standing wide open. Poking through it was like a treasure hunt at Grandma's house. Handfuls of expensive cookies and other random items including fancy wheat crackers and organic granola bars were either shoved directly into his mouth or into the pockets of his coat. He was taking as few risks as possible. He did not yet know what he was going to do, but not having food later was not something he felt like dealing with. He was sure, having not grocery shopped in a couple weeks, that there would not be much at his own home. He might as well take as much from here as he could. Besides, Mrs. Rose would not be making use of any of it.

Full at last, Henry picked up the glass of water and sipped at it. He was back in front of the window, listening to the hum of the open refrigerator. The dog was gone. So was the crow. Everything outside was just as it had been before. All the cars were still parked in their respective driveways or on the side of the street and many of the people who had once driven them were scattered about the neighborhood, dead. Some had collapsed in the most interesting positions, draped over one another somewhat comically. Others were alone, mostly in piles as though they had fallen directly to the ground where they stood.

It felt strange to think that all these people had gone to bed just a couple of nights ago as they probably did every night only to wake as zombies. He shook his head. No, not like zombies. They had woken as something different. Zombies, to the best of his somewhat limited understanding, were the reanimated dead. These people had all still been alive while they wandered about aimlessly, moaning. At least, they had been alive until the supervirus had completely destroyed them.

Henry drained the glass and set it inside the sink next to the Tupperware. He felt his forehead with the back of his hand. It felt normal. He felt normal. He scoffed and went to the kitchen door, ignoring the still open refrigerator door as he passed it. He felt as normal as he could possibly feel, he corrected himself. Normal, these past few days, seemed to be changing. He wondered why, though, he was not.

Pausing with one hand on the frame of the door that led from the kitchen to the side of the house, he touched the scabs on his neck, feeling the dried blood. The pale woman had definitely punctured his skin. He had not imagined that. Why, then, was he not exhibiting signs of infection? The news had warned against contact with the bloodily fluids of those who were infected. They had not warned against puncture wounds. Perhaps she had not infected him at all since no spit or blood of her own had been transferred to him.

He felt a pang of guilt as relief flooded through him. That was it. She had not actually infected him. While this thought was reassuring, it did not change the fact that so many others had not been as lucky. Had they been coughed on? Had someone sneezed too closely to them? Whatever happened, they had been in the line of fire in the form of infected bodily fluids and had fallen ill before dying only a day or two later. They had not been lucky enough to have had an encounter like his own wherein his souvenirs were a few scabbed over puncture wounds and his life.

He paused, deep in thought.

Wounds.

Mrs. Rose had not been coughed or sneezed on. She had not encountered any infected bodily fluids. In fact, she had been wounded by the very same pale person as he had and, yet, she had become ill and died.

So, why hadn't he? Mrs. Rose had not lasted long at all from the time she had been scratched until the moment she died. She was not, though, as young or physically fit as he. Perhaps it had simply not been long enough.

Henry nodded. That was it, he decided. He was, indeed, actually infected and would soon exhibit all the symptoms he had been warned about online and seen in Mrs. Rose. Before long, he would lose his mind along with his pigmentation and roam the streets groaning until his heart stopped. Then his body would fall into a heap and where it would remain until whoever survived the supervirus, if anyone, did something about it. Would he be given a proper burial? Would they just burn his corpse along with countless others? Was that not what was done in cases of plague? He was sure the protocol for this sort of situation had to be pretty similar.

Henry could not help but laugh at himself. Here he was, a grown man, paralyzed with fear and uncertainty in a kitchen losing his sensibility in favor of the dramatic. He needed to stop thinking about it. There was only so much he could do if he was already infected, most of which entailed getting his affairs in order. Since the time between infection and death was so short, it was a good thing his affairs were so few. Considering that his time was probably halved since it had already been over a day since he was likely infected, he would be better off not wasting time on matters like writing a makeshift will.

A will would not take long to write, though. In fewer than ten words, he could be finished writing it and signing it; *Donate my stuff to charity, -Henry Lee Decker II.* He chuckled at the thought of even the most desperate of charities wanting any of his crap. No, he would not be bothering with a will.

The only thing he could do now was get on with living for however long he had left. And, of course, try not to speculate what it was like to fall sick enough to die.

WHEN HENRY WAS five years old, he overheard his mother bragging to a friend that she could count on one hand how many times her son had been ill in his life. He had inherited his father's constitution and, as a result, rarely ever got sick. When he did, however, it was never anything worse than the common cold and it rarely lasted more than a day or two. Henry, until that year, could not have clearly explained to anyone what it was like to feel truly unwell.

His mother had not been a particularly boastful woman. On the contrary, she had often told Henry that if he ever wanted to ruin a good thing, all he had to do was tell someone else about it. He had not been sure what this meant until a week after his mother had told her friend about Henry's own good thing.

The pneumonia had set in so quickly that no one, not even little Henry himself, had known it was coming. One day, he had been happy and healthy, playing in the street in front of his house with all his friends and the next, he was bedridden. It had taken him two weeks to recover and almost a month longer before he felt well enough to go back to playing in the street. He had also missed a lot of school and had fallen behind the other students.

Henry, as an adult, had a very vivid memory of his mother sobbing uncontrollably and telling the doctor who had been kind enough to make a home visit that it was all her fault; she had made him sick through her boastfulness. No amount of consoling could convince her otherwise. He had been confused, unsure how anyone's words could possibly have enough power to make someone sick. Later, in his teens, he wished his words had that sort of power when he was informed by a much disliked teacher that he would not be passing the class. Fortunately for the teacher, Henry's words were no more capable of killing than he was of passing American Literature.

It was also in his teens when his father let slip that the real reason his mother had been so upset was that Henry had almost died. His father told him about a trip to the hospital late one night at the height of the pneumonia wherein he had been admitted for a little over a week. Henry had not believed his father. All his memories concerning his bout of pneumonia were as clear as if he was watching them unfold right in front of his eyes years later. He had no memory of having been hospitalized and certainly not for a week. He argued that a hospitalization was not something people just forgot about. Still, his father insisted that Henry had, indeed, been hospitalized and Henry was left wondering why on Earth he could not remember a thing about it.

For the remainder of her life, Henry's mother never again bragged about her son's health and, if anyone commented on it, would all but spit and throw salt over her shoulder. Henry was never that ill ever again and, much like the first five years of his life, never with anything worse than a brief cold.

WHAT HE NOW feared was coming was far worse than any cold and would make his run in with pneumonia look like a frolic through the park on a sunny day. With his hand still on the frame of the kitchen door, he stared out into the yard. He knew he could not stay here, but the thought of leaving was terrifying. The reality of his situation had fully set in and had him trapped between the need to run and the desire to return to the crawl space and hide until death came for him, too. His heart was pounding and his stomach, full of food, was churning uncontrollably. He felt as though he was about to throw up.

He had to make a decision. He could either lie down and die or step outside this house and forge on, come what may.

There were two soft clicks from behind him, the suddenness of them jolting him from his morbid reverie. The constant humming that had filled the small kitchen was cut short. Recognizing the sound of a refrigerator door shutting, he turned slowly with the stark realization that yet another decision had probably already been made for him.

Eleven

Ifedayo Obadiran
Se gbogbo yin wa ok? Mo t'in pe fun ojo meta.
Gbogbo eyan ni ibi bai n'se aisan. Mo n'beru lati
lo s'ita.
Translated from Yoruba.
Are you all ok? I've been calling for three days.
Everyone here is sick. I'm afraid to go outside.
(15 hours ago)

    Olufemi Ajayi
    Mo gba brotha e soro l'ana. O wa ok
    n'igba yen.
    Translated from Yoruba.
    I spoke to your brother yesterday. He
    was ok then.
    (15 hours ago)

    Olufemi Ajayi: Se o wa ok?
    Translated from Yoruba.
    Are you okay?
    (11 hours ago)

    Olufemi Ajayi
    K'asan? Mo fe ri boya n'kan lo dada.
    Se o wa ok?
    Translated from Yoruba.

Good afternoon? I want to see if
things are going good. Are you ok?
(6 hours ago)

Olufemi Ajayi
Ku irole? Ife?
Translated from Yoruba.
Good evening? Ife?
(2 hours ago)

Olufemi Ajayi
Ifedayo Obadiran? N'ibo lo wa? Jo
dashun si mi.
Translated from Yoruba.
Ifedayo Obadiran? Where are you?
Please reply to me.
(3 minutes ago)
Ifedayo Obadiran, LifeFeed (Social Media Site)

FRANKIE'S EYES WERE fixed on James's. Her
eyebrows were raised and the look on her face told him
quite clearly that she was expecting a punch line. James's
mouth was set in a straight line, waiting solemnly for her to
process the information he had just relayed. He had been
loath to tell her, having realized that, based on how little
she knew about what was going on, she had absolutely no
idea the level to which her father was involved much less
the fact that he was involved at all.

When no punchline came, Frankie released a short
giggle anyway. "This is a joke," she said, dismissing his
words.

James's lips tightened until they formed a pinched
white line. He shook his head and drew a deep breath in

through his nose then blew it out slowly. Maintaining eye contact, he tried to figure out how, exactly, one divulges information such as he had to someone as closely linked to the situation yet so far away as Frankie. An image of a bandage popped into his mind. *Right,* he thought, *just rip it off.*

"Frankie," he began with more hesitation than he would have liked, "Your father helped develop the supervirus."

Frankie stood in stunned silence, her hand still pressed against the door. Her father? It did not seem right. It did not seem possible. Yes, her father had worked for the government, but he had not done anything even remotely interesting. He had said so himself. He certainly could not have been involved in the creation of a virus that had led to so many deaths and, before long, would lead to many, many more.

Could he?

"B-but," she stuttered, "he...I..."

"I know it's not an easy thing to process, Frankie," James said, looking down at her, "but it's true. Your father was the lead scientist on the project. He was the head of a division that focused primarily on the development of viruses that could be used as biological weapons in the case of war."

"Stop right there," she interrupted, her free hand shooting up to halt his explanation, "you're wrong there. My father wasn't a scientist. He was a – a...well, I'm not entirely sure what he was, but I'd have known if he was a scientist! He didn't ever do anything....sciencey! He didn't even help me with my science fair projects. My mother did that!"

135

"Frankie…"

"No! He was not involved!"

James held up his hands in mock defeat, but Frankie could tell by his eyes that she had not convinced him. She glared at him and, grabbing the door handle, jerked the door open and marched angrily up the hall to the living room. She could feel James following in her wake, but refused to look back or acknowledge him.

The curtains in all three sections of the front of the cabin were drawn back and bright sunlight was shining through. It was warmer at this end of the cabin, but Frankie drew her robe closer to herself when she saw Mack and Earl sitting on barstools at the island, already digging into their breakfasts. Earl did not bother looking up from his food, but Mack smiled and offered her "mornin'" from around a mouthful of eggs.

She nodded silently at him and pulled out the stool next to him. The only other stool available was on the far end of the island next to Earl. She had been wary of him the night before even when she had been referring to him by the name of a beloved cartoon character. She preferred some distance between them until she could find out a little more about him. James quietly took the empty place next to Earl and greeted Mama Jean who, as usual, was bustling around the kitchen.

Mama Jean turned around with a loaded plate in hand and, spotting the scowl on Frankie's face, stopped short. "Oh, dear," she murmured. Then, louder, "Oh, dear, oh dear. You didn't go telling her about…*all that*…Did you, Jimmy?"

James shrugged and, leaning forward over the island, took the plate from Mama Jean's hands. "Had to eventually, Jean." He set the plate in front of himself and focused on it as though eating would put an end to the conversation that made him uncomfortable. It did not work.

"You rile me up sometimes, boy," Mama Jean got another plate and filled it with eggs and toast. "You should have waited."

"Until?" James asked, the coolness of his words surprising Frankie. "She was going to find out soon enough. Sooner is definitely better considering, don't you think?"

From next to James, Earl slurped his coffee and held it up to Mama Jean for a refill as if she were no more than a waitress and this a diner. "He's right, Jean. The sooner the girl is up to speed, the better. It's a quarter to seven already and we're wanting to be on the road in no more than an hour. She's bound to have questions and I don't feel like putting up with a ton of chit chat or fussin' in the back of a van. Tell her now and get all the crying over and done with."

Mama Jean glared at Earl, ignoring the hand that still held out his empty mug. In response, he jiggled the mug and matched her gaze with indifference equal to her anger.

Scowling, she placed the plate in front of Frankie who was gaping down the island at Earl. Before she could find her tongue, Mama Jean collected the coffee pot and topped up Earl's waiting mug. She regarded the man sternly, "Now, Earl. Be kind. It's a lot for anyone."

Just then, Mick swept into the room and, shaking her head at the empty plate Mama Jean had picked up and was indicating to her with, went directly to the entryway and pulled on her boots. She took a jacket down from a hook and, without looking back at any of them, pulled it on and disappeared through the front door. Frankie was not sure about her either. The girl, younger than Frankie by at least ten years, had come across as cold. Frankie might even go so far as to describe her as resentful. Of what, though, Frankie did not know.

"You'll be fine, Earl," James said into the silence that had followed Mick's progression through the living room. "She's riding up front with me. There's more to tell than I can cover right now and I need her for directions anyway."

"Directions?" Frankie leaned forward and looked down the island at James. He did not return her gaze. His breakfast had suddenly become very interesting. In lieu of an actual response, he grunted and continued eating.

Frankie's head was swimming again. Turning her attention to her own breakfast, she reviewed everything she'd been told and tried to link it to memories from her childhood. None of what James had just told her made any sense. She could not fathom how her father was connected to this much less how he could possibly be the reason for it as James had implied. She had known that he was a doctor and that he worked for the government, but a doctor of what and what he did for the government, she did not know. She supposed it could have had something to do with science. It was as reasonable an assumption as any at the moment.

What if it's true? She stared at the food on her plate, not really seeing it. If it was true, how could she have never had so much as an inkling about it? She had lived with the man for half her life. Was it possible she knew even less about her own father than she thought?

She realized how odd it must have seemed to James that she, a grown woman, had reached this age without having any clue whatsoever as to what her father had done for a living. *He probably comes from a family that had actual conversations around the dinner table instead of uncomfortable silences,* she thought. As Mick had the night before, Frankie prodded at the food on her plate, pushing it back and forth as she thought. Then common sense and hunger took over. She finished her breakfast quickly. It sounded like she was in for a long ride. Who knew when she would next have even half as good a meal?

FRANKIE GLANCED AT the clock on the dash. It was only a few minutes past eight so they were, according to Earl, just about on schedule. Why there was a schedule in the first place was beyond her. James was still on the front porch talking to Mama Jean. She wished he had given her the keys. She could have started the engine and turned on the heat. The other three were already in the back of the van. Frankie could only imagine how it was back there. It was so cold up front. She wondered why it was so chilly for this time of year. Normally, even at the beginning of September, while it was cool, it tended to be a lot warmer than this. She rubbed her hands together and blew on them in an attempt to get warm.

She watched in the sideview mirror as James wrapped his arms around Mama Jean and held her for a moment. Although they did not appear to be related, they did seem close. Eventually, James ambled down the wooden stairs and across to the van. He opened the driver's side door and hauled himself up into the seat without acknowledging her in the slightest. He slid the key into the ignition then reached over his shoulder and rapped with his knuckles on the wall separating them from the back. Seconds later, the van had roared to life and they were rolling down a long and graveled road through trees that thickly lined either side.

"Where are we?" Frankie blurted. She could not believe it had only just occurred to her to ask.

"The Jemez."

"The Jemez?"

James glanced over at her, "Yes, just outside Ponderosa to be exact."

Frankie's brow furrowed in thought. She felt more disoriented than ever. "So, where was I before?"

"Before?"

They passed a small cabin not unlike the one they had stayed in the night before. She turned to look at it before it was blocked completely from sight by trees. She was sure she had seen someone in the doorway. "Um. Yeah. As in 'I passed out in my home in southern Colorado and woke up in some freaky facility being poked and prodded at before being dragged off to a cabin in the Santa Fe National Forest by a bunch of people I've never met who haven't bothered explaining who they are or where they are taking me now'. That 'before'."

James snorted. "Was that all one breath?"

"Let me try that again. What the fuck was that place, who the fuck are you guys, and where the fuck are we going?"

"Well," James coughed into his fist, "When you ask that way…"

James steered the van to avoid as much of a spot in the road as he could where rain had made it bumpier. They rode in silence for a few more minutes before the tree coverage became a little thinner. James pulled off onto a paved road. Far up the road, Frankie could see what looked like a main road. She could not see any movement on it and wondered how far into the mountains they were exactly that there was no traffic especially considering what was going on. She had seen plenty of apocalypse movies. Surely people would have tried to get themselves and their families out of the path of the infection. Maybe no one had thought to head for this forest. Maybe they simply had not been able to make it this far.

"To be brief for now," James finally answered, jolting her thoughts back to her angered question, "You were in the Swass Facility. It's a 'secret' medical facility in southern New Mexico that is funded by the government. It's not government owned, per se, but they've definitely given the Swass family enough money in grants that they probably have quite a say in what goes on there. It's one of the worst kept secrets, if you ask me. I mean, if you're going to have a secret facility that focuses on things that would freak out the general public, building it close to the Alien Capital of the World probably isn't the smartest idea. Some kook is bound to discover it and freak out. In fact, few did…The government can only suppress so much. Your father worked there years ago. You knew that, didn't you?"

"No, I didn't. Did you? Work there, that is."

"No. I didn't, but I knew people who did."

"Next question."

James adjusted himself in his seat. "Well, I'm James and they," he pointed toward the back of the van, "are my not so merry men. Except for Mack. He's pretty merry. And Mick. She's not merry, but she's not a man either. I guess that just leaves Earl."

Frankie eyed him silently. His attempt at levity had not escaped her. She was just too angry to react as she normally might have. "And together you are...?"

"Trying to fix a horrible mistake."

When they reached the road, Frankie saw that it was not empty as she had originally thought. Rather, most of the cars that had been driving on it were now off on the side. Some had been driven farther off the road onto the grass. A couple of cars sat motionless here and there in both lanes. Every so often, as they maneuvered past the vehicles, Frankie would spot a body. Some were hunched over steering wheels or strapped into cars seats and boosters or secured still by seatbelts. Others, seemingly having wandered away from their respective vehicles, were lying in various spots about the road. People had, it seemed, thought of running for the trees.

Frankie tried to focus on the people. It was difficult because James was driving faster than the posted speed limit and was veering around each stationary obstacle with a good measure of skill. The bodies she did manage to get a decent look at all had a similarly greyish tone to their skin and hair that was either mostly or entirely white. It was as though all the color had been sucked right out of them.

She cleared her throat. From her peripheral vision, Frankie could tell James had glanced over at her. Without looking at him, she asked, "Do I look like them?"

"Like who?"

She pointed at a body ahead that was draped over the hood of a blue Camaro. The deepness of its paint job was startling against the man's shock of white hair and his pale skin. She asked again, "Do I look like them?"

James was silent for a few moments before reaching up and swiveling the rearview mirror until it pointed directly at her. "Not exactly."

Frankie adjusted the mirror and peered into it. It took her more than a few seconds to realize that the face staring back at her was her own. Her skin, though on the lighter side naturally, had lost its rosy hue. Now, it was slightly pallid and sickly looking. Then there was her hair. While it was still mostly black, it had streaks of white throughout as if she'd had chunky highlights added by an overly enthusiastic stylist.

Her eyes were the most shocking of all. None of the iris' hazel hue had changed, but her pupils were completely clouded over. She imagined she looked a bit like someone with the advanced stages of cataracts. Her vision, however, was just as good as it had always been. It was strange seeing swirls of green and brown surrounding such a frosty blue where only black should have been.

"I look like a cross between Storm and Rogue," she said to herself.

James burst out laughing. "I didn't take you for a comic book fan".

"Oh, yeah," she replied, leaning closer to the rearview so that she could get a better look at herself. "Ever since I was a kid. There's still a couple boxes of comic books up in the attic at my dad's house. All still in the plastic, too. Mostly X-Men or superhero comics like Batman and Superman. I loved the idea of being different – of being special. I think, probably, because I always felt so normal. Except for my hair, that is. I was a bit of a Plain Jane growing up."

"I wouldn't have pegged you as plain." He glanced over at her. "What's this about your hair?"

143

Frankie smiled wryly. "Imagine Bozo the Clown."

"Bozo?" James snorted. Frankie nodded silently, lips pursed. "Sounds pretty special to me."

"I guess."

"Well, you're definitely special now," James said without hint of dryness.

An awkward silence followed. Frankie leaned her elbow against the window and rested her head on her hand. The further they got from the cabin and the closer to civilization they got, the more abandoned cars they had to avoid. Not all had been abandoned. Many still had drivers and passengers, but none appeared to be alive. In any case, most drivers seemed to have managed to pull to the side of the road before succumbing to illness. Some, however, had simply stopped in the middle of the road. Others had crashed into them. At one point, James had to slow the van right down to five mph to squeeze between a bunch of vehicles that had been stopped all together at odd angles from each other. There were skid marks as though they had slammed on their brakes with little warning.

Every so often, she would spot someone who was still alive wandering between vehicles, but it was obvious that they were at the tail end of their illness. Stopping to help would only put their own people at risk. Ignoring the sick people was difficult. A few were still aware enough to turn their heads to follow the motion of the van as it passed. One, a young boy, had even turned his body completely toward them and screamed as they sped by on a particularly clear patch of road. Although, with the windows up, his efforts had been soundless, it had shaken Frankie. She stared at his gaping mouth, reflected in the sideview mirror, until he disappeared altogether into the distance.

Eventually, as she knew it would, Frankie's mind drifted back to her family. Memories of her children, so sweet and innocent, came bubbling to the surface. She saw Colin taking his first steps and Lydia cheering him on. She remembered her husband on their wedding day and how, despite promising he wouldn't get any stains on his tux before the ceremony, he had indulged in a chocolate ice cream with his three-year-old niece and had attempted to cover where it had dripped onto his shirt with his boutonniere. He had been less than successful, but she hadn't minded. For some reason, she had been afraid the wedding would go off without a hitch. Having some imperfection made her feel more secure. Perfection, in her mind, was not normal. Life was never perfect. She believed that, if everything was perfect, that it was not truly real and would not last.

Frankie felt her throat constricting. Her life had not been perfection and, yet, it had not lasted. She squeezed her eyes closed tightly, but the images would not be banished. She could feel tears threatening to come pouring from her again. She took a deep breath and swallowed hard.

Opening her eyes, she choked out, "Tell me more. About the virus." She paused then added, "Tell me more about my father."

"He's a great man."

"Okay."

"Really. He is. I've admired his work for my whole career. I've read every article he published and attended every lecture he offered. Whenever possible. I traveled several times to hear him speak. I even hitchhiked once when my car broke down. There was no way I was going to miss that lecture."

Frankie blinked. Now she was sure he was talking about someone else. Articles? Lectures? That wasn't her father. James, reading her thoughts from the skeptical expression on her face, continued.

"I'm guessing he never discussed his work with you." Frankie shot him another look. "Franklin Ray Reed born May 4th, 1951. Married Sarah Rosenbaum in 1979. They didn't have you until 1983. You really had no idea he was published?"

Frankie shook her head. It was unquestionably her father he was talking about. He had traveled a lot for work so it was not impossible that he had lectured at universities as well during his stints away from home. "No, we didn't really talk much. He was…reserved."

James nodded. "Yeah, sounds like him. Kinda. Anyway, like I said, I went to every lecture your father offered and read everything I could get my hands on that had his name attached to it. I thought he was brilliant. I finally got to meet him years ago. I had just been accepted to medical school and he was lecturing at my university. It was a bit of a struggle getting through the crowd to talk to him, but I was determined to meet him. Man…He was amazing. He opened my eyes to so many things. He changed my life!"

He looked like a kid reminiscing about a trip to Disneyland. His whole face had lit up at the memory and he was becoming as animated as he had before when first telling her about the supervirus. With a grin still on his face, he went on. "Anyway, I guess he took a liking to me because we spent a few evenings together after that. I was very persistent so I'm pretty sure it was more that I'd worn him down at first. He invited me to join him and a couple of his friends for drinks. I was so nervous that I could barely speak. I was surrounded by virtual geniuses and terrified I would say something stupid so I mostly listened that night. I learned so much from them. From your father, mostly. That was the night I realized what I wanted to do with my life. It changed the entire trajectory of my studies. I had been going to be a doctor. Instead, I followed your father into Epidemiology."

James fell silent for a moment, his brow furrowing. "He only visited my university twice after that and I did everything I could to go and visit with him when he was elsewhere. The last time he came, I was finishing up my degree. He called and asked if I wanted to meet up. Of course, I said 'yes'. When I got to the bar, I saw that none of the people he normally had surrounding him were there. It was just me and him. I could tell right away that there was something different about him. Something had changed. He looked far older than the last time I had seen him and like he'd been very sick. His hair was far whiter than it should have been and his skin was ashy. It also looked like he had entered the stage of cataracts where it just becomes visible, but he didn't seem like he was having any trouble seeing. He was acting so strangely and, for the first time since we met, he got drunk. Really drunk. Whisky. Scotch. A lot of it. In fact, he'd started drinking long before I got there. I tried to get him to slow down, but he wouldn't listen. He started rambling on about an experiment he had conducted when he suddenly broke down crying. I couldn't figure out what had happened. He was fine one moment, relatively speaking, and just…different the next."

Frankie's eyes widened. She recalled the day her father had first appeared odd to her. James's description, minus the drinking and sobbing, was pretty close to how she remembered him looking. She had thought he had just been very tired from the trip. He had been gone longer than normal. Had this been when he was infected?

147

James swerved to avoid a body neither of them had seen. They both stared out at the road while he considered his next words and Frankie processed what he had already told her. It was becoming hard to focus with so many thoughts swirling about in her head. Something was tugging at the edge of her memory, but she could not quite put a finger on what it was.

There were fewer trees now lining the sides of the road and, once or twice, the area had looked vaguely familiar. She had managed to just miss the only sign she had noticed since before turning left onto the road. She had been so wrapped up in what James had been saying and, even during his silences, had found it impossible to rip her eyes away from all the bodies. She had completely forgotten to actively look for signs. She had a suspicion, based on what James had said so far, that they were heading toward Los Alamos. The roads up to this point, while congested in places, had not been all that bad. They had been able to maintain a relatively fast more often than not. Surely, if their destination was Los Alamos, they would have arrived by now.

She had just thought to ask where, exactly, they were when a highway appeared in front of them. A sign informed them that turning left would take them through San Ysidro to Albuquerque and turning right would lead to Cuba and Farmington. Her brow furrowed. If they were headed to Los Alamos, why had they gone this way instead of east which would have been more direct and far faster? James interrupted her thoughts with a rush of words. "He said it was a virus he had been working on. He kept saying he never should have done it, that he would be the cause of millions of deaths. He told me that he had been infected, but it had not killed him. It did kill one of his friends, though, a fellow scientist who had helped create it. He was harboring some major guilt about that."

James rubbed at his chin.

"I figured it was all just drunken ravings." James frowned. "No, I think I was just hoping that's all it was, but parts of what he was saying made far too much sense. It got to the point where I had to haul him out of the bar before they called the cops on him. I got him back to his hotel room and into bed. On my way out…"

This time, the pause seemed endless. Frankie studied James's face, wondering what he was avoiding saying. "On your way out," she repeated, hoping to jumpstart him back into his story.

James frowned again then continued hurriedly, "On the way out, I saw some files and a flash drive. I…I took them. I don't know what possessed me. Curiosity, I suppose. Anyway, I stole some of your father's files and read them. I had one of my Computer Science buddies help me with the flash drive. It had some encrypted files that my friend was able to hack into. The contents changed my life. They changed everything."

"What were they?"

"Essentially, those files held the formula, if you will, for engineering the supervirus. I didn't quite understand it at the time. Eventually, though, I realized that, if this supervirus was ever released, the world could be completely wiped out. That's when I got some of my most trusted colleagues together. It took a bit of convincing, but they saw the truth in the end. We gained access to a private lab, a favor called in by my friend Robert, and tried to recreate the virus. We were not successful until recently. Honestly, we were not prepared for success."

He swallowed hard and sped the van up. Frankie got the impression that this was all she was going to get for now. She did not want to press him. He had said it was important for her to understand everything. She was sure he would tell her more soon enough. She leaned back and closed her eyes, blocking out the dead bodies that were growing ever greater in number the closer they got to civilization. Even behind her closed eyes, though, she could see them.

She was surprised when he spoke again only moments later. "We were not prepared because, in reality, we were nowhere near having a treatment for the supervirus. We knew certain blood types held the key, but we still don't know how to use them to formulate a treatment. That's why we need you and your father, Frankie. I guess that's the answer to your third question. We're going to Los Alamos."

Frankie had always wanted to be special and, now, because of the luck of the genetic draw, she was alive while so many others were not. The way the world was beginning to look, she wondered if she really was the lucky one.

Twelve

Gemma: Granny! It's me! It's Gemma! Pick up, Granny, please! Mummy and Daddy won't wake up! I don't know what to do! The neighbours have all left and I tried ringing 999, but I can't get through! I don't know what to do! Granny? Granny, please! Please pick up the phone. I need you, Granny. Please!

Gemma, age unknown, Answering Machine Message

"YOU PACKIN'?"

The question came as a shock to Henry. He stared at the boy standing across the kitchen from him. He could not have been more than twelve years old and was awkwardly pointing a hot pink Smith & Wesson directly at Henry. He was definitely not who Henry had expected to see upon turning. He was not sure he was grateful it was not the pale woman or terrified that his fate now lay in the hands of a frightened child.

"That a Bodyguard 380?" Henry asked as he took a step toward the boy.

The child practically shook the weapon at Henry. He had been squinting before, but now his light gray eyes were round and wide. His voice cracked as he yelled, "Stay back! I'll shoot!"

Henry lifted one hand up, palm facing the boy. "That your mama's gun, kid?"

The boy scowled at him, trying to collect himself by puffing up his scrawny chest in an attempt to make himself look bigger. The expression on his face must have been one he thought hardened criminals used when pointing their guns at people. It didn't match his lanky build, though, or go well with his disheveled orange hair and slightly too large teeth. It was an attempt to look older, but he only succeeded in making himself look younger and more lost. "I'm not a kid. You packin'?"

Henry ignored his question for a second time. He leaned casually against the kitchen counter nearest to him and regarded both the boy and his gun. Henry could now see something that this boy obviously did not know. He was no longer as concerned for his own safety. The boy noticed the change in Henry's demeanor and took a step back toward the doorway into the foyer.

"It's okay, kid," Henry said calmly, "I have absolutely no desire to hurt you, but I'm sure there are other people who might feel differently, you go pointing a gun at them. And you might want to take off the safety if you want to be able to use that thing. Won't fire otherwise. It's right there on the side. See it?"

The boy glanced down at the gun in his hands, distrust flickering over his freckled face before realizing that what Henry had said was true. Fumbling, he flipped the

153

safety and aimed once again at Henry. His hands were trembling now and he was having a hard time keeping the gun steady.

"Your mama know you have her gun?"

"She wasn't my mother. She was my foster mother and she wasn't even supposed to have it anyway."

Henry caught the grammatical tense the boy had used. Still with the appearance of being completely unaffected by having a gun pointed at him, Henry asked, "Was?"

"Yeah," the boy replied, nonplussed. He puffed himself up again and affected what he must have thought was a more confident tone by deepening his voice and imitating the speech patterns of a street thug. "Was. Like, she was my foster mom until she went all zombie and I put a cap in her head."

Henry raised his eyebrows as though impressed. He was trying hard not to laugh. "With that gun?"

"Yeah, with this gun."

"Was the safety on then, too?"

The boy looked flustered again for a moment. Then, without warning, his whole face crumpled and he began to sniffle. He wiped the back of his left hand across his nose, his lip trembling. He looked even younger now than Henry had first estimated. He lowered his guess to about ten-years-old.

Henry sighed. "You didn't shoot her, did you?

The boy shook his head, tears beginning to stream down his cheeks. "Nah. She went all zombie and I hid under my bed. She came into my room right before…" The boy choked back a sob then restarted, "She came into my room right before she died. She just fell to the floor. Her eyes were still open and I thought she was looking right at me and I thought…I thought…"

Henry had never been a fan of children, but, in this moment, he had a strong urge to close the distance between them and wrap his arms around the boy. This child had seen too much for someone so young and, judging by what he had told Henry, he had already had a head start before the supervirus took another person from him.

"Is that why you took her gun?"

The boy shook his head again. "No. I took it when the white lady came."

Henry's heart skipped a beat and a chill ran through him. "The white lady?"

The boy nodded, his coppery hair falling into his eyes. He shook his head to knock it back, the gun beginning to lower in his hand. "Yeah, she had super white skin like she'd rubbed chalk all over it and her hair was like the lunch lady's at my school, but she didn't look like she was that old. She looked like she was my mom's age. My real mom."

Henry understood now. It was no wonder the child felt the need to be armed; He had seen the pale lady. Henry picked at a bit of lint on his jacket, trying to appear as though this topic did not make him feel like wetting his pants. "What happened?"

"She came after me," the boy was trembling now, "She screamed all crazy loud and ran at me. I didn't know what to do so I ran to my foster mom's bedroom and got her gun. I'd seen it there in her closet before when I was playing hide-and-seek with Mikey, but she didn't know I knew about it. I wasn't supposed to go into her room. I wasn't allowed."

Henry nodded, waiting as patiently as he could for the boy to get it all out. The gun was now dangling all but forgotten at his side.

"I hid in the closet forever. I swear she knew I was there, but she never opened the closet door. I waited until she was gone and I just ran."

"And Mikey?"

"Huh?"

"You mentioned a 'Mikey'. What happened to him?"

Tears were flowing freely down his face now, but he made no move to wipe them away. "He got sick. I think he was dying. These guys in white suits came and took him away. They were gonna take my foster mom, too, but she told them she hadn't touched him so they left her. They asked if there was anyone else in the house and she said 'no'. I don't know why, though. She knew I was home."

Henry's mind flashed back to his own encounter a few nights before. They, too, had asked if he'd touched her. He wondered if he would be in Mrs. Rose's house right now had he answered differently. The main difference between his men and those in the boy's account, though, was what they had been wearing.

"Were you hiding?" Henry asked. When the boy silently nodded, Henry continued, "Smart thinking. She was trying to protect you, you know. Your foster mom."

The boy swiped his arm across his face, wiping away the tears, but did not answer. Henry knew the boy had understood that. Still, he'd lost someone he had obviously cared about and was angry about it. He just did not know where to direct that anger. Henry was all too familiar with that feeling.

Henry reached slowly into his pocket and withdrew a granola bar. The boy watched with interest as Henry held it up to him. Then, like a wild animal expecting to be tricked, the boy took several cautious steps toward Henry and snatched the granola bar from his hands. He ripped the wrapper with his teeth and ate the bar with as much gusto as Henry had.

"You got any more?" the boy asked around a mouthful of food. Henry pulled out what he had left and handed it to him. Soon, wrappers littered Mrs. Rose's tidy kitchen floor and the boy was looking less ravenous.

He had put down the pink handgun so he could use both hands to eat. It now rested on top of the counter within Henry's reach, but he made no move for it. Instead, he turned and inspected the pantry one last time, taking from it anything he could pocket and carry easily. He then went back to the kitchen door and stopped halfway through it. He looked over his shoulder at the boy who was wiping crumbs from his mouth with his shirt and staring mutely after him.

"Come on, then," Henry nodded at the gun on the counter, "and bring that. We might need it." When the boy did not move, Henry stepped the rest of the way out of the kitchen and entered the yard at the side of the house. He glanced around and, seeing no motion outside, called back, "Unless you'd rather try making it on your own."

Walking toward the front of the house, Henry smiled slightly to himself. He could hear the scrape of the gun as it was lifted from the countertop and the slapping of the boy's tennis shoes on tile as he ran to catch up.

THE SUN WAS high in the sky by the time Henry had finished installing the replacement windshield he had ripped from another Jeep at the junkyard. He and the boy had ridden the whole way there without uttering a single word. The boy, despite the kindness he had been shown, was still wary of Henry. Henry didn't really blame him. Instead of pressing him, Henry opted to give him his space and time.

It had taken longer than usual to get to the junkyard due to having to go through so many residential neighborhoods. Each street had been littered either with dead bodies or vehicles, some with engines still running and dead drivers staring blankly. Henry had had to stop and get out more times than he could be bothered keeping track of to move a vehicle or drag a body to the side so they could get through. Of all the ways he had thought he might spend a day away from his job, this was not one.

Finding a new windshield and the extra tools he needed to install it was, by far, easier than the journey to the junkyard. The office had been wide open and a man wearing a work shirt with the junkyard emblem on it was sprawled out on the floor. Henry thought he recognized the guy as being a new hire, but was not sure. It did not matter now, though. It was not as if he was going to be bumping into the man at the grocery store.

Henry pulled himself up into his Jeep and glanced over at the boy. He had spent the whole trip there with his legs pulled up on the passenger seat and his arms wrapped around his knees. He had not once offered to help when Henry had had to stop the Jeep nor did Henry ask for any.

Henry was dripping with sweat and had shed a few layers of clothes ages ago. The boy, however, looked chilly. He wasn't even wearing a coat. Henry imagined that the boy had just run out of his house wearing what he'd put on the day before, not thinking to grab a sweater or a coat. Kids didn't think ahead like that. He decided to go hunting for appropriate clothes for the boy as soon as possible. In the meantime, Henry grabbed his jacket from the backseat and draped it over the boy.

"Robby," the boy said suddenly as the Jeep sprang again to life.

"Henry." He smiled reassuringly at the boy then nodded in the direction of the entrance of the junkyard. "So, where to?"

The boy turned quickly to look at Henry. "You don't know where we're going?"

Henry shrugged. "I'm just the driver. Thought you might make a good navigator." Robby stared at him for a moment as though gauging how serious he was about handing over big decisions to a child. Henry raised his eyebrows and tilted his head toward the road. In response, the boy grinned at him toothily. He pointed up the road in the opposite direction from which they had come. Giving the boy one sharp nod, Henry stepped on the gas and the Jeep surged ahead, kicking up dust as they pulled out onto the road.

There was no more silence for about half an hour. Until that moment, Henry had no idea how much a child could talk. At first, the boy only divulged the most basic information about himself. He was Robert John Smith and he thought he had the most boring name in the world. He had just turned eleven the month before and had been in foster care since he was about eighteen months old. He liked Lego and reading and had wanted a bike for his birthday, but got a secondhand scooter instead. He didn't mind so much. He was happy to get anything at all.

159

As he spoke, he pointed in different directions, guiding the two of them slowly around town. Henry had not wanted to waste gas, but he felt it necessary to give the boy time to open up and recover from the shock of what had happened. It might also afford him the time to figure out just where they should go and what they should do. He did not think sitting in a junkyard for however long it took to make a plan would be very encouraging to a child.

As they drove and the boy talked, Henry took note of where there were more bodies. Occasionally, they saw someone walking around, but it was never someone who was not obviously infected. Henry avoided these people at all costs. He did not want the boy anywhere near them.

Before long, Robby began to open up and give Henry the more intimate details of his life. A social worker had popped in for a well-check and had found Robby's mother passed out on the toilet lid in the bathroom with a needle sticking out of her arm. Robby, left completely unattended, was sitting on the couch watching cartoons. He was surrounded by empty cracker packages and covered in crumbs. His diaper did not appear to have been changed for some considerable time. These were details he'd overheard while eavesdropping on his social worker and foster parents some years before. Henry had figured as much. He was pretty sure no one would intentionally want a young boy to know exactly how messed up his only parent was.

Robby had liked his last foster mother a great deal. After having been shifted from one home to another, he had finally been placed where he felt he belonged. Even though he loved his birth mother and enjoyed their supervised visits, he had secretly hoped his foster mother would adopt him. He told Henry how his foster mother had enrolled him in a martial arts class that he loved and how she signed him up for baseball. She had never in the two years he had lived there missed a game.

Mikey had been a foster child as well. He had been placed with them shortly after Robby and had quickly become Robby's best friend. They often claimed to be blood brothers and would tell anyone who would listen that they were twins. They had so many similar interests and behaved almost identically that they might have been believed had it not been for the fact that Mikey had roots in Nigeria while Robby looked like he could don a green hat and pose as a leprechaun for St. Patrick's Day.

The boy's eyes filled with tears several times while telling Henry about his foster family, but he had not let them fall again. Henry was truly impressed at the strength this little boy possessed. He was handling the lot life had handed him with far more grace than Henry had his and Henry's life had been spectacular in comparison.

Just when Henry thought the boy had finally run out of things to say, he started listing every Lego set by number that he wanted. Henry was startled by Robby's ability to recall so many numbers as well as the fact that he could link each number to a detailed description of the set to which it belonged. Often, he even knew exactly how much the set cost depending on where you got it. Henry, on the other hand, often had trouble remembering if he'd had breakfast.

Henry's contribution to the conversation, by this point, consisted mostly of nodding and making appropriate noises every now and then. The boy did not seem to notice or care that he had taken over the conversation. He had started to smile and was swiftly becoming comfortable with Henry.

Both realized at the same time that lunch had come and gone, but it was Robby who complained first. Or, rather, it was his stomach. Both the boy and the man laughed aloud at the racket it was making.

"I guess we should find some grub, huh, kiddo?"

'Yeah," Robby sighed, "I could really use a burger right about now."

Henry followed the boy's eyes as they fixed on a fast food restaurant. Henry slowed, seeing that the neon open sign was lit. He had seen very few pale people in this area compared to in his own neighborhood. He estimated there were fifteen within shouting distance and none of them overly close to the front of the restaurant. He figured it was worth a try. He had worked in a joint like this in his teens. If everything was still running, he was sure he would be able to cook something up for the two of them.

The excitement on Robby's young face was palpable as they pulled off the road into the parking lot of the restaurant. He noted that it even had an indoor play structure. This, aside from getting as far away as possible from where they had seen the pale woman, was turning out to be the best decision he had made all day.

It had felt like hope against hope, but the front door of the restaurant swung open easily and the smell of burgers and French fries immediately filled their noses. Henry glanced down at Robby. The boy was grinning up at him. It warmed his heart to see him have some happiness, however small it might be. He reached over and ruffled Robby's hair then gave him a small shove toward the play area.

"You go on. I'll fix us up something."

Robby dashed off, flinging himself against the door to the play area to open it. Henry watched him disappear as he climbed farther and farther up the brightly colored play structure. It felt good to do something right. With a smile still on his face, Henry turned around and came face to face with his second gun of the day.

Thirteen

私死にそう
Translated from Japanese
I am going to die

Kaito Takeda, Shout It (Social Media Site)

FRANKIE OPENED HER eyes and, yawning, stretched as well as she could with limited space. She had not really wanted to sleep, but it had seemed a far better option than counting bodies so she had closed her eyes and tried. The clock on the dash now read 11:12 a.m.

She had slept through about three hours of driving. She felt a little guilty at having not held up the conversation with James to keep him company, but she did have to admit that she felt better for having slept. In fact, she felt better than she had since first falling ill.

She looked out the windshield and watched as the road winded up around the side of a mountain and realized with a start that she recognized exactly where they were. They were no longer on the highway. The road straightened and she saw that they were heading toward an all too familiar little town. The road was completely clear and James, taking full advantage, sped up. Her gaze soon landed on the brown stone where bold white letters read *'Los* Alamos' and, below it in black on grey stone, *'Where Discoveries Are* Made'. She yawned, watching with interest for the animal clinic she had worked in part time one summer and then, farther up, the small airport. There were half a dozen small planes, some under covers, lining the fence.

When the road eventually split, James went right, choosing Central Avenue over Trinity Drive. Frankie's eyes scanned the streets as the van proceeded steadily up the main road. The first thing she noticed was, although it was eerily quiet, there were no scattered or abandoned cars and no bodies littering the streets. From what she had gathered, the supervirus was spreading faster than wildfire. Was it possible it had not yet reached her hometown? If it had not, where were all the people?

James, noticing for the first time that she was awake, glanced over. "This is where I'll need your help. I didn't have time to search for your father's home address. He isn't listed. I only knew the name of the town because he mentioned it a few times in passing."

"It's not hard to find," Frankie peered out the window. None of the shops on Central Avenue were open. She tried to think what day it was. Was it Saturday? Sunday? She tried to remember how long it had been since waking from the coma. She had slept so much since then that time seemed to go by in small flashes. If it were Sunday, it might explain the silence. "Just keep going up this street. It ends at Diamond which runs north or south. The labs are to the south so you're going to want to head north. I'll point you on from there. It'll still be a way up. It's right before the Parker's farm, my Dad's house. Well, it's not really a farm. The Parker's, that is. It mostly goats for rent, chickens, and a small crop."

She was beginning to babble. "Anyway, what's today?"

"Saturday."

Saturday. Not all shops would be open here this early on a Saturday. The diner would be open, for sure. Dinah's Diner even stayed open on Sundays to catch the after-church crowd. Curious, she watched for it out James's window.

"Sorry," she said absently.

"For what?" He looked at her, honest confusion spread across his face.

For you having to rescue me from that place I was being held. For crying like an idiot. For trying to kick your ass, she thought then settled on, "For falling asleep."

James shrugged her apology off. "From what I hear, it took your father a whole month to fully recover. I think you're doing really well, personally, although I wouldn't be surprised if you sleep a ton more before you're completely better."

"Why did we go that way, anyway?"

"Hmm?"

"Through Bernalillo. It would have been quicker to go through Jemez Springs."

"Oh." James replied, "The Forest Service had the road shut down just north of La Cueva. Not sure why. I didn't want to take the long way. It was riskier for a couple reasons, but what can you do?"

166

Dinah's Diner was up on the left. Her eyes fixed on it, her head turning so that she could stare into it as they passed. It was empty and all the lights were off. A cheerfully worded closed sign hung in the doorway, its curved writing promising that they would "Be Right Back, Y'all!". Furrowing her brow, she searched for any sign of life. Everything was so still and quiet. She remembered that, for being such a small town, it had always been full of noise and life. It had felt like there was always some sort of carnival or festival or parade going on.

She recalled the few parks they had always having a handful of children in them especially at this time of day. Mothers with younger children tended to get together for picnic lunches under the guise of socialization for their young ones. Everyone knew it was more to get the mothers out of the house for some adult conversation as well as to get them free from the tug of little fingers for a while. There was always someone hosting a bicycling club or a running group. It was what you did in small towns. If you didn't amuse the town folk, you were likely to lose them to bigger cities.

They were reaching the end of Central Avenue. As she had said it would, the road split off into two directions. Frankie gestured that he should turn right then went back to looking for people. She occasionally signaled that he should keep going or turn.

Frankie frowned. There had been no cars in the library parking lot and the handful parked in the Lemon Lot with "For Sale" signs posted on them had a thin layer of dust on them. She had peered as far down a couple of streets as possible as they passed by and had noted that every car was parked neatly in driveways or in front of houses. None seemed out of place.

It was like all the people who lived here had been zapped away by some unknown force. Frankie's mind went back to her reference to aliens the day before. The emptiness of this town made it seem like, if there were aliens, they were not taking over the planet but rather abducting everyone on it. She snorted to herself, ignoring James's sidelong glance.

She could not imagine any intelligent alien life form being interested in the people who lived in her hometown. It might have been full of scientists and engineers, but most would likely have bored the socks off whatever poor alien had the misfortune to abduct them. That was, if aliens even wore socks. *Maybe,* she thought, *they are not such intelligent life forms or they're just taking what they can get.*

A motion to her right caught her attention. A cat had leapt from the roof of a car to the hood and was racing down the street. She watched it for a moment before it dashed across the street and disappeared into a bush. She smiled, grateful that her imaginary aliens, intelligent or otherwise, did not seem to like cats enough to abduct them as well.

"Up here," Frankie said, pointing to a road on the left that they were approaching.

The drive had taken longer than she remembered it being. "This road leads to the Parker's. Dad's is about half a mile before it on the left. You can't miss it. It's the only one." Sure enough, a solitary two-story house came into view from behind a row of trees. There was a long drive that led from the road to the house which had been built at the edge of a patch of woods. Frankie had loved having so many trees right outside her back door. She had enjoyed building tree forts and playing make believe in it with Janie Parker when they were little.

James slowed the van and turned onto the dirt road that ran up to a largish open graveled patch that served as parking. Frankie recognized the only car as a black sedan belonging to her father. He had bought the Ford Taurus in the mid-1990s and had found it to be fairly reliable. He'd had to replace a few things here and there, but, all in all, it had lasted well enough to not warrant an upgrade to a newer model. Frankie wished she had fond memories of it, but there were no exciting road trips or vacations taken in this vehicle because her father had purchased it some years after the summer of the missed camping trip.

She noticed, for the first time since arriving in Los Alamos, an abundance of ravens hopping about around the back of the car and the trash bins. As the van approached, they took flight, heaving themselves up past the tops of the tall pines that surrounded the house. She had forgotten how huge they were.

"Well," said James as he pulled the van next to the Taurus, "we're here."

As soon as he cut the engine, he was out and around to open up the side of the van. She heard him asking how everyone was and listened as each person responded. Then, taking a breath, she got out of the van and made her way up to the front door. A raven cawed loudly from above her, drawing her eyes upward. Far above where the noise had sounded were two hawks circling slowly. Her father used to have a painting of a hawk in his study. She wondered if it was still there.

It had been a few years since she had last seen her father. The awkward silence had become too much for her and had been impossible to explain to her inquisitive daughter. Both she and Hugo had decided that it might be best for everyone if they backed off until something changed. Deep down, Frankie did not believe that her

169

father would ever change. Whatever happened to him so many years before had seemed to have had a permanent effect on him. It had had a permanent effect on her as well, both then and now. She agreed with Hugo that they could not subject their children to their grandfather's strange behavior. Children needed warmth.

Behind her, James was leading everyone up from the van. Frankie, already at the front door, had her hand raised in a fist to knock, but found she could not. It dropped limply to her side. A large hand rested on her shoulder, the weight of it reassuring. She looked up at James and smiled weakly. Seeming to understand what she was feeling, James knocked on the door loudly. The others scattered themselves about the porch and waited.

At first, when there was no answer, Frankie had thought that he might not be home. She discounted it immediately, her eyes shooting to her father's car. Worry began swelling up inside her. Had she left getting back in contact too long? What if he had been sick? What if he had fallen and had lain on the floor unable to call for help until he died? All the emotions she had felt when first grieving for her husband and children were beginning to flood back to her. She felt as if she were about to drown. Then, with a soft click and a scraping noise, she heard the deadbolt sliding back from inside the house. Relief swept over her as the door cracked opened and caught on the security chain.

Her relief was immediately replaced by confusion.

A woman's face peeked out through the slit and studied them. Her expression was of clear mistrust. Her gaze swept over all of them, but paused on James, her eyes looking him up and down as if pegging him as their leader. "Who are you? What do you want?"

"I'm James Wester," he replied, his voice softer than it had been. "We're here to see Dr. Reed."

"Oh? 'bout what?" The woman's eyes were darting from one person to the next. She settled on Frankie, her eyes narrowing distinctly. "She sick?"

Frankie shook her head. "No, ma'am. Not anymore."

"But you were."

Frankie nodded. She was unsure what to say to convince this woman she was no threat. She was not even sure yet herself that she was not. For all she knew, she really was still contagious. But, then, no one had treated her like she was. Also, James had said that her father had been infected and surely, if the virus was something that lingered to infect others even after recovery, she would have been infected years ago.

James patted Frankie's shoulder. "She's fine, ma'am. She's safe. We really do need to see Dr. Reed, please."

The woman looked him over once more then shut the door on them without another word. It was silent for so long after that even James was showing signs that he was not sure the door would open again. Then, as James raised his hand to knock again, the security chain scraped back and the door opened wide. The woman, dressed in pink nurse's scrubs with hearts printed all over them in purple, swung her arm in toward the inside of the house. Frankie felt a pang of guilt. Had her father's health declined so much that he needed a home healthcare assistant?

"Well, come in, then. And hurry up."

James led Frankie into the house, smiling amiably down at the woman who was now patting her greying black hair back into place where it was coming out from a tight bun. Earl nodded at her as he passed, but chose not to speak. Mack was more polite, offering her a "Ma'am" and a tip of his imaginary hat as he passed. Mick ignored the woman completely. She was looking even more sullen, Frankie noticed as she glanced back over her shoulder, than ever before.

Once they were all in the entryway and the door had been shut and bolted, the woman squeezed past and waved for them to follow. Frankie knew, by the direction in which they were headed, that she was taking them right down the hall to her father's study. Her father had never cared for sitting around in the living room. Entertaining guests had been her mother's thing. Whenever anyone came to see him, a rarity in later years, he always took them in his study.

Somehow, as they had all filed into the entryway, Frankie and James had fallen to the back of the group. She could hear the woman speaking to Mick and Mack as she started up the hall.

"You two twins?"

"That obvious?" she heard Mick mutter in response.

"Identical?"

This time, it was Mack who responded, his tone playful, "I'm the pretty one."

Frankie had not been in her father's study for longer than she could remember. It was where she and her father played board games like Candyland and Chutes and Ladders when she was small. Her father had always been secretive, but had become more so as the years passed.

Eventually, he stopped inviting her in altogether. In response, she stopped asking. She could still picture the room as it had been when she was small. He had always kept it perfectly tidy and ordered, just like everything else in his life. It was a perfect reflection of himself.

Frankie had loved the smell of the books mixing with her father's aftershave. Occasionally, it had been mixed with traces of pipe smoke or cigars. Her mother had hated that, claiming that, on top of it being horrible for his health, the smoke would ruin the books. To mollify her, Frankie's father had promised he would stop. Frankie knew he had not, though. She knew he would just crack a window and sit next to it so most of the smoke would go wafting out. Afterwards, Frankie still knew what her father had been up to as soon as she poked her head into the room.

The woman rapped her knuckles against the door to the study, but only waited for a few seconds. She must have heard something the rest had not because she then opened it and ushered them through.

The room was nothing like she remembered. It was dimly lit and smelled a little of lavender. Books were piled about the room on just about every surface and papers were stacked randomly about, some spilling from their piles onto the floor. The whole room was in complete disarray. To Frankie, it looked more like a poorly organized storage room than a study.

Her shock was complete when her gaze, having flitted about the room in search of some trace of familiarity, stopped on an old, frail looking man who was seated in a time-worn leather armchair behind a desk so littered with papers, books, and files that not even an inch of the top could be seen. She stared at the man, not quite recognizing him for a split second as their eyes met. She gazed into the clouded swirls of his pupils as the realization struck her.

173

"Frankie," he said, slowly rising to his feet and setting the quilt that had been draped over legs onto the chair behind him, "it's been a while."

The woman's expression went from a pinched mistrust to look of shock. "This your girl, Frank? The one you said lives up north?" Her father was nodding, a gentle smile pulling at his lips. The woman was now looking Frankie up and down with more consideration than she had at the front door.

Frankie, though sharing some features with her father, favored her mother. Her skin tone was, in comparison with her father's, very pale and she was slightly freckled across the bridge of her nose. Her eyes were almond shaped like his, but had distinct flecks of green mixed throughout the brown just like her mother's. The main similarity with her father was her hair. She had long ago stopped trying to relax her tight curls and, instead, embraced them and wore them with pride. It was a feature she had passed down to her children.

The only real difference between her hair and her father's was the color. While her father's hair was jet black, hers was only so thanks to the regular ministrations of a very talented stylist. Most of the friends she had now would be surprised to know that, despite her heritage, she was a natural redhead. That is, they would be surprised to know after discovering her heritage.

Frankie had started dying her hair about ten years before she had met her husband and had kept it up after both her children had been born with dark hair like their father's. She figured it would be a whole lot easier than having to go through explaining over and over that they were, indeed, her children as her father had had to do when people they did not know saw the two of them together. It was one thing to be biracial. It was quite another to be comparable to Little Orphan Annie as well.

"I see it," the woman said squinting at her, "I see more of Sarah in her, but I see it."

Frankie, becoming annoyed at being placed under a microscope and a little perturbed at this woman's assumed familiarity with her deceased mother, snapped back, "And who are you, exactly?"

The woman bristled and folded her hands behind her back. Frankie's father was moving carefully around the desk, using it to lean on. He looked up at Frankie and grinned, recognizing this fire in her. "Now, Francine. Let's not get off on the wrong foot. This is Cora."

"Cora Jenkins," she woman added somewhat curtly as if the name alone explained everything.

"But who are you?"

"A friend," she replied simply as she back against a bookshelf. She smiled over at Frankie's father who returned her familiar warmth. Frankie studied the woman closer. It was hard to gauge how old she was, but she was definitely older than Frankie. She was also at least a good twenty years younger than Frankie's father and, while no great beauty, was rather nice looking now that she wasn't scowling at anyone or looking at them like they might be enemy spies. Frankie wondered exactly what sort of friend this Cora was to her father.

Her father, grabbing a cane that had been resting against the wall next to his desk, leaned on it and made his way unhurriedly toward Frankie. "They sent me Cora about a year ago after I sent away all those silly gum-snapping little girls the agency kept sending me."

175

"'They?'" Frankie asked.

"Healing Hearts Homecare Assistance," he replied, panting slightly.

"And he didn't 'send away' anyone," Cora added, "He scared them. No one wanted to work with him. He was a real grouch, this one."

"'Was' being the operative term, Cora. 'Was'." He paused and the two smiled affectionately at one another as though they had known each other for years. It was obvious to Frankie that there was a lot more to their relationship than the professional aspect, but how much more, she did not know.

Dr. Reed then turned to Frankie and held up one arm to her. "Why don't you meet me halfway, Francine?"

Frankie looked at her father. He looked so much older than the last time she had seen him. His hair was now almost entirely snow white and he moved with the strength of a man well into his eighties instead of midway through his sixties. Frankie felt very much like the unsure six-year-old she had once been, staring at her father after an absence and not quite recognizing him. With more hesitation than then, she closed the distance between them and allowed herself to be wrapped in her father's arms.

She could have cried. He still smelled like her father even though so much about him had changed. He still felt like her father. No amount of change, no length of time, apparently, was so great that it could wipe the memory of his embraces from her mind. She buried her face in his neck and squeezed him, her sole remaining family member.

Frankie pulled away, tears beginning to stream down her cheeks. How was she going to tell him that his only grandchildren had died less than a week ago? How was she going to tell him that he would never again see the grandchildren she had essentially kept from him? He had only ever met his grandson once and Colin had been so young that the child had retained absolutely no memories of the man. She had kept them from him and now it was too late. She braced herself, searching for the right words and knowing that there were none.

Her father shook his head slightly, his eyes squeezing shut for a second before opening again and meeting hers. "I know, Frankie, I know. I'm so sorry, honey." He pulled her back into him and held her tightly. Frankie, the relief of not having to speak the word aloud, took a moment to collect herself before pulling away once more.

"Come on, Daddy. Let's get you back in that chair." She was surprised at how heavily he leaned on her. If she had not known this was her father, she would have guessed him to be far older.

Once again in his chair, Frankie's father immediately began fussing with the stacks of papers and the files that were splayed across his messy desk. "I know why you are here, James," he began before something occurred to Frankie.

"Wait," she said, holding up one hand, "How did you know about the kids?" She looked over at James who, eyes widening, shook his head.

Dr. Reed sighed. "Francine, Hugo was A-positive, right? His blood type?"

Frankie nodded mutely, not following.

"Honey, you are O-negative. With that sort of combination, the chances of your children being type O were only about 25%. There was a similar chance that their

177

RH factor would be negative. They…" He paused, looking right at her, "Francine, they aren't with you and I know the only way you would leave those children behind would be if they were…if they weren't around to bring." He choked the last words out, maintaining eye contact.

She felt glued to the spot. Her own mother had been B-positive. She wondered what the odds had been that she had inherited her father's blood type instead of her mother's. How much luck did she have to have in order to be alive right now? She looked away from him, her eyes searching for anything else to focus on. They landed briefly on Mick who was staring at her, her face unreadable. Frankie felt like an open book right now. She hated that her emotions were on display for everyone to witness.

"James," Dr. Reed continued, "I've collected every scrap of data concerning the Leucocelerosis Virus that could find. I'm ready to assist you in any way I can."

"The Leucocelerosis virus," James repeated, "It's strange having a name for it. All of your research called it L24X. It always did feel like too general a name for something so…so…"

Frankie's father shuffled a few files, "Yes, that was the name we used to discuss it outside of the Swass Research and Development Facility. Sounds like a trendy exercise regime, doesn't it?"

James smiled wryly and nodded.

"It was an ambiguous name," Dr. Reed continued, "and it was ambiguous for a reason. Everything about the virus was classified due to the nature of it. This wasn't the next Ebola or the Hantavirus. This was something far, far worse and, unlike many viruses that came before it, I know without a shadow of a doubt that the Leucocelerosis virus was specifically engineered to serve as a biological weapon. Its power simply hadn't been harnessed. Imagine the chaos if the general public had found out about it!"

"We don't have to imagine," came a feminine voice from the back of the room, "The general public already knows about it. Or don't you watch the news?"

Mick had stepped forward. Her face was masked in anger and she was trembling slightly. One had was balled into a white-knuckled fist. The other shot up and she jabbed a finger toward the window behind Dr. Reed. "Unlike *some* people, holed up in the comfort of their houses, *we've* been out there. *We* know what's going on because *we've* seen it. We've seen people dying in the streets and, unlike some people, we already know *we're* next."

"Now, hold up there, missy," Earl started, stepping forward with his hand outstretched to her.

"She's not wrong to be upset," Dr. Reed admitted. He looked like a schoolboy who had just been chastised by a fuming nun wielding a wooden ruler. "I haven't been out there. I've never been out there. Not since the outbreak, at least."

James had pulled up a chair and was sitting at the far end of the desk sorting through files. Frankie wasn't sure if he was keeping out of this or if he was simply too wrapped up in what he was reading to notice the shift. His finger was pressed firmly into a sheet of paper and his brow was furrowed as though in thought. He would have had to be completely oblivious to have not noticed Mick's outburst. Still, he did not look up. He just kept staring down at the same spot marked by his finger.

"Out there," Frankie said suddenly. Everyone except James turned to look at her. She could feel the heat of Mick's glare burning a hole into her. "I noticed something on the way in."

Dr. Reed looked up at his daughter as he pulled his quilt back over his legs and smoothed it down. "Yes?"

"Where is everyone?"

From the looks on everyone else's faces, it had not occurred to them that, like so many other towns across the country, the streets here might not be littered with bodies. Unlike Frankie and James who had had front row seats as they drove in, the rest of the group had ridden in the back of the van where, while vented, had no actual windows. They had not seen the empty streets or the closed-up stores. As far as they knew, they had driven across a dying state from one devastated town to another.

"What do you mean, 'Where is everyone'?" Mack had been leaning against a bookshelf near the door. The sound of his voice turned almost every head in his direction. "Aren't they…didn't you see…"

"No," Frankie leapt in, trying to save him having to put death into words, "There's no one out there. It's like a ghost town."

Dr. Reed cleared his throat. "Most people are 'holed up' in their homes," he said, using Mick's words. "We told them to stay put and not answer the door for anyone until we gave the all-clear."

"Who's 'we'?" Frankie asked.

"Cora and I," he said without elaboration.

"And they all just listened to you?" Mick's anger was building again. She was a petulant child who had had her toys taken away without what she thought was good enough reason.

Frankie's father was silent. He looked pensive.

"No," Cora answered for him, "They didn't. Not at first. But then they saw the news. They all listened after the news told them how bad it was. I've been out to get a couple things and check on a few people. Heard that the labs called up a lot of their own right about when this all started."

"So, no one here has died from the supervirus?" Mack straightened, his arms folding across his chest.

"No one here has died from the supervirus," Dr. Reed agreed.

Cora sniffed loudly, "But you all probably scared the wits out of them driving in. We don't get a lot of visitors here. Mostly truckers. And we haven't seen one of those for about a week now."

The room fell silent as everyone processed this news. They were in a town that had, so far, remained completely untouched by the Leucocelerosis virus. The looks on the twin's faces as well as Earl's was one of relief. They were safe here. They could let down their guard a little.

In the silence, a soft tapping caught Frankie's attention. James's finger was no longer stationary on the page he had been studying. He was mouthing something over and over. Frankie watched him as his expression gradually transformed to one of worry. A pit began to form in her stomach.

"AB-negative," James said aloud. He then looked up at Frankie's father. "That lab assistant. Cabot. Remember him?"

Dr. Reed thought for a moment. "Strange fellow."

"The trials we ran based on the files I borrowed from you - "

Dr. Reed's eyebrows shot up.

"Stole from you," James corrected himself with the hint of a smile, "Anyway, we all donated blood in order to run the trials. I'm trying to remember what Cabot was. I want to say he was AB-negative."

"And?"

"No, I'm sure he was AB-negative. I'd swear I saw it on his paperwork. I'm also pretty sure he fu-" James jabbed his finger into the paper, pausing to check his language, "messed with some of the AB-negative samples. Their results came out strange."

Dr. Reed looked interested. "Strange how?"

"Well," James looked pensive, "I suppose it would be more accurate to say that the virus acted strangely. It sort of…bounced off the protein coating. It was like the virus was the polar opposite of the sample. At least, that's what I thought I saw happen. I didn't get to retry it."

The room fell silent. Everyone was trying to process what he was saying. It was heavy information and, from the look on Mick's face, all the details had yet to sink in. It was impossible to tell how Earl was taking it. His face gave away nothing and he was as quiet as usual.

"Thing is," James continued, looking back down at the paper, "Cabot reacted to the virus when it was released. He got infected."

"He couldn't have been AB-negative then,' Dr. Reed rubbed his chin. He jabbed a finger in the direction of the files James had been reading through. "Every trial I ran back in the eighties had the exact same results as you claim yours did, as you can see. The AB-negative samples were essentially unaffected by the virus."

"Unless your trials were a fluke," James interjected. "Like I said, I only saw it once and that was right before I caught Cabot messing with them."

Dr. Reed gave his head one sharp shake. "No. My trails were no fluke. I ran several, all with the same reaction. Every AB-negative sample displayed the same reaction to the virus. It never managed to break through and begin the infection process. There is no possible way Cabot was AB-negative if he was infected."

Frankie furrowed her brow. "So, what happened to this Cabot guy? Did the virus killed him?"

James looked up at her, his finger still pressing down onto the paper. The look on his face startled her. It was a while before he spoke again, the silence somehow shattered by the hushed quality of his voice.

"No," he replied finally, "I did."

Fourteen

Mrtvy. Vsichni jsou mrtvy. Vsichni jsou mrtvy a
ja jsem dalsi na rade.
Translated from Czech
Dead. Everyone is dead and I think I'm next.

Evzenie Dvorak, Shout It (Social Media Site)

THE IRONY WAS not that Henry had managed to have
two guns pointed at him in the span of one day after
avoiding such a situation for his whole life. It was that,
within a matter of hours, he had had two young boys
pointing guns in his face. This time, however, the boy was
older and did not appear to be unfamiliar with the piece of
cold, black steel in his hand. In fact, he looked as though he
was so used to holding a weapon that Henry would not
have been surprised if it was something the boy had been
introduced to at a young age by older boys of a particular
ilk.

The boy, or rather, the young man, appeared to be
eighteen or nineteen years old. He was dressed in loose
blue jeans that were cinched tightly well below his waist so

that they would not slide entirely off him. His A-line shirt was stained with sweat and what looked disturbingly like blood. Henry hoped, considering where they were, that he had just had a run-in with the ketchup dispenser.

Strands of stringy blonde hair poked out from underneath a grimy black ballcap that he wore tilted off to one side and an equally grimy red bandana lay on the floor behind expensive looking Nikes that, at one point, must have been white. He was covered in a light layer of sweat, but as far as Henry could see as the boy squinted down the barrel of his 9mm at him, his eyes appeared clear.

Henry quickly assessed his options. There was no way he could reach his own gun before this punk kid unloaded his into Henry's face. Maybe he could talk him down like he had done with Robby. Granted, Robby had been a scared little boy. This guy looked more like a seasoned wannabe gangbanger.

"What's your name, son?"

"I ain't your son, mothafucka." The choice of words confirmed his assessment of the young man before him. The gangbanger jerked his chin slightly at Henry. "You alone?"

Henry, his face devoid of emotion, breathed a mental sigh of relief; the punk had not seen Robby. Henry hoped the boy would say put and quiet long enough for Henry to get them out of this situation. The boy was no match for this punk. Remaining as emotionless as possible, Henry replied, "Yeah. Sure am. Tell me your name."

The punk stepped back from Henry a couple feet, his eyes quickly scanning the area to see if Henry was telling the truth. "You packin'?"

His request for a name had been ignored again, but Henry got the distinct impression that he would not get away with avoiding the punk's question this time. He considered lying, but realized that this kid, while no genius, probably had enough street smarts to know that no one in their right mind would be wandering around unarmed in the current climate. Grudgingly, he nodded once.

"Take it out and put it on the floor. Slowly."

"What's your name, kid?"

"I ain't no kid neither," the punk spat, indicating with his gun that Henry should hurry up.

"I'm Henry," he said, moving slowly. Henry began to bend into a crouch, reaching toward his pant leg. His gun was still tucked into the waistband of his jeans with his blue flannel shirt hanging loosely over it. Henry could not be sure the punk had not seen the bulge of it under the shirt. "Tell me your name so we can talk like men."

The punk cocked his weapon, visibly annoyed. "We ain't gonna be talkin' like anything, dumbass. Just put your fuckin' weapon on the floor before I blow your fuc-"

There was a resounding bang from behind Henry and the punk's neck jerked back, his ballcap flying from his head. The punk, face frozen with his mouth open in the shape of a shocked O, fell backwards to the floor, a perfectly round hole in his left temple. In the same moment, Henry threw himself forward, grabbing his own gun from his jeans as he rolled behind a trash receptacle. The punk's head was a few feet away from him, a pool of blood already forming around it already being soaked up by his filthy hair.

Henry peered cautiously around toward the play area, suddenly terrified. The shot had come from where

186

Robby was. How could he have been so stupid? Why had he not scouted the place before bringing the little boy in? Why had he not, in the very least, have had his gun ready?

To his surprise, it was not another gangbanger standing in the doorway to the play area. It was not even an adult.

Robby stood staring blankly across the restaurant dining room at the body of the older boy on the floor. His gun, bright pink, was still pointed up where the older boy had been standing only moments before. Henry rose, numb from the realization of what the little boy had just done. He stepped out from his hiding spot. "Robby..."

"He was going to kill you," the boy interjected, looking up at Henry. His voice sounded dull and flat.

"We don't know that."

"I do," Robby said. He lowered his gun and carefully clicked the safety back into place. "He killed that other kid."

Henry knelt next to the body and felt for a pulse. He realized belatedly how ridiculous this action was. The wannabe gangbanger was very obviously dead. "What other kid?"

"The one at the top of the play thing. I thought he was alive at first. He was all hunched up like he'd been hiding. Then I saw the blood."

Henry turned the body on its side and searched the back pockets. He found a battered old wallet which he flipped open. The cash section held a few tens and twenties as well as what looked like a card. Henry slipped it out far enough to see that it was a school photo of a little girl with blonde pigtails in a frilly pink dress. She looked to be about five or six years old. Was this the punk's daughter? His little sister? Henry wondered where she was and who was taking care of her. He gently slipped the photo back into place and turned his attention to an ID that was visible behind a clear plastic slot. His eyes scanned it before he closed the wallet and tucked it back into the punk's back pocket.

"Not a good day to be you, Wesley Studdard," he murmured to the corpse.

HENRY STARED OUT the windshield of his Jeep as he chewed a mouthful of burger. He had been concerned that Robby might withdraw back into himself after what had just happened, but, on the contrary, he seemed just fine. Between mouthfuls of fries, the little boy was trying to explain some game he and his friends really liked that involved a lot of imagination and playing cards with pictures of peculiar creatures on them. The names of the creatures bordered on ridiculous. Henry had no idea what the boy was talking about, but was more than happy to sit and listen.

Henry had double checked the restaurant, packing up all the premade food as well as the fresher items he guessed their buddy Wesley had been making. Then, he and Robby got back into the Jeep, neither caring to eat right next to a dead body, and got back on the road. He did not know where they were going. Henry did not have any family to go to and, as far as he understood, Robby had no idea where his birth mother was so trying to hunt her down was not an option. It was just the two of them.

Besides, Henry was sure that there were twice as many pale people milling about than when they had gone in. He could also have sworn that he had seen one, a middle-aged man about half a block away, stop and look in their direction. He did not know if the pale woman in Mrs. Rose's house had been an anomaly or if they could expect more like her. Either way, he was not about to stick around to find out. Henry thought it might be a good idea to get moving.

Remembering his phone, he pulled it from his pocket and plugged it into the car charger. The screen blinked to life, the flashing battery bar at the top telling him that it had been just in time. While he waited for it to charge, he listened to Robby babble on and began keeping a mental tab of how many pale people he saw in each area of town that they went through versus how many bodies were scattered randomly about. The more populated the area, the higher the counts went.

Eventually, Robby's chatter died down and he took to staring out the window. Henry wondered if the boy was counting like he was. Even though this child had done something that he, a grown man, had never done and with greater ease than he believed he could have, Henry felt the urge to protect him. He also felt a twinge of caution. He glanced sideways at this child who had pointed a gun at him before breakfast time and killed a man by lunch. He was more thankful than ever that Robby had not known about safeties.

"Hey, kiddo," Henry said suddenly in a bid to redirect the boy's attention, "You know how to work these things?"

Robby followed Henry's finger to the cellphone between them. He snorted. "Yeah. Who doesn't?"

Me, not too long ago, Henry thought. It had been a silly question. It seemed like all children were better versed

189

with technology these days than were adults. His eyes flickered to the rearview to see if he had suddenly sprouted white hairs. "You mind getting online and seeing what's what? Search for 'news'. Darn thing doesn't work too good without the WiFi, but it should pull something up if you wait."

"WiFi," Robby said, picking the phone up and clicking the search engine tab, "You don't need to say 'the'. It's just 'WIFI'."

"Ah."

"And you're right. This thing sucks."

Henry gave a barking laugh. He was liking this kid more and more. He especially appreciated the child's honesty and bluntness. All too often, Henry felt, people hid behind politeness and neglected to say what they really thought. It always seemed to lead to trouble and misunderstanding. Henry reached over and ruffled the boy's hair.

"Seriously," Robby exclaimed, pulling slightly away with a grin. "Like, how old is this thing?"

"Well, I got it right after people stopped sending telegraphs, so..." He winked at Robby who giggled and went to work on the phone.

Several moments passed. In an attempt to get away from the bodies, Henry had steered them to the edge of town toward Broadway. He pulled off just before the end of the road and turned off the engine. Robby was staring intently down at the phone. His eyes were scanning words faster than Henry would have thought possible. It certainly would have been impossible for Henry to read that fast. He had never been a poor student. He just hadn't been a great one.

"You find something?"

"Mmm hmm."

Henry waited for a moment then asked, "You gonna share what you found?"

Robby did not respond right away then, handing the phone to Henry said, "It's all weird."

Henry looked down at the phone, curious as to what was 'all weird'. His own eyes scanned the page slower than had Robby's. There were no articles from major news outlets. Most of the articles that had come up under Robby's search topic of 'news' appeared to be private blogs and a few websites that looked quite a bit like the owners might be fond of wearing tinfoil hats.

He tapped 'CNN' into the search bar and waited. Eventually, an error code popped up so he tried NBC. When news outlet after news outlet came up with either an error code or a 'Down for Maintenance' page, Henry grudgingly resorted to trying Fox News. *Hell,* he thought, *anything's better than nothing at this point.* However, that search was just as fruitless.

He typed in 'news' again and 'supervirus' then, after a long pause while everything loaded, Henry scanned the article headlines and time stamps. They all sounded sensationalist and not a single one was more recent than four hours ago.

Henry frowned, wishing he had paid more attention to the annoying college kid who had sold him his phone. The guy had been explaining about cell towers, but Henry had only been interested in turning on his service and getting out of there. Cell towers and how things worked did not interest him.

Now, he found himself wondering if the lack of recent articles and the failed searches for major media outlets had anything to do with cell towers. He honestly could not see how it could. After all, they were still able to get online however slowly.

He glanced at Robby who was absently picking at a thread on his shirt then shifted his gaze up to the rearview mirror. Where there had been no one before, he could now see a small group of people moving slowly in the general direction of the highway. He could not tell yet because they were still quite far away, but Henry would have put money on all of them having ashen skin and white hair.

A chill ran through him. Maybe it had less to do with connectivity than having people to actually connect.

Henry tapped on a random article, figuring it was as good as any at this point, and watched the progress of the people in his rearview as he waited for it to load. They were moving almost as slowly as his internet connection. Sooner or later Henry would have to make a decision as to where he and Robby should go. Sitting here for very much longer would only get them surrounded by infected people.

The screen on his phone flashed as the article he selected popped up. The author of this particular piece, a Marquez H. Roybal, did not appear, judging by his photo, to be off his rocker as the religious tone of the title of the article suggested. In fact, dressed in a white button-down shirt with a crisp collar and wearing a beige fedora with a black band, he looked more like someone you might meet in the fishing section of a Sportsman's Warehouse and have a nice, but somewhat forgettable conversation with about the benefits of using nightcrawlers over red wigglers.

There was an extensive list of article titles running underneath the author's photo. The majority sounded very scientific and the list of credentials in the man's bio was more than impressive. Based on this, Henry guessed that Roybal's last few article entries, all dated within the past few days, were not the man's standard. The titles alone sounded like something you might see in one of those leaflets door-to-door religion salesmen tucked into door jams when no one answered. The article he had opened was the final entry. He read over it as quickly as possible.

WE ARE SODOM AND GOMORRAH

This is it. We are reaching the end of our civilization. We are reaching the end of all human life on earth. We should have expected it. We should have seen this coming. I turned my back on scripture years ago in favor of science, but, in the end, it was scripture that gave us the real warning. We just chose to ignore it. I don't often tell people because I always felt a bit embarrassed about my roots, but I was raised in the bosom of Catholicism. As a child, I found great comfort in reading the words in my bible, but, as I grew older, I found that they no longer gave me solace. By the time I was a teenager, I had far too many questions that my faith simply could not answer so, as a result, I turned to science. Science used to give me the solace I had been missing. It used to give me answers. Now it terrifies me. They are all dead. They are all dead or dying or missing. Sharsti Reddy, Franklin Reed, Robert Miller. I am so sorry. They are all gone and I believe I am next. Even if I am not destroyed by this, even should I somehow be spared, I will surely look behind. How could I not? Better a pillar of salt than to live with what

I know. Scripture tells us that angels of the Lord
came to Earth and forewarned that the Lord
would destroy Sodom and Gomorrah for their
evil ways. Just as Sodom and Gomorrah, the
Lord is destroying us for ours. We can only pray
that, like Lot, some of the innocent, the pure
might be spared. I should have listened to
Franklin. He warned me years ago not to follow
this path, but I did not listen. He told us this
would happen. We did not listen. We had to
pursue it. Our curiosity, our desire for power and
fame. Our love of money. It was our greed that
got us here. Our greed and selfishness. We
should have left all this in a deep pit in the desert
instead of cultivating it in a lab in New Mexico.
We were warned. We were warned and we did
not listen. We tampered with nature and now it
will kill us all. We are Sodom and Gomorrah
and L24X is our sin. We are being punished. I
am so sorry for what we have done.

'Article', Henry soon realized, was the wrong word
altogether. This was more like the deluded ravings of a
madman. For the most part, it was disjointed and made very
little sense. L24X? And who were the people he
mentioned? Did they have something to do with the
supervirus? It certainly sounded like it.

"Henry?"

Henry jerked his gaze away from the phone. Robby
was watching him, a curious expression on his small face.
"What's happening? I mean, I know everyone is getting
sick, but why?"

It had never even occurred to him to explain to Robby what was going on. He had assumed, based on what the boy had said, that Robby had understood the nature of the situation. The child likely watched twice as much TV as he did and he had, but the news was probably not on his watch list. Even so, Henry was sure that the news would have overtaken even children's stations and that there would be no need for any further explanation. The fact that the boy was uncommonly smart also didn't help keep Henry from making assumptions.

Henry set his phone down and considered how to put into words what he had read. It was not easy. While Robby seemed well advanced intellectually for his age, he was still a child. He found himself wishing he had spent more time around children.

"It's a virus," he said, watching Robby pick up the phone. He made no move to stop the boy from reading the article. It would only alarm him to think Henry was hiding something from him. "You, know. Like the flu. I don't know how it started. I haven't seen anything explaining that. All I know is that it's fast and it's bad. It's okay, though, because the news says we're fine so long as we keep our distance from anyone who's infected."

Robby looked thoughtful, but did not look up from the article. He was amazed at how well the boy could multitask. The older he got, the more Henry felt he was a breathing 'can't walk and chew gum' stereotype. At least he was still breathing even if he couldn't figure out why considering what he knew about the supervirus. According to the article he had read, he should have been dying by now. Or dead.

"We should go to New Mexico," said Robby suddenly, handing Henry back his phone.

195

Henry raised an eyebrow. "Why New Mexico?"

"Well," Robby jerked his thumb over his shoulder indicating the approaching pale people, "we can't stay here and you did say I could be the navigator."

Henry chuckled, glancing back at the advancing mob. He hadn't realized that Robby had noticed them. "Right on both counts. But why New Mexico?"

Robby pointed at the phone in Henry's hand. "That guy was talking about it. I think we should look for his friend. The one he talks about most."

"Franklin Reed?" Henry frowned down at the screen. "Roybal also said that everyone was dead. And, besides, this is crazy talk. Likely has nothing to do with anything. He's probably just freaked out and drunk. Talking nonsense."

"Maybe."

"More than maybe."

Robby was chewing his lower lip, his face screwed up as he thought. Behind them, the pale people were closer than ever. Henry turned on the engine, still unsure where to take them. "Please?"

Henry looked at the boy, "You really think so? New Mexico?"

Robby nodded, looking a little excited. "Yeah, and I read about the labs in New Mexico. They sound super cool. And New Mexico has Area 51!"

Henry laughed, watching the boy as he stuck his fingers at awkward angles from is head like alien antennae. "I think that's actually in Nevada."

"Then we'll go there next!"

Grinning, Henry put the Jeep in gear and started to pull back onto the road that led toward Broadway. They would make their way up West Broadway and along US 62 W to TX 256 W. More decisions could be made as they went.

"Henry?"

"Mmm hmm?"

"Are we gonna be okay?" Robby asked as he stared out the window.

Hello, heartstrings, Henry thought. The boy was more scared than he let on. Henry hated lying and believed the boy would see right through him if he tried. Instead, he opted for the truth. "We'll be fine so long as we don't get any blood or spit or anything like that from one of them on us."

Robby's head spun suddenly toward Henry. Henry was surprised at the sudden look of terror on the boy's face. "Robby? What is it?"

"The white woman," the little boy said, his voice barely more than a whisper, "at my step-mom's house? When she screamed at me, I got her spit in my mouth."

Fifteen

Ich denke, es waren die Russen. Es sind immer
die Russen. Die Bastarde haben uns alle getötet.
Translated from German
I think it was the Russians. It's always the
Russians. The bastards killed us all.

Dieter Schmidt, Shout It (Social Media Site)

ALL EYES WERE on James. Even Mick, who had looked
so disinterested in the discussion only moments before, was
staring wide-eyed at James with disbelief. James, who had
returned his own gaze to the paper he had been reading, did
not seem aware of the shocked silence he had caused.
Frankie wondered what sort of person could make such a
wild statement and not seem to notice the effect it had on
those who heard it.

"I'll rustle us up some brunch," Cora mumbled,
looking uncomfortable as she excused herself from the
study.

For several moments, the only sounds in the room
were the occasional tapping of James's finger and the

rustling of papers as Frankie's father looked through the varies piles in front of himself. Frankie looked from James to her father then back again to James. They were both acting as though this admission was nothing out of the ordinary.

She looked back at the rest of the group. She had been wrong in thinking what James had said had shocked everyone. Earl, while watching James, did *not appear to be surprised in the slightest. He probably already knew,* she speculated. *They are friends, after all.* But, then, he seemed to be friends with the twins and they were obviously completely taken aback.

Finally, the silence became too much for her. Frankie turned and, staring at James, blurted, "Really? You tell us you killed a man and then just drop it like you told us something stupid like your favorite color or, or...?"

James looked up at her, his eyebrows slightly raised, "What more is there to say about it?"

"You killed a man! There has to be more to say about it."

Mick, looking recovered from the initial shock of what she had heard, shoved her way between her brother and Earl. Turning her back to the desk, she leaned her palms against the top and pushed herself up onto it, oblivious to the papers upon which she sat. She had placed herself directly between Frankie and James, effectively blocking him from her view. She cast a sidelong look at Frankie then, while looking at James, spoke to the room as a whole. "If Jimmy killed some guy, he deserved it. 'nough said."

"It is not 'enough said'", Frankie insisted, noting the somewhat comical expression on her father's face as he adjusted to the sudden appearance of a young woman's posterior not only sitting on what appeared to be most of the messy collection of his life's work, but to the fact that said posterior was directly in front of his face. Frankie stepped out in front of the desk so that she once again had a clear line of sight. "Why did you shoot him? Are you in the habit of killing people?"

"In the habit of-," James started with a chuckle. "In the habit...No, Frankie. I don't normally kill people. In fact, he was my first."

First, Frankie thought, *but was he the last?*

James turned away from the paper he had been reading and leaned forward, resting his elbows on his knees as he had done before. He looked right at Frankie, ignoring everyone else in the room, and smiled. It was not a particularly happy smile nor was it necessarily sad. It had a strange middling quality as though James himself was stuck between how to feel about what he had said and how to feel about now having to explain himself.

"To be honest, while I never liked the man, I really didn't dislike him. Well, not enough to kill him. He didn't give me much of a choice."

"What," Frankie asked almost dryly, "did he point a gun at you first?"

"In a sense."

Frankie stared at James, waiting for him to continue. From the corner of her eye, she could see Earl lean farther back until his rear was balanced on a bookshelf. It did not look altogether comfortable, but he did not seem as though he wanted to complain. Mack had slumped to the ground with his arms resting on his knees and his back against a filing cabinet.

"In what sense?" she asked with more than a small measure of frustration when he did not elaborate.

James's gaze remained even with hers. "As I said, Cabot was infected. I didn't know it at the time. He'd looked like he was coming down with something, but he insisted that he was just tired from staying late the night before and that he felt fine. I took his word for it and assumed he was developing a cold as well. It made sense. Well, anyway, since there were two of them to monitor the new samples we had set up the day before, I told him and my colleague Shar that I would be out for the day. I needed a break. I felt like I was on the precipice of finding the solution we had been searching for, but something just wasn't clicking and it was getting the better of me. I decided to take a little time way from the lab. Catch a movie. It didn't matter what movie, you know, just so long as it distracted me. I needed to get my mind off it all so that inspiration might just have the chance to come on its own."

"And did it?"

"I forgot my wallet at the lab," he continued, ignoring her question. "I didn't realize right away because I ran into a friend who was going in the same direction. Because he was walking and it was a nice day, I thought I'd skip the drive and join him instead. It was only about a mile or so. We stopped at the movie theater and chatted for a while longer before he went on and I went in."

"Is all this important?" Frankie demanded impatiently.

James gave a wry smile. "Only because of the time I wasted. It took about half an hour to walk there because we weren't in a hurry then at least another ten minutes was spent before I realized I couldn't pay for a ticket. It only took a little over twenty minutes to get back to the lab because I didn't have someone to walk with. By the time I got back, I had been gone for about an hour."

He paused, his lips tightening and his brow furrowing. Drawing a deep breath in, he lowered his head, finally breaking eye contact with Frankie. Between them, Mick leaned toward James with one hand outstretched as if in an offer of comfort. When he did not look up at her or take her hand, Mick withdrew it with a distinct look of disappointment. It suddenly struck Frankie why Mick had been behaving in such a hostile manner toward her. Mick considered her to be a threat.

Before Frankie could fully process this, James looked up again at her. His brow furrowed and his voice took on a slightly harsher quality. "If I had driven, I would have been there and back within ten minutes. If I had driven, I might have got back to the lab in time."

He stopped. Frankie waited, watching his face which was now far less masked than she had ever seen it. Raw emotion filled his eyes. He was, she recognized, reliving a loss right in front of them. Feeling as though she already knew the answer, Frankie asked softly, "In time for what?"

James leaned back in his chair and stared at the ceiling. "When I got back, Cabot was all but delirious. He…he had her pinned underneath him."

"Your colleague?"

He did not answer her. Instead, he rubbed his hands down his face and got to his feet. Leaning around Mick, James pushed the paper he had been reading across the desk at Frankie's father. "You're sure this is accurate?"

"All my research is accurate," Dr. Reed responded, looking somewhat offended.

James scratched his cheek and went on, thinking out loud rather than directing his comments at anyone in particular. "This study states flat out that AB-negative samples were successful in deflecting the supervirus. I got the same results with my AB-negative samples, but I had been so sure that Cabot had done something to them to make them react that way. This proves he didn't. This is fascinating…It-"

Frankie threw her hands up with exasperation. She turned her back on James and went to the window. She was getting really sick of him not finishing his explanations. Everything was confusing enough without him muddling things even more. From behind her, she heard Mick ask what her problem was.

"She's probably sick of all the deflecting Jimbo is doing," Earl answered.

"I'm not deflecting," James said defensively, raising his eyes to the ceiling then back down. Although Frankie could feel him looking at her, she refused to acknowledge him. A moment passed, then James sighed. "Fine. I'm deflecting. What happened at the lab is just not something I want to get into right now."

Frankie shrugged and peered out the window into the trees behind the house. It was a beautiful day outside. There was a gentle breeze and a few small birds were diving in and out of the golden yellow leaves of the aspen trees. In the bushes below, she could see a small movement before a white-tailed rabbit came bouncing out into the light. It all looked so peaceful. In the brief hush that had fallen on the room, Frankie could almost forget that what was going on out there was anything but beautiful or peaceful.

"Anyway, I'm now positive that there was no way that Cabot was AB-negative." Someone shuffled some papers as James continued, "In theory, if he was, he would not have become infected which I have no doubt he was. I'm thinking, based on his swift reaction to the virus, that the sample he donated was one of the Rh positives. All samples that were Rh positive had very quick reactions, some within hours of exposure to the virus, but none more than 24 hours or so. Cabot must have become infected the night before when I thought I caught him messing with the AB-negative samples."

James banged his fist against the desk, "If I could just get my hand on Robert's notes."

"I, too, thought they had been a fluke," Frankie turned at the sound of her father's voice. "The tests we ran years ago. AB-negative had been the last blood type I had experimented on. We had started much as you did, James, with samples that were Rh positive. They were all overrun by the Leucocelerosis virus within twenty-four hours. Because of the strange reaction the A-negative and B negative samples had, we decided to redo them. It was only after I was infected that I realized that there was far worse to this new virus than simply death."

"Wait," Mick slid off the desk, eyeing Frankie's father as she took several steps away from him, "You were infected?"

"Well, yes," Dr. Reed replied, returning her gaze with a quizzical look. "I thought we all knew that." James and Earl were nodding. Mick glanced around the room to see if she was the only one. Frankie joined the nonverbal assertion mostly because had figured as much based on what had been said along with her own memories. It was also becoming fun to irk Mick who, seeing Frankie's response, scowled.

Dr. Reed coughed then continued, "It was my becoming infected that showed us the real-life effects of the Leucocelerosis virus on someone who is O-negative. As you can see, I survived.

"How did you become infected?" Frankie asked, her eyes focusing on her own reflection in the window.

"Damned lab assistant dropped a vial containing the virus. We were lucky it was just the two of us in a sealed room. Well, I was lucky. He, not so much."

"What happened to him?"

Dr. Reed's voice grew grim, "Well, the short of it is that he gave us an example of the real-life effects of the virus on someone who is B negative."

"And the long of it? How did he react?" Frankie turned at the sound of James's voice. He was leaning forward again, looking extremely interested. "I've only even seen the whole reaction under a slide."

"I'm not so sure that's true, James," Dr. Reed tented his fingers, his knuckles cracking softly. "I believe your own experience with young Mr. Cabot parallels my own experience."

A soft snore rose from across the room. Slumped against the filing cabinet with his lips parted was Mack. He was fast asleep. Earl nudged the young man with his boot and, getting no response, delivered a harder kick to Mack's side. Mack grunted and swatted a couple times in Earl's general direction, but did not fully wake. Dr. Reed held up one hand to Earl, shaking his head.

"It's alright. Let the boy sleep." He turned back to James. "The lab assistant and I knew the protocol. Within minutes of exposure, we were both run through decontamination then placed in quarantine. I was sure I was going to go first, being older than he, but, in the frenzy of it all, I hadn't considered the difference of our blood types. He was terrified. He was young with a family, I think. I can't recall his name anymore. He was Subject A on all the reports when it was over. I was Subject B. We both fell ill around the same time. The symptoms came on so suddenly that it was difficult to discern who felt them first. In any case, I don't remember much because I lost consciousness on the second day after infection. When I awoke three days later, the lab assistant, was behaving erratically. He was…violent."

Dr. Reed pointed at an open file in front of himself. "Here it is; the first ever human trial of the Leucocelerosis virus, however accidental."

James grabbed eagerly at the file and flipped it open. He was immediately engrossed in the information it contained. Without waiting for James to finish reading, Dr. Reed picked up another file and continued. "My lab assistant and I had been restrained with leather straps to our beds. When they saw I was behaving within normal expectations for having been ill, they entered our room to remove the straps. The sound must have attracted his attention because the boy became wild. He was bucking at his restraints and all but foaming at the mouth. It was as though he had lost his mind altogether and behaving similarly to how an animal might were it infected with rabies."

Frankie's father paused to cough. "But this was far worse than rabies. Rabies does not change a person's outward appearance so drastically. It doesn't sap melanin from hair or cause the skin to gray. It most certainly does not cause cloudiness in the pupils of one's eyes. I could not believe what I was seeing. I remember thinking that it looked like someone had taken an eraser to the boy and somehow rubbed the color from him."

Dr. Reed fell silent as the door to the study opened and Cora reappeared carrying a tray laden with mugs, a teapot, and a plate of cookies. He began to clear a space for the tray. Without looking up from the file before him, James started stacking papers and files and setting them aside as well.

"Thank you, dear," Dr. Reed smiled fondly up at Cora as she set the tray down and began pouring tea into mugs. Earl stepped forward and claimed the first mug just as soon as it was set down. On her way out, Cora looked down at Mack and tutted, but left him alone.

"I had not yet seen myself, of course," Dr. Reed said the second the door shut behind Cora. "I did not know, at that point, how much I had changed as well. You saw the changes in me, Frankie. I know you did. Granted, by the time they released me to return home, I had regained much of my natural coloring. I see you are regaining your own."

He patted Frankie's hand. "The other effect the virus had on my assistant was one we did not share. When I woke, I felt weak from having been ill. He, on the other hand, had never lost consciousness. He had, I am told, remained in a state of perpetual wakefulness. During this time, he seemed to take on strength he had not before displayed. He was pulling the straps out by the metal bolts that connected them to the bedframe."

"A-negative," James said suddenly, "Subject A was A-negative and Subject B was O-negative. I've seen firsthand the effects of the virus on O-negative." He shifted his gaze to Frankie.

"Yes," Dr. Reed said, sipping at his tea. "I'd wager they were similar to what I experienced. And she is recovering well. It bodes well for you, James, should you become infected."

"And I see the parallel now," James said, understanding lighting up his eyes. "Cabot must have been A-negative."

"Well, he might very well have been B negative." Frankie's father suggested from over the top of his mug.

"I suppose," James conceded, "The reactions I saw in the A-negative samples were pretty close to the reactions I saw in the B negative samples."

Dr. Reed stuck one finger into the air and, setting down his mug, handed James the second file that he had been holding in his lap. "But not exact."

James took the file and opened it. The room fell quiet again as his eyes scanned the pages within. Frankie took a cookie from the tray and bit into it. It was warm and delicious like it had just come out of the oven.

"Second human trials?"

Frankie looked over at James and was surprised by the expression on his face. It was a mix of anger and excitement and the two emotions were warring with each other. She glanced at her father who was nodding solemnly.

"Second human trials?" James repeated. "I get that the first were accidental, but these appear completely intentional."

"They were," Dr. Reed conceded, "I did not want to do them. In truth, I was very much against them, but I was afraid of what might happen with the virus if I did not participate. I was afraid of who might take over. In the end, it did not matter."

"'Test Subject AP1: Deceased. Test Subject BP1: Deceased. Test subject ABP1: Deceased. Test Subject OP1: Deceased. Test Subject AP2: Deceased. Test Subject BP2: Deceased. Test subject ABP2: Deceased. Test Subject OP2: Deceased Test Subject AP3: Deceased'…" James's head jerked up, disgust spread across his face. "How many people did you kill?"

Sadness had been creeping onto Dr. Reed's face as James read aloud and grew with mention of each test subject. "Far too many."

"Who were they?" Frankie asked.

"Mostly homeless people," her father responded with a heavy sigh, "Not that that made it any better. They were lured in with the promise of a hot meal and a payday."

"'Test Subject AN1: Exhibited violent tendencies…lack of conscious control…Terminated. Test Subject BN1: Exhibited violent tendencies…semblance of conscious control…Terminated. Test subject ABN1: No reaction. Terminated. Test Subject ON1: Experienced brief coma…recovery. Terminated.'" James had stated reading from another page. He was shaking slightly.

"They are all the same," he whispered, "Regardless as to outcome, they are all the same."

"Yes." Dr. Reed sipped his tea, watching James come to a full understanding of what he had done.

"Even the AB-negative test subject." It was a statement rather than a question, but Dr. Reed nodded in response to it anyway. He was about to say something else when Mick suddenly spoke up.

"Terminated?"

"It means," Frankie interjected, "that no matter how the virus affected or did not affect them, all the test subjects either died or were killed. Even those who recovered completely."

Mick looked horrified. It was the most non-selfish emotion Frankie had ever seen the girl express. "But why?"

"There was too much risk. What if they were released into the general public and started talking about what we had done to them in the lab? One or two 'crazies' ranting about being injected with an engineered supervirus is one thing. When it's several, all spouting the same insane story, people start taking notice. It was a risk higher ups at the Swass Facility were not willing to take."

"Weren't they afraid you would talk?"

Frankie was not surprised at the girl's naivety. She had already figured how her father had been kept silent. "No, they probably weren't." Mick's head swiveled around to face Frankie who only pointed at herself.

"That's right," Dr. Reed agreed solemnly, "They needed me and Frankie was just a little girl. There was so much they could have done if I had opened my mouth and no one would have been the wiser. Children get sick. They have accidents. It was a risk I couldn't take so I kept my mouth shut."

"Except you didn't," said James. "You told me everything when you were drunk."

Dr. Reed smiled, but it was humorless. "No. I was not anywhere near as drunk as you think I was. I told you enough to get you investigating on your own without too much culpability on my end. Even years after, they would have killed Frankie if they thought I was actively discussing what we had done."

"What?"

"You think it was a coincidence I had those particular files on me that night, James? You think I go everywhere with classified information on super viruses I helped engineer?"

James looked completely taken aback. It had never occurred to him that he had been set up to 'steal' those files. Dr. Reed had wanted him to find them and had given him just enough inspiration to secret them away. The older man had wanted him to begin his own research and had provided the path to it.

"And, before it comes out on its own, which I'm sure it will eventually, the access you got to that lab was thanks to a few strings I pulled. I made the suggestion that it be opened to students who needed space to work on their theses then put Robert Miller's name right at the top of the list for consideration. I knew it would not be long before you asked him for help. He was the logical choice to partner with, was he not?"

James sat back, still gaping at Dr. Reed. "And Shar? Was she there because of you, too? Did she die because of your meddling?"

Dr. Reed sighed. "I accept responsibility for the deaths of all those we experimented on. I did not speak against any of this until it was too late. I am culpable. I also accept responsibility for all those who are dead now or dying and for all those who will die because I did not fight hard enough to stop this. The Leucocelerosis virus is mine. I claim it and all the deaths that come from it. However, I did not personally put Dr. Reddy in your path. Her presence and participation were chance, but her death…"

"Did that Cabot guy kill her?"

James turned to Mick. "No. But he tried. I shot him before he could."

"So," Frankie decided to press James on this, "how did she die?"

James's face went cold. "She died at the Swass Facility after infecting the Midwest."

Sixteen

After all I've gone through, THIS is how it ends?
I don't think so. Come at me, bro.

Keryn Glassman, Shout It (Social Media Site)

IF THERE WAS anything Henry was truly awful at, it was comforting others. Robby's sudden announcement had caught him off guard causing him to jerk the steering wheel slightly. He corrected and continued toward the end of the road.

"When was this?"

The boy shrugged. "This morning, I guess. Right before I found you in the cookie lady's house."

"The cookie lady?" Henry asked with a smile. That certainly sounded like Mrs. Rose.

"Yeah," Robby still looked terrified. "I live just a couple streets up from her, but there's this kid who lives on her street and we play sometimes. The cookie lady always comes out and gives us cookies whenever we ride by on our bikes."

The boy was still speaking in the present tense. Henry wondered exactly how much of their situation had really sunk in with the boy. "Well, that was nice of her."

"Yeah," Robby chewed his lip and stared at Henry, "Am I gonna die?"

Henry turned right onto West Broadway, steering around a pickup truck that was halted right in the middle of the road. He had not seen a single moving vehicle other than their own in a very long time. It was comforting and worrisome at the same time. After their experience in the restaurant, he was unsure of the type of people they might run into. Still, the idea that they might be completely on their own bothered him.

Robby's question managed to bother him even more. Once again, he considered lying. He did not know this boy well, but he seemed more than ever to be the sort who would see through any lame attempt at avoiding the truth that Henry could make. He tried anyway. "We're all going to die, kiddo."

"But how soon?"

Henry shot the child a look. He appeared a little frustrated by Henry's answer so he decided to be as truthful as possible. "You know, I don't know."

Robby nodded, pulling his legs up onto the seat underneath himself and adjusting the seat belt so that it was no longer across his neck. Henry made a mental note to see about finding some sort of seat lift for the boy. He knew there was a name for such a thing, but he could not think what it was. Children and their safety in vehicles was not within his realm of knowledge. It was not something he had ever needed to know.

"What if I get you sick?"

Henry pointed to the scabs on his neck. "I'm not so sure you could, buddy."

Robby peered over at him. "What are those?"

"I got clawed by a pale woman. Maybe even the same one that you saw."

"You think there are more like her?" Robby squeaked. Henry had said the wrong thing. Fear was returning full force to the child's face.

Henry reached over and awkwardly patted Robby's shoulder. He had not really thought about it before, but now he saw that it was a distinct possibility. After all, there were so many infected people roaming around. What were the chances that none of them were like that woman? "I don't know, kiddo. You pretty much described the woman I saw. Point is, if she infected you, chances are she infected me, too. Either way, infected or not, we're both in the same boat."

"Jeep," came the whispered reply. Henry chuckled at Robby's joke, grateful for a break from the tension of their conversation however brief. *He really is a neat kid,* he thought as he grinned at the boy. Robby smiled in return, but it was half-hearted. Despite being smarter than most adults Henry knew, he was still a child and a scared one at that.

They rode in silence for several minutes. It was slow going near the highway entrances because of having to maneuver around abandoned vehicles and the occasional body. Looking into the vehicles as they squeezed past,

Henry could see that many had not been abandoned at all. Some contained only one person slumped at the wheel while others had what looked like entire families strapped in nice and snug. These vehicles were laden with suitcases and other belongings both inside and on racks on top. None of the people were moving anymore. They were all pale and had varying degrees of white hair. People had been trying to escape infected areas not understanding that they themselves were already infected. The supervirus was hitting even harder and faster than Henry had thought.

"Either way," Henry said, breaking the silence, "we're prepared. I feel pretty safe with you around, hotshot."

Robby smiled grimly. "You won't be saying that if I get you sick."

"Well," Henry said, "Keep your spit to yourself." The boy gave an honest smile this time. Maybe, Henry thought, he was not as bad at providing comfort as he had thought.

Reaching forward, Robby turned on the radio and began fiddling with the scan button. Station after station greeted them with either crackling noises or a single high-pitched tone. He cycled through twice then, giving up, turned it off again.

"You didn't try the AM stations," Henry suggested.

Robby turned the radio back on and switched the setting from FM to AM. "Who listens to AM anyway?"

Henry chuckled. "I do. There's a great sports program on-." He broke off, holding up one hand to the boy. A voice had sounded through the crackling. "Go back."

Robby pressed the left scan button one time. Henry had definitely heard a voice. Keeping an eye on the empty road ahead, he adjusted the setting until there was less crackling and more voice. It still was not very clear, but they could now make out most of what it was saying.

"-warning us to avoid all metropolitan areas. The supervirus is moving faster than expected. New York City is all but- *crackle* -looting and *crackle* -reports from other major cities are similar. Washington, D.C., Atlanta, GA, Little Rock, Arkansas…*crackle* …City, Oklahoma…Columbus, Ohio…Chicago, Illinois…*crackle* -spread over the whole eastern- *crackle* -and the majority of the Midwest. I'm hearing reports now from Los Angeles, California and Las Vegas, Nevada…*crackle* -Minister of England announced- *crackle* -so we now know it- *crackle* - only in the United States. It is suspected that Americans traveling for business or on vacation carried the supervirus to- *crackle* -and Germany as well as Japan and- *crackle* numerous reports coming in from Chi- *crackle*

It was everywhere. From what he could make out, people had been infected and then had hopped on planes and gone about their lives, spreading the virus like free candy on Halloween as they went. Who knew how many people one infected person could touch from the time they contracted the virus to the moment of their death? He wondered where it had started and if the point of origin had played a part in how quickly it had spread.

The voice on the radio had mentioned Atlanta, Georgia. Henry was sure that was where the CDC was located. Could that have been the point of origin? Henry was not entirely sure what the CDC did beyond announce the latest not-so-greatest virus. It was yet another subject his education was lacking. A place like Atlanta, Georgia made sense, though. Really, any big city made sense. The bigger the city when the supervirus was released, the quicker the spread. There were more chances for an infected person to run into people than there would be in a small town. Although, as evidenced in his own small town, the supervirus spread like wildfire, wiping out just about everyone within days.

Another thought sprang into his mind. Had the supervirus been released or was it purely luck of nature's draw? Was it intentional or was this like many natural viruses that just cropped up every now and then? This led to an even more frightening thought; considering that it was now all over the world, was this biological warfare gone horribly wrong? If so, who had created it? The U.S.? Russia? North Korea?

There had been a lot of tension in the news over the past year. The President, not even in office for a year, had approval ratings lower than any president in the history of the United States. His behavior had been described as erratic and his mental stability had been put into question. Some of the President's comments about other world leaders had become cause for concern as a few of those world leaders had made generalized threats in response. Henry wondered if this was one of those threats that had actually been followed through. If it was, then the joke, however poorly made, was on the attacker. The supervirus appeared to be spreading all over the world.

*"-has stated numerous times that there is no known treatment- *crackle* -but has made assurances that progress is being made. She also stated that The Swass Research and Development Facility has reached out to Dr. Fran- *crackle* -but has so far not- *crackle* -who, sources tell me, resides in Los Alamos, New Me- *crackle* -once again, Spencer reminds us that it is essential to avoid*

major metropolitan areas. Stay in your homes whenever possible and avoid making physical contact with anyone who is exhibiting any symptom of illness. The supervirus, I am now being told is called the Leucoce- *crackle* -and is highly contagious as it is spread by any bodily fluid however minute it might be. Once infected, you can expect illness to last between twenty-four and forty-eight hours before- *crackle* -death. The mortality rate for Ebola was around fifty percent whereas the mortality rate for the Leucocelerosis vir- *crackle* closer to eighty-five or ninety percent. It is unknown at this time how many- *crackle* -is devastating. This is deadlier than any virus or war we have ever known- *crackle* -even Smallpox was not- *crackle* - killing upwards of three hundred mil-*crackle* *crackle* - riots and- *crackle* looting *crackle* a smell unlike any I have ever-"

Henry hit the power button, cutting off the voice. He could not take listening any longer. It was too much for him and had to be way too much for a young boy regardless of what that boy had gone through or done in his own life. Henry looked over at Robby and was surprised to see the child had had a completely different reaction to what they had heard on the radio.

"Did you hear that?" Robby said excitedly, "Did you hear what she said?"

"Well, yes," Henry started uncertainly.

"The part about New Mexico! Did you hear it?"

It had not struck Henry at the time, but it occurred to him now that Robby was right. The voice had mentioned something about New Mexico. He did not get a chance to answer because Robby was all but dancing in his seat.

"She said, 'Los Alamos, New Mexico' and I think she was saying something about 'Dr. Franklin Reed', too."

Robby's eyebrows drew together and his voice had affected a child's perception of an adult's professional tone as he repeated what the voice had said. "Remember? Remember I told you about the labs in New Mexico? They're in Los Alamos and I think that's where that guy Franklin Reed is, too. Remember what that guy wrote? He talked about him then that lady talked about him!"

Henry had to give it to him. It did seem too much of a coincidence to ignore. "I remember."

"Are we still going?" Robby bounced in his seat, unaware of several bodies that Henry was now steering around as they passed the exit for a Texas visitor's center. He had completely missed the sign announcing that they had left Oklahoma. "We *have* to go now! It's Kermit!"

"Kermit?' Henry's eyebrow raised in confusion.

"Yeah! You know, Kermit! Like when something is meant to be!"

Henry barked out a short laugh. "I think you mean kismet."

"Kermit, kismet. Whatever! Can we go?" Robby was bouncing more excitedly in his seat, his face pinched into a pleading expression.

"I guess we do have to," Henry conceded. Robby thrust one fist triumphantly into the air. *Besides*, Henry thought grimly as he watched the boy celebrate his small win, *it's not like we have anywhere else to go.*

THE DRIVE BETWEEN the Texas border and Memphis, Texas took an hour longer than it should have. This was the route Henry was used to taking when making a trip into Amarillo, Texas and this leg of the journey should have only taken about half an hour. He had not, however, taken into consideration how much stalled traffic would be out in this direction. If anything, he had assumed there would be less as it was more of a backroad than anything else.

Several times, he had had to get out of the Jeep and move a group of vehicles off the road so they could pass. Robby had wanted to help, but part of moving the vehicles entailed moving bodies and, despite everything, Henry wanted to spare the child that grisly task.

The gas gauge had just made a dinging noise as they pulled into Memphis, indicating that they were running low on fuel. Henry frowned at it. He could have kicked himself for having forgotten about filling up before they left Hollis. They had even passed three gas stations on the way out of town. Now that the tank was close to empty, he worried that he would not be able to fill up at all. Most places were electronically controlled these days and required payment at the pump or with a cashier before they would work. He hoped that this town was still up and running.

The randomly placed cars and bodies scattered here and there as they drove in stole his hope. More likely than not, he would have to siphon gas from another vehicle. The first few businesses they passed were packed with unmoving vehicles and did not appear to have any electricity. None of the businesses around them seemed to have power either. It was looking more and more like this little town had been hit just as hard by the effects of the virus as had his own town.

Since there was no power, it must have been worse here. It might simply be that more time had passed and there was no one to monitor power grids or whatever it was people did to keep electricity running. He wondered if the lack of power here was recent. Perhaps his hometown was blacked out now as well.

Henry figured that power plants were relatively automated and would keep running for a decent amount of time before requiring human intervention. If that were true, then, seeing as though his hometown had had power no more than two hours ago, he thought it unlikely that this particular outage was due to a lack of human intervention. From what he understood, the virus only appeared on the scene about a week ago. Surely whoever designed power plants had implemented some sort of failsafe to ensure that things would keep running on their own longer than this. The only other explanation for the lack of electricity here had to be something outside the plant itself. He wondered what had happened to knock out the power to Memphis altogether and so soon. There were, after all, several crashed cars. It was not inconceivable that one or more had crashed into a transformer.

Feeling as though his choices were limited and not trusting that the few gas stations here would be accessible, Henry veered off Noel Street at 1st Street and headed north, He was sure there was a farm supply or something similar up in this direction. It would have the things he would need to get his own gas. Henry was just beginning to doubt his memory as the road curved at Bradford Street. Then, a block up on the right, he saw it.

He pulled into the dirt parking lot of a farm supply store and checked out the few vehicles that were parked out front. A beat-up Toyota and an old Ford pickup seemed to be his best options. He spotted a gas can in the bed of the pickup. His luck appeared to be on the upswing. Now all he needed was some tubing.

With one hand resting on his gun which was still tucked out of sight, Henry surveyed the area and, after instructing Robby to stay put, headed toward the front door of the store. Robby, not pleased about being told he could not go, crossed his arms over his chest, but stayed strapped into the front seat. Henry could feel the boy's sullen gaze following him as he walked away. He understood Robby's frustration. He would not have wanted to be left behind, either, but he did not know what to expect inside the store. There might be people hiding and, even if they weren't infected, he could not guarantee they would be friendly. Whether he liked it or not, Robby was safer in the Jeep.

Henry pulled the bar on the front door and was relieved to feel it give. The door opened easily and a bell attached to the top tinkled lightly. He paused, looking around the store, then stepped inside after seeing no motion. As quickly as possible, Henry went up and down the aisles searching for tubing. After each aisle, he returned to the front and peered out to make sure that Robby was still where he was supposed to be. Each time, the boy was. He did not look happy, but he had listened and minded the instructions he had been given. It felt strange to have any sort of control over a child's actions beyond the stereotypical yelling of "get off my lawn" and having children scatter in mock fear.

He found some tubing meant for irrigation that he thought would probably work for now and grabbed some pruners off a shelf as he walked by. Remembering a rack of clothes with long sleeved shirts for boys on it, he circled back and grabbed a couple. Robby could double them up until he could find him a proper coat. He draped the shirts over his arm and went back to the front of the store with the tubing and shears tucked under his arm. There was a map display next to the door that he had not noticed on his way in. He selected a couple and, folding them, tucked them into his back pocket. He then pushed open the front door, the bell tinkling again and froze mid-step.

There was a tall man with his back to Henry standing facing the Jeep.

At the sound of the bell, the man turned around, his movements swift and jerky. His skin was ashen and his thick hair was a shock of white, but he looked to be somewhere in his seventies or eighties. There was a split second wherein Henry was sure this was just a normal old man. Then, seeing Henry, the man's mouth opened, growing impossibly wide as a high-pitched shriek pierced Henry's ears. Before he could reach for his gun, the man came tearing toward Henry faster than seemed possible for a man his age even when fully healthy.

About three feet away and with the man's fingers just beginning to brush against his skin, Henry whipped the pruners out from under his arm and rammed them forward as hard as he could into the man. There was a sickening squelching noise as they tore through the man's upper midsection and were buried in his body. The man released a breath of air and fell forward onto Henry who dipped his left shoulder and spun out and away from the man. The old man fell to the ground, the pruners piercing him through with the impact.

Staggering away, Henry stared wide-eyed at the still twitching man, waiting for him to get up and come at him again, but he did not. He reminded himself, as the convulsing gradually slowed then stopped, that this was not a zombie movie. The infected were still human. They were still alive. Well, not this guy. Not anymore.

Henry stood panting for several seconds before turning back to the Jeep. Fear swept through him. He could not see Robby.

"Robby!" Henry stumbled toward the Jeep, clutching the shirts to his chest. "Robby!"

From beneath the window, Robby's small head appeared. Henry swallowed hard, nodding at the boy with relief. Keeping his eyes on the still motionless body, he cautiously took a few steps toward it to collect the tubing from where it had fallen. The pruners were a total loss at this point. He had very little desire to attempt to retrieve them from their new home and even less to go back into the store for another pair.

Moving faster now, Henry chucked the shirts to Robby through his open window and went to the pickup. He grabbed the gas can from the back and placed the gas can on the ground. He then wrenched open the driver's side door and dug around between the seats. He found a couple of old rags on the floorboard which he tucked into the pocket of his jeans.

Leaning farther in, he popped open the glove compartment. Inside was a pack of peppermint gum, a brown leather wallet, and a black cased hunting knife. He pocketed the gum for Robby and grabbed the knife, flicking it open. The blade was at least two and a half inches long and looked very sharp. It would serve more than a few purposes.

Henry palmed the knife and, ignoring the wallet altogether, exited the pickup. With one eye on Robby who was watching his every move from his hunched position in the Jeep, Henry opened the cover to the gas tank and removed the cap. Flicking open the knife again, he cut two pieces from the tubing, one distinctly longer than the other.

He opened the gas can and put one end of the longer tubing into it then fed the other two ends into the tank. He took the rags from his pocked and packed them around the tubes. Picking up the free end of the shorter tube, Henry took a deep breath and forced it all back out through the tube. He had to do this a few times before he heard gas

225

splatter from the long tubing into the gas can at his feet. His eyes drifted back to the body on the ground. He had known it would be a good thing to bond with the boy now that they were stuck with each other. While he had hoped to find they had something in common, he would have preferred it was something more along the lines of a love of baseball or fixing things.

Far up Bradford Street, something moved, catching his eye. He paused, staring, but could not make out what he had seen. He shifted his attention back to the task at hand. He had to get this done or they would not be going very far. Henry knelt next to the gas can and peered inside, monitoring how much was going into the can. When it looked full, he withdrew the long tubing from the can and, with his thumb over the end, held it up so that anything left in the tube would go back into the tank. He then collected the tubing and the rags and, picking up the gas can, went back to the Jeep.

"How'd you learn to do that?" Robby sounded awed.

Henry chuckled, "You pick up skills here and there. This will be a good one to know, I'm guessing."

"Don't you get gas in your mouth?"

"Nah," Henry scanned the parking lot again as he transferred the gas from the can to the Jeep's tank, his hand trembling slightly. He had not realized how much he had been affected by killing the old man. "Haven't for a long time. I did the first few times, though."

"Yuck," Robby's tongue poked from between his lips, "I bet it tastes even worse than it smells!"

"Sure does, kiddo." Henry agreed. His eyes shot up again to the far end of the road. He could have sworn he had seen something move again. There was always a chance it had been another vehicle passing through on the main street. He had seen a few other moving vehicles since the start of their trip. It was likely just people like them; survivors searching for a safe place. Henry tapped the last of the gas out of the can and stuck it and all his new siphoning supplies into the back of the Jeep.

He got into his seat and started the engine, his eyes darting back and forth from his immediate surroundings to the end of the road. He was being paranoid, but then, who wouldn't be after killing a man?

Opting not to mention anything to Robby, Henry got back on the main road. To get back to the highway, he would have to drive farther up this road. He rolled up his window and, pulling out the gum, offered it to Robby. "Roll up your window."

"Why?" Robby took the gum and began unwrapping a piece.

Henry did not respond. His eyes were sweeping from one side of the street to the other. He was driving slower than necessary. Part of him wanted to get the hell out of there, but another part of him was curious and wanted to figure out what he had seen. He reached behind himself and took out the maps from his back pocket. Holding them out to the boy, he said, "Here, look for a route into New Mexico that doesn't involve going though Amarillo. I have a feeling we're going to want to avoid big cities."

Robby opened up a map and stuck his nose into it. As an afterthought, he reached out without looking up and rolled up his window. If the boy had noticed how edgy Henry was now, he certainly was not letting on. In any case, Henry was glad the boy was happily distracted. If there was nothing at the far end of the road, then he was just being paranoid and he could brush it off and move on. However, if there was someone or something lurking, it might be good to know.

He thought about the man he had killed and shuddered. The man had looked and behaved very much like the pale woman. This, to him, was proof enough that she had not been an anomaly. The realization was unnerving and made him wonder how many more people like the pale woman and the pale man were out there.

They pulled up the stop sign at 3rd Street and paused despite the lack of traffic. Henry wanted to give the boy a minute to find the way they needed to go himself so he turned left slowly and proceeded without haste back toward Noel Street which, if they continued west on, would lead them on a route that avoided Amarillo, Texas. Henry already knew which way to go, having been through Memphis before, but he felt that, like siphoning gas, finding his own way was another skill that would do the boy good.

Henry looked over at Robby. Movement behind the boy forced his eyes to rise up past the boy's face and he stared out the window with growing dread at a church on the corner that they were passing. There was a pathway that had been shielded from sight until just now. Even before they reached it, Henry could see that it was packed with people, all of whom were pale. They were milling about aimlessly and, for the moment, completely unaware of the soft rumble of the Jeep's engine. Remaining calm, Henry glanced at the boy and maintained his speed, afraid a change in direction would attract attention. Robby's nose was still well into the map.

"You see where we need to be, kiddo?" He kept his voice low as the Jeep rolled past the crowd. Robby, on the

228

other hand, had found the route they needed and the excitement in his eyes reached his voice.

"Yeah! We need to get back onto…TX 256 West…That's Noel Street again so we need to-"

This time, it was not a solitary shriek that cut through the air, but three or four. Both Henry and Robby's eyes shot up in the direction of the crowded pathway. Four pale people were facing them, all with their mouths stretched open in that ghastly screaming mask. One, a little girl in what looked to be her Sunday best, was pointing directly at them. As one, the crowd of pale people lifted their heads and turned to face the Jeep. Henry slammed his foot down on the gas and the Jeep lurched forward, wheels screeching, just as the crowd surged toward them.

Almost two blocks up, Henry swerved to miss a pile of people who had apparently dropped one on top of the other in the middle of the road. Robby clutched at the door to hold himself in place, his eye fixed on the sideview mirror. Behind them, forty to fifty men, women, and children were running full speed after them. They were impossibly fast and closing the distance between them and the Jeep almost as fast as Henry was making it. Their hair, in varying degrees of whiteness, made them look like a wave of people in the sea.

The Jeep bumped over something. He was sure he had just driven over someone, but he could not slow down or stop to see. Only days before, he would have been horrified by the thought of running over someone, dead or alive. Today, there were more pressing matters than the possibility of flattening someone who very likely had not been alive to care for several hours.

"That way!" Robby yelled, pointing left as the road merged at Front Street.

Hoping the boy had enough sense to keep holding on, Henry slowed just enough to veer left then again to make the right turn onto Noel Street then stomped back down on the gas and sped up the road. He could no longer see the pale people chasing after him, but he knew they were still coming.

"Henry?" Robby's voice was shaky which really was no surprise. Henry's own heart was pounding. In his rear view, he could now just make out someone rounding the corner far behind them as they went over the train tracks.

"Henry?" There was a fresh urgency in the boy's voice.

Henry tore his eyes away from the rearview and followed where Robby's finger was now pointing. The sight before him caused him to slam on the brakes. The Jeep skidded to a halt in the intersection of Noel Street and Boykin Drive. There was a semi overturned across the north side of Boykin Drive. The roads south and west were littered with cars, pickups, and a few vans, some of which had crashed into each other.

They were completely trapped.

Seventeen

MACK WAS PERCHED on a tree stump in the backyard. His sister was standing next to him, her hands very animated as she ranted about something Frankie could not hear. Mack seemed not to care in the slightest about whatever Mick was going on about, but like a good brother, he was letting her talk.

He looked a bit like an impossibly big frog ready to make a huge leap from atop the stump. Frankie clutched her mug to her chest, a lump rising in her throat as she thought of how Lydia used to sit just like that whenever they came upon a stump or large rock.

"Morning." Frankie tore her gaze away from the sliding glass door and looked up at James. He was holding a mug of his own which he used to indicate the chair behind her. "Mind if I join you?"

Frankie shrugged. She leaned back in her chair and sipped at the steaming hot coffee Cora had made for her. James pulled the empty chair up so that it was next to Frankie's and lowered himself onto it. Together, they stared through the window in silence at the twins. After a few minutes, Frankie tucked one leg up underneath herself and turned so that she was twisted more toward James.

"That was the Swass Facility I was in, right?"

James did not answer right away. He nodded slowly as though considering his next words. "Yes. It's the Swass Research and Development Facility."

"And you work there." It was more of a statement than a question.

"No."

Frankie raised her eyebrows in surprise. Before she could ask for clarification, he continued. "I took the badge and the uniform off a new guy. He said it was his first day. I figured he wouldn't be missed."

"'Wouldn't be missed'? What did you do with him?"

Outside, Mick gave her brother a forceful shove. He flew off the stump and stumbled down the slight hill, kicking up pine needles as he went. He did not seem upset with Mick. Instead, when he turned around, Frankie could see that he was grinning at his twin. His hands were raised, palms up, as if professing innocence and asking what he had done to deserve such treatment.

James laughed. "Those two. Always getting at each other."

"What's up with her?" Frankie asked, pointing her mug in Mick's direction.

"Mick? She's the polar opposite of her brother. He's the joker. She's always been more serious. You've never seen such a serious little girl. Mack always saw the funny side of things no matter what it was, but Mick was always looking for more. She had to know the ins and outs of everything. I think she thought she could fix anything so long as she knew how it worked. There was no telling her that some things didn't need fixing."

"Are you related? You seem to know them pretty well."

"Oh, no," James chuckled, watching Mick pelt Mack with pinecones. "I knew their father. He was my high school biology teacher, actually. After I graduated, I moved into this crappy little studio apartment off campus because I couldn't get into the dorms at the university. I was working at a fast food restaurant and barely making rent. One day, he and his pregnant wife came in for lunch. She was massive…"

He smiled at the memory. Outside, Mack had scooped up of couple pinecones and was playfully chucking them in his sister's general direction. Unlike his sister, he was making no effort to actually hit her. Frankie smiled. Mack had been the one against whom she had slept in the van on the way to the cabin. The longer she knew him, the more she liked him. He was the sort of young man she had hoped her own son would grow to be. Her throat constricted as an image of her sweet little boy flashed in her mind. She swallowed hard, choking back her emotions before they could well up far enough to consume her.

"It was around Thanksgiving," James continued to Frankie's relief, "and I was hanging up these cheesy placards of turkeys holding burgers. Anyway, we got to talking about being thankful and I joked that I was thankful for the food people sent back or didn't finish because it made up the most of what I had been living on that month. His wife, that's Mama Jean, had freaked out. They invited me to dinner that night and couldn't get rid of me after. Not that they tried."

Frankie finished her coffee. She gently rocked the mug back and forth by the handle. "So, you're family after all."

James looked thoughtful. "I suppose we are, in a sense."

Through the glass, they could just make out Mick yelling at Mack that he was an asshole before she stomped away around the side of the house. Mack's whole body was shaking with laughter. They watched as he gathered up the pinecones she had thrown at him and piled them up next to where he repositioned himself on the stump as though preparing himself for her inevitable return.

"So, you took a badge and uniform…" Frankie prompted, hoping to get James back on track. "Did you do that to get me?"

"Not originally," James admitted. He stood up and, taking her mug from her, went into the kitchen. She could hear him pouring more coffee into their mugs. Normally, she would have stopped at one cup, but this seemed like a good way to get him talking. There was so much she still did not understand. "I'm pretty sure they brought you in on the same day I arrived, though. A lot of people were being brought in. I was there because my friend Sharsti had been taken there."

There was something, a certain softness, about the way he said her name. Frankie watched him as he came back in with their refilled mugs. She took her mug back from him with murmured thanks and cupped it in her hands. "She was more than just a friend, wasn't she?"

James sat down again and stared out at Mack who, since his original target had failed to return, was now throwing pinecones like baseballs from his tree stump pitcher's mound. He released a slow, heavy sigh. "Yes."

It was clear that she was not going to get much more information if she kept focusing on the personal aspect. She switched tacks. "You said you were working together with a fellow called Richard, right?"

"Robert," he corrected her. "Robert Miller. There were a few others, but it was mainly the three of us."

Frankie prickled at the name. There was something familiar about it as though she had heard it years before. "And your friend, Sharsti, ended up in the Swass Facility like me. What happened to Miller?"

James became quiet again. He sighed and shrugged. "I'm not entirely sure, but I'm guessing nothing good. I haven't heard from him since I snuck into the Swass Facility to get Shar."

Frankie nodded, waiting. She was becoming even more frustrated. James reminded her so much of the conversations she had with her daughter after school. Sometimes, Lydia would come home bubbling over with stories about her day. Other times, it was like pulling teeth to get the smallest detail out of her daughter. Getting information from James was even more difficult. She had tried being patient and polite. Perhaps a more direct approach would work better.

"Look," she said, trying to keep her voice even and calm, "my entire world just turned upside down. In the span of a week, I've lost my whole family, recovered from what I'm being told is a virus that very few people have the chance of surviving, and I've been yanked about by a bunch of people I don't know who really haven't told me much about what's going on. I'm really going to need you to be a little more forthcoming with…with, well, everything."

James turned and met her gaze. "I know this has been hard for you. It hasn't been easy for me, either. We've both lost people. My life has been taken from me as well."

"And that's why I think you should just be open with me. I understand how you must be feeling. I just don't understand much else. I have this huge gap of time that you happen to be able to fill in on top of the fact that it's sounding more and more like you are the reason for that gap."

He nodded soberly. "You're right. It's just…painful."

Frankie really did not want to push him too much. She was afraid he would stop talking altogether. Instead, she waited again and sipped at her second cup of coffee. Mack was still pitching pinecones and hitting his imaginary mark on one of the trees more often than not.

Colin had loved baseball. Even at two-years-old, he was showing signs of being a promising player. She and Hugo had got him a little plastic t-ball set for the backyard and he had surprised them by actually being able to hit the ball pretty far. They had been so excited about getting him on a team in a few years, and now it would never happen. She turned her face slightly away from James so he would not see the tears that were stinging her eyes.

"Cabot was on top of Shar when I got back to the lab," James continued suddenly. "I didn't know what he was doing, but she was screaming and it was obvious that he was hurting her. I didn't think about it. I just grabbed him by the back of his lab coat and hauled him off her. I'll never forget the look on his face. He looked wild like he was possessed or something. He didn't look like the meek guy I'd hired on to help. He was sweaty and, at first, I thought he'd got something white in his hair."

Frankie wiped her eyes furtively and returned her gaze to Mack who was still pitching pinecones. Next to her, James sipped his coffee, his eyes on Mack. "I threw him off her pretty hard. I was sure that I had broken one of his bones because he crashed into the table that had the samples on it and damn near broke it in half. Several of them got knocked to the ground. I didn't have time to think about that because he got up like it was nothing and charged at me. I threw him off again, but he just got up. I couldn't get him to stop."

Frankie turned her attention completely to James, leaving Mack and the memory of her dead son outside. "Then Shar started screaming again. I don't know why, but she did and Cabot rounded on her. He looked like he was going to kill her. He'd already scratched up her face pretty badly. She was bleeding. I...I didn't know what to do. He was going for her again so I..."

"You shot him," Frankie said when he became quiet.

"Yeah," he said, "I have a concealed carry license. I didn't think about it. I just shot him."

"Did you call the cops?"

James looked uncomfortable. 'No. Shar didn't want me to and it kind of made sense. What we were doing in that lab...well, it would not have been easy to explain. And Shar just wanted to go home. I thought she meant to her

237

apartment at first so I started to drive her there, but she told me she wanted to go home to her parents for a while. I begged her to stay. I guess I knew something was wrong, but she convinced me to take her straight to the airport. She could have convinced me to do just about anything."

He paused, his lips pursing tightly. With a deep breath, he rushed on. "Anyway, I put her on a plane to Oklahoma. She said she had family out in Hollis."

"And that's how she infected the Midwest?"

"I suppose it would be more accurate to say that that is how *I* infected the Midwest. I mean, if I had just kept her there in the lab, the virus might have been contained. But there's also Robert."

Frankie swirled her cup, watching the coffee spin in circles. "What about him?"

"Cabot, Sharsti, and I had been the only ones who were supposed to be there, but Robert decided to come in for some reason. I never got the chance to ask him why. He said he had heard the gunshot downstairs and had followed the sound to the lab. I was sure he would call the police even if I didn't, but he told me to get Shar out of there and not to worry about anything. He said he'd take care of it."

"Did he?"

"I thought he did," James admitted with a hint of regret. "I mean, the body was gone by the time I got back to the lab. So were the samples. I got Shar to the airport and onto a plane. We were lucky to get a ticket. It was hard to let her go. I just wanted to take care of her…she looked so pale…she was obviously still in shock from the attack. She was normally so graceful…so beautiful…"

James shook his head as if it would clear the memory then continued. "As soon as she was up in the air, I headed back to the lab. Halfway there, I got a text from Robert saying that he was heading to Colorado."

"Why Colorado?" Frankie looked up at James with curiosity.

"Well," he replied, "considering that it was Durango he was heading to…"

"Durango?" Frankie sat up straighter. "That's where I'm from!"

James looked grim. He set his second cup of coffee down on a table nearby and ran his fingers through his hair. "Yeah. I'm pretty sure you are the reason why Colorado."

She was confused. "Are you saying he was trying to find me?"

"I believe so."

"Why me?"

James was rubbing his temples. "Remember how your father said he kept his mouth shut about the supervirus because he was trying to protect you?" When Frankie nodded, he went on. "Well, I think Robert had decided to use you as a bargaining chip."

Now Frankie was even more baffled than ever. Her confusion must have been clear from the look on her face because James offered up the explanation without any further prompting.

"Robert had tried to bring your father in on our tests several times. He kept getting turned down, though, and it was really beginning to piss him off. He felt that we were missing some vital piece of information that your father would have and was frustrated that he was too afraid to join us. I think Robert decided that the only way he was going to convince Dr. Reed to help was to scare him more than he was already scared. That meant using you."

"So, he went to Durango to, what? Kidnap me?"

James did not answer, but Frankie understood that this was exactly what Robert had intended to do. She leaned over James and set her mug next to his. She no longer could even pretend she wanted it. She lifted her other leg up onto her chair and wrapped her arms around her knees. She felt sick.

"The last text I got from him said, 'I am not afraid to die. I am afraid to live'."

"What does that mean?"

James shook his head slowly. "I don't know. But that was almost a week ago. I haven't heard anything from him since. Considering that I found you in the Swass Facility, I'm guessing he never found you."

"And Sharsti?"

He took a deep breath, pain flickering across his face. Frankie had the urge to switch topics to spare him whatever memories of her were causing him so much pain, but her curiosity kept her quiet.

"I called her phone the same night everything happened at the lab." James rubbed at his left temple. "Her mother answered and told me that Shar had arrived safely, but that she had appeared to be ill. She had gone to bed, but, when Mrs. Reddy went to check on her, she wasn't in her room. She wasn't anywhere in the house. Nothing looked disturbed and there wasn't a note. Her purse was still on the table in the hall. She was just gone."

"Gone?"

He nodded. "Mrs. Reddy was about to go driving around to look for her when a couple of guys rang the doorbell. They said they were looking for Dr. Reddy so Shar's mother called her husband to the door. It hadn't occurred to her that they would be looking for Shar and not her father since she didn't even live there."

"What did they want with her?"

"I'm not entirely sure, but, from the things they said to the Reddys, it sounded like they were from the Swass Facility. I think they somehow knew that she was infected. I'm not sure how they knew." He paused again then scowled as realization crossed his face. "They must have been watching us the whole time."

Frankie frowned. "You said that's where you found her, right? The Swass Facility? How did you know they would take her there?"

"I didn't know for sure," he clasped his hands together. "There were a few places they could have gone, but this made the most sense. It was a lucky guess."

"Lucky for sure," Frankie said, thinking more about how James had found her there as well than about how he had been right in looking there for his friend. "So, you hopped a plane to wherever this facility is, stole some guy's badge and uniform, and rescued me."

He tilted his head, nodding. "Just outside of Roswell, New Mexico and, yes, that's pretty much how it happened. They had you under the name Reed and I recognized your name from conversations with your father so I went through your chart. It was obvious who you were and I figured why they wanted you."

"And your friend?"

James looked as though his whole body was deflating. He sunk down more into his chair, squeezing his hands together. "She was dead before I got there. There wasn't anything I could have done anyway. Turns out she was B-positive. Her blood type was a death sentence."

Frankie reached out and put her hand on his shoulder. He did not shrug it away or move. They sat quietly for several minutes while he recovered from rehashing his memories and she processed the new information. The death of his friend was affecting him just as much as her own losses were still affecting her. She wondered why he insisted on using words like 'friend' and 'colleague' when this Dr. Sharsti Reddy was obviously so much more to him.

"I keep thinking about all those people who were on the plane with her. If she touched anyone or shared a drink…Hell, if she even coughed or sneezed even once…She was probably infecting people the whole time and didn't know it. I'm lucky she didn't infect me, too."

Frankie had not considered this before. Sharsti could have infected several people on her way to her parent's house and those people would have passed on the supervirus to countless others as they made connections, rode in taxis, or went home to their families. Some of those people might have been traveling overseas. It was no wonder this supervirus was spreading was as quickly as it was.

"James," she began.

"Who is that?"

The question confused her. For a second, she was sure he had suddenly lost his memory and no longer knew

242

his own name. Then, following his gaze, she looked back out the sliding glass door and saw that an older man dressed in overalls and a red checked shirt was standing a few feet behind Mack. Mack was still pitching pinecones and completely oblivious to the presence of the man who was now reaching out to him.

Frankie rose swiftly to her feet, fingers pressed against the glass and squinted out at the man's back. He was very familiar. "I think that's Mr. Par-"

A piercing shriek cut her off. Mack fell forward off the stump and tumbling through fallen leaves, twisted around onto his rear end to face the man who was now advancing quickly on the young man. James leapt up and began struggling with the latch on the sliding door as Earl, dressed only in jeans and a t-shirt, came running into view. The older man lurched forward, falling over the tree stump as though he had not seen it and, flying forward, rolled on top of Mack.

Earl, reaching the two, grabbed the old man by his shirt and tried to haul him off Mack, but the man had too firm a grip on the younger man. James, finally unlocking the sliding glass door, wrenched it open and barreled out onto the back deck and down the stairs. Frankie, barefoot and far shorter, followed several paces behind.

Together, James and Earl managed to get the man off Mack. The man, seemingly unaware that his target was not the same as it had been moments before, began to tear at Earl's face with his bare hands. Then, throwing himself forward, the man sunk his teeth into Earl's shoulder.

Earl yelped as the man's teeth pierced his skin through his thin t-shirt and shoved hard at the old man to get him off him. James had one arm around the man's chest and was pummeling him with his free fist, but the older man seemed to be completely impervious to the assault. Frankie skidded to a halt, her eyes widening as the top half of the older man's face came into view.

"It is Mr. Parker!" she cried out, leaping into the struggle as James pulled a black handgun from a holster at his side and placed it near her childhood best friend's father's head. Then, as Frankie screamed, he pulled the trigger.

Eighteen

Shawn Wiggins
Fukkin zombies everywhere. You turn I dont
care who you are. imma blast your fukkin head
off just like Mallory. Fukkin sad but you gotta do
what you gotta do right?
(16 minutes ago)

> **Derek Jones**
> You murdered your girlfriend???
> (5 minutes ago)

> **Shawn Wiggins**
> Nah man! She was a fukkin zombie!
> She was screaming all high n shit. I
> had to do it. I'll miss you baby girl! RIP
> (4 minutes ago)

> **Derek Jones**
> Dude! She wasn't a zombie! She
> wasn't even dead! She was just sick
> and you fucking murdered her!
> (3 minutes ago)

> **Tyrone Telar**
> Trust me, bro. what Shawn did was
> mercy u gotta do what u gotta do.
> (2 minutes ago)

Shawn Wiggins, LifeFeed (Social Media Site)

"HENRY! THEY'RE COMING!"

Robby, twisted around in his seat to look out the back of the Jeep, was practically shrieking with terror. Henry could see the crowd of pale people coming toward them far faster than they should have been able. He scanned the area, realizing that there was absolutely nowhere they could go in the Jeep except back in the direction from which they had come or back east on Noel Street. Either way, he had to turn the Jeep around and was bound to run into the mass of pale people. Without a cowcatcher on the front of the Jeep, ramming through so many people seemed like a very bad idea.

"Come on!"

Henry reached over and unbuckled the boy's seatbelt then hauled him out the driver's side door. As much as he did not like their only other choice, wending their way through the vehicles and heading for the nearest building seemed like their best bet. He knew their options were limited. There was a residential area across Boykin Drive as well as a few small businesses to the right and a truck stop to the left. He doubted they could make it to any of the houses before being overrun, but maybe they could make it to the truck stop. It had, although not by much, the clearest path. Barring that, they would have to duck into another vehicle and hope for the best.

Practically dragging Robby behind him, Henry raced through the vehicles toward the truck stop. He could hear the boy panting and felt his fingers digging into his flesh as he pulled him around a brown pickup. He could also now hear the footsteps of the pale people thundering toward them. He realized with a sudden sense of finality that they were not going to make it. They were simply not fast enough.

A loud crack echoed against the vehicles around them. Henry's head whipped around in time to see a pale man who had been leading the crowd fall to the ground mid-stride. There was another bang and the pale man who had replaced the first as leader fell to the ground and disappeared behind a blue car.

"Look!"

Henry followed where Robby's small face was pointing. At the edge of the truck stop was an old, timeworn Toyota Dolphin RV with flaking salmon-colored trim. A figure dressed all in black was leaning slightly over the hood from the driver's side door, pointing some sort of rifle in their general direction. A third shot whizzed by uncomfortably close, but, judging by the pale woman behind them with whose hag-like head it made contact, it was clear that the shooter was not aiming for them.

Taking this as a good sign, Henry redoubled his efforts and yanked Robby around the back of a blue sedan that had crashed into the group of cars in front of it. Their path was now clear and the RV was only few yard away. The camper door was slightly open and Henry saw the shooter wave them forward as he switched to shorter, stouter gun and took aim. He fired again at a fourth runner who, having managed to make his way around the sedan, was right on their heels. The boom from the weapon was deafening.

Henry pulled the door open wider and shoved Robby through it, following right behind him. Once he was inside, he slammed the door shut and locked it. Panting and wheezing, Henry stumbled over to the couch and collapsed onto it, still pulling Robby with him. There were a few more shots then he felt the RV rock slightly and heard a door up front slam shut. A dark curtain which separated the cab from the rest of the camper opened and the shooter came through. He slid a wooden board over the opening and secured it to the wall with metal clasps on either side.

He was shorter than Henry had first thought when he had seen him behind the hood of the camper, but then he had also been leaning out of the cab to fire instead of from the ground. Henry watched as the shooter checked the lock on the door they had come through then peered out the curtained windows. His face and head obscured by a black fleece half-mask and some expensive looking sunglasses as well as a black zippered hoodie with little demons in various poses painted on both the front and back. A few strands of dark brown hair were poking out from under the hoodie, but no other part of the shooter was visible.

A thump against the side of the RV drew Henry's focus away from the shooter. Another three thumps followed in quick succession making Robby jump. The pale people were throwing themselves against the side of the RV and, each time, Robby clung harder to Henry. Henry wrapped one arm around the boy and squeezed, his eyes moving back to the shooter who had slipped into a chair opposite them.

He rested leaned his rifle against the wall and his black shotgun on the table next to him then raised two fingers of black gloved hand in greeting to them. His hand, like him, was relatively small. It suddenly struck Henry that this was not a man who had rescued them and given them sanctuary; it was a boy.

They sat in silence listening to the thudding of the pale people grow farther and farther apart. Every so often, the shooter would twist in his seat to peer out the corner of the curtains behind him. Henry, unable to see what the shooter could see, was not sure if the pale people were losing interest or if they even had enough awareness to be interested in the first place. Either way, they seemed to be going away and Robby was gradually loosening his stranglehold on Henry's arm.

When several minutes had passed without incident and the shooter seemed satisfied that they were no longer in danger, he pulled down the half mask and set the sunglasses on the table next to his weapon. He then shoved his hoody back and shook his head slightly to release the mass of unruly brown curls that had been hidden away.

He was a she.

"You hungry, kid?" the girl asked, scratching at her scalp with both hands. "I have enough for both you and your dad."

"He's not my dad," Robby replied meekly, "but, yeah. I'm super hungry."

"C'mon," she said, waving him into the kitchenette. "I have chicken nuggets. You like chicken nuggets? They're my favorite." Robby, governed by his stomach just like most children his age, readily released Henry's arm and followed her.

Henry gaped at her. The girl had been completely covered by shapeless black clothing and had wielded a more than impressive gun with amazing skill and precision. Because of the climate in which he had been raised, it had never occurred to him that there was even a possibility that the shooter would be female much less a young and attractive one. He was inwardly kicking himself for the preconceived notion that only a male was capable of handling himself the way this girl had handled herself. She had certainly done so with greater expertise than he had so far.

He watched the girl move around the small kitchenette, chattering to a very engaged looking Robby as she pulled a box from a small freezer and, after pulling the lid back a bit, stuck it into a microwave. The girl was not much taller than Robby. She only had about half a foot on him, standing around a little less than five and a half feet tall. Her face heart-shaped reminded him of a young actress he had recently seen in a movie, but whose name he could not remember. She was nothing short of gorgeous and seemed completely unaware of the fact.

The girl, shifting her crescent moon shaped brown eyes to Henry, smiled wryly. There was a mischievous upturn to her full lips. "Yeah, yeah, yeah. I'm a chick. Moving on…"

Embarrassed, Henry looked away, taking in the inside of the camper with open appreciation. The outside had not been much to look at, but the inside had been well cared for by someone with an attention to detail. He wondered if that person had been the girl. He leaned forward, resting his elbows on his knees to get a better look at the gun she had left on the camper's small dining table. She might have been young, but she certainly had good taste in guns. It was far shorter than a shotgun, but far larger than a pistol and had the words 'The Gatekeeper' embossed in white on the side. It was a beautiful weapon.

"You like it?"

Henry looked up. The girl was standing next to him, smiling brightly. Her eyebrows were raised inquisitively, but Henry had no doubt what she was really saying. He leaned back, creating a respectful distance from the weapon. Robby squeezed past them both and flopped back down onto the couch next to him. He was clutching a container of microwaved frozen chicken nuggets.

"That's an impressive gun." Henry commented.

"And that's why I have it," she answered, taking it from the table and laying it across her lap as she sat back down in her chair. "I wanted one for years and now I have it. Thank you, Apocalypse!"

He nodded, wondering if she was implying having looted it. He looked up at her, meeting her gaze. "Henry."

She tilted her head slightly to the side. "Tess."

Without looking up from his plate of food, Robby pointed down at himself and spoke around a mouthful of chicken. "Robby."

"Well, that was easy," Tess said cheerfully, "Now what?"

Henry shrugged, "Well, I guess we thank you for your help and hospitality then see ourselves out."

"Just like that, huh? Bang, bang, thank you, ma'am!" She pointed her fingers up in the shape of guns and blew on the tops of each once. When she got no response from her play on the old saying, she asked, "Where are you headed?"

Henry jerked a thumb over his shoulder. "West. To New Mexico."

Tess pursed her lips, her eyebrows lifting again. "New Mexico, huh? Well, I see a couple problems with that plan."

"Oh?"

"First off, it's a long way to go by foot. Your Jeep is on the wrong side of that jam out there."

Robby shoved another chicken nugget into his mouth. "Henry'll move the cars. He's done it before."

"Lot of work for one person. What if the freaks come back?"

"We'll figure something out," Henry said. While he appreciated Robby's faith in him, he had to admit that Tess was right; it would be a massive job and likely to cause enough noise to draw attention back to them.

"Or," Tess leaned forward, patting her gun, "I could help. My uncle always said I wasn't much of a driver, but I'm not a bad lookout."

Henry smiled, "You're a fantastic shot."

The girl grinned, accepting the compliment.

Robby rose and took the empty chicken nugget container back into the kitchenette. Finding the trash, he threw it away and came back. "What's the other problem?"

Both Henry and Tess looked at him blankly. "You said there were 'a couple' problems with us going to New Mexico."

"Oh, yeah," she said, tucking her hair back behind her ears. It was a fruitless effort. Her curls were so thick that they popped right back out as soon as she moved her hand. "Last I heard, it's worse out there than here, if you can believe that."

Henry shrugged. Tess help up one hand. "Unless you wanna get yourselves infected, I say you're better off sticking it out here until it's over."

He shrugged again. "We'll be fine."

"We're probably infected anyway."

Tess looked sharply over at Robby. "What's that, now?"

"Yeah," Robby said with a hint of regret for having spoken. He did not seem to like being scrutinized by the girl, having taken to her so quickly, "I got spit on me and Henry was scratched or something."

Tess's eyes narrowed, but she didn't move. 'And you got into my RV? With me?"

This was another thing that had not occurred to Henry. He had been so occupied with getting himself and Robby away from the mob of pale people that he had completely forgotten that they had both been exposed and might be putting anyone they encountered at risk. Still, it had been longer than the news had said it would be before he should have started experiencing symptoms. He felt fine. On the other hand, it was right around the time when Robby should start showing signs of infection.

"You're fine," he said casually, "We're fine. We were both exposed almost two days ago and we don't have so much as a sniffle."

It was a partial truth. For him, it had been over a day and a half since the pale woman had pierced his skin with her sharp nails and exposed him to her sweat. It had been less than twelve hours since Robby had been exposed. He could feel Robby's eyes on him, but he did not acknowledge the boy. He was not sure why he had lied. He did not honestly think this girl would shoot them so soon after showing such open hospitality. On the other hand, she had shot four pale people that they knew of and, from her complete lack of hesitation, Henry wagered there had been more before they had all met.

Tess still seemed skeptical, but appeared to be a little less wary of them. Her eyes moved back and forth between them as if weighing her options. Then, without warning, she rose, taking both her Gatekeeper and her rifle with her, and checked the windows one more time. Staring out at the waning daylight, she said, "Well, it'll be dark soon. I only have two places for sleeping. The first is where you are right now and the second is my bed up there above the cab. The couch pulls out. You should both fit. You're welcome to stay, I guess. It's getting dark and moving cars will take a while."

"Thanks," Henry said softly. She was putting herself in a potentially dangerous situation by allowing them to stay. For all she knew, they were lying about everything and would either infect her or kill her in her sleep. Maybe both.

He had not realized how tired he was until just now. His body was aching and his eyelids were drooping. At this rate, he would be asleep long before Tess and Robby and he would be the one putting himself at risk. He stood and stretched then signaled for Robby to move so he could pull out the couch. Robby was looking pretty tired himself. An early night would do both of them a world of good.

Tess clambered up onto her own bed out of their way and, lying on her stomach with her gun next to her, she peered through the curtains around her head. After a few moments, she made a gun shape with her fingers and aimed it through the glass. "Still some of them out there. I could probably pop the window and get a few more of them."

Henry sat on the pullout bed and looked up at her. "Doesn't it bother you at all?"

"Doesn't what bother me?" She glanced down at him, one eyebrow raised.

"Shooting them," he replied as Robby crawled onto the other side of the bed and curled up. Henry pulled off his jacket and laid it over the boy.

Tess's lip curled. "Nah. Why would it?"

He frowned. It had bothered him a great deal when he had rammed the pruning shears into the old guy at the farm store and he was certain it had bothered Robby to shoot the gangbanger at the restaurant. He was beginning to reevaluate staying with the girl. He was not sure how a girl as seemingly nice as Tess could not be bothered at all by the idea of shooting the infected people.

"You're okay with killing people?"

"But I'm not," she laughed, "I'm downing freaks."

"Tess," Henry said slowly, another realization dawning on him, "Those 'freaks' are still alive."

"No," Tess said, her voice matching Henry's slow cadence, "they're freaks. You know, like, zombies and shit."

Henry sat up, his forehead knitting together. "No, Tess, they aren't 'like zombies and shit'. Those people out there are very much alive."

Tess rolled onto her side and sat up as much as she could from the loft. She was small enough that she did not have far to hunch over in a seated position. She stared almost blankly down at him for several seconds.

"No."

"What do you mean, 'no'?"

"I mean, 'no'," she said, shaking her head. "I'm not killing people. I'm…"

She went silent, her gaze fixed on Henry. He wondered how old she was. At first, he had placed her around twenty-two or three, but she now looked as young as fifteen or sixteen. It was obvious that she had honestly

255

had no idea that the pale people she had been shooting had been still alive. He did not really blame her. Her assumptions, given the current popularity surrounding all things zombie apocalypse, made complete sense especially if she had not been following the news closely.

"It's okay, Tess," Robby sleepy voice came out from under Henry's coat. "I killed someone, too. I had to just like you had to. They were gonna kill us."

Tess was still staring at Henry, but the expression on her face was a mixture of pain and disbelief. Henry felt the urge to hug her and laughed inwardly. When had he become such a softy? He had never cared for kids or young people in general. He had never had the patience for them. Now, in the past twenty-four hours, he had essentially adopted Robby and was feeling sorry for this girl who was having to rethink her own morality.

Without another word, Tess swung her legs back up onto the bunk and rolled onto her side facing away from them. Taking a cue from her, Henry lay down next to Robby and stared at his back watching as it gently rose up and down with each peaceful breath.

Only minutes before, he had had every intention of waking early to move vehicles from the path of his Jeep then grabbing Robby so they could continue on their journey to New Mexico. Adding anyone else to their duo had definitely not been on the agenda before meeting Tess. Now he was unsure that he could just leave this young girl behind to deal with her misinformed actions all alone.

He smiled to himself. He was collecting people faster in one day than he had in his whole life. At this rate, they would be able to start a football team by the end of the week. Besides, Tess seemed like a pretty good kid. Maybe collecting her would not be such a bad thing. She was, after all, a great shot and Robby seemed to like her quite a bit. Robby was snoring softly next to him. He adjusted his coat over the boy then rolled over. Yawning heavily, he stretched one more time then closed his eyes

"Henry?" Tess's voice sounded shaky and very much how Robby's had sounded when they had first met. She did not wait for him to answer. "Please don't leave me tomorrow."

The decision was made. The duo was officially a trio.

Nineteen

Casey,

   I didn't know how to get ahold of you. My phone isn't working anymore and the landline is dead. Dad got sick so I'm driving him to the hospital just as soon as your brother get home to help me with him. That's where you can find us if you decide to make the drive home. I know you'll find this note if you do. You always go for the fridge first. Don't eat anything inside. The electricity went out late last night.
                        Love,
                                Mom

FRANKIE FELT NUMB. She was sitting near the stump, her bare heels dug deeply into the cold dirt beneath the bed of pine needles. Her eyes were blurred from crying. The old man in overalls lay on the ground only feet way, pale and unmoving. The only real color he had to him was the bright red blood that was now pooled around his white-capped head.

She had known this man her whole life. He had been like family to her and now he was dead. Both her father and Mack tried to comfort her, reminding her that he had been infected and would have been gone soon enough anyway had James not put him out of his misery, but it was poor consolation. Frankie could not shake the possibility that, like she had, Mr. Parker might have recovered.

James had kept his distance. Instead of trying to help with her, he had taken Earl inside to see to his wound. Cora had met them at the screen door, but seeing blood on Earl's shirt, had quickly excused herself to some other part of the house and did not come out for some time after. Mack, shaken, but seemingly no worse for wear, had eventually given up trying to talk to Frankie and taken himself in as well. Her father had stayed with her longer, but even he got up and went back inside when he could tell his words were falling on deaf ears.

Frankie's eyes were fixed on the hole in the side of Mr. Parker's head. Although she had seen several dead bodies over the past few hours, but she had never expected to see one like this. No movie she had seen had prepared her for this. She found herself thinking that the hole looked so small and the damage surprisingly minimal considering the close range at which the gun had been fired. She could not recall if the barrel had made contact with Mr. Parker's head or not.

She shivered violently, scrubbing at the tears that were still streaming down her face. In no time at all, she had lost four people she had loved and, if James and her father were right, their deaths were only the beginning. When they had first said as much, however, she assumed that they meant that people would be dying from the supervirus. She had not considered that the supervirus would not be the only cause of death.

"C'mon," a voice said impatiently from behind her. She looked up over her shoulder and saw Mick standing there with her arms crossed over her chest. "It's cold out. Get up."

Frankie looked back at Mr. Parker's body. It, too, would be cold before long. They would have to bury him. This made her think of Janie, Mr. Parker's daughter and her childhood best friend. They had not spoken in quite some time. Both their lives had become busier and busier with each passing year. She could not recall the last time they had chatted on the phone. In fact, if had been a few years since either had sent so much as a holiday card to the other. Frankie had always regretted how time had pulled them apart and often thought she should bridge the gap, but something had always cropped up and, before she knew it, her intentions were inevitably forgotten. There had always been a 'next time'. Now, it might be too late. Frankie wondered if phones were still working. Someone had to tell Janie about her father.

When Frankie did not move, Mick sighed with annoyance. "Seriously, get up. I know this sucks, but you have to get up." Frankie squeezed her eyes shut. Behind her, she could hear the swish of Mick's jacket as she threw her hands up with exasperation. "Fine. Stay here. Whatever."

Mick's footsteps started to crunch away as she walked over the pine needles. Frankie slowly rose and, still feeling numb, followed her back to the house and up the steps. Inside, she went to the kitchen, tore a sheet of paper towel off its holder, and wiped her face dry with it.

"I had to do it," James said gruffly.

Frankie turned slowly to face him. She could feel anger welling up inside her. "You 'had to do it'? 'Had to'?"

James lifted his hands slightly as if defending himself from the possibility of physical assault. "Yes. I had to. He was going to kill Earl. He probably alre-"

"You don't know that!" Frankie spat at him. "You don't know what he was going to do! He was sick! He wasn't himself!"

"Frankie, he bit Earl."

"So?" she practically shrieked even though she knew perfectly well what the implications of a bite would be. If it was bodily fluid that transferred the supervirus, then it was all but a sure thing that Earl was now infected.

James sighed, backing away to lean against the adjacent counter. "Earl is A-positive."

The words hit Frankie hard even though she had only just met Earl. Regardless, he was now just another person who was going to die. She turned back away from James and stared at the abandoned coffee mugs on the counter. She felt James come up behind her, the warmth of his body spreading to hers. He placed a hand on her shoulder.

"That's not all." Frankie looked up at him, her brow knitting as she waited for him to continue. He took a breath. "We got blood on us, Mack and I. I'm not sure whose blood it was. It might have been Earl's, but there was some blowback from when I..."

"What if it was Earl's?"

"I suppose it'd be a fifty-fifty chance of infection. The transfer from him to us after the bite might have been too soon after exposure. But, if it was from your neighbor..." His voice trailed off again.

James removed his hand and crossed his arms awkwardly before uncrossing them again and walking over to the coffee pot. He picked it up and stared for a moment at its base before replacing the canister and heading back to his chair in the next room. He gave the sleeve of Frankie's shirt a small tug as he passed her and, taking the hint, Frankie followed and sat again in her own seat. It was not, she realized as soon as she sat, the best of ideas. Mr. Parker's body was still out there, lying in direct sight from their position. A lump formed in her throat. She forced her eyes away from the body and focused on James. He appeared to be too wrapped up in his thoughts to notice.

"What's going to happen?" Frankie wanted to curl up and sleep until she woke from this nightmare. She had thought before that it was all too much, but it just kept getting worse.

James looked pensive. "Well, worst case scenario first. The blood was from your infected neighbor and now all three of us are infected. Earl is A-positive and Mack, as far as I remember, is AB-positive."

Frankie swallowed hard. Both blood types were a death sentence. "And you are O-negative like me." James nodded wordlessly. "So, you'll be okay. Right?"

"Maybe."

She looked sharply at him. "What do you mean, 'maybe'?"

James scratched his head thoughtfully. "We don't know for sure that being O-negative is enough to assure survival. Granted, the few tests I ran seem to match the majority of the tests you father conducted years ago so, if we're not missing something, it's looking good. For me, at least. In theory, if I get sick, I'll likely fall into a coma for two to four days before I begin recovering."

262

"And that's your best-case scenario."

"Yeah. Kind of," he agreed, "The worst being death, of course."

Frankie frowned, catching what he had said. "How is it 'kind of' the best-case scenario?"

James was rubbing his hands together and looking a little nervous now. Frankie searched his face. Was he worried he might not make it through the coma? Was it possible that he would not even make it to that stage? He spread his hands out, palms up and stared down at them.

"You were in a coma for four days. Your father told me his was only three."

"Yeah?" Frankie bit her lip. "That's good for you, then, you think? I mean, maybe yours will be shorter."

"Maybe." He rose and went to stand in front of the sliding glass door. Frankie followed his eyes, could tell he was seeing Mr. Parker now and probably having similar thoughts about removing him. "But what if it isn't?"

There was movement behind them. Frankie turned in her seat to look, but James remained still. Mack had wondered in, rubbing his wet hair with a towel. He smiled cheerfully at her and cast a look into the kitchen. "Any more coffee?"

"In the pot," Frankie said pointing to the far corner of the kitchen. "Nice shower?"

She had meant to sound casual, but her voice came out with a squeak. If he noticed, Mack did not show it. With his towel thrown over one shoulder, he searched the cabinets for a mug. "Oh, yeah! Think I got the last of the hot water, though. And your dad seems to be out of Virus-

Be-Gone shampoo. He's got plenty of the minty dandruff stuff. Maybe that'll work."

Mack laughed at his joke, oblivious to the fact that no one was laughing with him. Having found a mug, he poured himself some coffee whistling tunelessly, and took the seat James had vacated. He raised his mug at Frankie in a sort of toast before taking a big gulp.

James turned suddenly and, patting Mack once on the shoulder, walked out of the room without so much as another word. Frankie watched him go then turned to Mack. She did not know what to say to him. Everything that came to mind sounded trite or inappropriate considering what he had just gone through and what was likely going to happen to him. She settled on a simple, "How are you doing?"

"Better now than I'll probably be tomorrow!"

He sounded so nonchalant. Frankie blinked at him, "How can you be so..." She fought for the right word. "So not scared shitless?"

Mack met her eyes His smile was as wide as ever, but his eyes were showing a hint of sadness. "What's the point in wasting what may or may not be the final moments of my life on being scared? If this isn't it, I'd like to be able to look back on this and laugh."

Frankie had to give it to him; he had a point. Where most people would be losing their minds to hysterics, Mack was choosing to be positive. It really was not a bad way to be especially considering that the alternative was freaking out or wallowing in misery.

"I wish I had your outlook."

Mack grinned boyishly at her. "It's not as easy as it looks."

"No," Frankie said softly, "I don't suppose it would be."

Neither spoke again for quite some time. The silence that hung between them was surprisingly comfortable. Frankie, for once, felt no urge to fill it with questions or even mindless banter. Instead, she relaxed against the back of her chair and enjoyed it as best as she could.

When Mick entered the kitchen, neither Frankie nor Mack bothered looking over. In her peripheral vision, she could just make out Mick's long blonde hair whipping around her as she opened and shut cabinets.

"Top left. Over the coffee pot," Mack offered.

One more cabinet opened then closed and a mug clinked against the counter. Frankie heard the coffee pot scrape against its base then what was left of the coffee splash into Mick's mug. She then set the pot down on the countertop instead of back into its place.

"Well, that sucks."

Frankie glanced over at the younger woman, frowning. It was just like Mick to complain about not having enough coffee left to fill her mug instead of just brewing a new pot. To her surprise, Mack responded, "Yeah, that's what I thought."

Frankie shifted her gaze to him. "What?"

Mack jerked his thumb over toward the kitchen. "Power is out.'

"We can get on without power, can't we? It doesn't mean the end of the world." Even as the words spilled out of her mouth, Frankie realized, wincing, that they might be truer than she had intended them to be.

"It means," Mack said with sudden solemnity, "that we can't run an EKG, an IV, or even a ventilator should one be needed."

Frankie looked blankly at him, trying to think of a reason for any of those things in the first place. Mick smiled wryly at her brother. "Unless we find a generator."

"We could borrow the one at the Parker's." Frankie suggested. Then, feeling very much like it was a silly question, she asked, "But why do we need all that?"

Mack looked more serious than ever. "Frankie, you were in a coma for four days. During that time, you were hooked up to machines that helped keep you going and gave you the chance to heal. Your body holds the key to being able to fight back and recover from the Leucocelerosis virus, but it was not a guarantee that you would survive the recovery itself. Your body was in a weakened state and required assistance breathing as well as nourishment. Without a ventilator and an IV, you might not have made it."

His words sounded like one of James's explanations. They seemed far too serious to have come from Mack. She ran them over in her mind, her eyes fixed on the young man. It was beginning to click. If James was infected, he would almost surely fall into a coma. Without the outside assistance of life preserving machinery, his chances of survival, despite having a natural resistance, were distinctly lowered. Without electricity, that outside assistance would be meaningless.

Frankie stood up and looked around the room. Mick and Mack were watching her with interest and she knew it was because her demeanor had gone from mewling and unsure to determined and self-possessed. In this moment, she felt more like herself than she had since before she had fallen ill. She knew what needed to be done.

"Well, then," she said resolutely, "we have a generator to relocate."

"One thing before we get right on that," Mack said, drawing his words out. "Was your neighbor married?"

Frankie raised an eyebrow. "Yeah. Why?"

He pointed one finger at the sliding glass behind Frankie and she started to turn, following where the twins were looking. Mack's next words were all but overpowered by an ear-splitting screech from the other side of the glass.

"Because I'm pretty sure that's his wife and I doubt she's looking to borrow a cup of sugar."

Twenty

Linda,

I am so sorry. I never wanted it to end this way. I never wanted to hurt you. I just can't let myself become one of those things. I can't. I'm sorry to go this way and I'm sorry that you'll probably be the one to find me. Please understand. I didn't have a choice. I love you.

Adam

TESS WAS ALREADY up when Henry rolled stiffly from the foldout bed. They locked eyes then, as quietly as possible so as not to wake Robby, went out the side door of the Toyota Dolphin, Tess leading with her Gatekeeper in hand.

They spent the first five minutes scouting the area, making sure there were no pale people lurking about, before Tess took up a position atop the hood of her RV. She had put all her black colored gear back on and was once again looking like the intimidatingly skilled force she was. Henry turned his attention to the cars. The majority in the way had crashed into each other, but most looked like they should still be operational. Henry, pulled on his gloves and set about the grim task of pulling bloody dead bodies from drivers' seats and piling them out of the way. He was grateful that most of the blood was already dry. Even with gloves, it was an unpleasant job and he was not exactly enthusiastic about getting anyone else's bodily fluids on himself, dead or alive. He then started each vehicle, one after the other, and backed them out, parking them either on the side of the road or in the parking lot of the truck stop.

It went far smoother than he had expected. So far, all the vehicles started and ran fairly easily. Even the ones that had crashed into something were relatively drivable. He was definitely having a run of good luck. Henry had just about finished when Robby's head poked out from behind the side door of the RV. "I'm hungry!"

Henry snorted. It was typical. He really had not expected the boy to offer any help anyway. At Robby's age, Henry, too, had been governed mostly by his stomach. Tess pulled her half mask down to speak. "There's cereal in the kitchen. I'm out of milk, though, so you'll have to eat it dry."

Robby shrugged with indifference and disappeared back into the RV. Tess scanned the area one more time then lowered herself to a seated position on the hood before sliding down to the ground. Henry wiped the sweat from his forehead. The sun had only been up for a little over an hour and it was still chilly out, but hauling dead weight was no easy task.

"You okay?" Tess asked, eyeing him.

"Yeah, sure," Henry cracked his knuckles and peered around the road.

269

He had two more cars to move before the Jeep would have a path clear enough to drive through to the other side of Boykin. The rest of Noel Street looked relatively clear. As far as the RV went, he would have four more vehicles to move so it could get through. He considered for half a beat suggesting they leave it behind, but could see that not going over very well with Tess. Besides, Henry preferred the idea of being able to sleep inside something that locked well than the alternative. His Jeep was not exactly spacious and was nowhere near as secure as the RV. It would be good to have it as an option at least for a while.

"You ever siphon gas?" Henry asked as an afterthought.

Tess shook her head. "Nah, but I can learn."

"Good," Henry replied as he walked away to the next vehicle. "Robby'll teach you how."

Tess pulled down her sunglasses, exaggerating an impressed look toward the RV. "Kid knows how to do that?"

"He watched me yesterday."

She laughed. "He watched you yesterday and he's going to teach me today?"

Henry stopped at the first of the two cars he needed to move from the Jeep's path, turning to face her. "Don't doubt the kid."

"It's not that he's a kid," Tess said. "It's that it's hard to believe that anyone can teach something they've never done themselves."

"Don't doubt the kid," Henry repeated as he hauled a large woman's body from a red sedan and dragged it to the side. He had complete faith in Robby's ability. He had listened to the kid recite enough random information from memory to know that there would be no missed steps. Having both Tess and Robby able to siphon gas would make things that much easier. "You have an extra gas can?"

"Nah, but you can go tank to tank, right?"

"Yes, but it couldn't hurt having extra on us if we get stuck without another vehicle to syphon from. Do me a favor. Look in some of these trunks for extra gas cans just in case."

Tess nodded and began to saunter off. Several feet away, stopped and jutted a finger toward the truck stop. "I need to stock up. Want to join me for a little 'shopping' when you're done?" She waggled her fingers to form quotation marks in the air.

Henry looked over at the truck stop. He did not really care to go wandering into a place so large that might have pale people roaming about, but it would not do to continue up the road without plenty of supplies. Who knew when they might be able to find food or water again?

"Sure. Sounds like a plan."

"NOODLIE-O'S…VIENNA SAUSAGES…peas?"

Henry chuckled as he swept one arm across a shelf of toilet rolls, knocking them into a wheel barrow he'd found in the back of a pickup truck out front. "Any canned food will do, Robby. Who knows? You might be grateful for those peas someday."

There as a sharp smashing sound then the tinkling of glass falling on the linoleum flooring behind them. Henry looked up sharply to see Tess standing on a chair so that she was positioned over the glass counter by the registers. Grinning mischievously at Henry, she tossed the fire extinguisher she had used to break into the display aside and carefully reached inside.

"Sweet," she murmured to herself, pulling out boxes of bullets and dropping them into a container behind the counter. "I love shopping."

Henry looked over the items in his wheelbarrow and, satisfied, steered it around the clerk's body and toward the front door. "Okay, you two. Time to head on out. I don't want to push our luck."

After yesterday's events, Henry had no desire to linger anywhere that was not inside one of their vehicles. Their supply run had been surprisingly uneventful. The only pale people they had seen inside the truck stop had already completely lost the battle with the supervirus. Henry had, when passing the door to the showers, heard a rhythmic banging coming from within like someone was walking over and over into something immovable. He had opted not to investigate nor did he bother telling Tess and Robby. He had little use for a shower room in a truck stop that had no electricity and figured neither of his young companions would be very interested in a cold shower either.

Tess came skipping from behind the counter, a wicker basket hooked over one arm. She looked a bit like a goth Dorothy. Henry was torn between laughing and cringing. The world was certainly becoming as strange as the Land of Oz, but with a sickening twist.

"Robby," Henry called out again, "get a move on!"

"Shake a tail feather!" Tess said in a sing-song voice as sashayed away with her haul toward the entrance.

"I'm…" Robby sounded hesitant, "I'm coming.'

Henry paused, looking back for Robby. He spotted him standing in the wide doorway that led to the restaurant area of the truck stop. The boy was standing deathly still, staring down at something on the floor. A chill ran down Henry's spine. He let go of the wheelbarrow and, pulling out his gun, slowly made his way toward Robby.

As he rounded the display blocking his sight, Henry saw what Robby was looking at. Curled up on the floor in pink princess pajamas was a very small girl. She looked at first to be sleeping, but the ashen pallor or her skin combined with her snow-white hair told another story. Henry stood wordlessly next to Robby, his hand resting heavily on the boy's shoulder. Together, they stared at the tiny child. Their pause and consideration were likely the only memorial this child would ever receive. She was alone which told Henry that she had probably been infected after her parents and wandered off in search of them before ending up here in a doorway in a truck stop.

Henry turned and took a decorative blanket down from a nearby display then draped it over the child's small form. It was nowhere near what she deserved, but Henry knew they could not go around burying every person they found no matter how much the idea of leaving them hurt his heart. He turned and walked away slowly, leaving Robby to pay his respects to this nameless girl.

Tess was waiting at the front door with her wicker basket laden with ammo, knives, and even a couple of guns. Henry had not seen any handguns on display, but decided not to ask. One looked pretty old and he had seen more than a few bodies lying about. Tess had tied a black bandana around the lower half of her face and was scanning the parking lot while whistling just as tunelessly as ever. Henry picked up the handle of the wheelbarrow again as Robby came to join them at the door.

"Ready?" Tess nodded at him and switched up her whistling to something that actually sounded a bit like a spy show theme song. Robby was pushing a laundry cart filled with canned goods and various pastries, chips, and candy. Henry peered in at the junk food then up at Robby.

"I'm a kid," he smirked, reading Henry's expression, "What did you expect me to get?"

"True." Henry laughed, pressing his shoulder against the door to open it. With a little help, he got his wheelbarrow out then held the door for Tess and Robby. They crossed the parking lot quickly, eyes darting around for any signs of motion. They reached the RV without incident and loaded up quickly. Tess was particularly pleased with their haul and celebrated by snatching up one of the pastries before it made it into the RV.

"C'mon," Henry heard Robby say to Tess. "We gotta get this hunk of metal some gas."

"Hey, now!" Tess said with mock insult. She followed him, shoving most of the pastry into her mouth at once.

Henry watched them go. To anyone watching, they looked like a brother and sister enjoying each other's company without a care in the world. Tess ruffled Robby's gingery hair then gave him a playful shove which resulted in Robby leaping on Tess and wrapping his leg around her. The two fell to the ground in a twisted pile, giggling as if they had known each other for years.

Henry smiled. Robby had a way of making people drop their guard. He had done it with him and now he was doing it with Tess. Watching the boy, he had a momentary flash of gratitude for the deadbeat mother whose actions had put this boy in his path. Because of her, Henry had, for the first time in more years than he cared to count, some semblance of a family.

"ON THE ROAD with them," Henry sang, his thumb jutting backwards to the road behind him, "Like a band of gypsies...and sickies on the highway..."

They did look a bit like gypsies, he in his Jeep leading the way and Tess and Robby in the Toyota Dolphin close behind. The past couple of hours of driving had been relatively easy going. They had run into fewer blockages than Henry had expected there would be and only one mob of pale people. All other pale people they had seen had either been confined by vehicles, alive or dead, or far enough away that they did not pose any problems.

Each time they approached a town, a strange hopefulness spread through Henry, filling him up. A few times, he was sure he had spotted a person, a real person and not some infected facsimile trudging mindlessly around. Every time, though, there would be a flash of white hair or the cold gaze of vacant, cloudy eyes. Every time, the hope that had risen in him would sink heavily into the pit of his stomach and churn angrily.

He was not sure why finding people who were truly alive was so important to him. He had never before cared for people, but then, he had never had anyone like Robby and Tess. "We're the best of friends," he sang.

He was glad the kids had made friends so quickly. It was comforting watching them interact. In his rearview, he could just make out Tess bopping behind the wheel of the RV to whatever awful music she had playing in her cd player. Robby was taking full advantage of riding without restrictions like having to remain seated or belted in. The one thing they had not encountered was any more moving vehicles. The chance of a crash seemed highly unlikely. Unrestrained and with a look of pure bliss, Robby was leaning partway out the window with his face tilted up against the wind. He looked a bit like a red setter minus the panting and drool.

"Wishing that the world had kept turning our way." He broke off, the edited verse echoing in his mind. The world was still turning, after a fashion, but he did not know in whose way anymore.

They were approaching a town called Nazareth after which they would only have about an hour's travel before they reached the border of New Mexico. He laughed inwardly at the name of the upcoming town, thinking of the article by that Roybal guy that he and Robby had read and its biblical overtones. He had never been into such things himself, but he could certainly now understand, given the apocalyptic atmosphere the world was currently taking on, how people could hold so much faith in what the Bible had to say.

Something on the side of the road far up ahead moved. Henry leaned forward in his seat and squinted. It was probably just another pale person or, at best, an animal. The closer they got, however, the less he thought it might be the latter. For one, animals do not carry packs and bedrolls. *At least*, he thought wryly, *not of their own volition*. They also did not wear jeans and white undershirts shirts. *Wife Beaters*, Henry thought absently, his eyes struggling to focus on the figure as they fast approached it. It was definitely not an animal nor did it appear to be a pale person. In fact, Henry could now see that it was a man with short cropped black hair.

The man turned at the sound of their engines. He began walking backwards, his right arm stretched out far with his thumb sticking up. He was sweating from the heat of the midday sun and had a healthy-looking tan. As far as Henry could tell from a distance, he was not exhibiting any symptoms of the supervirus whatsoever. The man was not smiling. He was staring almost blankly at them. Not blankly, Henry realized. He was emotionless. Something about that made Henry uncomfortable.

Henry pressed his foot against the gas pedal slightly harder than before, gently and subtly accelerating. Behind him, he could see Tess's confusion as she first slowed, spotting the hitchhiker, then sped back up to match Henry's pace again. The upper half of Robby's body twisted to face the road behind them and the hitchhiker turned to face forward again as they passed.

Henry shivered violently. There had been something about the man that made him nervous, but he could not pinpoint what it was. Looking in the rearview mirror, he could see the man's receding form standing still with his arms raised up from his sides as if to ask "what the hell" as they sped away. As the figure disappeared behind them, doubt niggled at the edge of Henry's mind. He wondered if he should have stopped for the man after all. Aside from Robby and Tess, this man was the only person he had seen who did not appear to be infected. It was looking more and more like this was going to be a real rarity. Then he thought of the man's face, emotionless even after their refusal to stop, and shook off all doubt.

He had done the right thing.

NAZARETH WAS A ghost town. It was the first place they had been that did not seem to have any pale people. He had not seen so much as a body. Every vehicle they passed was completely vacant. After what they had already seen of this new world, the lack of horror was somehow more unnerving.

Having seen a few vehicles close to the beginning of the small town that might serve well for syphoning, Henry signaled to Tess and turned the Jeep around. She followed suit and pulled around a muddy patch into what must have served as a parking lot for the Swift Café.

Henry barked a laugh. The place was anything but swift now if it had ever been in the first place. Looking around it, he was not sure how it had ever passed for being a café in the first place. The place had probably meant a lot to someone and to travelers who found themselves out in the middle of nowhere with nothing for lunch. He was grateful for Tess having suggested the trip to stock up at the truck stop. They would not be like those other travelers. Lunch was in the RV.

Robby swung himself down from the cab of the RV and trotted about the dirt lot scooping up random rocks and chucking them as far as he could. Each time he ran out of rocks, he did a sort of ninja roll toward the nearest one he could see. He was getting himself absolutely covered in dust. It didn't matter. It was not like they had anyone to impress anyway. In any case, the boy deserved to play however messily. After a few hours trapped in a moving vehicle that stopped only twice and briefly at that, it was no big shocker that the boy felt the need to burn off some pent-up energy. Henry could not help but think that Robby was exactly the sort of boy he would have been friends with when he himself was a child.

Tess slid from her own seat in a more serpentine fashion. She had piled her mass of brown curls on top of her head where it was, for the most part, out of the way. She sidled up to Henry with exaggerated steps as though she were in the old west and looking for either a showdown or a saloon. "Howdy, cowboy."

"Howdy."

"This here town ain't big enough for the two of us." She swung her face to one side and made a noise as if she was spitting into a metal spittoon.

Henry grinned. "Good thing we'll be getting right back outta Dodge just as soon as we fuel up.'

Tess nodded, surveying the vehicles parked in front of the café. They had agreed back at the truck stop that the safest thing to do would be to fill up every chance they got. She pointed a finger gun at three of the vehicles and pretended to fire at them one after the other. Rolling his eyes, Henry grabbed the gas can and his syphoning tools from the back of the Jeep and headed for the first of the three. Tess did her cowboy walk back to the RV to collect her own gas can. She had had enough sense to pick up extra tubing at the truck stop in Memphis after Robby had explained how it worked. Two sets of tools were always better than one.

They were not really in much of a hurry, but this would be pretty fast considering they had hardly used any gas since the first fill up. His plan was to fill up the cans now, topping up the tanks, and still have plenty farther down the road should they find themselves in a place without access to more.

He was not much worried about taking long in this town. He did not really think, having seen no signs of life so far, that they were likely to see anyone at all. Still, part of him was anxious to get back on the road. He supposed it was just Robby's excitement that had rubbed off on him, but the more he thought about it, the less he felt like that. There was something niggling on the edge of his mind. Everything about the journey itself had been relatively easy so far. He was beginning to feel anxious about how the rest might be. Like it or not, Henry had a more realistic idea about their trip than did the boy.

For one, he did not think they would find anyone alive in Los Alamos by the time they got there. If they did run into anyone, they were more than likely to be pale people on the verge of death. The supervirus was doing its thing frighteningly fast. Henry could not see how Los Alamos would be much different from the past several towns they had gone through. There were really only three ways they could find it; overrun with pale people, littered with the dead, or silent and ghostly like Nazareth.

He and Tess almost tied for first filled up. She was still learning, but was a quick study. It also did not help that her RV had worse gas mileage than his Jeep. He replaced his gear in the back of the Jeep and went to stand next to Tess. He leaned against the RV and watched her with appreciation. She really was quite impressive. He could count on one hand the number of people he knew who could pick up a new skill as easily as she had. "How old are you anyway, kid?"

Tess rose, straightening as much as she could so that she stood ever so slightly taller. A look of indignation spread across her face. "Who you calling kid, old man?" She poked him in the stomach with the butt of her pocketknife.

Henry made a noise as if the action had knocked the wind from him and staggered back, clutching at his midsection. "Hey! Watch out or I'll shake my walker at you."

Tess snorted. She gathered up her own syphoning gear and packed it carefully away. "I'm twenty-one."

Henry raised an eyebrow. "Twenty," she amended somewhat grudgingly.

When Henry's eyes remained fixed on her, she threw up her hands with a cry of exasperation and walked away. "Fine! Nineteen. But my birthday is, like, a month away."

He laughed loudly, still skeptical, and followed her around the front of the vehicle. "Whatever, ki-,"

He stopped short, almost running into Tess who had frozen near the driver's side of the RV. He put one hand out to steady himself against the hood then looked up over the top of Tess's hair. Robby was standing facing them, terror blanching his face even more than his normal light freckled hue. Behind him stood a man with short-cropped black hair and a travel pack and a bedroll on his back.

Against Robby's gingery hair, he had pressed a shiny silver gun.

Twenty-One

MISSING
HAVE YOU SEEN THIS MAN?
Pawel Nowak
47
BLACK HAIR, BROWN EYES, 6'1
LAST SEEN AT O'HARE INTERNTIONAL AIRPORT
IF YOU HAVE ANY INFORMATION,
PLEASE LEAVE A MESSAGE AT ANY
CHICAGO POLICE STATION

FRANKIE WOULD NOT have recognized Mrs. Parker as being this banshee-like woman who was now slamming herself over and over into the glass of the sliding door had she come across her anywhere else. The supervirus had all but ravaged her once rosy appearance leaving her with a sickly grey pallor and hair steaked heavily with white.

So much of her hair was still the rich brown that she had been dying it for years that Frankie absently wondered if that was why so much of her own hair had remained black. It made sense. The supervirus seemed to affect the melanin in hair. She could not see how it could alter hair that had been dyed. The melanin would have been sucked from every strand of hair, but only the natural strands would be noticeable. Only the strands that were older and dyed, as evidenced by the fact that Mrs. Parker still had quite a lot of brown in her own hair, had any color left.

It was her eyes, though, that struck Frankie most. While her actions appeared wild and involuntary, Mrs. Parker's cloudy blue eyes were focused intently on Frankie. There seemed to be awareness in them. Was it possible that the woman was still conscious and trapped in a body she could not control?

Frankie snapped back to attention quickly as Mrs. Parker's body flew into the glass once more. Her mouth seemed to be permanently open and her screeching was continuous. She had not yet paused for breath. It was a strange, hollow sort of sound that emanated from somewhere deep within her and echoed right through Frankie's bones. She had never in her life heard anything like it. It reminded her of a battle cry or, perhaps, a call to war.

She backed away slowly, her eyes fixed on Mrs. Parker. A hand wrapped around her arm and pulled her firmly away from the window. Mick stepped around her, drawing a handgun from a holster at her side. She was at the door with her hand outstretched to slide it open when Frankie cried out to her.

"What are you doing?"

Mick turned to her, a look of confused frustration on her face. "I'm putting the bitch down."

"That 'bitch'," Frankie yelled, "was like family to me!"

Frankie started forward again only to have Mack leap up and bar her with one arm around her midsection. He spoke softly, but firmly into her ear. "Regardless, she's got to be put down."

"No!"

Frankie knew what Mick intended to do was the only logical option. Still, it did not make it any easier a pill to swallow. Mick rolled her eyes and, gripping the door handle in one hand and her gun in the other, nodded over at her brother who pulled out a gun of his own and aimed it beyond his twin at the bansheelike woman outside.

Frankie looked frantically around the room, looking for an ally, but James was the only other person there and she already knew where he stood on this matter. He already had his own gun out and was circling around the back of the room with it pointed in the direction of the sliding glass door. The expression on his face confirmed for her how he felt about the need to kill Mrs. Parker.

She knew what she was feeling was completely irrational, but she was simply not ready to give up her sense of morality. Somehow, admitting that people like Mrs. Parker were in need of being 'put down' more than anything else meant losing her humanity. It meant, for her, forfeiting the last shreds of innocence she had managed to maintain from childhood. If killing people was now acceptable, then she had stepped into a world she no longer understood. The most frightening thing was that there was no door leading back home.

Frankie turned away, her hands on either side of her face. She closed her eyes and waited. Behind her, despite blocking out as much as she could with her hands, she could hear Mick shoving the sliding glass door open as hard and fast as she could so that it crashed against the stopper loudly. Several shots followed in quick succession and then there was silence. It was briefly broken by a muffled thud. Without looking around, Frankie walked slowing from the room and up the hall. She opened the door to the guest bedroom and disappeared into it.

Mick slid the glass door open again and, slipping through, shook her head with disgust. "Pathetic."

"This isn't for everyone," Mack said softly, replacing his gun in its holster and wiping at a thin layer of sweat that had beaded across his forehead. "Not everyone grew up with guns. And, besides, this woman was her friend."

Mick shrugged disinterestedly. She grabbed the handle of the door and slid it back closed, nudging Mrs. Parker's hand out of its way with her boot. She locked the door and rounded on her brother. "I don't know why you keep defending her. She's annoying as fuck."

"Michaela," James started.

"Don't fucking 'Michaela' me, Jimmy. I'm not a child."

"No," her brother agreed, "But you definitely act like one."

She glared at him and stormed from the room. James and Mack shared a look of understanding. Mick had always been hot tempered. Given time alone, she would eventually calm down and be easier to talk to and reason with. Mack, ever the optimist, hoped she might even warm to Frankie sooner or later. Things were beginning to look bleak. Friends and allies could very well become scarce.

Mack lowered himself into closest chair, suddenly looking very tired. James, noting a distinct change in his young friend, hurried over to Mack and took him by the wrist. As soon as James touched his clammy skin, Mack pulled away. They met eyes, fear springing to Mack's.

"If I'm…" he started, "If you aren't…"

James stared down at his hands for a moment then looked back up at Mack. Without breaking eye contact, he deliberately took hold of the younger man's wrist again and felt for his pulse. Frowning, he released Mack and rose. He offered his hand, speaking quietly, "Let's get you to bed."

FRANKIE HAD NOT given any thought to where James and Mack had taken Earl. Standing now in the guest room, she stared down at the bed closest to the door and watched as Earl's chest rose and fell rapidly. He looked as though he was overheating, but there were no covers to remove and the window had already been opened. A cool breeze drifted through the room causing Frankie to shiver.

"Earl?" His eyes were open and fixed on a spot on the ceiling, but he did not appear to be actually seeing anything. She stepped cautiously closer to the bed. If this were a horror movie, this would be the moment the demon possessing Earl would cause him to levitate over his bed and spew obscenities at her.

"Earl?" She spoke a little louder, her voice shaking. She reached down to touch his arm, but snatched her hand back only inches away. She was not sure why she was so scared of him. It was not as though he could infect her again. He posed no danger to her.

Or did he?

She thought of the Parkers. Both had wandered over the property line and attacked them. Why they had attacked, she did not know. Her brow furrowed as she recalled James explaining about the lab assistant's reaction to the supervirus. He had attacked the other researcher, hadn't he? But why?

Earl groaned loudly, his body spasming and wrenching around suddenly in the bed. Frankie stumbled back at the sudden motion, bracing herself against a vanity so she would not fall. She watched, unable to move, until he became still again, then, steeling herself, pulled the chair from the vanity and walked around between the two beds and placed it down facing him. She lowered herself into it, resolving to stay put through whatever course the supervirus would take. According to what James had said, the outcome would be bleak.

But will he…turn? She thought.

The bedroom door creaked open and James came through as though the very thought of him had summoned him to the room. Close behind him, Mack entered looking as though he were developing the flu.

Frankie half rose, seeing Mack's condition, but he waved her back into her seat. She watched as James helped him onto the second bed then turned to him, whispering sharply, "How is this happening so fast? I thought it took a while, a day at least, before we would see any signs of infection."

"Every immune system, for all that they are constructed the same, is different. For Earl, it likely hit him hard because his skin was broken and blood was drawn. It probably didn't help that he was in remission. For Mack…" he paused, searching for an explanation, "I just don't know."

287

"Remission?" Frankie shook her head slowly. "You mean he survived cancer only to have this happen?"

James did not respond at first. When he did, it was with careful and slightly punctuated words. "He understood the risks."

Frankie looked back at the young man. He was getting himself settled on top of the comforter and looking as though the effort of lying down had zapped his last bit of energy. He was conscious and aware, but was either ignoring their hushed conversation or was just too tired to focus on it. She wondered if he, too, had understood the risks.

"Are they going to turn?" Frankie asked without thinking.

"Turn?" James looked at her with confusion.

"Like…like the Parkers. Are they going to turn like them?"

James sighed, lowering himself onto the end of Mack's bed, facing the window. "They weren't zombies, Frankie. They were alive."

Horror filled her at his words. She had known this, but part of her did not want to fully accept it. Part of her wanted to believe that, once the supervirus took hold and all consciousness was lost, the person who had fallen ill was completely gone. It was far easier to accept ridding the world of zombies than it was to accept that these were real people, alive despite their lack of consciousness, that were being, as Mick had so eloquently put it, 'put down',

"They were alive and you killed them anyway?"

"It's not like that," he said tiredly, "It's not that simple."

288

"Make it simple."

He was silent for a few seconds. Turning slightly to look at Mack, James continued, his voice as calm and measured as before. "They were alive, but they would have died eventually on their own. The human body can only go for about three days without water and three weeks without food. They would have dehydrated and starved sooner rather than later because they have no real consciousness. They can't care for themselves."

"So why didn't we care for them instead? Help them get better?"

James looked away again. "Because they would never get better. It's a wasted effort."

Frankie looked over at Earl and then at Mack. She hardly knew these two and, yet, she wanted to do everything possible to help them get better. She could not comprehend not trying at all. "How can you call anyone's life a wasted effort?"

'I wouldn't have before," he admitted, "Before all this. But I've spent some time reading more of your father's files. Frankie, there's no recovering from this if your blood type is positive. There's no coming back if it's A or B negative, either. It just takes longer and…and what we saw today always happens. I'd put money on the Parkers both having being A or B Negative."

"But they aren't zombies."

"No," he smiled wryly "but that would have made things a little easier to bear."

It was the first time he had let on that killing the Parkers had bothered him.

289

Frankie chewed her lower lip in thought then spoke softly. "It's a kind of mercy."

James was silent for so long that Frankie assumed he had not heard her. Then, rubbing his eyes with one hand, he replied, "Yes, I suppose it is."

From his bed, Earl spasmed again, his groans becoming louder and more prolonged. Both Frankie and James turned their full attention to him. James watched broodingly as a change began to sweep over Mack. His hair was changing rapidly and the color draining from his skin. Frankie was shocked at the rapid progression that was taking place right in front of her.

James rose and went to the side of his bed to look him over. After several moments, he murmured, "I wish it would make this easier."

Frankie did not have to look to know what James was about to do. Instead, she turned the chair around away from Earl's bed to face Mack and leaned over his bed. Mack met her eyes, but did not speak. She tried to smile at him and, when she found she could not, scooped up his hand into hers. She squeezed it gently. On the other side of the room, there was a rustling noise followed by the sound of Earl spasming or jerking around on the bed. Then, with a sudden finality, Earl fell still and the noises stopped.

"James?" Frankie whispered, still unwilling to look at what she knew he had done. Mack turned his head and looked over at the two men beyond Frankie. Tears glistened in his eyes.

"I had to."

"I…" Frankie sighed. "I know."

"I had to," James repeated as though trying to convince himself. "I couldn't let him…"

A heavy silence fell upon the room, the weight of it pressing down on the both. Outside, the day was cool and pleasant. It was so strange to be sitting inside so close to death on a day that felt like it should one should be out celebrating life. James made a strangled noise causing Frankie to turn and look. Earl was motionless on the bed. James, however, was clutching a pillow to his chest and shaking as though sobbing, but there were no tears or cries.

"He asked me to,' James said softly, "I couldn't say no."

IN THE END, it had been Frankie, James, and Mick who had set out up the road in the van. Her father had come out and, after hearing of Earl's death, had suggested that the generator be collected as soon as possible. They had searched both Mr. and Mrs. Parker's bodies, but had not found any truck keys on them. Frankie could distinctly recall where they had always hung their keys. The hope was that this would be where they would be found. Using the Parker's truck would be the best way to transport the generator back to the house although it might just fit inside the van.

Her father had pulled her aside before they had left. His face was shadowed with concern as he waited for the others to walk out the door. Once they were out of earshot, he leaned closer and said, "That was a very quick progression."

She shook her head slowly in response. Dr. Reed's eyebrows rose slightly as his eyes followed hers out the door. James was getting into the van, his face now devoid of the emotion she had seen on it earlier. He looked back at Frankie, nodded sharply once at her, then turned to go back to his study.

"Dad?" Her father paused, leaning heavily on his cane. A thought had leapt into her mind. "If everyone here has been keeping to their homes, how did they get it?"

"The Parkers?"

"Mmm." She watched as he looked down at the floor for several seconds without answering so Frankie pressed. "Did they go out of town?"

His brow furrowed. "No, not that I am aware."

A sinking feeling fell over her and a familiar pit began to form in her stomach. Without another word, she stepped out the front door, and closing it behind her, headed down to the truck. Mick had already claimed the passenger seat in the cab of the van. She gave Frankie a sullen look as she approached, but Frankie ignored it and spoke through the open window at James.

"The Parkers haven't been out of town," she said with meaning, looking pointedly past Mick.

His mouth pursed then he swore under his breath. He ran both hands through his hair and swore again. Mick looked from him to Frankie then back again. "What?"

Frankie slid the side door of the van shut and opened up the passenger door. She got in, pushing Mick farther in as she closed the door behind herself. "Shove up. I'm not hiding back there on my own."

Mick scowled as she moved closer to James and repeated her question with clear irritation. "What?"

James put the van into reverse and backed up and around until he was facing toward the road then put the van in gear and pulled out toward the Parker's farm. Only then did he address Mick's question.

"It means," he rumbled quietly, "that someone gave it to them. Someone here."

"How?" she asked, baffled.

Years ago, before having had children who asked similarly silly questions on a daily basis, Frankie would have rolled her eyes. Barely managing to refrain from doing so now, she answered as patiently as possible. "Well, we weren't here before the outbreak, were we?"

Mick looked confused for a moment longer. Then her mouth rounded into a silent O-shape and she turned to face straight ahead. Frankie turned away, wondering who else had come to town and if the Parkers had been their only victims.

In the van, it did not take long to reach the Parker's farm. It was pretty much exactly as Frankie remembered it. The only real difference was that there were goats and chickens roaming around the front unattended. Mr. Parker would never have allowed that under normal circumstances. Frankie knew that he would have kept on working even after falling ill. Business had been waning for several years and he could not have afforded to take time off from his daily duties. He would have kept going until he absolutely could not continue. He must have been feeding them when the supervirus took him over completely.

The front door was wide open and, aside from the bleating of the goats and the cluck and flap of unnerved chickens the whole place was utterly silent. Frankie had spent many days here as a child and was used to a lot of hustle and bustle. She often jokingly compared Mrs. Parker to the old woman who lived in a shoe, but, in truth, she and Mr. Parker had stopped at six children. Even having grown up around it, six seemed like a frightening number to have. Frankie had found she barely had enough energy for two.

She swallowed hard, shaking off the pain that was creeping back into her heart. She motioned to James with her head that they should go around back the shed and followed closely behind as he took the lead. Mick, gun drawn took the rear.

After a particularly bad winter many years before, the Parkers had purchased a generator. It had, more than once in the years that followed, come in handy when the small mountain town suffered a power outage. It would quite literally be a life saver once relocated to her father's house.

Frankie studied James as he inspected the lock on the shed. He looked to be in peak condition. Earl and Mack had fallen ill with frightening swiftness. She wondered how long, if James was also infected, it would take him to show signs.

Feeling her eyes on him, he glanced over, one eyebrow cocked. "Yes?"

"I was just thinking," she said, looking back quickly at Mick. "How they got sick so fast."

James took a breath, stepping back from the lock. "Like I said, not all immune systems are created equal. I, for example, rarely got sick as a kid."

"Did Mack?"

"Not really," he frowned. "There's just so much we still don't know and I'm afraid we're running out of time."

"So, you might still be infected?"

He shrugged, turning his attention to Mick who was pacing back and forth irritably around back of the house. "Hey, Mick, any ideas on how to get this lock off?"

The young woman stopped her pacing and stalked toward them with purpose. Frankie's eyes were still on the lock. A thought had sprung to her mind. It was a memory that seemed to appear from nowhere, inspired by nothing in particular. They had come to the Parker's to collect a generator when, surely, it must have been one of the things her father had collected when stocking his bunker. She had, until now, completely forgotten about the bunker. She wondered why her father had not mentioned it. She and James stepped back to either side of the shed to give Mick room to work, the subject of the bunker just reaching Frankie's tongue. Then, without warning, Mick raised her gun and, pointing right at the lock, fired.

The shot rang out, echoing against the house and through the trees. The lock, shattered, fell uselessly to the ground. James, his face a mixture of surprise and anger, looked from Mick to the lock and then back again. "What the fuck, Michaela?"

"What?" she demanded. "It's off, isn't it? Let's just get in there and get the fu-"

Her words were drowned out by a high-pitched shrieking directly behind James. He spun around as a woman flung herself at him, fingers stretched into sharp-looking claws. Frankie, taken by surprise by the sudden noise and motion, stumbled backwards and landed hard on the cold, hard ground while Mick stood frozen to the spot in shock, her gun dangling at her side.

"Mick!"

The pale woman had her fingers wrapped tightly around James's neck, her mouth still stretched in a macabre fashion. The noise that came from her was continuous and even more penetrating that Mrs. Parker's had been. James grabbed at the woman, attempting to shove her away.

"Mick!" James slammed his fist into the side of the pale woman's head causing it to twist at an odd angle before snapping back into place. The blow did not seem to have had much of an effect, if any, on the pale woman. It had not so much as interrupted her screeching.

Mick blinked hard and, shaking, raised her gun and took aim, but she had no real shot. James and the pale woman were moving so much that any shot would be just as likely to hit James as it would be to hit the woman. Frankie, still stunned, stared open-mouthed at James and the pale woman. She was far more affected by the supervirus than either Mr. or Mrs. Parker. Her hair was pure white and her eyes were so clouded that no natural color showed whatsoever. Her skin was probably the most changed. Instead of the ashen grey Frankie had seen before, this woman's skin was almost as white as her hair. As she stared in horror, Frankie realized that there was something very familiar about this pale woman.

Frankie scrambled to her feet, circling around the shed toward Mick. She kept her eyes on the pale woman, recognition slowly coming to her. "Janie?"

The pale woman did not respond to the name, but Frankie knew it was her. She was drastically changed by the supervirus, but this was her friend. This was Janie. She must have come home to her parents when she had first fallen ill. She had not married and had not had children so she would not have had anyone else to go to for care except her parents.

James punched again at Janie's head, but she would not release her grip. Droplets of blood were springing up on his neck where her nails were piercing his flesh and he was beginning to gasp for air. Frankie turned to Mick, her eyes flashing to the gun the young women still held.

"Mick!" Frankie grabbed Mick's free arm and shook her. "Mick! You have to shoot her!"

With a final burst of energy, James managed to throw Janie off himself. He stumbled away, panting, his hands up at his neck. Janie had her arms at her side. Her head slowly turned from James to Mick and Frankie, her clouded eyes focusing on the two women. She raised her arms and, with her clawed hands outstretched, she shrieked louder than before. Then, with alarming speed, she ran directly at Frankie.

Twenty-Two

I love yu daddy cat doge mommy love cris

Christopher Nielsen, 4 Years Old
(Drawing found next to body in home)

ROBBY'S FACE WAS so shockingly pale that, had there not been a man with a gun standing directly behind him, Henry would have thought that the boy had suddenly fallen ill with the supervirus. He was visibly shaking and staring at Henry, his eyes pleading for help. Henry tore his eyes from the boy's face and met the gaze of the man who was holding his gun against Robby's gingery head.

The man was smiling. It was almost a genial smile like one he might have reserved for his closest friends, but there was a smarminess behind it. His eyes did not reflect the smile in the slightest. They were guarded and intense. Nothing about him matched the expressionlessness he had exhibited when they had passed him on the highway.

"Well, hello there!" The man drew out the words with exaggerated casualness. Still smiling, he nodded in Henry's direction, but the brunt of his attention was focused on Tess. He tipped an imaginary hat at her and winked. "Ma'am".

"Let him go," Henry said lowly, his eyes fixed on the stranger. He covertly reached for his own gun, hoping that the man's attention would remain on Tess.

"Ah, ah, ah!" The stranger cocked his head, his eyes shooting back to Henry. He waggled one finger in the air like a parent chastising their child. "You shouldn't do that unless you want to see how quick a shot I am. And I don't have to be very fast at all really. I mean, the kid is already kinda lined up. It wouldn't be much of a challenge now, would it? Hell, I could probably put a bullet through the kid's head and one in each of yours before you could even touch your piece."

Henry froze. He was in no position to test this man. "Let him go."

"You've said that," the man turned to Tess. "Is he always so verbose?"

"What do you want?" Tess, as far as Henry could tell, was unarmed. At least, she did not have her Gatekeeper and he could not see any other weapon on her. The lack of pale people had caused them to let their guard down.

The man tapped his chin in mock thought. Then, raising one finger into the air as though an idea had just sprung to mind, he replied, "Well, your RV would be a good start."

"Fine," Tess replied without hesitation. Her voice was firm and steady, "You can have the RV. Keys are in the ignition. Just let the kid go."

Henry watched Tess. She had only known Robby for a day and she was willing to give everything up she owned for him. The love she was showing for the boy shook him to his core. In truth, he felt it as well. He could not think of a single thing he would not give up to ensure the boy's safety.

The man was nodding slowly, his lips pursed. His eyes were fixed on Tess's. "And what if there's something else I want?"

She did not respond right away. She was glaring at the man, hatred plain on her small face. "And what would that be?"

The man broke into a hearty laugh. The sound of it made Robby jump forward. The man reached out and, grabbing the boy by the back of his shirt, hauled him back into place. His eyes never once left Tess's.

"That your daddy?" he asked, nodding in Henry's direction.

"What do you want?" Tess repeated, ignoring the question.

The man raised his eyebrows. "Not your daddy, then. Maybe he's your sugar daddy." His eyes slowly shifted toward Henry. "Is that what you are, friend?"

Henry's eyes narrowed. "Just take what you want and let the boy go."

The man looked down at Robby and ruffled his coppery hair in a playful manner. Tess looked like she wanted to rip the man's throat out with her teeth. Henry could not help but share the sentiment. He wanted the man's hands off Robby. "Maybe he's your daddy, huh?"

"Yes!" the boy cried out. Tears were streaming down his face freely now. "Please let me go, mister. I just want my dad!"

Henry's heart stung. He had never wanted children and now, whether it was desperation or honest desire, a child wanted him. There had to be a way out of this. Without any better ideas, he pulled out the Jeep keys that were dangling from his pocket and chucked them at the man's feet. They landed in the dirt and slid then came to a stop against his booted foot. "Take the Jeep. I'll hitch it to the RV."

The man laughed again. "That piece of crap? What would I want with that? Besides, I don't think that RV could take pulling a load. It looks kinda old, but it will do for now." He kicked the jeep keys to the side, still chuckling.

"What do you want?" Tess asked through gritted teeth, each word punctuated.

"Maybe you are his kid," the man said thoughtfully, "You're verbose as well!"

"Enough!" Tess exploded, risking a step forward. "Just tell us what you want and let Robby go!"

"Verbose *and* obtuse!" He tutted and shook his head. "Those aren't the most flattering qualities, little Miss. Good thing you more than make up for it."

Tess cringed visibly as the man's eyes slid up and down her body. He noticed and pouted mockingly at her. "Aw, c'mon. I'm not *that* bad, am I?"

She did not respond. He was waiting for her to answer, feigning a lack of patience through a series of eyebrow raises and lip twisting. On anyone else, it might have been comical. On this particular man, however, it was nothing short of daunting. Henry was not sure if this man was entirely in control of his sanity. "She's not going with you."

The man stopped pulling faces to address Henry, but did not get the chance.

"Yes, I am."

Both the man and Henry looked at her, one with obvious surprise and the other with horror. The surprise swiftly melted from the man's face and was replaced by a smarmy smile. He shifted his weight from one foot to the other, looking very pleased with himself as though he had just secured a major business contract. In a sense, he had.

"Well, now! Verbose and obtuse, but at least you have your looks and some measure of common sense." He shot a look over at Henry. "You. Why don't you go stand right over there were you can't cause trouble? I'll be with you in a minute."

Henry grudgingly backed away, circling around to where the man had indicated. It gave him a clear view of the door to the RV. It also put him farther away and gave the stranger a clear view of him. Henry watched as the man gestured at Tess with his gun. "Go on, girl. Lead the way. You can drive. I'm powerful hungry and I'll bet my new camper comes fully loaded."

Tess, struggling to mask her emotions, spun on her heel and headed for the RV. She cast a furtive glance of desperation at Henry. She mouthed something at him that he thought might have been "don't move", but he could not be sure. He had absolutely no idea what to do. The man shoved Robby forward, shifting his gun so that he could walk with it still pointed at the boy. His attention was split between Robby as he stumbled forward, Henry, and the unintentional sway of Tess's hips as she walked away.

"I'd stay right where I was, if I was you," he called over to Henry. "Remember, I'm a crack shot."

Tess opened up the RV and hurried inside without a backwards glance. At the step up to the RV, the man swiveled Robby's body then shrugged his pack off his back, belatedly realizing that it was far too large to get through the doorway while still on. He would have to release the boy altogether to manage the task. He cast a look over at Henry who had not budged an inch and, deciding he was no threat at all, tried to shift the pack one-armed while still holding his gun.

As soon as the man's back turned, Henry made the decision to act. He knew it was a risky move, but he was banking on the man being more bark than bite. After all, if he was half as good a shot as he claimed to be, why had he simply not shot both Henry and Robby instead of bothering with all that back and forth?

Henry whipped out his gun and pointed it at the man's back just as his foot landed on the first step up to the side door of the RV. Hearing the movement, the man twisted around, his arm swinging awkwardly to aim at Henry. Robby took advantage of the distraction and sprinted away from the door, heading to the back of the RV.

A shot rang out. It was immediately followed by two more, both from different guns. The man stumbled forward, a look of surprise frozen on his face. There was a wound near his shoulder from where Henry's bullet had struck him, but that was not the first shot nor was it the one that stopped him. A drop of blood slid down his forehead and fell onto the ground at his feet. Then, as if in slow motion, the man followed it, dropping first to his knees then falling face first into the dirt.

Henry gasped. He had not realized that he had been holding his breath. Tess emerged from the RV clutching her Gatekeeper. She looked down at the man's corpse and spat at it. "Not as good a shot as me, bitch."

"Tess!" Henry dashed forward. "Jesus!"

She leapt down and allowed him to envelop her with his arms. He squeezed her tightly, pressing her head against his chest. His heart was still racing, but she seemed surprisingly calm. She had formulated a plan and carried it out flawlessly while he had been busy mentally fumbling for even a semblance of a solution. He had never been more impressed or proud of a person in his entire life. "Yeah," she whispered, "Me, too."

Henry was trying not to shake. He had come so close to losing both her and Robby. Suddenly remembering the boy, he released Tess and frantically scanned the area around the RV. "Robby! Where is Robby?"

Tess bolted in the direction she had seen him go and came skidding to a halt at the rear of the RV. Henry followed, the man's corpse completely forgotten.

"No..." Tess was shaking her head over and over. "No, no, no!"

Henry came to a stop next to her and followed her eyes. There in the dirt looking impossibly small and sickeningly motionless was Robby. A red flower had spread over the back of his shirt and was pooling in the dirt around him.

Twenty-Three

To whoever finds this. I am looking for my kids.
They are all blond w/blue eyes. Jonny is 13, Jean
is 11, Jenny is 7, and Joey is 6. They were living
with my mom on the north side of town. If you
see them please bring them to Freddy's stop and
shop. I'll be checking there every day at noon.
Please help!
Jessica Sanderson

**Jessica Sanderson, Note found posted to a
telephone pole**

FRANKIE WOULD NEVER have touted herself as an
exceptionally brave person. She was able to admit that her
specific skillset did not include the ability to come up with
ideas or answers to problems with any real swiftness.
Thankfully, the career she had chosen did not require much
speed. Most of what she used to do took weeks, sometimes
months, to plan before any real action was taken.

None of that mattered now.

What mattered was that she was neither an exceptionally brave person nor was she a fast problem solver and these two flaws would be the cause of her death. It was death that now raced toward her. She found herself unable to move. She could not tear her eyes away from Janie's beautifully manicured and pink polished fingernails tipped with blood and reaching for her.

"Frankie!"

James's voice jolted Frankie back. She felt as if she were going to throw up. At least she could move again. She turned to Mick for help, but saw that the young woman no longer had her weapon raised. It was back at her side and there was an odd expression creeping onto her face. Desperate, Frankie reached for the closest thing to her. She lurched to the side and ripped the gun from Mick's hand then shoved the younger woman as hard as she could. Mick, unprepared, fell gracelessly and landed roughly on her side.

The grip felt warm in Frankie's hand and far heavier than she would have thought, but she had no time to think about it. She lifted the gun up and pointed it shakily at Janie. Janie's eyes were devoid of all their natural color. They were also missing Janie herself. She was completely unaware of the gun that was aimed at her as she raced toward Frankie.

Frankie squeezed her eyes closed and the trigger of the gun at the same time. The bang was deafening. She found herself staggering backwards and willed herself to reopen her eyes. Janie had stopped short as if she had been punched in the torso and was wobbling in place. On the left side of her chest was a bullet hole out of which an unexpectedly small amount of blood was dripping. Frankie found herself marveling that, with as changed as Janie was, her blood was as red as anyone else's. She barked a laugh.

Had she really thought the color would have been sucked from that as well?

Janie suddenly crumpled to the ground, her body heaving slightly and her arms flailing limply. Frankie took a few steps forward, her eyes on Janie. She looked like anyone else might were they dying from a gunshot wound. This was another thing she had not expected. All three of the Parker's had behaved so very much like zombies that she had unconsciously begun to think of them as such.

Yet, here was Janie; pale, white-haired, and dying a human's death.

Dry-eyed and unable to stop the senseless giggles that were bubbling over her lips, Frankie turned and walked away. She paused next to Mick and dropped the gun at her feet then walked on past James. His eyes followed her, but he remained where he was. He did not know what to make of her reaction and was still stunned by what had happened.

Frankie needed to get away.

She wandered into the trees that lined this side of the property and stopped at the tire swing she and Janie had used as children. She had not been able to save Mr. and Mrs. Parker and her hand had been forced when dealing with Janie. She knew she had had no other viable option. Still, it was not quite guilt she was feeling. The whole ordeal had taken mere seconds.

To Frankie, everything had moved far more slowly. She could not understand how she had managed to react as quickly as she had. Then there was Mick. The look on the younger woman's face when Janie had charged at Frankie was not one of fear or concern. She could not place exactly what it had been.

"Frankie?"

Frankie looked over her shoulder and, seeing Mick, sighed. She sat on the swing and clutched at the rusted chains Mr. Parker had used to hang it. She had nothing to say to Mick. She had nothing right now to say to anyone. Now that she had stopped giggling, she felt numb.

"Frankie," Mick was shuffling her feet, "Frankie, I'm sorry. That should have been me doing that, not you. I...I don't know what happened."

Frankie did not know what to say. She honestly was not sure what had happened back there herself. Only seconds had passed from the moment Janie had attacked her to the moment she had fallen. Yet, to Frankie, it seemed to have happened so much slower. She had never even fired a gun before. The closest she had ever been to one was when she was standing behind a police officer in line at the checkout in a grocery store and his had been securely strapped into its holster. She turned her head away from Mick making it clear that she had no interest in talking.

There was a soft scraping noise from where Mick stood then James's voice echoed through the trees calling for her. Something plopped to the ground followed by the sound of Mick's foot slicing through the leaves. Her boot found the just fallen pinecone and sent it flying. She turned and went back to the clearing without another word. Frankie looked around and watched her go, still feeling curiously emotionless.

The side of the shed was visible from where she sat, but she lost sight of Mick as the young woman rounded it. She could not see James or, thankfully, Janie's body. That was the last thing she wanted to see or think about. Instead, she tilted her head away toward the front of the house and the road and, pushing against the ground, began to swing.

"YOU HAVE BLOOD on you," James said.

Frankie had been swinging fast for several minutes and had only just tucked her legs against the tire to slow down. She had always loved the way it felt when the wind whipped through her hair. When she was younger, she had thought that, if she just swung hard enough, she would be able to touch the high branches with her toes. She knew now that, no matter how hard she tried, that would be an impossible feat.

She looked down at herself. Sure enough, there where splatters of blood on her shirt. She dropped her feet and dragged herself to a complete stop, staring down at the dried red marks. "Oh."

"You probably saved her life, you know," he said, reaching out to pull her up from the swing.

She furrowed her brow then said, "Oh. You mean Mick."

He nodded, still holding her hand. "She can't afford to get any blood on her. The risk of infection is far too high and, as you know…"

"Her blood type," Frankie murmured.

"Yes. I told her she likely had her life to thank you for."

That explains the lame apology, Frankie thought.

James gave her hand a little tug and started back toward the shed. "We found the generator. It isn't very big and has wheels so I just put it into the van myself. Mick and I thought we'd go ahead and get supplies from the farmhouse if that's okay with you."

There was a small, round rock on the ground where Mick had been standing. Frankie looked from it to James, distracted by his words. "Why wouldn't it be okay with me?"

"They were your friends."

"Oh." They walked back into the clearing. Mick was facing away from them with her hands on her hips. Janie's body was nowhere in sight. "Well, they aren't going to be using their things."

James sighed softly, nodding once. Mick, hearing their approach, turned. Her eyes fell immediately to their clasped hands and her face pinched immediately. Without speaking, she turned again and all but stomped to the front of the house. James and Frankie followed and, at the steps, he released her hand. Frankie had quite forgotten that he had been leading her by it. His touch was gentle and familiar. It was comfortable.

The inside of the Parker's house had not changed much since the last time she had seen it. It was chilly from the door having been left wide open, but cozy nevertheless. Mrs. Parker had been fond of shades of blue and cream and had decorated almost every front room similarly.

They found Mick in the kitchen. This had been Frankie's favorite room. She had spent a lot of time here with Janie and her sisters learning from Mrs. Parker how to make pies and cookies. Her own mother had not been much of a baker. Frankie leaned against the island in the middle of the room and inhaled. It still smelled sweet and fresh like Mrs. Parker had been baking recently. She resisted the urge to check the oven.

Mick had busied herself piling canned goods and non-perishable items on the far side of the island. She looked up at Frankie with her typical glower and grudgingly asked, "Couldn't find the truck keys. We'll have to make everything fit into the van. Anything to transport this stuff in?"

"Oh. Yeah." Frankie moved around the island and reached under the kitchen sink. She took out a bunch of reusable grocery bags that had been neatly folded into a larger bag. "These do?"

Mick grunted and took them from her. Frankie, waking up a little mentally, took back a bag and began loading it with items from the counter. James had disappeared up the hall toward the back rooms. The woman worked together in silence before Frankie cleared her throat and paused.

"You know," she began quietly, "One of Janie's older sisters was quite the fashionista. Judith…She left a lot of her own creations here when she went off to college. Never did come back for them after she married."

Mick cast her a glance, "So?"

"You're about her size. Her size back then, that is."

"And?"

Frankie sighed heavily. "You should check them out. I noticed that you didn't bring any clothes with you. I'll probably see if there's anything I can wear in one of the other rooms before we leave. Anyway. Third door down the hall on the left. I'll finish up here."

Mick eyed her suspiciously, but put down the can she had picked up. "Yeah, okay," she said as she moved toward the kitchen door. "Third door on the left?"

Frankie nodded, turning her full attention to the task at hand. She knew this kitchen far better than Mick and would be able to pack up anything useful in no time at all.

Her motive for sending Mick to look at the clothes had not been entirely selfless. It was true enough that neither of them had any spare clothing, but what Frankie wanted more than anything else at the moment was just a little bit more time to herself and her thoughts. She did not have it for long. She had only managed to pack two more of the bags when James came wandering in with his arms full of random items including towels, toilet paper, and tooth paste. He dumped everything on the counter and started to pack it all into bags. Frankie watched for a moment before continuing with her own task.

"How are you holding up?"

Frankie looked up quickly, startled by his sudden question. "Fine," she said, "Good."

He was watching her carefully, his eyes searching her every movement. "Good?"

"I'm great. Really."

"You're not," He pushed aside the bag he'd been working on and went around the island to her. "You've lost a lot of people in a very short period of time. It's okay not to be okay."

"I'm fine," she insisted, avoiding his eyes. She was not fine, but there would be plenty of time later to grieve. There was too much to do and breaking down yet again before it was all done would only needlessly slow them down.

He wrapped an arm around her shoulder and gave her a squeeze. "Listen. I've been your dad's friend for a while now and I know how to read him. You are a lot like him and he's a terrible liar."

"He convinced you that you had stolen those files."

312

"True," he laughed. "But I can still tell you aren't okay."

Frankie shoved another full bag to the far side of the island and rubbed her temples with her fingers. He was right. She was far from fine. After losing her husband and children, she had thought that nothing could hurt her so monumentally ever again. Watching the Parkers die had almost been too much. Killing Janie had just about driven her over the edge. She had felt it coming and had pushed back the emotion as hard and as far as she could. Having too much to get done was only an excuse. What she was really afraid of was that, if she let herself feel again, grief would overwhelm her and swallow her up.

"You're right," she heard herself admit. "I'm not okay."

James pulled her in toward himself with the arm he had wrapped about her shoulder. She did not stop him. The warmth from his body was comforting. She spoke softly against his chest, "But I can't allow myself to deal with it right now. I just can't."

"I get it. I understand."

Frankie closed her eyes, her hands finding their own way up to hug James back. Both she and James had lost people. It felt good to have companionship even if neither was fully ready to deal with their own grief yet. It made sense to Frankie. Deep down, she knew these would not be the only losses they would experience. They could ill afford to break down every time.

Someone cleared their throat.

James released Frankie who stepped back and turned toward the entrance to the kitchen. Mick stood in the doorway in a sleek, black shirt with silver trim and tight

313

jeans altered at the bottom to flare for boots. The very boots Frankie would remember Janie's sister wearing every time she thought of her were now on Mick's feet. Her long blonde hair had been swept up and twisted into a neat, fat bun on the top of her head.

Mick was somehow managing to look more sullen than ever. Her eyes were moving back and forth between Frankie and James. Her lips were twitching angrily and her hands were balled into white-knuckled fists. With a surprisingly even voice, she asked, "Ready to go?"

Frankie glanced over at the bags she had packed. "Yeah, in a minute. I'm going to go get some clothes for myself. You look great, by the way." She picked up an extra bag and squeezed by Mick who didn't budge an inch for Frankie. She headed down the hall, peeking into rooms as she went. From behind her, she heard James complimenting the young woman and Mick grunting in response.

It was in Janie's old room that she found boxes that contained Mrs. Parker's old clothes. She would look a little outdated, but she supposed it really did not matter. Clean clothes were clean clothes and she was in no position to be picky. It was a shame, though, that she was not as tall and slim as Mick. She had not been exaggerating about Janie's younger sister's sense of style. If she were to be honest, she was a little envious that she, too, could not pick from the closet that had prettier and more stylish options. While she had always been fairly slender in her youth, she had never been as slim as any of the Parker sisters. After two children, her hips would forever be far too wide for either of their old clothes.

These, she thought as she pulled a pair of what she and her friends had once jokingly called mom jeans from the box, *will have to do.*

When her bag was full, she went back through to the kitchen and found that everything had already been cleared out so she headed for the front. James and Mick were loading the last of the bags into the van as she walked out. She shut the door behind herself thinking how pointless the action probably was and rejoined the others. James smiled at her as she approached, but Mick was right back to ignoring her.

"You feeling okay?"

James shrugged once. "I'm well enough."

She eyed the puncture marks around his neck and, spotting a long scratch that ran from his ear down to his chin that she had not noticed before, asked, "Are you sure about that?"

He chuckled and cast her a reassuring look that did anything but.

Once they were loaded, all three of them piled back into the front of the van again. As before, Mick was sure to secure her spot next to James. Frankie could not help but wonder what sort of relationship Mick had fashioned in her mind for herself and James. He was as good as an uncle to her and did not appear to be romantically or even just physically interested in the girl whatsoever. She was almost twenty years his junior which, for many men, might have been a draw. It was clearly not for James. If either was the sort of relationship Mick was imagining, Frankie could not see how she posed a threat. She had just lost her entire family which happened to include a husband she had loved very much. At the moment, while grateful for the comfort she had so far received from a few of the people she had met recently, she was not in the slightest interested in a romantic attachment.

315

As they pulled out onto the road back to her father's house, Frankie considered James's actions toward her. He had been extremely understanding and comforting right from the beginning. Perhaps this was the cause of Mick's apparent jealousy, but then, her own brother had been just as kind to Frankie and Mick had not inserted herself between them as she had with James.

She leaned against the window and stared out into the trees as they sped by. James had little regard for speed limits. Considering that they had not seen a single vehicle being driven in this town so far, it seemed to be yet another thing that no longer mattered quite as much as it did before the supervirus was released. Frankie, having grown up here, would still have driven with more caution. There was a lot of wild life in this area and you never knew when a deer or rabbit would spring out from behind the trees onto the road.

Something in the trees moved, catching her attention. She craned her neck to look back as they drove on, but she could not see anything move again. It was most likely just a deer or a figment of her imagination. She had, after all, been thinking about what might be out there. Either way, there would be no telling now. She straightened back up and noticed James watching her.

"What's wrong?"

Frankie waved her hand. "Nothing. Just thought I saw something in the trees."

"A bear?"

"Maybe." She had not thought of that, but it had not seemed large enough. It was the right time of year. Bears would be coming down the mountain to raid the trash bins of the people who had encroached more and more upon their territory over the years. Bears knocking over bins had

316

been a long-standing issue here and resulted in various types bear-proofing being adopted. Her own father had tried without success using bungee cords to strap down the lids until trash pickup day. He had assumed he had not attached the cord tightly enough when he found the bin tipped over and open in the morning. It had not been fun cleaning up the trash that was strewn across the front yard. However, it became apparent after several attempts that these bears were far smarter than the average person.

"Probably one of those massive crows," James mused. "They're everywhere!"

"Yeah," Frankie agreed, but whatever she had seen seemed bigger than a crow.

"Seriously, what are they eating that makes them so huge?"

Frankie shrugged, "Probably trash. They're as bad as the bears. Worse, maybe."

Her father's house was now visible. Frankie leaned forward in her seat, bracing herself against the dash. There was another vehicle parked alongside her father's black sedan. It was silver and sleek, but dusty and the bottom was lined with mud as though it had been driven in less favorable conditions. When they pulled in and got out of the van, she could hear it was making soft ticking noises. Whoever had been driving this car had arrived only moments before.

Concerned, Frankie hurried to the front door where she was greeted by Cora. The woman seemed a little more at ease as she ushered Frankie through the door. Frankie, clutching her bag of clothes, peered into the living room and found it empty. "Who's here?"

Cora dismissed her question with a wave of her hand and called out to James. "Hurry up! It's almost as cold in here as it is out there. I started a fire, but it's not enough."

"Sure thing, ma'am," James heaved the generator out of the van, "I'll get this set up right away."

Frankie, agitated, repeated the question. "Cora, who's here?" In response, Cora turned on her heel and disappeared back into the house without another word. Frankie threw up her hands and turned back to the van where James, oblivious of the interaction, was struggling with the generator.

Remembering all the bags of supplies in the van, Frankie dropped her own bag onto a chair in the foyer and went back out to help. Mick, her arms laden, shoved past Frankie without even looking at her. Frankie rolled her eyes and grabbed a couple of bags. *It going to be a long day*, she thought wearily as she headed quickly inside, *if Mick keeps up this childish nonsense.*

FRANKIE STOOD OUTSIDE the room Mack was in with her hand up ready to knock. It was not so much that she did not want to disturb him as it was her own fears that gave her pause. When she had left for the Parker's, Mack had been showing signs of flu. They had cropped up so suddenly and right after his interaction with Mr. Parker that there was little doubt he had something far more serious than the flu. She was afraid, remembering Earl's relatively fast decline, that she would not find the young man she remembered behind this door.

Bracing herself, she knocked gently and waited. At first, she was met with silence. Then she heard bedclothes rustling and a quiet voice call out for her to go in. She took a breath and opened the door, peering behind it as she went in. Mack was propped up in bed looking distinctly paler than he had been before. His skin was glistening with sweat despite the room being quite cold. She crossed immediately to the window and slid it shut.

"That's better."

Mack smiled weakly at her. She returned his smile, grateful that he was still aware enough to recognize her. She lowered herself into the chair she had used before and took Mack's hand. He squeezed her fingers and closed his eyes before she could get a good look at them.

"Has Cora been in?"

If she had not been looking directly at Mack, she would have missed the barely perceptible shake of his head. She looked around for a glass of water and frowned when she did not find one. It did not look as though anyone had been in to check on him since they had left some hours before.

"Has anyone?"

"No," he whispered, "I'm glad you're here."

"Me, too." Frankie smiled down at him with feigned happiness. He was dying. No one should have to go through that alone and the last thing he would want to see upon opening his eyes again was her getting weepy over him. She patted his hand. "I'll just go get you some water. I'll be right back."

Eyes still closed, Mack smiled weakly. Frankie released his hand and quietly slipped from the room. She was halfway down the hall when she met Cora coming out of one of the rooms. Frankie reached out and gently touched the other woman's shoulder. Cora recoiled noticeably from Frankie's touch. It made sense that the woman would be afraid of Mack, but Frankie was no longer contagious.

With great effort, she managed not to roll her eyes at the older woman. "Has no one been in to see Mack?"

She knew the answer, but did not know how to ask her real question. She would have liked to believe that there was an innocent reason no one had gone into that room while they were gone, but something told her that she did not really want to know the answer.

Cora wrinkled her nose. "No, of course not!"

"Of course not?" Frankie repeated. "The man is sick. He needs someone to take care of him."

"Well, it won't be me." The older woman sniffed and continued hurriedly away to the study leaving Frankie standing alone in the dim hallway.

She shook her head. Fear always seemed to trump compassion. She made her way to the kitchen and poured a glass of water then headed back to Mack's room. The front door opened as she passed through the foyer and James stepped in rubbing his hands together briskly. He looked tired, but healthy otherwise.

"Getting cold out there."

"It's pretty cold in here already," Frankie muttered, looking up the hall toward the study.

"The genny is up and running so that should be fixed soon."

She smiled wryly. "I wish that's what I meant." He looked at her with interest, but she did not feel like elaborating. Instead, she pointed up the hall with her chin. "I'm on my way back to see Mack. Care to join?"

He nodded immediately. "Of course."

There had been no hesitation either time those words had been spoken. She marveled at how people could respond so differently to the same need. Both people likely had the fear of infection, but that would have been the last thing on James's mind, the first thing being Mack.

At Mack's door, Frankie tapped gently and listened. When no response came, she knocked harder, but again heard nothing. Worried, she opened the door and went in. Mack was lying very still. He appeared even paler than before and his blonde hair was beginning to streak with white. She rushed to his side and felt for a pulse. It was there, but extremely weak.

James had followed close behind her and was leaning over Mack, listening and watching carefully. He sighed with relief. "He's still breathing."

"But not for long." She had not meant it to sound harsh, but it was the truth and both she and James knew it. "Maybe you should get Mick in here."

James looked confused for a second then, realizing why, rose and left the room. Frankie slid her hand around Mack's and sat quietly. She was surprised at how much her heart hurt for this young man she barely knew. It was a separate pain from the constant ache she had been feeling since hearing of the deaths of her family members. It was sharp and it was fresh. The intensity of it was bordering on overwhelming. She had not been able to sit with her children or husband as they died. At least she would be able to do this for Mack.

Frankie was not prepared when Mack began convulsing. She was just as unprepared for Mick's entrance. Both had happened within seconds of each other and with rivaling levels of intensity. The only indication that something had changed with Mack occurred less than a minute before Mick came bursting through the door.

It began with Mack suddenly gripping Frankie's hand as though she were a lifeline. Frankie gasped, but made no effort to take back her hand. Instead, she allowed him so squeeze it harder and harder, wincing as his fingernails threatened to break skin. His eyes then flew open and his once kind eyes, clouded by icy white swirls, stared coldly at the ceiling. He gulped a breath, his back arching and neck twisting at a dreadful and unnatural angle before collapsing back onto the bed and beginning to shake.

It was then that Mick appeared followed closely by James. The younger woman's eyes widened in fright as she watched her twin's body begin to lurch uncontrollably on the bed. She rushed forward and, grabbing Frankie by the arm, yanked violently at her. Frankie, still held by Mack's iron grip, could not be moved from him.

"Get away from him!" Mick shrieked, "Get away from my brother!"

James wrapped one arm around Micks waist and hauled her away from Frankie. Mick had not let go of Frankie. She was now being wrenched violently in two different directions. Pain seared through her and she shrieked, tugging desperately and without success to free herself from both twins.

The bedroom door slammed open and a petite woman came dashing in. Her rich, dark skin stood out in contrast against the creamy colored silk blouse she wore and the bright yellow skirt that billowed about her with each step. Her quick, dark eyes assessed the situation before she pushed herself into the spot between Mick and Frankie. She grabbed Mick's wrist and twisted slightly until Mick yelped and let Frankie's arm go.

"Take her away," she calmly directed James over her shoulder. Her heavily accented voice was deep for a woman and almost musical. James did not question the order. His arm still around Mick, he carried her kicking and screaming from the room.

The woman turned her attention to Mack without another thought to James or the banshee-like girl he was carrying out. She took hold of his wrist and applied pressure. Within seconds, Mack had released Frankie's hand and was convulsing unrestrained. The woman, ignoring this, guided Frankie to the far side of the room where they stood, backs to the wall, witnessing the young man's death.

It did not take long. They watched for a few minutes, respectfully silent as the convulsing lessened into sharp sporadic jerks. Each lurch was punctuated by a shriek from another room in the house. It was as though both twins and not only one were dying.

Frankie absently rubbed the spot on her arm where Mick's hand had been. She felt helpless and stupid for just standing there, but there was nothing else she could do. If anything, she was grateful for not having been expelled from the room altogether by this new force who had appeared as if out of nowhere and taken control of the situation.

She glanced at the woman next to her. She was slightly shorter than Frankie, but held herself as if she were a giant. Sensing Frankie's eyes on her, the woman met her gaze and offered a small smile. She gave Frankie a nudge forward, waving her to one side of the bed while she went to the other.

"He will go now," she said simply as she took hold of one of Mack's hands. Frankie, taking her cue from the woman, covered his other hand with her own. He had stopped convulsing and was lying very still with his icy blue eyes wide open and staring blankly at the ceiling. If she had not spotted the faint movement of his chest, she would have thought him already dead.

The bedroom door opened once more and a far more sedate version of Mick stepped through with James very close behind. She came to a stop at the end of the bed and looked at her brother, tears streaming down her cheeks. James stood behind her and rested his hands on her shoulders. This, Frankie understood suddenly, was as close to her twin as she would be allowed to get.

It was good timing as well. With a small shudder, a wisp of breath escaped Mack's lips and his chest did not rise again. Mick spun around and buried her face in James's chest. He wrapped his arms around her and held her with obvious caution all the while murmuring softly into her ear.

Frankie realized that James was taking care not to allow any part of his skin to touch the girl. She looked closely at him for the first time since they had returned from the Parker's. There was a thin sheen of sweat on his face and he was looking a little ashen. He had, she reminded herself, just had to physically restrain a strong young woman and, before that, had lifted and set up a generator on his own. He could simply be tired.

The woman was drawing Mack's eyelids down over to shut his eyes. She whispered a few words in a foreign language that Frankie thought might have been a prayer then pulled the sheet below Mack's comforter up over his head. Frankie found herself staring at the woman's hair. It was jet black and had been put into many thin braids that fell halfway down her back. The length of her hair was held together in two separate places by orange hair ties so that the braids would not move independently as she walked. Slapping her hands against her thighs, the woman rose to her feet and looked around the room. "Shall we return to the study?"

It had been a question, but Frankie got the distinct impression it was more of a statement than anything. She rose and followed the woman out of the room, leaving James and Mick to have more time alone to process their loss.

FRANKIE'S FATHER BEAMED at her as she entered the study behind the woman. "Ah, Frankie! Bunmi! I see you have met!" Cora stood as soon as the two women were through the door and made some excuse about seeing to dinner as she slipped out the door.

"We have not met formally," the woman replied, smiling brightly. "But the resemblance between you and your daughter is strong." Frankie raised her eyebrows. It was the first time anyone had ever said that she looked a lot like her father. She had become used to people squinting slightly at her and then at her father for a few moments before agreeing that they did share a similarity or two. Bunmi winked and pointed to the wall across the room. "And I have seen photographs."

"Oh!" Frankie found herself briefly distracted from the knot of grief in her chest by the musical quality of the woman's voice. Her accent sounded West African and had hints of British influence.

"Bunmi came as soon as she heard that the Leucocelerosis virus had been released," Dr. Reed said, indicating that they should sit. "She thought she might be of some assistance."

The woman, Bunmi, seated herself on the chair Cora had vacated. Two extra chairs had been added in front of her father's desk since she had last been in this room. Frankie took the one immediately to Bunmi's right, feeling an odd affinity to the woman despite their having never before met. She appeared to be in her mid-thirties, if not younger.

"How do you know my father?"

"That is a long story." Bunmi paused and cast a meaningful glance at Dr. Reed before turning back to Frankie with a soft smile. "Perhaps another time?"

"Dad," Frankie cleared her throat. Her curiosity could wait. She had news for her father anyway. "Mack just…died…and James seems sick now, too."

Her father gave her a measured look. "That is because he is, Francine. I have never before seen anyone fight the supervirus as fiercely as James is. I wish I could study his progression closer."

Bunmi nodded. "Yes, it is most intriguing."

"You wish?" Frankie furrowed her brow. "But you're right here. You can study him, can't you?"

"To a degree, yes." He admitted, "But my mind is not what it used to be and I am afraid I do not have the stamina to manage a man such as James should he become violent."

"Is that a possibility?"

"It is," Bunmi answered, "but I do not believe he will. However, there is still so much about the Leucocelerosis virus that remains unknown. While the end result never varies and is dependent on blood type, everyone's progression through the illness is individual to them. For example, two brothers fall ill, but one dies quickly and peacefully while the other takes longer and is fitful. It is the same for those who might expect recovery."

Dr. Reed shifted uncomfortably in his chair. "James tells me your illness and recovery took a day longer than mine and that the process was far more peaceful."

It was the first information, however minimal, he had ever willingly offered her about that time. "So, it was bad for you?" she probed. He nodded grimly. "It was bad for Mack, too."

"It wouldn't have been if he had let me help him like Earl did." Frankie had not heard the door to the study open. James was standing in the doorway looking even more tired than before. His eyes met Frankie's for a split second before he nodded a greeting to her father then turned all of his attention to the new woman.

"Dr. Olubunmi Bola," James said, his eyes widening with surprise. "I've read just about everything you've written."

"Bunmi." She rose and faced him, her face tilting slightly at the compliment. James took two long strides into the room and reached out to clasp her hand before, with embarrassment, drawing his hand back into himself. Bunmi smiled and stuck out her own hand to him. "It is safe for me to touch you. I am immune."

James eyed her hand, confusion spreading across his face. "Immune? But is that possible? I've never known anyone to be, that is. None on of the people used in Dr. Reed's trials were kept alive long enough to prove immunity."

"It is not impossible. I stand before you, do I not?"

"But how? All blood types reacted to the virus in their own way, but none proved to have any true defense against the supervirus."

"Not so," she said, sitting again and waving toward the chair on the other side of Frankie. She paused long enough for James to take a seat. "The Leucocelerosis virus infiltrates and remains present in all blood types even after recovery. It reacts in a devastating manner to O-positive blood types within a day or two of infection without exception. It is only fatal to A-negative and B-negative blood types in the sense that those infected die not from the virus itself, but because they are unable to provide nourishment for themselves during what I can only describe as a hostile takeover. Even if nourishment was supplied, however, those with A or B-negative blood types would never come out of the fugue state the Leucocelerosis virus puts them in. Those who are O-negative, as you know, have the ability to recover, but most require medical intervention to help sustain their bodies during recovery. As a result, you can imagine that very few people who are O-negative will survive the virus simply because they have no medical help."

"That leaves those who are AB-negative." James said, leaning forward with interest.

"Yes," she agreed. "That leaves people like me. As I stated before, the Leucocelerosis virus infiltrates our blood just as it does anyone else. The difference is that, unlike everyone else, the virus has no hold on us. It cannot attach itself to host cells. It is present, but cannot harm or alter us in any way."

"Are you sure of this?" James asked, his question sounding more like a demand. Bunmi gave him a confident smile.

"As sure as I am that I have been infected with the Leucocelerosis virus for the past five years and have seen no symptoms whatsoever, neither have I infected others." She stepped forward and took hold of his hand for herself. "This is a cull, James Wester, and we have been chosen. We have been spared."

Twenty-Four

It is with great sorrow that I announce that this is the final issue of The Seattle Journal. Due to an ever-decreasing staff, it has become extraordinarily difficult to continue functioning and those of us who remain now understand that it will soon be impossible to continue at all. It is our duty to report the news and we did so as long as we could. This virus, to say the least, has been devastating. I regret that we cannot use these final words to offer advice better than that already given over the past week. All we can offer is hope and well-wishes. We need to take more precautions now than ever, but we must remember to never allow ourselves to simply accept our fate. Fight. We must fight with all we have. Carl Sagan once said that "Extinction is the rule. Survival is the exception". For the future of our species, we must fight to be the exception.

Jake Henderson, Executive Editor, The Seattle Journal

WHEN HANK LEE Decker died, Henry felt, with a twinge of guilt, relief. Their relationship had been strained since Henry's mother died and neither had been able to get things anywhere close to where they had been when she was alive. It was not that Henry did not love his father. He loved him very much. The relief he felt was because he no longer needed to look for ways of connecting with a father who was so overwhelmed by his own grief that he put in the least amount of effort possible with his son.

While barely eighteen, Henry had handled his father's death with dignity and a stoicism far beyond his years. As his father had all but emotionally cut off most of the family, there was no one to help Henry prepare for the funeral and very few people attended. The majority of them were people who had worked with Hank over the years. Only a handful were relatives and distant at that. Henry, at the time, had not thought much about this. Years later, it occurred to him that his own funeral was likely to be even bleaker and more sparsely attended. He did not socialize with his coworkers and he had not kept in touch with any of his relatives.

None of that mattered anymore. There would be no funeral for him now. Who would hold it? As the supervirus swept across the nation, there would soon be far more bodies to bury than people to bury them. He had never given his own death much thought before, but, in the back of his mind, there would at least be someone to put him in the ground. It had never occurred to him that he might spend the rest of his physical existence rotting on the spot where he fell.

Henry had eighteen years with his father. With Robby, he had had only days. Yet, somehow, it was the boy's death that was the loss that brought him to his knees.

Tess had refused to leave Robby's body while Henry found a quiet spot to bury him. She sat cross-legged on the ground in front of the RV with her head hanging until he returned to collect them both. Her face was streaked with tears and dirty from having sat on the ground in the dirt while little gusts of wind blew dust about her. Her nose and cheeks were flushed red with cold and her eyes, now dry, were pink from crying.

Henry had not known what to say to her. He had not known what he would have wanted said to him. It felt strange to have developed such a strong emotional attachment to a boy he hardly knew in such a short amount of time. Still, it had happened. He had no real measure for comparison aside from what he had been told by others, but the ache in his heart felt very much like how he expected it must be for any parent who lost a child. In his last moments, that was exactly what Robby had called himself; Henry's son. He had filled a hole in Henry's heart that he had not known existed.

He watched Tess pull herself up into the Jeep and the ache in his heart intensified. Tess was hurting and he could not make it better. He could not take away her pain any more than he could his own. There was no logic behind it, but he was sure that was something he should be able to do for her. He put the key in the ignition and paused. Tentatively, he reached over and patted Tess on her leg. She lifted her head and looked at him and, with a shock, he realized that he felt just as strongly about this girl as he had Robby.

He could not lose her, too.

They rode in silence to Holy Family Catholic Church with Robby's small form wrapped up inside Henry's coat in the back of the Jeep. Henry was not a religious man and certainly not a Catholic, but he felt

332

compelled to bury the boy in a cemetery. Anywhere else seemed less than the boy deserved.

After locating the church, he walked up and down the graveyard's rows of headstones and selected an empty place beneath a tree where someone had, with the aid of a backhoe loader, already begun digging a grave. As he finished the task of digging, he wondered what had happened to the digger and for whom the grave had originally been meant. The fact that it lay open and unused was sign enough to Henry that this was where he was meant to leave Robby.

Henry, with Robby's body cradled in his arms, slid down into the open grave and laid him gently down. He would not have, as all the others laid to rest here, a fancy coffin of oak or redwood. He would not have a coffin at all. His tiny body would have no barrier between it and the cold dirt around it. He clambered out, hating that he had to leave the boy here. With use of the backhoe, Henry covered the boy's body with layer upon layer of dirt.

This had been too much for Tess. The girl fell into a crouch and, hugging her knees, began to sob uncontrollably. She did not look up again until Henry had finished and had returned from parking the backhoe far away from Robby's grave.

Lacking the necessary tools, he knew he would be unable to properly mark Robby's grave. It felt wrong leaving him nameless, but he comforted himself with the fact that there were two people who would know who was put to rest in such a beautiful spot. In place of a real headstone, he selected a small, blank square of marble from a storage shed behind the church and placed it at the top of the grave.

Tess rose and stood over the fresh grave, staring down at the blank stone. Henry wanted to hug her. Deciding to give her a moment alone instead, he wandered back out of the cemetery toward the front of the church where they had left the Jeep. Although he did not truly expect it to, he had hope that the walk might help clear his mind a little. He realized before even rounding the building that it had not. He sank down onto the cold stone step in front of the church's main entrance and rested his head in his hands.

He had been sitting for several moments before he noticed a dull and randomly spaced thudding coming from behind him. Slowly, he stood up and walked up to the entrance. The thudding had stopped. He peered through a pane of glass on the left side of the double doors and squinted into the dark. There was a small lobby just beyond the door that was sparsely decorated with flowers that looked as though they had been dead for several days. At the far end, between two solid and windowless doors, was an elaborately decorated holy water font. Henry stared at it for several seconds before the thudding resumed.

His eyes shot toward the doors.

Henry backed away from the entrance slowly then, faster, turned to head around the side of the building. He had a theory about this ghost town, but he certainly did not care to test it by opening any doors. Just as he turned off onto the grass to circle the building again toward the cemetery, he stopped and glanced back at the Jeep. Another idea had popped into his mind. He rushed to the Jeep and, leaning through the passenger side, opened the glovebox and rummaged around until he found what he was looking for. Pocketing the item, he headed back toward the cemetery keeping close to the side of the church.

There were several windows along the side. Henry rushed past the first few and crouched low to peer through one just beyond the middle of the building. The glass was tinted, but still gave him a relatively clear view of the sanctuary beyond. It also gave him a clear view of a packed church. It looked as though the whole town had gathered in what they must have assumed was the safest place to be. Gauging from the number of bodies that were draped over pews, slumped against walls, and littered on the floor, they had been horribly wrong.

At the far back of the sanctuary was a group of about ten to fifteen people. Some were milling about listlessly while others only stood swaying. One, a rather large man in a cassock, was walking over and over into one of the doors that led to the lobby. Satisfied at having found the source of the thudding and confident that the people trapped inside posed them no threat, Henry rose and returned to the cemetery.

He found Tess much as he had left her. Henry reached into his pocket and withdrew the item from the glovebox. Silently, he handed it to Tess. She looked down at the object in her hand and then back up at Henry.

"A marker?"

"Yeah," Henry shoved his hands into his pockets. It was getting chillier. "It's permanent. Well, permanent enough."

Understanding, Tess dropped to her knees in front of the blank marble and uncapped the marker. "Do you know his full name? Birthday?"

"Robert John Smith…'most boring name in the world'," he added, remembering what Robby had said, "And his birthday was a month ago, but I don't know the day. He…he just turned eleven."

335

Tess nodded and began to write with flourished letters. Henry was glad he had had her do this. Her handwriting was far better than his. "Hey, Henry?"

"Hmm."

"What's your full name?"

"What's yours?" Henry countered. Tess shot him a look over her shoulder, but did not reply. "Henry Lee Decker."

Tess returned to her writing and, after another minute, rose to admire her work. Henry looked down at the once bare stone and read: Robert "Robby" John Decker (née Smith), Eleven Years Old.

THE SUN HAD set by the time he and Tess, exhausted, returned to the RV. The stranger's corpse still lay outside the door where it had fallen. Tess paused next to it and stared down with a chilling look of calm. Several moments passed before she swung one booted foot back then planted it squarely in the side of the corpse's head. Whatever release the action provided must have been significant because she drew her foot back and kicked again. Over and over, Tess's foot connected with the stranger's head. She did not speak, hardly making a noise at all, and Henry made no move to stop her.

He understood the pain that had brought her to this point. He was feeling it as well. The only difference, perhaps, was that he believed his own release could only have been found with this action had the man still been alive.

When Tess finally stopped and stepped over the battered corpse to enter the RV, Henry took hold of it by the legs and dragged it as far from them as possible. He dropped the legs on the other side of a building and stared down at the it for a moment. Then, with one swipe with his foot, he gave it a light dusting of dirt and walked away without a backwards glance. This man did not even deserve as much burial as that.

The microwave was beeping as Henry closed and locked the door of the RV behind himself. He knew there was no point in trying to convince Tess to drive on tonight. To that point, he wondered if they should even continue to Los Alamos at all. It had been, after all, Robby's idea to go and it was solely for Robby that Henry had been going.

He sat in one of the two chairs at the small table and accepted the frozen dinner Tess placed in front of him. She sat across from him and leaned her head against the wall. She had not heated a dinner for herself. He hated that he was hungry. It felt like a betrayal of sorts. He was here, safe with Tess and about to have dinner, while Robby was some six feet beneath the cold earth. *At least*, he thought as he looked down at the plate of what he believed was meatloaf, *it is not chicken nuggets*.

"I wish I had said something," she said suddenly, breaking the silence they had held for the past few hours. Neither had been able to come up with the right words once Robby's body was in the ground nor had they found them once Henry had covered him with blankets of cold dirt. They had simply stood quietly, Henry with his arm around Tess's shoulder and Tess with her head tucked into him. No words seemed adequate so they had settled for none at all.

"Mmm." Henry said as he shoved a forkful of meatloaf into his mouth.

"I mean, don't you think we should have said something?" He looked up at her. Her face was pinched with pain. "Or done something for him? Some sort of gesture. You know?"

He swallowed hard, the processed meat sticking in his throat. "Beyond what you already did? We still can. We can go back in the morning. Whatever you like."

Tess did not speak again until Henry had finished his meal and had, without rising, tossed the container up into the small sink in the kitchenette behind him. The she turned slowly to face him. "Anything?"

"What's that, now?"

She rested her elbows on the table and propped her head in her hands. "You said we could do something for him. Anything I like."

He nodded. 'Yeah. What are you thinking?"

Tess's eyes were fixed on his. "I want to go to Los Alamos."

Twenty-Five

DUE TO THE lack of power, the automatic doors to the emergency department of the Los Alamos Medical Center had to be pried open. It had taken surprisingly less force than Frankie had expected and, for that, she was grateful. Once in, she had fallen behind Bunmi, bowing to her far superior knowledge of medical instruments and supplies. Bunmi made a beeline for Triage and, selecting a few items, handed them to Frankie without instruction and headed for a door at the back of the room. Frankie shoved the items she had been given into one of the backpacks she had brought and followed Bunmi to the back.

It was eerily quiet and, as another result of lack of power, chilly and darker than it was outside. At least, outside, they had moonlight. The hairs on Frankie's arms were prickling uncomfortably. Something about all this seemed off.

"Um, Bunmi?"

Bunmi, while lacking in height, could have rivaled the pace of someone far taller. Frankie wondered if being a doctor and having to react to emergency situations was what made her so speedy. Frankie was slightly taller than Bunmi, but had to jog to keep up.

"Bunmi, wait."

The other woman slowed without stopping and looked over her shoulder. "Yes, Frankie?"

"Don't you think it's strange," she panted, "that no one is here?"

"Dr. Reed told me that the residents reacted quickly to the threat. Perhaps they are all in their homes."

Frankie frowned, pointing up at the ceiling, "But, surely, there are sick people here. You know. Up in the rooms. Wouldn't someone have stayed for them? There were only a few cars in the parking lot that I noticed." She skidded slightly as Bunmi came to a sudden halt. The thought obviously had never crossed the other woman's mind. Frankie, now having Bunmi's full attention, continued, "And another thing. There's no power. Why is the generator not running?"

"I could not tell you," Bunmi said as she absently rubbed at her cheek. "I am afraid I do not know much about engineering. I can tell you, as a doctor, that hospital generators have failed many times for various reasons. I remember there was a hospital somewhere on the east coast some years ago that had a generator fail during a hurricane, but I do not know exactly why it failed. There were generator failures in New Orleans during Hurricane Katrina as well, but I do not believe either example would explain what has happened here."

"A 7,000-foot elevation does make it a little difficult to be affected by hurricanes," Frankie joked.

Bunmi was nodding, her attention not completely on Frankie. "Also, in San Diego during a blackout, there were generator failures. There could be any number of explanations as to why there is no power, but I agree that it is unlikely hospital staff would have deserted their patients."

"Maybe we should avoid floors with patient rooms, then."

Bunmi's face took on a quizzical look. "Why is that?"

"Well," Frankie explained, "If what my father said is true, then everyone is either in their homes or confined to one area of the hospital. If we barge into that area, we might cause a panic. We're strangers."

Bunmi thought for a moment. "Agreed. We will avoid any floor that might house patients. What we need can be located elsewhere."

With a tilt of her head in the direction she had been heading moments before, Bunmi continued her search for equipment. Frankie followed, noting that their pace was significantly slower and more cautious than before. Despite their footsteps echoing off the tile floor and minimally decorated walls, Frankie doubted they were loud enough to attract any attention. Patient rooms were elsewhere. There was no way the noise they were making would attract attention unless someone was in the same hallway with them. As far as she could see, the dim hallway that extended in front of Bunmi was completely empty.

Frankie did not care for the dark corridors. Had this been a movie, a monster would have had several opportunities to jump out at them. She wished James had been able to come. He had wanted to, but there was no ignoring the fact that he had finally fallen ill. His presence would only have served to slow them down. Should the progression of the illness be as swift as it had for Earl and Mack, the women might have found themselves with a whole lot of deadweight to somehow transport back to the house. It made far more sense for him to remain behind. Her father obviously could not have come as he was slow on his feet and tired quickly, and Cora would never even have entertained the idea of helping with such a task.

That left only one person. Even having the company of the sullen Mick would have been better than just the two of them doing this alone, except Mick had been swallowed up by her grief and had closed herself into a spare room. She had refused to speak to any of them. Even James could not persuade her to come out. In the end, he had left her to her thoughts and carried on with things that needed to be done and could wait no longer.

James had removed both bodies himself from the room Mack and Earl had died in and, with Frankie and Bunmi's help, had tidied up both beds in preparation for what was to come. As soon as the two women were ready to leave for the hospital, James had turned over both Earl's and Mack's gun to them just in case they should find them necessary. He had then put himself to bed in the freshly cleaned room. Exhausted from his efforts, he had fallen asleep before Frankie and Bunmi walked out the front door.

Neither woman had known what to expect when they pulled up in front of the emergency department in James's van. They had not seen anyone out and about on their way, but Frankie had, in the back of her mind, expected to be greeted by someone here. It was so surreal to be in a place like this without the familiar hustle and bustle of doctors and nurses tending to the sick and wounded.

Frankie was feeling no more comfortable with her surroundings by the time Bunmi led them through a door to a doctor's office and into an examination room. Without hesitation, Bunmi begun to unplug machines similar to the ones Frankie herself had been hooked up to. She pointed to an IV stand without pausing her own task or speaking. Frankie grabbed it and wheeled it from the room into the hallway.

Bunmi came out, pulling a machine with her, and looked up the hall. "Take these to the front. I will go looking for the rest of what I need."

"Are you sure that's a good idea?" Frankie was loath to leave the woman on her own. Bunmi waved her away and, taking the empty backpack from Frankie, started up the hall before she could argue further.

"I will not be long," Bunmi called over her shoulder.

Shoving both the machine and the IV stand while lugging a full backpack proved even more difficult than she had expected it would be. It took much longer to get back up to the triage room and through to the front than she would have liked. She wanted to get it out to the van so she could get back to Bunmi as quickly as possible. Thanks to the distraction her cumbersome load provided, the trek back to the van was less eerie than it had been going in with her companion.

If not for the almost full moon and the bright twinkling of the stars, the night would have been completely black. Without streetlights and neon building signs, there was just enough light. Frankie, not wanting to be out alone in the cold for long, pushed the machine and the IV stand up next to the van and started back in.

She paused, looking back and wondered how she and Bunmi would manage to get the machine up into the van. The IV stand was easy enough, but the machine was heavier and unwieldy. She stepped back inside and scanned the waiting room area. Finding nothing of use, she went back through triage and started opening up cupboards and storage room doors.

After several minutes, she found a storage closet that contained random items. From the thick layer of dust on everything, she guessed that this was where things were sent when no one knew what they should do with them. They were then left to be forgotten altogether. It worked in her favor. Up against the back wall were several sturdy looking sheets of metal. She pulled one out and dragged it back out to the front.

At the van, she chucked her backpack onto the front seat then wedged one end of the metal sheet into the curb and let the other fall into the open side door. Then, shoving with all her might, she pushed the machine up the makeshift ramp and into the van.

The IV stand, wonderfully light in comparison, went in easily after. She turned the metal sheet on its side and slid it inside the van as well. The ramp could make removing the equipment easier once they got back to the house. Since no one was around, she thought it safe enough to leave the van door open for the remainder of the supplies.

Exhausted, Frankie leaned up against the side of the van to catch her breath. At the far end of the sparsely occupied parking lot, she saw a few rows of vehicles she had not noticed before. They were all parked in a lot that was set back a bit from entrance to the main parking lot. It was no surprise that they had not spotted them before. A row of bushes would have obscured their view of the lot coming in. She wondered where the owners of those vehicles were now and if they were employees of the hospital. She pushed her questions aside. She had to get back to Bunmi.

Sweating and still shaking slightly from effort, she walked back into the hospital and retraced her steps. Frankie smiled to herself as she walked, pleased with her problem-solving efforts. All in all, loading the van on her own had not taken very long at all. Bunmi, however, was taking longer than she had expected. In the amount of time Frankie had been gone, the smaller woman could have made it all the way around the building a few times. Frankie would not have been surprised should she learn that Bunmi competed in some sort of racing sport.

Frankie passed by the elevator doors for the third time since she first arrived. She had noticed before that one was stuck in the open position. What she had not noticed until now was the elderly man slumped in the corner.

She stopped and stared for a moment before realizing that the man was trembling almost imperceptibly. Cautiously, she put one hand on the elevator jamb, but remained outside of the elevator. After the events of the past few days, she did not want to get too close to this unknown man.

"Hello?" The man stirred at her voice. "Sir? Are you all right?"

He raised his head so that she could see his face. While his hair was heavily marbled with white, the skin of his face was completely smooth. He was several decades younger than she had first thought. He looked up at her, his cloudy eyes traveling slowly up the length of her and stopping when they met her eyes. When he finally spoke, his voice was no more than a raspy whisper. "They're...out there."

"Who?" Frankie leaned back, looking first up the hallway in the direction she had been heading and then back in the direction from which she had come. Aside from herself, it was completely empty.

"They're out there," he repeated with strained urgency, one hand raising slowly and shakily to point into the hallway.

Frankie backed away into the hallway, looking up and down it once more. She took a few steps farther into the hospital, her eyes passing over the small glass window of the doorway that led to the stairs.

Something caught her eye.

Slowly, she approached the door and peered through the window. In the dark stairwell, lit only faintly by the moonlight that shone in through a window above them, were about a dozen people. Most were in scrubs or white lab coats, but a few were in street clothes and one was in a hospital gown and looked as though she had, at some point, been hooked up to something. She was facing away and the back of her gown had fallen open exposing her bare back and powder blue underwear.

All the people had varying degrees of white hair and ashen toned skin. None appeared to have any awareness of either herself or each other. Movement farther up the stairs caught her attention. There were more above.

She took an involuntary step back from the window. The man in the elevator was speaking again, the urgency in his voice growing as his clarity of speak declined. Frankie understood now who "they" were.

A loud popping sounded from up the hallway causing Frankie to jump. It was followed by three more pops in quick succession. Her eyes darted in the direction from which they had sounded then back to the glass of the stairwell doorway.

A man's face was now behind the glass blocking her view of everyone else inside. He was looking directly at her, his eyes all but consumed by swirling white. Frankie stood frozen, her gaze locked with his, unable to move. The man opened his mouth and began to shriek, the earsplitting sound passing easily through the window and metal door, sending chills right through her. Through the deafening noise, Frankie could just make out another gunshot, but she could not yet manage to tear her eyes away from the man. Although he did not move, the door shook suddenly as something slammed suddenly against it.

"Frankie!"

The screaming man had not paused to take a breath. Frankie, still frozen to the spot, marveled at how he was managing it. If they were still alive as her father, Bunmi, and James had claimed, then how were they able to make such high-pitched extended noises? Frankie recalled having seen a documentary some years before that involved humans who were able to do extraordinary things when put into stressful or frightening situations. Perhaps, like those people, these, too, were running on adrenaline.

"Frankie!"

She jerked her head toward the sound of the voice. Bunmi was racing down the hall toward her. In front of her, there was another thud against the stairwell door which was followed by two more in quick succession. It was as though the people inside were, at the screeching man's bidding, hurling themselves against the door.

"Frankie! We must go! Now!"

Bunmi took hold of Frankie's arm and yanked her away from the door, practically dragging her back toward the front of the hospital. Frankie, her body jolted back to life, stumbled and, catching herself, ran behind Bunmi. The other woman let go of her arm and darted at full speed toward triage, her bright yellow skirt billowing behind her, with Frankie at her heels.

Behind them, the door to the stairwell burst open and the people who had been trapped behind it came pouring out. A voice from behind them, amid the din, began screaming. "They're out there! They're out!"

Neither Frankie nor Bunmi slowed at his voice. Only Frankie risked a look back over her shoulder as they skidded through the door into triage. Behind them were several people running blindly after them, their faces turned in different directions as if they had no choice but to go where their bodies took them. She could just make out the shrieking man in a white lab coat following at a more sedate pace behind the crowd.

Frankie slammed the door behind herself and began to push a filing cabinet in front of the door. Bunmi, without stopping, called out to her over her shoulder, "There is no time! We must go!"

Leaving the filing cabinet to mostly block the door, Frankie swiveled on the balls of her feet and ran to catch up with Bunmi. Outside, Bunmi had thrown the backpack she had been wearing into the back of the van and quickly slid the door shut. She clambered into the passenger side of the cab and reached for the door.

Frankie ran around the front of the van and climbed up into the driver's seat as Bunmi closed her door. Slamming her own, Frankie fumbled as she ripped the van key from her pocket and crammed it into the ignition. There was a thunderous crash from inside the hospital as the van roared to life. Frankie mashed her foot down on the gas causing the van to lurch forward, wheels squealing, as the van drove away from the building. In the sideview mirror, several people with pale skin and white hair spilled out of the building into the street.

Frankie and Bunmi had made it safely away, but, in the process, had unleased a small swarm of infected people into Los Alamos.

Twenty-Six

IM SORRY I LET U DIE

Unknown, Graffiti found on wall

OF ALL LIFE'S modern technological perks, the one Henry missed most was one that had already begun its journey into obscurity several years before. He could do without a lot of things, but he really missed being able to turn on the radio and scan through the stations until he came across a song he recognized or was drawn in by the friendly banter of a couple of disc jockeys. It seemed to him that most people in the past ten years or so were listening to their music on machines that seemed smaller and smaller each year or ordering it directly to their phones on various music applications that would provide exactly the song you wanted at the precise moment you wanted it.

Henry far preferred the joy of the hunt when it came to music. He liked to be surprised. Sometimes, he would have to go through the stations several times before settling on one. He did not see it as being an inconvenience. Rather, the effort seemed to increase the joy he experienced once the numbers on the screen came to a halt on a station and a song he recognized filled his Jeep.

Now, he drove in silence.

Since it was just the two of them now, Henry had hitched the Jeep to the back of the RV. Tess, he felt, would need company after what had happened in Nazareth, but he did not think she would ever have asked for it. He had made the decision that they would ride together and Tess had not argued. He took it as a good sign that he had been correct.

He had set the radio scanner in the RV so that it would cycle through the stations on their own, but it rarely paused. When it did, only static or dead air came through his speakers in the brief moment before the radio moved on in search of the next station. It had been three days since he had heard so much as a voice come from either the FM or AM stations.

It had also been three days since Robby had died.

The curtain separating the cab from the back of the RV opened and Tess slipped through. She flopped down in the passenger seat and tapped the off button on the radio with the ball of her bare foot. "That's enough of that."

Henry could not have agreed more. It was becoming difficult to decide which was more depressing; the widespread radio silence or the fact that most of the people they had seen in at least a day were all obviously infected and, from the way they lurched slowly about, on their way out. More than a few times in the first day after they had left Nazareth, they had spotted a hitchhiker making their way along the side of the highway. Two or three times, they had spotted what seemed to be a whole family. Eyes set firmly on the road ahead, they had driven past each person or group without slowing.

351

After what had happened in Nazareth, they were taking no risks. They would not be stopping for people and they would be keeping their guard up whenever a traffic jam or other road block forced them to stop. Both knew the probability of running into another person like the man in Nazareth would have been unlikely before the release of the supervirus. Now, the possibility of encountering people who had been made desperate from hunger, thirst, or loss was far greater. Tess and Henry had, in comparison with most, a lot. In a sense, with an RV packed with food and a fully functional vehicle in tow, they were rich.

In the past two days, however, they had seen no one who was truly alive. There had been no hitchhikers thumbing for rides or small groups perched on top of cars or resting beneath overpasses. There had been no one watching them disappear far up the road. There had been plenty of sick and dying people, too many to count, but even their numbers were dwindling the closer Henry and Tess got to their destination.

Henry had become numb to the infected for the most part. He was cautious around all pale people until he could be sure none were the sort that screeched and seemed to draw others to attack. Even that sort was becoming fewer and farther between. With Tess's help, they were easily dispatched within a second of opening their mouths. Few got out so much as a squeak before Tess put them out of their misery.

For the most part, having Tess put the pale people down really did not bother him. They were going to die anyway, so far as he could tell. From watching them, it appeared that the ones who roamed about would eventually be worn down from the illness and not eating or drinking to the point that their bodies could no longer keep them going. They would simply drop wherever they were and die.

It was the small children and infants that got to him. He had lost count how many tiny bodies he had found strapped into car seats or lying along the road. It had been clear that many had been killed by the supervirus, but some had just been unable to care for themselves once their guardians had died or disappeared and had died from exposure or starvation. It was because of these that he refused to allow Tess to help him when he had to clear a path for the RV to get through. He wanted, at least, to spare her this.

What they were seeing was more and more bodies in each town they passed through. They had also encountered more traffic jams since the beginning of their journey. Henry assumed that, as the supervirus swept the country, more people began to take to the highways in an effort to outrun or escape infection. Most, as evidenced by the cars in ditches or rammed up against other vehicles, had not made it wherever they had been heading. Most had not been able to get away before they had discovered that they were already ill.

It was clear, by now, that Henry had not been infected. The marks the pale woman had left on his neck had scabbed over and appeared to be healing perfectly. There were no signs of infection, supervirus or otherwise. Henry had somehow managed to escape falling ill.

For that matter, Robby had never shown any signs of illness. He wondered what it was about them that had protected them both from the supervirus. What made them special? For the hundredth time, thinking about Robby caused a lump to catch in his throat. The boy had survived infection only to die at the hand of a madman. He glanced over at Tess and hoped that she, too, would prove to be special. With all the precautions she took, he was unsure he would ever have to find out. He would do all that he could to protect her from everything else.

The remainder of the drive to Los Alamos beginning in Nazareth should have taken a mere five or six hours. Three days would have been enough to frustrate the average person. Henry, however, had not really minded that it was taking so much longer than it would have under normal circumstances and Tess had not yet complained. Instead, they both made their way with a quiet sort of patience. Despite all the death around them, they were both, in their own ways, actually enjoying the journey.

"Where are we anyway?" She had picked up Henry's cell phone and was bouncing it absently back and forth between her hands. He hadn't bothered turning it on since early the morning before. There did not seem to be a point. Nothing had come up on the screen when he'd tried pulling up the internet. He doubted anything would come up now. Still, he could not seem to part with this relic from his previous life.

Henry squinted at a sign and read it slowly, enunciating each sound "Poh...joe...a...que."

Tess followed Henry's gaze to the sign and burst out laughing. "Pojoaque," she corrected him.

"Po-ah-kay," he tried again. "Never was good at Spanish."

"Close enough. And it's not Spanish," Tess rolled her eyes at him. "It's Tewa."

"What now?"

Tess reached down between the seats and grabbed a bag of potato chips. "Tewa. It's a language, Native American, you know?"

"I do now," he replied, snatching the bag from her and, popping it open, crammed chips into his mouth. The girl made a tutting noise at him and reached down for another bag. Henry considered snagging that one as well, but, catching a glimpse of her expression as she opened the second bag, thought better of it. "How do you know?"

"My mom was from around here." Henry could see it now. Tess had fairly high cheekbones and almond shaped eyes. Neither were overly pronounced, but obvious now that attention was drawn to them.

"What happened to her?"

Tess did not answer. Dropping the phone into her lap, she tilted her face toward the window and traced a finger along it as though outlining something in the distance. Henry crumpled up his chip bag and chucked it at her. It bounced off her arm and fell to the floor. Tess did not turn or smile as she normally would have. He tried a different tactic. "Who taught you to shoot?"

"My uncle," she said softly. "This was his RV."

"Where is he?"

Tess turned and looked at him for a moment then returned her attention to the world outside. "Dead. They're both dead, okay? And, before you ask, I don't know where my dad is. He left years ago."

Henry pointed up at a green sign that read 'Los Alamos'. Tess, seeing it, sat a little straighter. She did not comment. They had chatted on and off over the past few days, but only Henry had really opened up. No matter what he tried, the girl simply was not ready or willing to share personal details with him. Henry was used to being shut out. He'd had almost a decade of being shut out by his father. This, for some reason, bothered him far more than his father's silences.

He took the exit that steered the car toward Los Alamos, noting that he had seen very few bodies in this area. To that point, he had not seen any pale people for at least half an hour. He wondered if it had something to do with the area or, more reasonably, the fact that it had now been about two weeks since the news had first announced the outbreak. It was not unreasonable to assume that most of those infected would have died by now. Still, he would have thought that, like everywhere else, there would be at least a few bodies in the streets.

Henry glanced at Tess, worry cropping up again. Had the supervirus run its course? Had it been long enough that the virus could begin to just die out as its last victims perished? Or would she become infected? She had certainly been in close proximity with plenty of infected people. There had been several opportunities for her to contract the supervirus. Perhaps her love of body covering clothes truly had worked in her favor. Maybe she was like him and Robby and would, for whatever reason, remain unaffected despite being exposed.

His heart stung as he thought of the boy.

He shoved the memory of the boy far back into his mind. He could not keep doing this. Every time he thought about Robby, he felt as though he might fall to pieces. That would not be such a big thing in the world they had come from. There had been psychiatrists and therapists or priests to help you cope with grief. This world had none of those things. Grief sat and became heavier with no real release. He could not afford to allow himself to be consumed by it.

As if reading his expression, Tess suddenly reached over and took hold of his hand. She gave it a squeeze and offered him a smile which he returned with one of his own. Together, they stared up the clearest patch of highway they had seen in quite some time. The mountains were quickly closing in around them. He gave her hand another squeeze. "Not long now."

Tess looked nervous. She had become increasingly so as the RV winded its way up and around the twisting mountain road. They had just passed the welcome sign which seemed to capture all of her attention.

"'Los Alamos'", she read aloud as she rolled down the window, "'Where Discoveries Are Made!'"

Henry kept his eyes focused on the road ahead. He did not know what about their arrival was making Tess nervous, but he knew what was having the same effect on him.

There had been no cars blocking their way up the mountain nor had there been any parked or crashed vehicles along the side. There had been no bodies, no pale people, and definitely no healthy-looking people anywhere. It was eerily still as they entered the town.

"Look!" Tess leaned against the dashboard and pointed farther up the road. "Airplanes!"

Sure enough, there was a small airport with about a dozen small planes lined up along the side closest to the road. Henry had always wanted to learn how to fly a plane. Now, he would be hard-pressed finding someone to teach him. These planes would probably remain where they were until they rusted and became completely useless.

Tess stretched her arms out as best as she could and, with one hand catching the wind outside of her window, closed her eyes. Henry did a double take. She was pretending to fly. It was very much the sort of thing a young child would do. Henry grinned, glad to see that this young woman had managed to retain this small innocence when everything else seemed to have been ripped from her. She opened her eyes and sighed happily. It was the first real joy he had seen her experience since before Robby's death.

"A co-op," Henry noted a minute later. Tess had put her arms down and was leaning a little out of her window. Her head turned to keep looking at a large greenhouse that stood near the co-op. Both parking lots, he noted as his eyes flickered briefly past the girl, were completely empty. Strands of thick curls pulled free from the bun on top of Tess's head and were whipping around in the wind. She looked so very young to Henry in that moment, closer to fifteen or sixteen rather than nineteen as she had told him.

"Oh!" Tess clapped her hands together, her eyes on a brightly colored play structure on their right. "A playground!"

Henry raised an eyebrow at her. "How old are you again?" She shushed him then, for good measure, stuck her tongue out at him. He grinned, turning his attention back to their surroundings just as they came to a point where the road split into two.

Henry slowed, looking first left then right. He could see a large grocery store to the left and the right appeared to be the classic main street most small towns had. Tess, without putting much thought into it, waved her hand to the left. Henry, taking the cue, turned the RV left to go up Trinity Drive and increased his speed.

"It's quiet here."

"Mmm." It was quiet and it was making Henry even more nervous. His skin was beginning to prickle uncomfortably and he could not keep his eyes from darting around. He was not sure what he thought he was going to see, but he could not shake the feeling that something was off.

There were a few vehicles in the parking lot of the grocery store and none at the bank on the other side of Trinity Drive. There did not appear to be any people inside the vehicles or on the streets. It appeared they had entered another ghost town. Henry wondered which building, in a town rife with scientists and engineers, people would have gathered in. Would it still be a church?

None of the traffic lights were working nor did any building appear to have electricity, but that was par for the course in all the towns they had been through for days. Henry looked down at the gas gauge. They were running low. They would have to fill up sooner rather than later just to be on the safe side.

He scanned parking lots on either side of the street as they drove slowly by, his eyes pausing briefly on a rectangular blue sign with a bold white H printed on it. Oddly, majority of the lots were empty or mostly so. In every other town, cars had been scattered almost randomly. It was almost as though the people who lived here had known about the outbreak ahead of time and had hidden themselves away. It was a ridiculous thought at first, but then it began to make more sense. Even if they had not actually known what was coming, this was a town of scientists and other logic-driven people. As soon as the news broke, they would have taken every measure to protect themselves.

"And a pond!" Tess was sitting up on her knees, looking out the passenger window. Henry made a noise of acknowledgement, but his attention was now firmly on his search for a good vehicle to syphon. He had just spotted an old pickup at a gas station just before Oppenheimer Drive that might serve their need when Tess spoke again.

"What was that?"

Her head had whipped suddenly to the left and the tone of her voice had changed. It was no longer bubbly and sweet. This was older, serious Tess again. He hated that her childlike innocence could be wiped so easily from her.

Henry looked from Tess, squinting far up the street where she was looking. He had not seen whatever had caught Tess's eye, but he was not about to assume it had been a figment of her imagination or that it was something completely harmless. Not following up on hunches had not proven wise in the past. Thinking it best to investigate, he drove past the gas station and over Oppenheimer drive, leaning forward in his seat to get a better look.

Whatever Tess had seen was gone. Perhaps it had been something innocuous. They were up in the mountains surrounded by trees and desert life. It was not unheard of to have deer run right across the road in towns like this, especially as you got closer to the where the trees were thicker. He was just about to tell her this and circle back to the gas station when something darted across the street a little farther up.

"There's another!" Tess reached back through the curtain without looking back and pulled out her Gatekeeper. She kept her eyes on the road ahead as she held her gun at the ready. "That was definitely human."

Henry slowed the RV slightly, but continued, his curiosity needing to be satiated. They were both so focused on the corner of a building where they had seen the second figure disappear that they almost missed the third. It darted out in front of them then, noticing that there was a moving vehicle on the street, it spun and dived back into a line of bushes.

"What the...?" Henry had slowed completely to a stop. Both he and Tess looked from one side of the street to the other several times before she continued. "Okay, this is kinda freaky. Maybe we should go back. I mean, Robby said this town has labs and does experiments and stuff. What if those are, like, mutated freaks or something? What if they've experimented on the freaks and made them into blood-thirsty soldiers with superhuman speed? They're fast enough without help, you know? Maybe we should just go back."

"You're babbling," Henry muttered. He let his foot off the brake bit by bit and crept farther up the road. He was almost at the spot where he had seen the third figure vanish.

"Babbling doesn't mean 'not making sense'. Seriously, dude. Maybe we should jus-"

Henry held up a hand, shushing her loudly. "Look. There."

Tess grudgingly followed his gaze then sucked in a breath as she saw what he was seeing. "Dude."

"That's a kid."

Henry came to a stop again directly in front of the bushes that held the child. He rolled down his window and rested his arm on the door so that his elbow dangled out, his eyes searching the bushes. As he opened his mouth to call to the child, a vision of a creepy man driving a windowless white van popped into his mind. *Hey, kiddo. Want some candy? I have puppies in the back. Climb on in.* He snorted at the thought. Most kids were lectured on a regular basis about the dangers of strangers. He would not have been surprised if this child took off running the moment he spoke.

"Hey, kid," he began, wincing at the creepy start, "You okay? Where are your parents?"

"Hell," muttered Tess, "where's anyone?"

Henry ignored her. He was not surprised when the child did as well. He tried again, opting for a slightly less disturbing approach. "Is there an adult we can talk to?"

They could just see, through the leaves, the child shifting its dark legs. Henry scanned the other side of the road. Whoever the child had been with was either long gone or extremely well hidden. He threw the RV into park and, turning off the engine, opened his door.

"What are you doing?"

He waved dismissively at Tess, his eyes back on the bush. The child was still there, but seemed to be becoming more nervous as he stepped down from the RV. He put both hands up and took a couple tentative steps toward the bushes. The child twitched then burst from the bushes. Barefoot and poorly dressed for the chilly autumn weather, she sprinted across the street in the direction Henry and Tess had seen the other figures go. Her long, black hair whipped behind her as she rounded the corner of the building.

One thing about the child really stood out to Henry. While her parents seemed to have neglected to remind the child to put on shoes before going out, someone had seen fit to be sure, at least, that her mouth and nose were covered. She was wearing a white mask not unlike those worn in hospitals. Outside of a hospital, the sight of it put him in mind of photos he had seen of New York subways and the streets of China where it was crowded and the air was so polluted that masks were a necessity. And Michael Jackson. It also made him think of him.

Curiosity fully piqued, Henry walked around the front of the RV toward the building. He heard Tess open her door and jump down onto the road, but he did not look back. "Wait!"

A face appeared from behind the building, its sudden appearance shocking Henry. He stopped and stared back at the young Asian girl who was looking at him. The majority of the lower half of her face was obscured by a scarf and her hair was cut in a bob just below her ears. She was taller and looked slightly older than the first girl, but looked very similar around their eyes which made him wonder if they were related. She was also terrified.

"It's okay," he said as gently as he could, "I'm not going to hurt you."

Without making a noise, the girl put one finger to her lips in a shushing gesture. Tess came to a stop next to Henry, her Gatekeeper resting against her shoulder. He sighed inwardly. Even to Henry, he and Tess did not seem like safe, trustworthy people. He was a creepy old guy and Tess was locked and loaded.

"Is your mom around? Your dad?" he tried again.

The girl made the gesture again, exaggerating it as she waved her free hand in a shooing motion. Tess sighed. "Look, kid, we'll go. Just tell us if there are any grown-ups around we can talk to and we'll be on our way."

The girl was beginning to look desperate. She had given up trying to silence them and was merely pointing up the road. Both Henry and Tess turned their heads at the same time. Not too far up, the top of a building poked up over the tree line. It looked like some sort of administrative building or, perhaps, a hospital. Whatever it was, Henry did not think it was what the girl had been indicating.

Slowly, Henry walked forward and a little farther up the street to bring more of it into view. Tess followed closely at his heels. When Henry came to a sudden stop, Tess had to catch herself and skirt around Henry to prevent running into him. Together, they lowered their gaze to street level where the child more than likely had meant to point. There was something spread across the road up where the street began to curve. Henry took a few more steps, his face still turned to look up the street.

It was Tess who saw it first. From her vantage point, the end of the street was now in view as was the source of the little girl's fear. Tess gasped sharply and took a step backwards before freezing altogether. Henry's heart thumped suddenly faster and heavier in his chest. Slowly, he took the few extra steps necessary to place him next to Tess. With a sickening jolt, he realized what the girl had been trying to warn them about.

In front of them, some standing and swaying, some collapsed in the road, was the largest crowd of pale people they had seen since Memphis, Texas.

Twenty-Seven

Veni, vidi, perivi

Unknown, Note pinned to hanging body

IT HAD BEEN three days since the power had gone out. On the first day, Frankie and Bunmi had sped back from the hospital in the van with the equipment that would be necessary to care for James should he slip into a coma. Their unexpectedly rushed arrival brought everyone except Frankie's father to the front door to discover the source of the commotion. Their questions were brushed aside and the van was unloaded hastily before any explanation was given.

Once inside, Bunmi had gone immediately to the study, closing the door behind her. Frankie, however, double locked the front door before checking and locking every door and window in the house. She knew this house inside and out and was determined to be extra sure nothing and no one would be able to get in without their knowledge.

Cora and Mick watched Frankie with growing concern as she rechecked the front and back door for the second time. Cora had all but demanded answers as she followed Frankie from room to room, but Frankie paid her no mind until she collapsed at last into an armchair in the front room.

She looked across the room at James who had wandered in and seated himself on one end of the couch to wait for her to finish. Cora wore a frightened expression and was leaning away from James despite having several feet between them. Judging by the look on James's face, Frankie knew that he already suspected what she had to tell him.

Frankie was loath to confirm his suspicions.

She had kept the explanation as short as possible, editing details so that Cora would not become even more afraid. She cast pointed looks at James to convey that there was more she could not say just yet. During the short drive back to the house, Frankie had decided to let everyone know that there were infected people in the hospital, but not to reveal to Cora that they were now outside.

Cora, shaken by the limited news she had been allowed and either satisfied with the explanation she had been given or realizing that this was all she was going to get, disappeared down the hall. Frankie did not know if Cora truly believed that the people she and Bunmi had found inside the hospital were still securely inside.

James and Frankie stared at each other as they waited and listened for the click of the study door. The hallway had never seemed longer to Frankie. She was anxious to share what had really happened with him and to see what he thought they should do. When the click finally sounded faintly, she released a breath she had not realized she was holding and, with it, two simple words. James was nodding even before she spoke. Frankie, in two words, had confirmed his fears.

"They're out."

ALTHOUGH THE ENTIRE excursion, from leaving the house to their return, had taken only a little over an hour and a half, discussing it with James took almost all night. James had insisted on hearing every detail at least twice and had asked question after question, some of which she had thought irrelevant.

"What does it matter whether they were doctors or patients?"

"Well, for one, we could use as many healthy doctors as possible." He swiped at his forehead with the sleeve of his shirt. "Also, people tend to trust doctors. Nurses, too."

"So?"

"So, if you saw someone who looked like a medical professional collapse on one side of the road and some regular Joe collapse on the other side, who would you be more likely to run to help first? Be honest. I'm not judging you."

Frankie cringed inwardly. She liked to think of herself as a fair person when it came to compassion, but James's question brought her natural bias into the light. While she would feel sorry for the other person, she would have run to help the person dressed professionally.

"Yeah," he said, shrugging, "I would, too. Most people are typically taught at a very young age to be wary of strangers. People in uniform, however, we are told are safe. If you are lost, find a policeman. Need help? Ask that fireman. Worried? Let a nurse ease your mind. See that man reading on the park bench? Better stay away from him lest he offer you puppies and candy to lure you into his van and kidnap you."

"Sounds vaguely familiar," Frankie joked.

James chuckled softly. He had sunk farther back into the cushions and was really beginning to look as though he was coming down with flu. The gleam of sweat that he had wiped away had already returned and the color was rapidly draining from his skin. There were thin streaks of white throughout his hair that she had not noticed until just now.

"Essentially, I am concerned that the people of Los Alamos might be lured from their homes if they see a doctor or a nurse walk by who was visibly in need of help."

"What about the patients? I only saw one, I think, but surely there are more."

"Maybe," James pulled himself up and rested his arms on his knees while he caught his breath from the effort. "But I'm less concerned because only friends or relatives would recognize them. It's unlikely many people would be tempted to rush to help them. Sounds cruel, but…"

"This is a small town." Frankie rose and offered her hands to James. He accepted them, gripping her and hauling himself up with her help. The exertion was almost too much. He swayed and Frankie, being far smaller and knowing that she could not support his weight should he fall on her, sidestepped him while maintaining her grip to help keep him steady. "Most people know each other here. And most are super friendly."

James met her gaze and shook his head slowly. "They did start out sick so most probably won't make it to the exit. You're right, though. I suppose they do pose an additional risk." That fact made matters worse. Still, there was nothing he could do about it now. He was far too ill to attempt to contain the issue himself. Someone else would have to do it for him.

A silence hung between them and then, with a heavy heart, he tore his eyes away and started down the hall to the guest room. His words echoed in the hallway as she watched him go.

"You know what you need to do."

IT WAS TWO days since James had succumbed to coma. After a long night mulling things over with Frankie, he had taken himself to the guest room and collapsed onto one of the beds without bothering to pull back the covers or get undressed. With help from Bunmi, Frankie managed to roll James onto his back, but settled for covering him with an extra blanket from the linen closet instead of trying to undress him or get him under the comforter.

Bunmi had set up the equipment James would need to survive his coma shortly after she and Frankie got him better situated on the bed. It had not taken her long and her only regret was that she had not had time to get a catheter while they had been in the hospital. They would have to make do and, for James's sake, omit some of the details concerning the time he spent in his coma after he woke.

According to Frankie's father, James had managed
to remain aware far longer than anyone he knew of had
after contracting the Leucocelerosis virus. Once collapsing
onto the bed, however, James lost consciousness almost
immediately and had slipped into a coma soon after.

Frankie and Mick had taken turns, at first, sitting
with him, but Frankie quickly became so irritated by the
other woman's glaring and generally childish behavior that
she began avoiding the room altogether. Bunmi, after doing
routine checks, reported back to Frankie and her father
about his condition. It was better than nothing and certainly
better than having to put up with Mick.

Cora, who had been keeping mostly either to her
own room or the study while James had been awake, now
busied herself around the house disinfecting everything that
James might have touched. She was not one for chatting,
but Frankie pried from her that she had been an RN for
several years at a hospital in the Midwest before moving
west and switching to home healthcare for people like
Frankie's father. The two had taken a liking to one another
and, after quite a bit of finagling, Frankie's father had
convinced the company Cora worked for to remove all
other patients from her caseload and station her for all
shifts permanently with him.

Whatever Dr. Reed saw in the woman, Frankie did
not know. She was a bit of a cold fish and avoided
interaction with everyone except her charge whenever
possible. A portion of Cora's aloofness, Frankie guessed,
came from her fear of infection. According to Dr. Reed,
Cora had told him that her own blood type was AB-
positive. Infection, for her, like Earl and Mack, would
prove fatal. Still, the woman's personality probably had a
great deal more to do with her attitude than anything else.

Frankie found herself rattling around the house with no real purpose for the first day after of James's coma. She knew what she needed to do. She had already allowed the contagion to spread by not addressing it immediately. So much time had been wasted already while she and James had sat up talking. Part of her hesitation lay in knowing that the infected people who had followed them out of the hospital were already wandering the streets and would be difficult, if not impossible, to locate and dispatch before they came into contact with anyone else.

So far, however, they had not seen any more infected people wandering through the yard or even up on the street that led up to the main road. Her father's house was, while not exactly remote, far enough away from the hospital that the possibility of one of the people making it this far was slim.

Her hesitation was also caused by fear, pure and simple. She knew she was safe from the effects of the contagion, but the behavior of the infected she had seen so far absolutely terrified her. It made little sense to her why they should act in such a volatile manner. She had heard James and her father discussing it, but most of what they talked about was well above her education level and had gone right over her head.

Now that James was incapacitated, it was Bunmi who sat up late into the night in hushed conversation with Dr. Reed. Frankie had tried a few times to join them, but found she was the cause of conversational shift more often than not. Whatever they were discussing was apparently not meant for her ears. They were treating her exactly as she had Cora; she was someone who could not mentally or emotionally handle the difficult information they possessed.

She stood now, outside the study door with her hand raised, fist balled and ready to knock. It was a mixture of curiosity and frustration from being left out of whatever loop Bunmi and her father were in that stayed her hand. The voices behind the door were barely audible. She held her breath and listened.

"…experiment on one," her father was saying, "…incomplete in the past so there is no conclusive evidence…"

The rest of what he said was too low for her to discern, but Bunmi's words were clearer due to being seated closer to the door. "I am not entirely comfortable with that sort of thing, Doctor. They have no way of providing consent and locating family members to agree to let us perform autopsies on their loved ones much less experiment on them while they are still alive will be all but impossible."

Frankie pressed her ear up against the door, eager to hear her father's response. She felt like a small child as she stood there. She would have a fun time explaining herself to Mick or Cora should they come out of their respective rooms.

"Dr. Bola," said her father, ever respectful, "we are past the time when consent is our biggest worry. In my opinion, it should not be a consideration at all."

Frankie stepped away from the door, surprised. She had, until recently, always known her father to be a stickler for rules. He had, on more than one occasion, preached the importance of maintaining a high moral ground. It was strange to hear him casually dismissing something that had once been so important to him. Even so, it would mean that she would have at least one person who would back her up on what she was about to suggest.

She had put off James's unspoken instruction long enough. Raising her hand again, she rapped twice on the door. The conversation inside the study cut short the beginning of Bunmi's response and, after a moment, the door opened. Bunmi, seeing Frankie, put on a smile, but it did not extend to her eyes and Frankie could see her poorly masked weariness.

"Come in," she said as she stepped aside, "I must check on James."

Frankie touched Bunmi's shoulder to halt her. The topic she was about to broach would be easier if she could do so with just her father, but Frankie felt she would be doing Bunmi an injustice if she purposefully excluded her. She had a feeling she knew where the other woman would stand on the matter.

"What I have to say concerns us all."

Bunmi nodded and, still smiling, guided Frankie into the room. When both women had seated themselves, Frankie found she did not know exactly how to propose what she meant to do. She did not even want to do it herself however necessary she understood it to be. Her father, seeing her discomfort, waited patiently until the words finally came to her.

"We need to kill them."

Bunmi gaped at her. "Kill who?"

Frankie drew a deep breath and turned to address Bunmi. She knew it would be Bunmi who required the hard sell just as she had, but they could not take another day to agree. Another day and Los Alamos might be completely overrun. That is, if it was not already. None of them had been outside since the night they returned from the hospital.

Aliens could have landed and offered up tickets to Mars for all they knew.

"The infected people from the hospital," she spat out. "We need to kill them and anyone they might have infected and we need to do it now. Then we need to dispose of the bodies just to be sure. I'm thinking fire, but we'll have to be careful. We wouldn't want the mountain to catch on fire. They're still recovering from the last one. Anyway, you and I are the only ones who can do this because James isn't awake yet and Mick has A-positive blood type. She can't take the risk. I've already been sick and you…"

Frankie paused, looking at the shocked expression on Bunmi's face as the woman tried to absorb everything Frankie was hurriedly spouting, "Well, you're a miracle."

"Immune," Bunmi said softly, not quite ready to respond further.

"How's that for immoral?" Dr. Reed asked wryly.

Bunmi slowly turned her head to him. "I suppose you agree with this?"

"Absolutely." Dr. Reed's response was firm and without a shred of hesitation. Frankie, as much as she hated the idea, knew it was necessary and was grateful to her father for the support. Her father turned his attention from Bunmi who was beginning to lose what remained of her composure to Frankie. "Do you think you can capture a few of them?"

"Capture?"

"Yes. You might as well know that I intend to perform experiments on those infected who exhibit violent behaviors due to the Leucocelerosis virus. I believe it is affecting a particular portion of their brains and-"

"Is that really as important as trying to figure out what it is about us and her," Frankie interrupted, jerking her head toward Bunmi, "that lets us all survive the virus?"

Frankie turned to her father. His expression was difficult to read. Frankie looked back and forth between the two. When neither replied, she continued. "Don't you think we should be focusing on a cure instead of trying to figure out what makes some infected people act crazy?"

Her interjection was met with a brief silence then her father spoke gently. "Frankie, understanding how the virus affects specific brain centers in the brains of the infected is critical in helping us determine why certain blood groups are immune or able to recover while others are not."

"So, we shouldn't be looking for a cure?" Frankie, never having been very medically minded, was feeling lost and confused.

He shook his head. "No."

"It cannot be cured."

Frankie raised her eyebrows at Bunmi. "What?"

"It's a virus," Bunmi said quietly. "Viruses do not have cures. We can treat their symptoms, but we cannot cure them."

"That, then!" Frankie's frustration was reaching new heights. "Shouldn't we be focusing on a treatment?"

Bunmi looked at Dr. Reed. He did not respond for several seconds. Then, pursing his lips, he nodded sharply once. "Yes. I should not be waiting for James to wake to restart my research. I can begin immediately. Between the four of us, I should have plenty of blood to conduct the necessary tests."

"But we still need to take care of the infected out there."

Again, her father nodded his agreement. Bunmi frowned, but nodded as well. "I do not like it, but I agree they cannot be left to their own devices. I will help you, Frankie."

Dr. Reed rose suddenly, leaning on his cane. Both women looked up at him, surprised by the motion. Then, in a tone that did not allow for disagreement, he said, "I will go as well. You two will need to be able to focus on the task at hand and I will be requiring some things from the hospital if I am to begin testing. We will have to stop there."

He rounded the desk with more ease that she had seen since they arrived. He paused in the middle of the room and looked back at them. "I'll drive."

Twenty-Eight

And I looked, and behold a pale horse: and his
name that sat on him was Death, and Hell
followed with him.
Revelations 6:8

Unknown, Graffiti found on wall

"GET BACK IN the RV." Henry, his eyes fixed on the
crowd of pale people, backed slowly toward Tess. He
reached for her and spoke again under his breath. "Now,
Tess. Go."

Tess turned on her heel and dashed toward the RV
and Henry followed, wincing as he heard her door slam
shut. He cast a glance over his shoulder as he clambered
into his side. None of the pale people looked like they had
noticed the door shutting. They were not aware of them and
made no movements in their direction. In front of the
steering wheel with his door still open, he searched for the
little girls, but there was no sign of them. He paused with
his hand on the key he had left in the ignition.

"What?" Henry looked over at Tess. She was staring at him, looking a little anxious. Without answering her, he shut his own door as gently as he could and watched for a reaction from the crowd. Seeing none, he breathed out slowly and turned the key. The engine roared to life far louder than he had remembered it would. There was no way the sound of it had not been heard by anyone within a block of them. The crowd, Henry had estimated, was almost two blocks away although a handful of pale people were somewhat closer. Not a single one moved.

Henry dropped his shoulders, feeling the tension in them ease slightly. He threw the RV into reverse and, focusing now on the rearview mirror, began to back down the street. He was saddened to find that Los Alamos had also been affected. Part of him had assumed, for some reason, that this would be a safe place. The empty streets and lack of chaos had been eerie, but far more promising than any other town they had been in. He had subconsciously decided that the town was healthy and the intelligent people within it were hidden safely away. He was disappointed that the virus had reached these mountains, but a sort of relief spread through him. At least now he knew what to expect.

"Henry?"

He broke from his thoughts shooting Tess a quick look as he continued his slow progress backwards. "Hmm?"

"Henry?"

He looked at her again, this time noticing that she did not look as relaxed as he was beginning to feel. "What is it?"

"Look." Henry stopped the RV and looked back up the street. Most of the pale people had been moving sluggishly or swaying in a drunken fashion, but none had seemed very active. Now, though, through the middle of the crowd, Henry could see a man with a shock of white hair coming toward them with purpose. His face was turned up directly at them and he walked with long strides. A white lab coat swished behind him in the gentle breeze.

"Oh, shi-"

The man opened his mouth and shrieked, the sound of it echoing and drowning out Henry's words as if it was coming from within the RV and not several hundred feet away. The pale people in the crowd, those who were still standing, all looked up as one. With an eruption of energy, every one of them turned and started toward the RV at varying speeds.

With the Jeep in tow, Henry could not just slam on the gas and reverse quickly. He cast around for options, but saw only two. He could keep going in reverse and hope that he could get back to the intersection where he could back up enough to drive forward down Oppenheimer Drive before the crowd overwhelmed them.

Or he could throw the RV in drive and just plow through them.

He and Tess exchanged a look then both grabbed their seatbelts and strapped in. Tess planted her feet firmly against the floor and the jamb of the door. She gripped her Gatekeeper with one hand and braced herself with the other. Henry shifted into drive and slammed his foot down on the gas. He hoped they could gain enough speed to make this worth the effort.

The crowd was surging forward at an alarming pace. With gritted teeth, Henry bore down, lowering his profile in case any of them should fly up into the windshield. Just before the RV connected with the first pale person, Henry spotted a white van coming around the corner onto Trinity from the top of the street. The pale person hit the front of the RV with a sickening thud and disappeared beneath them. It was followed by two then three more. Henry gripped the steering wheel harder as the tires of the RV bumped over a few of the bodies.

Beyond the chaos, the white van swerved slightly and slowed before speeding up and swinging into a parking lot on their right. Henry's attention was firmly on the man in the lab coat who now had a clear path toward them. He had not stopped his shrieking once that they had seen. Not even to catch his breath. Henry floored it, and plowed directly into him, the impact cutting off the piercing noise he had been making. Because he had been moving faster and was taller than the pale people before him, the man's body flipped up on contact with the front of the RV and went crashing up over the hood. He slammed into the windshield in front of Tess and flew off the side of the vehicle where he tumbled along the side of the road before coming to a stop in the gutter.

Henry did not slow at all. The RV cut down more pale people than he could keep track of and, by the time they had made their way all the way through the crowd, the front of the RV was splattered heavily with blood and a trail of mangled bodies lay in their wake. They came to a screeching halt in the middle of the street across from a large building. It was, as Henry had suspected from afar, a hospital. The white van they had seen had come to a stop in front of the entrance to the emergency department. Two petite women wearing backpacks leapt out of the passenger side and ran toward the open door.

One darted into the building without a backward glance. Henry watched as her long hair, bunched together in what looked like braids, whipped behind her like the tail of a scorpion about to attack. The other skidded to a halt at the entrance and spun around. She called something to a man who had stayed in the driver's seat before twisting to dash in after the other woman. As she turned back to the entrance, dark curls bouncing around her head, her eyes locked on Henry's.

Henry had read about moments where time seemed to stand still, but he had always thought they were a load of crap. He knew that time sometimes felt like it was going faster while, at other times it felt like it was going slower. However, it did not stop. In the few seconds when their eyes met, Henry could have sworn that time had, indeed, stood still.

He had not noticed that Tess had exited the RV until he heard a gunshot. He jerked his head up away from the woman and saw Tess making her way back down the street pausing here and there to put a bullet through a mangled pale person. A few had been missed altogether, but they were no longer trying to get at Henry and Tess. Instead, they had gone back to their stationary swaying or mindless slow roaming. Tess sent them on their way as well as she passed them. She had her black mask pulled up over her mouth and nose and was wearing her sunglasses. Her rich, brown curls were falling out of the band that had held them in a bun at the top of her head and were spilling around her face. She looked powerful. She looked dangerous. Henry was glad she was on his side.

Remembering the woman, Henry looked back at the entrance to the hospital, but she was gone. He unfastened his seatbelt and, putting the RV into park, jumped down to the ground and strode over to join Tess. He pulled out his own gun and pointed the barrel at the head of a nearby pale woman. This was not a task she should have to do alone.

Twenty-Nine

Someone needs to know what they did to me. Someone needs to know how they hurt me, how they used me. Someone needs to know how they left me for dead. Someone needs to know about the horror I experienced and how for three hours all I could think of was how I wanted to die just to escape the pain and humiliation. But I can't bring myself to put it into words. I don't want to risk another girl reading this and having to live what I lived even if it is only second hand. My attackers will soon know for themselves. They thought I was just a bit of fun, something to use and toss aside. They didn't know that I had already begun to die when they snatched me and that they will soon follow.

I am Bridget Benally and I will have my revenge from the grave.

Bridget Benally, Note found in hand of body

THERE WAS A hard lump in Frankie's throat. She was filled with anxiety and could not keep herself from checking the guns James had given her. One, which had belonged to Earl, was resting on Bunmi's lap and the other, Mack's, was gripped firmly in Frankie's hand. It was, when she had first been handed it by James for the first trip to the hospital, strange to be holding a weapon. She had not then expected to have to use it at all. It had simply been a precaution. So much had changed. She had once again taken hold of the weapon and had winced at how bitingly cold the metal felt. Now it was hot and slick with her sweat. They had been unable to locate James's gun and Mick was nowhere to be found so Dr. Reed had had to go unarmed. Frankie had made him promise to stay in the van and to honk the horn like mad should anything happen.

When Frankie, Bunmi, and Dr. Reed rounded the corner from Diamond Drive onto Trinity Drive, the last thing they had expected to see was an RV about to plow its way through a mob of infected people. They had heard the familiar shriek before they had completed their turn and had braced themselves for a confrontation. When Frankie saw what the RV was going to do, she had hastily instructed her father to just drive behind the crowd into the parking lot of the hospital as quickly as possible.

The van squealed to a stop in front of the automatic doors she and Bunmi had left open three days before. Bunmi flung open the passenger side door and, slipping on a backpack, leapt out. Frankie jumped out and slammed the door behind her, her gun in hand and her own backpack slung over her shoulder. She paused at the open door and, turning around to face the van, called back to her father.

"Stay in the van!" She turned again to follow after Bunmi who had already disappeared into the hospital. The RV had come to a stop in the street across from the hospital. She could now see that it was towing an old, tan Jeep behind it, but it was the man driving the RV who had caught her attention.

From a distance, she could not make out exactly what he looked like except that he had short dark hair and did not appear to be sick. He was staring directly at her which, for some reason, made the lump in her throat drop into her stomach. The passenger door of the RV opened and, from the corner of her vision, Frankie saw a dark-clothed person circle around to the back. Frankie shivered then broke eye contact with the man and ran into the hospital. She had a job to complete and no time to worry about who the man was. Besides, he had taken care of the second part of their mission for them.

She jumped when she heard the first gunshot, but did not slow her pace. Bunmi was heading farther into the hospital to collect the supplies Frankie's father would need to restart his research. Frankie's task was simpler. All she had to do was gather more antibiotics and medicines from a cabinet Bunmi had broken into when they had last been here.

As she passed by the open elevator door, her eyes caught sight of the man who had tried to warn her about the people who had been trapped behind the now open stairwell door. He had toppled over at some point and was no longer moving. Frankie, knowing it was impossible to think he might still be alive considering the pallor of his skin, the whiteness of his hair, and how still he was. The stairwell, she saw as she ran by, was completely empty except for one slumped body dressed in a hospital gown.

Repeating to herself the directions to the room Bunmi had been in, Frankie sped up. Her eyes swept back and forth each time she passed a door or hallway. While she believed herself to be as mentally prepared as she could be to encounter an infected person, she was not looking forward to having to put one down. She knew she could do it, having done it once before, but that did not make it any easier in her mind. It was a necessary evil.

She found the room with little difficulty and pulled her backpack off. She unzipped it and began filling it with the contents of the open security cabinet. The smashed glass front and discarded metal bar must have been what had made it possible for Bunmi to open the cabinet. She slipped the bar into the backpack as well, knowing she would most likely need it again.

Once the cabinet was empty, she zipped up the backpack and shouldered it again. Checking her gun for the hundredth time, Frankie slipped out the door and down another hall that Bunmi had assured her would take her to one last place before leading her back out toward the emergency department. She would have to take the stairs to get up to it. It was something she was dreading because of her last experience with a stairwell, but Bunmi had stressed it was important to get the contents of a particular secured cabinet on another floor so she had no choice except to get over her fears and just do it.

The second room had been slightly harder to find. She passed by it twice before realizing that it had been almost right next to the stairwell she had come up. The elevator doors next to this stairwell were frozen open and cool air wafted from the dark elevator shaft. The elevator itself was somewhere either below or above this floor.

She turned her attention to the door that held the second security cabinet. She chuckled to herself that she had missed it at all. It wasn't exactly obscured from sight like a secret entrance to a hidden room or some trapdoor to a hidden bunker. She paused, her fingers lightly gripping the handle.

A hidden bunker.

She had completely forgotten about the bunker her father had built in their backyard. She knew for a fact that he had kept it well stocked with everything from food to toiletries and guns. There was even a generator. A frown pulled at her lips. Why had he not mentioned this when the power went out?

There was no time to think any more on it. She would ask her father about it as soon as they were finished collecting supplies. She entered the room and glanced around. The cabinet she was to gather from was, as expected, locked. To top it off, the front was made of metal and not glass as had been the first cabinet. This was not a problem the metal bar would solve.

Grudgingly, she pointed her gun at the lock and pulled the trigger. The gunshot rang out and echoed through the halls and down the stairwell she had propped open for a quick escape should one be needed. She hoped that the noise would not attract anyone, but it had, at least, done the job. The lock was shattered and the door swung easily open at the prod of her foot.

She opened her backpack for the last time and swept the contents of the cabinet in with her arm. She quickly gathered what had not made it into the backpack then zipped it back up before heaving it over her shoulder. Because to was so heavy, holding the gun was difficult. She set the safety and hastily tucked it into the waistband of her jeans then took hold of the backpack's straps to alleviate the pressure on her shoulders.

Bunmi, she was sure, would be done with her own task by now and should be on her way back to the van. Frankie hurried to the stairwell. She was grateful that this stairwell had been relatively close to the entrance of the hospital. It meant she did not have to haul her load too far.

Frankie slid as she came to a stop in front of the closed door that led into the stairwell. The trashcan she had used to prop it open was now against the wall next to the door. If the door had been too heavy, it would have pushed the trashcan into the hall. Instead, it was beside the door as though someone had come through and pushed it aside. Quietly, she pulled off the backpack and set it next to the trashcan. She took the gun back out from her waistband and held it low as she pressed her shoulder into the door and pushed it slowly open. The stairwell appeared to be empty.

"Bitch."

The word had come from behind her. Frankie whipped around, drawing her gun up to chest level and found herself a mere six feet away from a black-clad figure.

THE CAR HAD pulled up behind the van so quickly that it had taken Dr. Reed a full minute to realize that it was his own. By that time, the driver, dressed in black, had all but disappeared through the entrance. Confused and with no small measure of concern, Dr. Reed carefully stepped down from the van and fumbled to draw his cane out behind him. As he shut the door and turned, he saw the two people he had been watching clear the infected getting back into their RV and continue up the road toward Diamond Drive.

Dr. Reed rushed in after the figure, but whoever it was had gone by the time he was through the door. He swore under his breath for not being able to move faster. He was about to go through triage as Frankie had described she and Bunmi had gone through the first time, when he saw the door to the stairwell down a hall to the right swing shut. He turned stiffly and went in that direction. He leaned forward to look up the flight of stairs. He saw the figure go through a doorway two flights up. With great effort, he mounted the stairs and began the slow journey upwards.

"YOU KILLED HIM."

Frankie stared mutely at Mick, but did not lower her gun. Mick had one of her own pointed at Frankie. The two guns were so close that they were almost kissing. Wisps of blonde hair were escaping from underneath her black beanie. She might have looked angelic had it not been for the hateful expression that twisted her features.

"You killed him," Mick repeated. "It's your fault he's dead."

"Mick," Frankie could not back away. The stairwell was behind her and the trashcan to her right. She had nowhere to go except directly at Mick. "You don't know what you're saying. Let's just calm down and put our guns aw-"

"Shut up! I know exactly what I'm saying! You killed him!"

"Mick-"

"He's dead because of you. If not for you, we'd all be home with my mom. James wouldn't be sick. Earl would still be here." She paused then choked out her next words. "Mack would still be alive."

Frankie could not think of a single thing to say that would calm Mick down. The younger woman was far too worked up. There was only one way this was going to end; someone had to die and Frankie would be damned if it was going to be her. Without warning, she squeezed her trigger hard.

Nothing happened.

Mick began to laugh. At first, it was a soft giggle. Then it bubbled up into a maniacal cackle. "You are so pathetic. I mean, who aims a gun without first taking off the safet-"

Frankie had lunged forward, smacking her gun into Mick's. It was not a perfect solution, but it afforded her the element of surprise. Mick yelped with pain as her gun flew from her hand and slid across the floor out of reach. Frankie continued forward, slamming her body into Mick who toppled backwards with Frankie on top of her. The two women rolled away from the stairwell and came to a stop a few feet away from the open elevator shaft. Frankie's thumb fumbled for her gun's safety while she tried desperately to maintain her advantage.

Mick was strong. She was far younger than Frankie and had obviously spent her after school hours in some sort of physical pursuit, unlike Frankie who gone from learning to play the clarinet to hanging out with her friends up in the woods. Frankie was not at all prepared for a grappling match.

Unable to reach her own gun, Mick took hold of Frankie's wrist and bashed it and the gun she was still holding into Frankie's head. Frankie cried out, dropping her gun as Mick once again wrenched her hand away from her head. It slid across the floor and bounced off the opposite wall. Now at a complete disadvantage, Frankie jerked her leg up and planted her knee squarely into Mick. If she could just pin her long enough to push herself back, she could roll toward the gun and put some distance between them.

The younger woman gasped as Frankie's knee dug into her. Then, switching her hold, she grabbed at Frankie's middle and yanked up as hard as she could. Frankie had already been precariously positioned. The motion forced her whole body up and over Mick's head. Disoriented, she reached out to grab anything she could. Her fingers grazed the edge of the elevator before she went tumbling down head first into the dark shaft. She let out a cry and swung both arms frantically, but could not find purchase.

Mick, still on her back, held her breath and listened for the thud. When it came, it took with it Frankie's voice. She lay there for a few seconds longer then, releasing her breath with satisfaction, rolled onto her side and stood up. She brushed at her clothes and looked up.

Dr. Reed was standing in the hallway just outside the stairwell, his hand still on the door. A look of shock was on his face as he stood mutely frozen in place. There was no question about it. He had seen what she had done to his daughter.

Without a further thought, Mick reached down and drew a second gun from a holster on her boot. She pointed it directly at Dr. Reed's head and fired.

BUNMI HAD BEEN carefully stacking boxes of unused slides and test tubes about a portable microscope in her backpack when she heard the first gunshot. Assuming it was Frankie trying to get into the secured cabinet, she had continued her task. It had been hard enough for her to break into the first one that she would probably have started by employing her gun immediately with the second instead of going about it as she had before.

She was on her way back toward triage when she heard the second shot. Pausing, she frowned and changed directions to head toward where she believed it had come from. She heard a door open as she approached the hallway that held the stairwell that led up to the room where she had sent Frankie. Pressing herself up against the wall, she peeked out down the hall and saw someone dressed in black dashing away toward the main entrance.

Unnerved, Bunmi shifted the backpack so that the weight of it was spread more evenly on her shoulders then went to the stairwell and climbed up to the third floor. She cautiously pushed open the door and peered into the hallway. At first, she saw nothing. She cautiously pushed the door father open and met with resistance. She took off the backpack and set it next to the door before squeezing through the small space into the hallway. Whoever she had seen must have been fairly slight as the door would open just enough for her to get through.

Once in the hall the cause of the blockage became clear. Sprawled on the floor in front of the door was the body of a man. Blood was pooling around his head and dripping from a single gunshot wound in his forehead. His eyes were wide and staring accusingly at the ceiling.

Bunmi fell to a crouch and, with a heavy sigh, drew her fingers down over his eyelids, closing his eyes. Without Dr. Reed, researching a treatment would be extremely difficult and far more time consuming than they had projected. No one knew his work as well as he had. It would be almost like starting from scratch.

Calmly, she rose and looked around. Frankie's backpack was sitting next to a trashcan on the right side of the door, but Frankie was nowhere in sight. Bunmi sidestepped Dr. Reed's body and went to look in the room she had sent Frankie to. It was empty. She slowly walked back up the hall, pausing at the open elevator shaft. She gripped the side and peered in, but could not see anything. She turned around and saw Frankie's gun discarded against the wall.

It was not difficult to piece together. Still, she was driven to confirm her theory. She collected the gun and went back to her backpack. Digging through it, she found a flashlight. She clicked it on to test it then, when it lit, returned to the shaft and shone it downwards.

Four floors down, at the very bottom of the shaft, was the basement level. On it, twisted in a grotesque fashion and unmoving, was the body of a woman. Bunmi's eyesight was keen. She needed no further confirmation that it had belonged to Frankie.

She closed her eyes and clicked off the flashlight. It was such a waste. While not scientifically minded like James or like Dr. Reed had been, Bunmi had rather liked Frankie. She was not especially good at showing people how she felt, but she had taken to Frankie almost immediately. While Bunmi was serious and often pensive, Frankie had been lighthearted and full of humor. Several times since they met, Bunmi had laughed inwardly at one of Frankie's jokes or puns. She wished she had let her know how much she had liked her.

There was nothing for it. Bunmi returned to Dr. Reed's body and, after patting his trouser pockets, located the keys to the van. She then opened the door to the stairwell and pushed Frankie's backpack through before squeezing to the other side herself. She put her own backpack, the heavier of the two due to the microscope, back on and carried Frankie's down the three flights of stairs. She opened the door to the main floor just enough to see through and, finding the hallway empty, stepped out and headed quickly to the emergency department entrance.

Outside, the air seemed to have grown even more chilly. She opened up the passenger side of the van and loaded the backpacks onto the bench seat. She then went around and pulled herself up into the driver's seat. She started the van and pulled away from the hospital entrance slowly so as not to shift the backpacks. Eyes scanning the parking lot, she made her way toward the exit that led back onto Trinity Drive.

Anyone who saw her at that moment might have thought her to be without worry. On the contrary, while her face remained calm, Bunmi's mind was swirling with thoughts and unanswered questions. With everything else that was going on, there was now a murderer who, whether they had known it or not, had quite possibly killed the one person who could save what remained of the world. Whoever it was either not interested in what Frankie had collected as the backpack had been left behind or they had not seen it. Perhaps they had not had time to take it. She had not taken long getting upstairs. Perhaps the killer had heard her and had run away as she arrived. Dr. Reed appeared to have simply been in the wrong place at the wrong time, but why had he been there at all? Why had he not waited in the van as had been agreed upon. She had known him for years. She could not convince herself that he would have gone back on that agreement without good reason.

She would have to hurry now. Aside from Mick and Cora, there would be no one to help her juggle taking care of James and setting up for her research. Mick, from what she could tell of the girl, was intelligent, but overly emotional. Bunmi could not be sure that any instruction would be well received. Cora, on the other hand, was useless to her. She would be even more so when Bunmi broke the news to her about Dr. Reed. The two had seemed close.

At Trinity, Bunmi paused, looking first to the right. The street was littered with bodies. Her eyebrows flew up with interest. She had been far too wrapped up in her thoughts about what she had needed to do that she had not even given a second look to the RV they had seen when they had first pulled onto Trinity Drive. She had thought she had heard something as she ran through triage, but had not been sure. There were far more bodies than the trajectory of a forward moving RV could explain. Several were off to the side of the road and many were on the sidewalks.

She wondered if this had been the work of the people in the RV. Inwardly, she thanked them. It meant less work that she would now have to perform alone or wait to do until James had recovered and Mick had collected herself. Without the help of the people in the RV, the supervirus would likely have spread through far out of her control by the time she was prepared to face it.

On the drive back to the Reed residence, Bunmi's mind drifted to the person she had seen running to the exit in the hospital. She had only caught a glimpse, but it was not enough to make any sort of ID. She struggled to remember any details, but came up with nothing. Whoever it had been had not taken anything from the scene and that bothered her. Had it been a scavenger, anything deemed useful would have been removed. The more she thought about it, the more like a hit it felt.

Bunmi pulled into the driveway and parked next to Dr. Reed's black car. She hopped out and circled around the front to unload the backpacks from the van. A faint ticking noise brought her to a full stop. She took a few steps back toward Dr. Reed's car and felt the hood. It was slightly warm. She recalled Dr. Reed having said that, because of the release of the Leucocelerosis virus, neither he nor Cora had used his car. Cora, he had told her, did not have one of her own as hers had been in the shop when the outbreak first occurred.

Someone had just driven this vehicle.

Bunmi grabbed both backpacks from the van and hauled them up to the front door. It swung open before she could set them down to open it herself and Cora appeared in the doorway looking very concerned. Her eyes went right over Bunmi to the van, searching for Dr. Reed. Not seeing him, she finally acknowledged Bunmi who had picked up one backpack and was trying to get past her into the house.

"Where is he?" She did not move to allow Bunmi entry. "Where is Franklin?"

"If you would please excuse me," Bunmi suggested, "I will tell you everything in a moment."

The woman huffed, but stepped aside. Bunmi immediately deposited the backpack on the closet chair in the living room and rubbed at one sore shoulder. Mick was sprawled out on the couch, flipping through a magazine. She glanced up at Bunmi and, nodding once in her direction, went back to her magazine.

Bunmi studied the young woman. She was wearing black jeans and a black tank top, but her boots had been cast off in the corner by the front door. Bunmi had noticed them as she came in. One bare foot was resting on top of the back of the couch while the other was stretched out along the length of the couch. Her blonde hair, usually pulled up into a tight, neat ponytail, was gathered loosely and messily near the nape of her neck. Aside from the state of her hair and cheeks which looked more rosy than normal, Mick looked just as she always did.

The figure Bunmi had seen had also been dressed all in black. She was sure, though, that there was more than one person in this town who liked to dress as Mick did. She frowned. It was altogether possible that Mick had had nothing to do with the goings on at the hospital.

Bunmi collected the second backpack and placed it next to the first, her eyes drifting back to the young woman. Aside from the car, one more thing was bothering Bunmi; Mick was a little too casual. It had only been three days since Mack had died and Mick had suddenly gone from mourning twin to indifferent and sullen distant relative. Rubbing again at her sore shoulder, Bunmi looked away from Mick to the sliding glass door and out into the yard.

"It is cold today." When Mick only grunted in response, Bunmi tried again. "Do you not find it is very much colder today than it has been?"

"Wouldn't know." Mick did not look up from the magazine. "Haven't been out.

"Not at all?"

"Nope."

The front door shut and Cora appeared next to Bunmi. "Where is Franklin? He's not out there. Where is he?"

Bunmi turned her eyes back to Mick and watched for a reaction. "I am sorry, Cora. Dr. Reed met with trouble at the hospital."

"Met with trouble? What do you mean? He's coming home, though, right?"

"No," Bunmi answered in almost a whisper. "Neither he nor his daughter will be coming home."

Silence filled the room. Mick had not yet looked up from her magazine. Bunmi glanced at Cora and saw she was trying to work out if she was truly understanding what Bunmi was saying. She took pity on the older woman and placed one hand on her shoulder.

"I am afraid both Dr. Reed and his daughter lost their lives." Mick was sitting up now.

"Lost their…"

Bunmi crossed her hands over her chest and, after a small pause, said, "They were killed." As she spoke the last word, Bunmi raised her eyes to Mick to gauge her reaction to the news.

The younger woman's face was completely devoid of emotion. She met Bunmi's gaze head on. They stared at each other for several seconds while Cora stammered, trying to process her shock.

"He's not," the older woman began, "They're not…"

"I am sorry."

Then, without shifting her gaze, Mick rose and left the room. She looked away only after she had passed Bunmi. Cora, fully realizing the meaning of Bunmi's words, burst into tears. While she would have loved to follow Mick to fully confirm her suspicions, she was now obligated to remain with Cora.

BUNMI WAS EXHAUSTED. Cora had finally wept herself to sleep on the couch and Bunmi, now free, covered her up with a patchwork quilt that had been draped over one of the chairs. She was long overdue to check on James.

Wearily, she picked up the backpacks to take with her. It would be easier than making a trip back for them after seeing to James. As she passed through the foyer, she paused and looked down around the front door. There were no black boots in the corner.

Frowning, she continued up the hall toward James's room. On a whim, she stopped in front of the room Mick had been staying in. She knocked twice then listened. No sound came from within so she tried once more. This time, when there was no response, she quietly opened the door and peeked inside. The bed was rumpled from having someone sleep on top of its covers, but it was still made and relatively neat. Her thick, black leather jacket was nowhere in sight. Looking around the room, Bunmi could spot no trace of the younger woman whatsoever.

Brow furrowing, Bunmi closed the door and went to James's room. She opened the door without knocking and found it just as she had left it. Thanks to the generator, all the machines he was hooked up to were beeping steadily. She needed to have a closer look, but she first needed to answer a question that had crossed her mind. She carefully placed the backpacks on a chair near the door and went to the window. Pushing the curtains aside, she squinted out into the dark night. The van was still there as was Dr. Reed's car. She frowned as she pulled the curtains back into place. Where was the girl?

Bunmi let go of the curtains. As they fell back into place, a movement outside caught her eyes. She pushed back the curtains and peered out again. Several seconds passed before she allowed the curtains to fall again. She was tired and had just been through an experience that would have traumatized most people. It only made sense that her eyes would be playing tricks.

At James's side, Bunmi took his wrist and placed two fingers over a vein to feel for his pulse. She found it quickly and was pleased with its strength. Pulling her flashlight from her pocket, she quickly checked his pupils. They were still cloudy, but better than they had been. It was a sure sign that he was on the mend. Lastly, she reviewed the printout the machine was issuing. Everything seemed to be going well for him. Everything, that was, except for the fact that he appeared to still be in a coma.

Bunmi's mind drifted back to Mick. If her theory proved true, it was quite likely she was in danger. She would have to take precautionary measures and hope that she was wrong. Bunmi collected the backpacks from the chair by the door. She was tired, but she could rest soon enough in the study. She could lock the door and begin her research while she waited for James to recover. Perhaps, in time, she would also discover that her suspicions about Mick were little more than that. Perhaps she had read too much into the girl's behavior and would find that her reaction to learning about the deaths of the Reeds had been typical of her.

Hope ever so slightly renewed, Bunmi stretched and, opening the bedroom door, quietly slipped out. The door clicked shut behind her and she headed up the hall to the study. Inside the room, the machines beeped on.

James opened his eyes.

Thirty

I saw another suicide this morning. I guess I shouldn't be all that surprised anymore that this would be the way people would choose to go especially when the alternatives are so horrific. I copied the note she had written into my log book and left the original on the desk in front of her where I found it. She meant for it to be seen. I doubt she thought it would be me who saw it first. I always leave the notes just in case the people they were written for ever return. I don't really think they will, though. I think they probably left their own notes.

I like to keep a record just in case I run into someone who is trying to find a loved one that I have already found. It's difficult, though, when the messages are written in languages I did not study. I'm kicking myself for not paying more attention to the romance languages. Still, who would have thought taking so many different languages in college would have come in useful this way? I admit I had thought I would use this skill in the world of business rather than the world of memorium keeping.

Someone has to do it. Someone has to
remember that these people were alive, that
they existed. I seem to be impervious to this
virus and I have nothing but time. It might as
well be me. I just hope I'm not alone.

Rebecca Joseph

IT HAD BEEN an excruciatingly long day. While both
Henry and Tess had understood that what they had done in
front of the hospital was necessary, it had, by no means
been as easy as they had probably made it look. The only
way Henry had managed was to push as far back into his
mind the fact that the people he was shooting were actually
still alive. He had no idea how Tess was justifying their
actions to herself. He did not want to ask. He did not really
want to know.

Once they were finished and all the pale people
were on the ground and unmoving, they returned to the RV.
Henry noticed that a black car was now parked behind the
van in front of the emergency entrance of the hospital. He
had somehow managed to miss its arrival. Part of him was
curious what these people were up to. They were, after all,
the first people they had seen other than the hitchhiker in
quite some time and, from what he could tell from a
distance, they had appeared healthy.

Henry stared over the bodies that were scattered
about the street. He had almost forgotten about the young
girls who had tried to warn them away from this end of the
road. They had not seemed to be sick either, but Henry
doubted they would allow themselves to be seen again any
time soon.

401

There was a chance, however, that the people who had gone into the hospital would know how to find Doctor Reed. Los Alamos was not all that big and people in small towns seemed to make a point of knowing each other. Asking survivors would probably be quicker than trying to find a phone book and hoping that he had an address that was listed.

Even if they did find the doctor, did it matter anymore? It had only been because of Robby that they had come to find the man and now, judging by what they had just seen, there was a possibility that he was not even still alive. Even if he was, what could he possibly do to change the current state of the world? He had seen so much death and very little life recently. Pretty soon, here might not be anyone let to save.

Despair began to creep over Henry as negative thoughts flooded his mind. Even if there were others yet untouched by the supervirus, he felt it was unlikely he would want to save many, if any, of them. There was no guarantee they would be worth helping. He turned toward the RV, his eyes skimming the dark windows of the hospital. The people he had seen go in were sure to be just like the man who had killed Robby; out for themselves. That was the way the world was now. The urge to discover more about them still niggled at him, but something told him he would be better off keeping his nose in his own business.

He and Tess climbed back into the RV and continued up to Diamond Drive where, for lack of any other idea, they turned right. They had not gone far before Tess broke the silence that had been hanging between them.

"Screw it."

Henry glanced over at her. She looked pensive and tired. "Screw what?"

"All of this." She waved a hand around, indicting either her distaste for mountain towns or the world in general. "Can we just stop for today? I need to just...stop."

Henry shrugged and pulled off into the parking lot of an abandoned gas station. It did not look as though it had been in business for at least a few years. It was not the most ideal place to stop, but it was large enough to accommodate both the RV and the Jeep. Given more warning, he would have liked to have scouted around for a better, more secluded spot. For the time being, it was as good a place as any to rest and gather their thoughts.

He turned off the engine and, together, they sat in silence staring out the front windshield. He knew what Tess had meant. They had come all this way simply because they had wanted to honor Robby's memory and, now that they were here, they found that this town was almost exactly like all the others they had been through. Within days, it would probably be no different. He, too, just needed to stop if only for the night.

It was almost completely dark out. The sun was sinking fast and so were Tess and Henry. He didn't figure it would take much to convince his young traveling companion to call it a night and save for the morning the chore of figuring out what they would do next. With a sigh, he twisted and pulled back the curtain to the back of the RV.

"Come on. Let's do something about dinner."

SLEEP CAME FAR more easily for Tess than it did for
Henry. He lay on the couch listening to her rhythmic
breathing for almost an hour before giving up. He had, in a
town just this side of the New Mexican border, picked up a
few random paperback novels. Even if none of them were
any good, he had hope that one would, at least, bore him to
sleep. He clicked on the light and began looking through
them. Choosing one to read proved almost as difficult as
trying to sleep. At this rate, he thought, he would bore
himself to sleep.

There was a soft rapping at the door.

Henry's head jerked up and the book he had been
holding fell to his feet with a muted thud. He remained still,
unsure if he had actually heard something or if his mind
was simply playing tricks on him. Then, just as he
convinced himself of the latter, he heard it again.

This time, the knocking woke Tess. She bolted
upright in her bed, banging her head against the ceiling.
Swearing under her breath and holding her sore head in
both hands, she looked down questioningly at Henry who
shook his head slightly and shrugged. He rose, picking up
his gun from the table and clicked off the safety. Tess
slipped down off the bed and collected her own gun then
moved diagonally behind him so that she would have a
clear shot past him through the door once it was open.

The knocking sounded a third time and, after
exchanging one final meaningful look with Tess, Henry
unlocked the door. He raised his gun up and aimed at what
would be average chest height for a man then threw the
door open.

Outside, with her arms wrapped tightly around
herself, was a young woman. Although dressed in black
jeans and a sturdy-looking black jacket, she was shivering

visibly. Her long blonde hair was loose beneath a black knit beanie and was been blown gently by the breeze. Her cheeks were rosy from the cold night air and her eyes were a clear, deep blue with no hint of clouding. She looked at them pleadingly, slowly extending her hands from her body and holding them palms up to show they were empty before speaking in a timid and shaking voice.

"Please," she begged, "I've got no one left here. I need to get home to my mother. Please. Take me with you."

Acknowledgements

First and foremost, I would like to thank my mother, Joan Glickler. Without you as my sounding board, I doubt this book would have evolved the way it did. Thank you for always believing in me and encouraging me to do my best.

I am grateful to my husband without whom I likely would not have started this book at all. His love and support made it possible for me to mash together an old short story with a new idea that had been swimming around in my mind. Thank you for your endless patience while I wrote, rewrote, edited, edited again, and fussed incessantly about this novel. Also, thank you for helping me understand what guns, weapons, and vehicles can or cannot do.

I am thankful for Gabby Swass who read my first attempts and gave honest and constructive advice on how to improve. You answered all my medically related questions and allowed me to bounce ideas off you even in the middle of the night. Thank you for always being there for me.

For providing me with translations or checking my own, I would like to thank Bumni Odumade, Irene Brink Gehre, and Jungae Hermanson. I know none of you think you did much in this area, but I promise you did. Your help made it possible for me to ditch the dreadful way I originally opened each chapter and replace it with far more interesting and relevant content. Trust me. It was bad.

Thank you, Jack, Mac, and Sean Duggins as well as the Franzoy family the parts you played in the creation of the cover.

Even though I've already mentioned her, I would like give a special thanks to Bunmi Odumade. I cannot tell you how grateful I am for you. Thank you for being my personal cheering squad. The whole story took a turn for the better because of you.

Thank you, Tim Marquitz, for your support and advice. I didn't always take it, but I always appreciated it.

As for all my friends and family members who asked me to kill them…you have no idea how much fun I had granting your wishes. Let's do it again soon.

Made in the USA
Middletown, DE
22 May 2020

95807731R00241